REVIEWERS
SOUTHERN SECRETS

"Enticing story set in the South where one's reputation is guarded with care and some things are never spoken about."

—*Rendezvous*

"Nelle McFather's *Southern Secrets* is an evocative, intricate and memorable tale of lies and deceit, laced with a strictly Southern flavor!"

—*Rave Reviews*

"We want to know what happens next—and, for that matter, what happened before in this story of love and greed in the new South. History, folklore and island superstitions—it all adds up to good reading."

—*Florida Times-Union*

"Young, tantalizing Tally Malone finds herself at the center of a swirling family tempest: an illegitimate child, near-incest, madness and land swindles."

—*Booklist*

"A love story garnished with adultery, incest, bigamy and sorcery. McFather succeeds with an often surprising, intricate plot!"

—*Publishers Weekly*

SOUTHERN SECRETS

NELLE McFATHER

SMP
ST. MARTIN'S PAPERBACKS

SOUTHERN SECRETS

Copyright © 1991 by Nelle McFather.

Cover illustration by Robert Gunn.

Library of Congress Catalog Card Number: 90-27341

ISBN: 0-312-95023-3

Printed in the United States of America

St. Martin's Press hardcover edition/July 1991
St. Martin's Paperbacks edition/March 1993

10 9 8 7 6 5 4 3 2

Acknowledgments

Although I grew up with Gullah stories told to me by the black women in the quarters, "De Buzzard and De Hawk," passed down from Aunt Rose to her daughter Queen to granddaughter Annie Mae (who helped raise me), is taken from another source. I am grateful for the authentic translation by Ted Williams, whose version of this story appears in Patricia Jones-Jackson's book *When Roots Die*. I also refreshed my memories of childhood visits to primitive churches, some of which practiced snake-handling, by reading accounts in *Foxfire* of this fascinating religious practice.

I am especially indebted to the following experts and entrepreneurs: Bill Jay of Nashville, L.O.P., who never stays anyplace very long, and my cousin I.W., formerly of the National Guard and currently a close neighbor. Thanks for your help, guys! I also wish to thank my readers, Marlene Bush and Aleece Jacques, and my school assistants, Marian Brigman and Rose Suttles, for cheering me on. My special thanks, too, to the dozens of courageous women who wrote me about their unwed mothers' homes experiences.

It would be impossible to acknowledge everything my wonderful agent, Meg Ruley, has done for me, but I'll try—thanks, Meg!

And, finally, what can I say, Mo? Just this: In my almost twenty years of writing novels, I have had some top-notch editors, but none better than Maureen Baron. So, to Mo the Slasher I humbly offer my most respectful "Thanks—I needed that!"

—*Nelle McFather*

SOUTHERN SECRETS

Part One

Summer 1951

1

Most full-time residents of the islands off the coast of Georgia take the magic for granted. Not so the visitors, the "off-islanders."

One member of the latter category, Cane Stephen Foster Winslow, stood on the balcony of a back bedroom of Camellia Hall, the mother plantation house of Moss Island, and took in a deep stinging breath of the salt-filled air blowing off the Atlantic Ocean. He had felt the magic of the place the very first time he had visited, as a skinny fourteen-year-old, back in '37. Now, fourteen years later, he felt it as strongly as ever.

The nights were the most memorable. Cane could remember clearly the first night he had visited the white beach, walking to it along the ancient shell road-path. The groaning sounds of the road had made him shiver. Island folk had explained to him about the uncanny groaning. They claimed that the shell for the roadbeds had been dug from prehistoric Indian mounds. It was easy for the imaginative to think, as the old blacks still did, that the sounds came from unhappy Indian ghosts.

It was easy, too, once he was on the beach with the phosphorescent lights on the lapping waves lighting up the eeriness of transparent shrimp and ghostly crabs, for Cane to imagine he smelled the fragrant steam from Lenora-de-Cook-Pot. Many a slave's descendant on Moss Island swore that the legendary soup pot was still heated up on moonlit nights, even though old black Lenora had long since taken her legendary "perloo" recipe to her grave.

The twenty-eight-year-old man settled back into his lounge chair to work some more on his suntan. He could easily see why the original plantation owners had left for cooler spots during the scorching July heat and miasmic swamp mugginess. Cane Stephen Foster Winslow, who was given his two middle names after the famous Dixie song writer, liked the heat. He, in fact, thrived on heat of all kinds. Basting contentedly in sweat and tanning lotion, Cane grinned when he thought of the way Poke Taylor had described the heat when he picked Cane and his guest up at the mainland ferry landing. "Hotter'n Sherman's backside in hell," the ferryman had wheezed, pulling off his baseball cap and wiping away the sweat with a tobacco-grimy hand. "I ain't shittin' you. Fifty-one'll go down as a real doozy of a summer."

Cane would think back to that prediction later. Right now he was enjoying the unaccustomed luxury of lazing under a hot sun in a place where the only annoyances were an occasional insect getting bogged down in the sticky, sweaty lotion on his body, or the raucous scream of a gull. Tri-Com Enterprises seemed very far away, even though the communications empire Cane was slowly building was in Atlanta, only two hundred or so miles from here.

Cane jumped up with a start as a yellow-fly, enticed by the smell of the tanning lotion, stung him sharply. "Damn! Even down here, everybody's out to take a chunk out of my ass!" Cane swatted the minute but nasty carnivore. "There, blood-sucker. I just wish some of those New York bastards would land that close when they take a bite out of me." Cane's good humor returned. It pleased him that his efforts to build a communications empire had not gone unnoticed among the eastern establishment. He had been mentioned in a few top trade publications, not always favorably but usually with an underlying message that Cane Winslow might be a man to keep an eye on in the business world.

Tri-Com was a young but vigorous company already. Cane was smart enough to realize that its rapid growth had not come about accidentally. He had used the modest inheritance left him by his mother in careful conjunction with opportunity and entrepreneurial genius. The results were gratifying. Cane's company now owned several newspapers and radio stations and would soon be branching out into television stations.

The intruding thoughts of empire-building were brushed away like the annoying yellow-fly. Cane reminded himself that he was on the island to relax. Moss Island had always been a soothing place. He had thought of it often during World War II, when he was a scared eighteen-year-old fighting a man's battle. He had come back here to recuperate, letting the island magic heal his wounds, physical and emotional, before going off to college as a much-matured twenty-one-year-old. His stepsister Lucy and her husband, Harm, were the only family he had left. They'd welcomed his occasional visits home from Yale and encouraged him to continue them during graduate school and these past two years of getting Tri-Com established in Atlanta.

Something flashing off the jagged line of surf brought his reverie to a halt. "Dolphins," Cane murmured with satisfaction. Dolphins with their airy domination of the ocean pleased him. He picked up his binoculars and watched the creatures playing in the deep water beyond the sandbar. They were beautiful, fascinating to watch.

The sound of crunching along the shell path beneath him diverted him from the dolphins. Cane swiveled the binoculars away from the ocean to focus on closer quarry.

No prehistoric Indians, these two. Cane grinned as he watched two girls, arm in arm, coming up from the beach. They weren't quiet about it; in time with the scrunching of shells beneath their tough brown feet, they were caterwauling "Young Love" at the top of their lungs.

He started to call down to them, but decided against it. Lucy had always been careful to keep him away from the island "natives," and he had never had much of an opportunity to satisfy his curiosity about these particular two. The dark-haired girl was, he was pretty sure, the daughter of the ferryman, Poke Taylor. Sexy little thing, he decided, as he zeroed in on

jiggling breasts and swaying hips. These island girls had a way
of growing up fast, like the lush yellow jessamine and acacia
that stretched their fragrant tendrils almost overnight.

Reba Taylor—that was her name. Reba. Fifteen? Looked
like she might have a dash of the dark blood in her, and it sure
as hell hadn't hurt her looks. She was as ripe as a peach-
plum. Cane would lay odds that every young buck in nearby
Ducktown, the island's so-called village center, had found his
way to this young beauty's shanty by the ferry dock. Maybe
even old Harm Cantrell, Lucy's husband, had smelled his way
there, too. The poor bastard didn't get much at home, he had
hinted to Cane after a few fingers too many of vintage bourbon.

Cane was enjoying his wicked role as Peeping Tom so much,
he almost didn't swerve his focus to the girl walking with Reba.

He drew back slightly when a laughing face turned up and
Tally Malone's eyes seemed to look directly into his. "My
God," he breathed. "Is that Genevieve's sad little urchin who
used to scuttle off like a fiddler crab every time I tried to speak
to her?" He looked closely, amazed at the changes that had
taken place since the last time he'd seen her. "She doesn't
look one whit like Vieve, not one whit. Look at that hair.
Where the hell did that color come from?" Tallulah Fontaine
Malone's mother was a typically pretty Southern woman, her
dark-haired beauty blurred by conventionality.

There was nothing conventional about Genevieve's daughter's looks. She was like wild honey, Cane decided—from the
gold-brown of the slender figure to the rich amber sheaf of hair
that fell to the girl's waist in one unbroken line. Warm honey.
Ten to one she had a few freckles, too. Golden, delicious
freckles.

"What is this? Cane Winslow, matrimonial object of at least
a dozen Atlanta Junior Leaguers, reduced to ogling innocent
young island girls?" Cane jumped guiltily when Gretchen
Lee's amused voice reached his ear. "Tsk, tsk. What would
Lucy say? You know how hard she tries to keep you from
tangling with the island 'trash.' " Cane followed as Gretchen
led the way into the welcome coolness of his bedroom and lit
up a cigarette. "I've finally figured that out, you know. The

witch doesn't want you hearing firsthand how her Daddy War-bucks stole this place away from Genevieve Malone's family.''

"Justin Randolph didn't steal the place, Gretchen." Cane took Gretchen's cigarette and puffed at it once, then handed it back. Their hostess kept delicate little cups of unfiltered Camels on every table in the house. Lucy Cantrell was proud of her plantation's product being used for the best-grade cigarettes. Cane made a face and picked the shreds of tobacco off the tip of his tongue. "The Fontaines lost their property fair and square. If Lucy's daddy hadn't picked up the mortgage to this place, someone else would have. He *didn't* oust Fontaine for reasons no one understands. You can't hold it against her that my stepsister inherited this place when Justin died back east. Or blame her for Andre Fontaine's suicide. The house legally became Lucy's. She had a right to claim it and move in.''

"Maybe not, but I think it's damned bad taste to keep the chair he was sitting in when he blew his brains out.''

"She had it recovered," Cane pointed out mildly.

"In the same dreadful black." Gretchen shuddered. "I notice Harm doesn't sit in it, even though it's in his study. But I'll bet dollars to doughnuts ole Lucy sneaks in there on dark nights and curls up in it like a witch's cat, thinking about the people she'd like to have zapped.''

Cane was trying hard to hold on to his initial amusement over Gretchen's and Lucy's immediate mutual loathing, but his fondness for both women was making it difficult. "Gretchen, Lucy likes to keep things as they were. The 'death chair' is a piece of history. Not just Andre, but his father, too, expired in that chair.''

"Maybe the chair will decide it's time for woman's equality and get ole Lucy. Didn't traitors posing as Confederate women get shot in the Civil War?" Gretchen giggled. "I just realized. 'Civil War' is an oxymoron.''

Cane came back from the closet with his robe. "And you're just a moron. I swear, I wish I'd known ahead of time that you were going to pull your Dorothy Parker act on Lucy. It's wasted. Lucy has no sense of humor. All you do is stir her up like a one-woman wasp's nest." Cane let out an exasperated sigh. "Gretchen, you are the light of my life and the best damned radio-show emcee I've got, but will you please cool it about my stepsister? As I've mentioned before, she's not perfect, but she's all the family I've got left."

Gretchen wrinkled her nose at him. "Is that why she glares at me every time I snuggle up to you when she's around?"

"That's another thing," Cane admonished. "I've had it with your little game of pretending there's something more than friendship going on between us. I know I promised to let your father think our radio-station merger might turn into one of another kind, but that was a temporary favor only. Lucy isn't your father. Lucy couldn't care less that you're twenty-seven and still single. Or that you prefer muscle-bound teenagers who . . ."

Gretchen grinned. "I wish that meant you're jealous, but I know better. I am sorry I started cutting up about you and me when we first came, but I'll stop if you promise to let me borrow your shower before cocktails. That witch put me in a room with a tub bath. I can't stand sitting in my own muck."

"You can use the shower—later. Right now I want to take a nap. This heat is finally getting to me."

But that was not what was getting to Cane. He was anxious to have a few moments alone to think about the girl he'd just seen on the path. Gretchen Lee would laugh at him if he told her how he had reacted to a twelve-year-old girl whom he'd hardly ever noticed before. He and Gretchen often confided in each other about their romances, but Cane didn't want to do that right now. It sometimes irritated him that Gretchen had taken it upon herself to govern his love life, though her gratitude to him for taking her out from under her father's smothering autocracy had turned into big-sisterliness that Cane usually appreciated.

"Well, maybe I'll push ole Lucy in the pool and you can jump in to save her." At Cane's threatening look, Gretchen hurried to the door, pretending to ward off blows as she went. "I know, I know! I'm going—I'm *going*." A moment later, she stuck her head back in the door. "What the hell is 'chicken mulligatawny,' by the way? That's what Essie Mae said she's serving tonight. It won't walk in under its own power, will it?''

Cane couldn't help laughing at Gretchen's comical look of alarm. She was a woman with plain features, but her repertoire of expressions made up for it. Someone had once likened Gretchen to a pinball machine with all that energy, flashing eyes, and perpetual movement. ''Not if Essie Mae had anything to do with it. She's murder at wringing a chicken's neck. But I'll admit, I haven't the slightest idea what it is. Lucy says we're having a meal just like the original plantation owners had way back when. That's all I know.'' Cane spotted Gretchen's straw sun hat on the bed where she'd left it and picked it up. ''Here, you better take this. And from now on, don't park your hat on my bed. The old Gullahs say that's a sure way to bring trouble to a house.''

Gretchen made another face as she took her hat from him. ''I never can decide if you're putting me on about all these old African superstitions or what. Okay, I'm gone. Have your beauty sleep.''

But Cane was still not in the mood for napping. He wandered around the room after Gretchen left, wondering if Genevieve Fontaine Malone ever had to clean this bedroom, which she had occupied as a blooming southern belle. Lucy never failed to justify using the former heiress to Moss Island as household help by reminding Cane that the Malones were dirt-poor. They could not, Lucy contended, get work anywhere else with Genevieve's chronic back problems. Not only that, she contended, but Daniel, Genevieve's husband, was barely competent at overseeing the tobacco-growing operations. Who else, she demanded hotly whenever Cane accused her of rubbing Genevieve's nose in her poverty, would have kept on a religious fanatic and his half-crippled wife who lived on sangaree punch and dreams of the past?

Cane always stopped arguing with his stepsister at that point. It was a shame that the Fontaines had lost everything, but he— an ambitious entrepreneur himself—agreed that the beneficiary of another's loss could not reasonably be brought to task.

Still, he sympathized somewhat with the man who had destroyed himself after his empire—Moss Island—was gone. Cane looked at the framed picture over an old chifforobe (that had probably held young Genevieve's party dresses—Lucy would take impish delight in keeping such an heirloom in plain view). The picture was apparently early 1900s vintage, judging from the fringed surreys that were parked on the lawn, where Andre Fontaine was hosting one of his famous picnics.

"So you had it all," Cane mused to the dapper mustachioed man in the picture—Genevieve's late father and Tally's grandfather. "You had it all passed down to you and lost it. Maybe that's why you lost this place—because you weren't the one who had to carve it out of the wilderness in the first place."

And a wilderness the island had been, too—in the beginning. No one had ever known much about the earliest dwellers on Moss Island, but the seventeenth-century remnants of the Guale Indian villages were later authenticated. The Spanish missionaries attempted to make the island theirs, but were unsuccessful, as the aged ruins indicated. An old tabby chapel, comprised of the peculiar mixture of lime, shell, sand, and water, survived through the plantation era, but few other missionary-constructed edifices did.

The island had had many different tenants. Plagued by Indians, pirates, and the English, the Spanish missionaries finally gave up the ghost. By 1733, Indians and Spanish were long gone. Around 1742, General Oglethorpe's officers' plantations, optimistically built for permanency, were razed by the Spanish in the Battle of Bloody Marsh on nearby Saint Simons.

Others moved in, restored the ruined plantations; most surrendered to the rigors of trying to grow large crops, such as cotton or rice, without enough labor. When Breneau Marchant Fontaine came from France to escape the Revolution, he was able to buy the largest tract of property for a song. Not only that, the increasingly available slave labor helped his rice-growing industry thrive from the start. Successful and confident, he bought more slaves, including some from the last slave ship (*The Wanderer*) ever to land in the Southern states.

Eventually, as they had for all the islanders before him, the tides turned against Breneau Fontaine. With the Civil War and

Sherman's subsequent Field Order number 15, which virtually gave island land to the slaves occupying it, Fontaine's empire began crumbling piece by piece.

Somehow Fontaine managed to hold on to the house and part of the acreage. Soon after he died in 1885, his heirs came up with a plan for converting the island into a private hunting club for sun-seeking northerners (and island-loving Atlanta financiers). Selling shares and limited time leases turned out to be a popular and lucrative venture. The Moss Island Club thrived for almost fifty years.

The great hurricane of 1924 destroyed many of the elaborate "cottages." The great crash of '29 destroyed most of the remaining lessees. The latter national disaster started the financial decline of island landowners like the Cantrells and the major landowner, Andre Fontaine. Justin Prelutsky (who changed his name to "Randolph" upon his advent into island society) bought up mortgages, including the Cantrells', and set his sights on the main property and Camellia Hall.

In 1933, Justin's twenty-one-year-old daughter Lucy was married to Harmon Cantrell. The couple's wedding gift was the deed to the Cantrell cottage. In 1935, Justin Randolph brought his new wife, the widow of a cotton-mill magnate and Cane's mother, to live on Moss Island. Lucy's father was not satisfied with the large shuttered cottage he and his bride occupied. He made his first bid for Camellia Hall, which Andre Fontaine turned down flat.

The mutual dislike of the two men turned into bitter enmity. Though the Fontaine property and mansion were dangerously close to foreclosure, Andre Fontaine made it clear that Justin Randolph would never own anything belonging to him.

Justin was equally stubborn about what he wanted. But the sudden death of his new wife after only a year derailed him momentarily. Then, after a year's mourning spent off the island, he came back to Moss. This time he brought with him his stepson, Cane. The fourteen-year-old boy reacted to the island much as any other southern boy freed from a strict boys' school after two years: he loved every inch of it.

Cane became attached to his new family as well. He formed

a close bond with his stepsister especially. He really liked Harm, but it was Justin Randolph on whom he cast an admiring eye. Someday, the young Cane Winslow promised himself, he too would be a powerful man in the world of business.

Changes came quickly that long-ago spring. Justin went back east on a business trip, and he died of a sudden heart attack while there. In June, Genevieve Fontaine married Daniel Malone, a quiet, rather good-looking sharecropper. The shock of the sudden marriage on islanders gave way to the larger shock of Andre Fontaine's suicide in August. People whispered that Lucy Cantrell had as much as pulled the trigger on Fontaine's shotgun when she came back from settling her late father's estate. She had with her the deed to Camellia Hall.

Andre Fontaine had sworn all his life that he would not leave his ancestral home except in a pine box, and that was how he left it. Lucy Cantrell paid for the pine coffin and the funeral in the little tabby chapel. She and Harm moved into Camellia Hall the day after.

In 1941, Cane Winslow, now a frequent visitor to Moss Island, was drafted. Like Daniel Malone, who was called up about the same time, he would not return to the island until close to the end of World War II. When he returned in '45, Cane soaked up the healing warmth of the island and thought hard about what he would do with the rest of his life.

Yale took care of four years of it; graduate school another year. Then Cane was ready to start building his empire. . . .

Cane knew Gretchen was probably chafing at the bit to get her shower, but he was in a reflective mood, thinking about this place and all the different lives it had touched, including his. He admired the way old Fontaine had built Camellia Hall so that most of the surrounding landscape could be seen and appreciated. Cane especially liked the view from the back of the house, where he had sunned earlier, because it overlooked the dunes and the ocean. The island wasn't all that large— maybe about eighty miles in perimeter—and shaped like a kidney. On that magical first visit, Cane had climbed up to the top of the tabby lighthouse and looked out over what he was sure was almost the entire island. He could see the stretch of beach until it disappeared around a bend, on the other side of which was a cove where he'd often gone swimming. The lagoon between the lighthouse and the cove was a mere sparkle of dark blue. He'd sneaked down there a few times for skinny-dipping, not trusting the privacy of the well-lighted pool by the main house.

The far reaches of the island—the marshlands, the swamp, the little community of Ducktown on the opposite side of the island, had all borne exploration by a curious young boy. Cane had been enthralled by several excursions into these areas, often in the company of the oldest living black on the island. Uncle Gibber, descendant of John-Gwine-Run-Away, a slave whose name had evolved from his penchant for numerous escape attempts, had taught Cane everything he knew about fishing, crabbing, frog-gigging, even gator-baiting. From Gibber Cane learned, too, all the scary stories that all the Gullahs knew and respected. Cane was not a superstitious person, but he never passed by the "Hainted Oak" at night without wondering if it was really haunted. Its "haints" were the ghosts of the three black slaves hanged by poachers who were afraid of being identified to the plantation owner. The "Ghost with Long Arms" lived in that tree, too, according to Gibber, who owned up even to a small boy that he was careful never to look at the swaying moss—just in case. If the ghost beckoned to you while you were looking at it, that meant you were going to die. . . .

Cane laughed out loud, wondering if he had been permanently trapped in the island's magical web of old mysteries. "The only mystery is how I'm gonna get showered and dressed before Gretchen bangs on the door for her turn."

Still he lingered, staring out the window that afforded a view of Lucy's exotic garden, which was religiously maintained as it had been laid out by old Fontaine. Persian date palms, fig trees, riotously flowering shrubs, some dating back to the Spanish missionary occupation, abounded. Cane wondered if anyone in the history of the island had ever actually seen the one exotic plant still missing from the garden: the fabulous "Lost

Gordonia.'' The legendary blossom was supposedly a flower
of such incredible fragrance and beauty that horticulturists still
came to Moss Island in search of it.

Cane thought about the vision of wild honey he had seen
through his binoculars. Perhaps the Lost Gordonia was, like
most other treasures, right there under one's nose all the time.

"Tally Malone—your Lost Gordonia.'' Cane walked toward
the bathroom, shaking his head. "Winslow, you better have
that shower before you get any deeper into this island-magic
shit.''

He made it a cold shower, which helped considerably.

Reba Taylor and Tally Malone finished a few more rows of
suckering tobacco after they returned from their swim in the
ocean. As they walked down the corridors of tall green plants,
one girl on either side of the stalk, they talked about Reba's
latest love interest, Jim-Roy Tatum.

Or at least Reba talked. "Honey, it's just gettin' outta hand,
how that boy wants it. Tally, I swear I ain't about to go all the
way till he says we're engaged, or something. Maybe engaged
to be engaged. You know. Anyhow, I just don't know what
I'm gonna do with that boy if he keeps carrying on like he's
been doing.'' Reba stopped and took a large swig of the RC
Cola she'd stashed at the end of the row. The peanuts she'd
put in the bottle had all floated to the top. "Want some?''

Tally shuddered, shaking her head as she reached between
the top leaves of the stalk they were both attacking. She snipped
off a parasitic sucker to keep it from drawing all the nutrients
out of the more important leaves of the tobacco plant. "You
could just tell him that, couldn't you? I mean, tell him how
you're not gonna do . . . uh . . . you know, unless he's serious
about making you his girlfriend.''

"Girlfriend,'' Reba snorted, shaking her dark curls off her
neck, which was covered with sticky sweat. Wisely, Tally had
pinned her long hair up on top of her head. "*Girlfriend!* Shoot.
Jim-Roy just wants in my pants and I ain't lettin' him. You
reckon we could save the rest of these rows till tomorrow
morning? I'm plumb whupped out.''

"Me, too. Want to go down to the lagoon?" Tally reached up under her halter top to scratch an old bite. Durn red bug, probably. Whatever it was, it was itching like aitch. She scratched the tormenting spot vigorously, wishing Reba would stop talking so she could go for another swim. She hoped that Reba didn't want to go, since she really needed some time to herself. With all the work in tobacco lately and Reba deciding they were best friends and her mother having an especially hard time with her back, Tally was really feeling the need to be alone.

"Nah." Reba laconically snapped off another sucker, looking at it as though she were really interested in it before tossing it over the row. "I gotta fix my pa some supper 'fore I go out with Jim-Roy. Pa wants grits, don't you know. Ever' night, ever' night—grits, grits, grits. I tell you, Tally, I ever get shut of this place, I ain't never gonna cook grits again. I swear it up and down, those gritty little devils will never be in my cooking pot, come hell or high water."

Tally brushed the sweat off her face and wondered if this much perspiring out in the heat was as good for the skin as Essie Mae swore it was. But Essie Mae didn't sweat, hefty as she was. So how did she know? "Well, I tell you, there are a few things I'm not gonna eat after I leave here, neither. Chicken, for one. That one I cut his head off today jumped all over the yard after I did the chopping. It's just downright eerie something could go hoppin' all over after his head's been chopped off."

"I still like taking the ax to a chicken's neck 'stead of wringing it like a dishrag. Jim-Roy Tatum and me was talking about that, how living on a farm has got some real cruel parts to it. He's a case, that boy." Reba's full mouth curved. "Got a case on me, too, I reckon. You want to know what he done the other night, after we finished puttin' in the barn at ole Hackebarney's?"

Later, as she floated alone in the cool water of the lagoon, Tally thought about what Reba had told her. She wasn't sure that her friend had really experienced all the things she said she had, but it was pretty interesting all the same. Only, Jim-

Roy or a boy like him wouldn't do for her, Tally had decided long ago. The man of her dreams would have to be a lot more sophisticated. She lay back in the water, paddling around lazily as she thought about that elusive fantasy figure. What would he look like?

A sharp voice calling her name scattered Tally's peaceful oblivion. "Tally! Tal-lee Malone, you down here? Lord, girl, can't you hear a body calling you?"

Tally dog-paddled over to the shallows to look up at her father, Daniel, who stood on the bank amid the palmettos and soft-brown cattails. She knelt so that the water was up to her neck, because Daniel hated seeing females, even half-grown ones, close to naked. Daniel Malone's religion did not hold with nakedness. In fact, the primitive church Perrie went to didn't hold with much of anything. Tally noticed that what other people called having fun Perrie and his group called sinning. She had on her skimpy halter and shorts, but they would be clinging wetly to her, and that was as bad as being naked. "I'm sorry, Perrie. I didn't hear you." The "Perrie" came from *père*, which Tally's mother had taught her was French for "father." The nickname had stuck, for some reason. Daniel, who usually disdained anything to do with his wife's fancy ancestry, unexpectedly liked it. "Did you want me for something?"

"Well, I was planning on you helping me with the un-stringing so we'd have us enough tobacco sticks for the barn we're puttin' in Saturday." Daniel ignored the girl's grimace at the mention of a job she detested even more than suckering. "Unstringing" the cured tobacco leaves from the sticks they had been tied to for the curing process was a hot, smelly, unpleasant job. "But that'll have to wait its turn. Essie Mae is in dire need of help up to the big house. That sorry F'Mollie's cut out on 'er again, just when Miz Lucy's company needs their supper."

"F'Mollie's not one bit sorry, Perrie, and it's mean of you to say so. She's been trying to make her some extra money with the tobacco puttin'-in's. Lord knows she'll never get anything doing for Miz Lucy." Tally had always admired F'Mollie's spirit and sass. She would call her her best friend if Reba hadn't already claimed that exclusive not-to-be-messed-with spot. Essie Mae proudly claimed that her daughter, "F'Mollie," had been named by the doctor at the Brunswick charity clinic. He'd written his choice of a name, "Female," right there on a pretty little bracelet on the infant's wrist.

"I just hope Miz Lucy doesn't make Essie Mae take a keen switch to F'Mollie. Her legs are skinny and marked up bad enough from all the mosquitoes that come in that ole shanty at night."

"I'm gonna take one to yours if you don't get yourself out of that pond right quick and get on up there to make yourself useful. Your ma said I wasn't to tell you to take her place tonight, Miz Lucy not having no patience with her feeling sick and all, but I don't see that Vieve's up to workin' again. And you know how Miz Lucy'll act if things ain't done right."

Tally forgot her tiredness at that. She came out of the water like a shot. "Mama's back's troubling her again? Perrie, I sure hope you made her lie down. I'm getting old enough to do for the big house. Mama's not able, even if she does keep on trying to do everything ole Lucy tells her to."

Daniel looked at Tally, perplexed as always by her spirit. "Sometimes, girl, I wonder who's the young'un—you or Vieve. You're as soft on her as she is on you. When I whipped you with my belt last Sunday for violatin' the Sabbath, she cried all night." Tally cringed a little, remembering the whipping. Daniel was not basically a violent man, but he occasionally took the belt to her. She sensed out of an uncertain wisdom that the physical outbursts were desperate attempts at playing some sort of fatherhood role with a daughter whom he neither loved nor understood. "Well, anyways—don't worry none about your mama. Mistuh Harm brought down some of the yambis and ham he said Essie Mae had left over from last night. Your ma won't go hungry, that's for sure. Never will, neither," he added, with a sly sideways glance at Tally to see how she was reacting. "Not so long as a certain party's soft as warm butter on 'er."

Tally couldn't help blushing. She and everybody else on the

island knew that Harmon Cantrell was sweet on her mother and always had been. Tally was sure Daniel had never revealed the jealousy beneath his obsequious treatment of the master of Camellia Hall to anyone else. The burden of that confidence was one Tally didn't enjoy, since it placed her square in the middle of her mother and father and their unhappy relationship. She was pretty sure that Daniel had heard some of the same remarks she had from old-time islanders about how the still-beautiful, once-aristocratic Genevieve Fontaine had married "beneath her." "Well, I just hope you won't say anything about that where Miz Lucy can hear it. Mama enjoys being treated like she's still a lady. She really does."

Daniel's eyes darkened dangerously, showing how he disliked Tally's implication that he offered Genevieve very little of the genteel life. "I despise it when you and your mama take up for each other like you're better'n anybody else on the island. You gonna skedaddle on up where you're needed, or you want me to break a keen switch right here to get those skinny legs moving?"

Tally scurried past him, wringing her hair out the best she could. Essie Mae kept a maid's uniform and apron up at the house for her, so Tally didn't worry about her wet clothes. But she did worry about what Lucy's company would think seeing a white girl working around the house in the same kind of uniform that the black folks wore. Genevieve had tried to convince her daughter that wearing a maid's uniform didn't change the way a person felt about herself inside, but Tally wasn't buying. That black sateen dress and starched apron Lucy insisted on her help wearing made Tally feel like—well, like dressed-up cow dooky.

The childish vulgarity of her thoughts cheered her. She pulled her shirt down over her skimpy attire so she wouldn't offend Perrie and scooted well ahead of him down the path to the big house. "Tell Mama I'll bring her something special when I come home tonight," she called to Daniel as they parted.

Essie Mae was on the kitchen stoop pouring a pan of water on her beloved benne patch. Benne seeds were like store-bought sesame but had greater powers. Good luck came to those who kept a healthy benne patch; but woe unto the gardener who ever let the patch die out. Tally had heard it all her life that once you planted the benne seed, you had to keep it up. Otherwise, "ole man death would catch you." Gullahs were always doing everything they could to ward off "ole man death."

" 'Scuse me, brother!" Tally devilishly called out the litany that traditionally accompanied the act of dumping out water. Essie Mae shared the island blacks' superstition that it wouldn't do to offend any spirits lurking about by dousing them with water. "Excoo-oose me!"

The huge black woman responded with laughter, though she put a menacing free hand on her hip and shook her head as Tally ran up the steps. "You look like a frizzled chicken, chile. Look at that hair. Lordee. You're a drownded rat, if I ever seen one, and Miz Lucy entertainin' company." Essie Mae hustled Tally into the kitchen, which was warm enough to hatch eggs. "Git yourself outta them wet clothes and let me see can I find one of them hairnets Miz Lucy has taken to likin' the he'p to wear on their haids."

"Shoot, 'fore you know it, she'll have us wearing chains on our ankles like those slaves that walked down into the sea."

But Tally quickly ducked into the pantry and changed into her uniform, obediently letting Essie Mae tuck her hair up under one of the infamous thick hairnets Lucy had ordered. "Umm, um," she breathed, taking in all the fragrant smells from the ovenlike kitchen. "Something smells so good, I can't hardly stand it. I just hope it's not fish, Essie Mae. I been eating so many of those boogers lately, I be breathing through my cheeks."

Essie Mae's bulk rocked with laughter as she tucked the last recalcitrant curl up under Tally's hairnet. The black woman was secretly tickled by her "chile's" comfortableness with old island Gullah and by the way she occasionally mocked it without even being aware of it. "Well, be that as it may, there's a bucket of crawdaddies over there waitin' to be biled and cleaned. It's got your name on it."

Tally shuddered when she went over to peer into the pail of squirming, crusty crawfish. "Yuk. Essie Mae, you know good and well how much I despise boiling up things that are still moving." The black woman had a heart of gold, Tally reflected, except when it came to cooking. Nothing that swam, crawled, flew, or walked on more than two feet was safe from Essie Mae's firm conviction that anything with meat on its bones was meant to be eaten.

Essie Mae softened, knowing how tenderhearted the child was. "Then you gits the hard part—mashing up the taters for soo-flay. And the biled chicken needs dee-boning for that crazy furrin' dish Miz Lucy ordered up."

"Mulligatawny. It's just plain old stew, Essie Mae, but Miz Lucy thinks she's serving up the same dishes that the old-timey people who used to live here ate." Tally waited till the black woman wasn't looking before she garfed down a handful of raisins meant for the soufflé.

Essie Mae saw what was going on but pretended not to notice that Tally was eating as many raisins as she was mixing into the potatoes. The marshmallows would be next, but that was all right, too. The black woman was well aware of how lean the Malones' larder was. Fish and grits, mostly. "I'll be sure to save some of everything so's you can take a good mess home with you when you git through tonight." Essie Mae pulled out the roast pig from the mammoth oven and pronounced it "fit to eat with yo' mouth."

"I'm glad to hear that," Lucy Cantrell said, entering the kitchen in a rustle of taffeta. "Good heavens, no wonder the whole house smells like a barbecue pit. You've cooked up every wild beast on the island." Lucy made a delicate face as she peeked into the crawfish pot. "No matter what people on this island think, God did not mean for those hideous creatures to be eaten." Lucy hastily replaced the lid on the offending soup and rolled her eyes at the sight of the still-intact pig's snout on the roasted carcass. "Well, at least the beast doesn't have just three legs. I'd hate to think that Aunt Monday would be staging a voodoo vendetta against me for serving up her pet pig."

Essie Mae looked shocked. Neither she nor anyone on the island joked about the island obeah who lived deep in the swamp with her ferocious, three-legged wild boar, Lionel. "Aunt Monday's not no hag . . ."

Lucy inspected her nails, which were polished in the latest color: Cherries-in-the-Snow. Her lips were the same brilliant deep red. "No, in fact I've heard she's quite beautiful. Very, very old—but still beautiful."

Essie Mae chuckled. "Miz Lucy, you still ain't got de Gullah talk down right. A 'hag' be a witchin' woman that's up to no good. But what I was sayin' was that Aunt Monday ain't one for puttin' spells on folks. She just knows all them good roots and yerbs for makin' medicine." Essie Mae stuck an apple in the roasted pig's mouth and stepped back to admire her handiwork. "Now ain't Mistuh Cane gone love that. I can just hear 'im now—'Essie Mae, you come to Atlanta and open you up a resterant and there won't be no more folks wastin' their money at Mammy's Shanty.' "

Lucy obligingly looked at Essie Mae's porcine masterpiece. "Sometimes I think that my stepbrother comes down here more for your barbaric cooking than to visit me. Is that one of those boars that my husband says descends from the original line?" Lucy was referring to the breed of boar that still roamed the island. They had been especially brought over by an eastern potentate visitor in the early days of resort opulence.

"Naw, this'un ain't one of them skinny razorbacks." Essie Mae's eyes grew thoughtful. "You know, next time Mistuh Cane come down, I gone find me a plump turtle and fix some of them rissoles he likes so much."

Lucy looked as if she might be on the verge of gagging. "For such an attractive man, my stepbrother certainly has peculiar taste in food." Lucy took a dainty flowerlet of cauli-flower from the platter of fresh raw vegetables she always had the cook prepare for large dinners. Lucy was not fond of south-ern cooking, though she made it almost a fetish to have com-pany menus reminiscent of the old plantation dwellers. "Peculiar taste in women, too. I declare, that woman he brought down with him is about the plainest, skinniest thing

I've ever seen. No spring chicken, either. She's thirty if she's a day.'' Gretchen Lee was, in fact, twenty-seven. Lucy sniffed. She liked it better when her stepbrother came down alone and regaled her with the latest gossip about Atlanta society. ''Cane says it's a business relationship, of course. Gretchen's father sold his chain of Georgia radios and newspapers to Tri-Com, and Cane has made the daughter part of his team.''

Tally, who was in the corner, out of Lucy's periphery, dropped her wooden spoon and Lucy whirled around at the noise, seeing the girl for the first time since she had entered the kitchen. ''Taking your mother's place again, are you, Tally? That's getting to be a regular thing these days. Be sure you wash that spoon before you dip it into the food again.'' Lucy's ice-blue eyes harpooned Tally into paralysis. ''Well, pick it up off the floor, child. I declare, I hope you're not going to turn out like one of those genetic accidents you see all over Ducktown.''

Tally's flush from working in the warm kitchen deepened as she stiffly retrieved the spoon and took it over to the sink to wash it. ''Miz Lucy, I don't appreciate you sayin' I'm a moron,'' she said in a quietly dangerous tone that made Essie Mae rally into divertive action.

''Lordy, Miz Lucy, what in the blessed world was goin' on a while ago down at the pool? All that squealin' and carryin' on like somebody had done drownded or something.''

Lucy smiled indulgently. At least Cane, despite his current involvement with empire-building, had not lost his playfulness. She patted her new poodle haircut and brushed off an imaginary fleck from her moiré taffeta dress. Gretchen Lee would have to do *her* toilette all over again, and that bleached hair (Lucy's was naturally blond) would be straight as a board. Lucy's pleasure showed in her smile. ''I suppose you could call what happened amusing. Childish, but rather funny. That silly woman pushed my stepbrother into the pool—the woman cannot hold her liquor, although very few people can drink *three* martinis and keep their senses—and he pulled her right in with him. His clothes were ruined, of course. . . .'' Lucy's eyes lit on Tally's face suddenly.

"You *can* be of some use tonight, after all, Tally. Poor Cane brought only the one pair of trousers. Unfortunately they're cotton. You do know how to iron, of course?"

Tally did not. The Malones didn't own an iron. Mattie, the washerwoman in the quarters, had always taken care of all the island's laundry. "Certainly I know how to iron," Tally said with dignity, ignoring Essie Mae's rolling eyes.

"Then our little problem is taken care of." Lucy brushed her hands of the matter and of Tally Malone. "Mr. Winslow is in his room, the one at the end of the hall. After you've pressed his trousers, do you think you could find him?"

"I think so," Tally said solemnly. "That was my mother's old bedroom and she showed it to me once when she was cleaning upstairs."

Lucy had the grace to turn pink. "Well. Be that as it may." She turned quickly to the black woman. "I want dinner served promptly at eight, before anyone gets drunk. And, Essie Mae, there's to be no wineglass at Mr. Harm's setting. You understand me? If he asks you for a glass, pretend you didn't hear. My husband has enjoyed himself quite enough for one evening." Lucy's pretty face took on an almost baffled look when she added, "Can you believe that the man actually, for an infinitesimal instant, acted as if he were going to throw *me* in the pool?"

Essie Mae and Tally did not dare look at each other. "No, ma'am, I can't believe it. But I'm sure enough glad he didn't go and do it!"

When Lucy had left, Essie Mae sat down at the kitchen table and started pulling the skin off the chicken Tally had deboned. "That Mistuh Harm come real close to dying out there by that pool—and it warn't from no drownding, neither. Now, Miss Priss, what's this mess you got yourself into this time? And I cain't git you out of it. I ain't got time to iron no pants. You'll just have to make the best of it."

"I'll handle it," Tally said, with not quite as much confidence as when she had claimed to Miz Lucy to have a talent she did not in fact have. "I'll handle it, even if it kills me."

* * *

It nearly did. Tally burned herself three times before she finally
got the awkward garment into position to press out the worst
wrinkles. A scorching smell made her panic. What if she
burned a hole in this Cane fellow's precious britches? Well,
everybody said he was rich, Tally thought; he could buy a
whole storeful. She had caught glimpses of him over the
years—not close up, but enough to recognize that he was a
man particular about the way he looked. Miz Lucy hadn't
seemed to think much of the woman he brought with him, but
it could be that Cane Winslow wouldn't take kindly to wearing
scorched pants in her presence. Reba had heard Cane was
twenty-eight, which was pretty old. Maybe this lady was someone he'd decided to marry and settle down with. Regardless,
Tally was pretty sure Cane Winslow would be cranky if his
pants were returned to him totally ruined.

She sighed as she folded the slacks over her arm and went
around to the back shutter-enclosed stairs that Miz Lucy liked
the help to use instead of the main staircase. When she reached
the door, she took a deep breath and tapped timidly. Just before the door opened, she snatched off her hairnet and stuffed
it in her pocket.

Then she was face-to-face with Lucy Cantrell's stepbrother,
Cane Stephen Foster Winslow.

2

The man in her dreams was real. Tally just stood there
staring. She had once overheard Miz Lucy telling Essie
Mae how her stepbrother's hair had started turning gray when
he was in his teens. Tally had always equated graying hair with
getting old.

This man had graying hair but he was far from old. Even
the crispy, iron-colored hair had a youthful vitality to it, springing back from a bronze-tanned forehead. Aliveness. That's
what it was, Tally thought numbly, amazed to see that Cane's

eyes were tiger-colored like her own—yellow-brown with dark rims and ringed with smutty-black lashes. She knew what she would tell Reba later about his face: *He's got these dark, pointy eyebrows, kind of like the devil's. And you never in your life saw such white teeth—like an Ipana ad; I'll swear to it on a stack of Bibles.* Reba would want to know, too, if Cane had a good body. Tally looked at the muscular chest that was showing through the loosely knotted robe and swallowed hard. She and Reba had once seen some convicts on the chain gang who were all muscled, some with hair on their chest like Cane's, and had whispered about it for a week, about how it would feel to be hugged by a man with all that muscle and hair.

By the time Tally's inventory had gotten to Cane's feet, she had an imprinted detailed memory that would keep her and Reba in delicious whispering conferences for weeks to come. But as Tally memorized Cane's lean bare legs and feet—which had the same lush, even bronze as the rest of him—she was brought back to her senses. Cane was clearing his throat and obviously wondering if she was one of the Ducktown retards ole Lucy had earlier accused her of resembling.

She tried to think of something brilliant to say. Her tongue betrayed her. "I . . . uh . . . I brought you your . . . uh . . . pants."

"By George, I thought I recognized those as mine. I've been caught with my pants down before—but never mind all that." He looked Tally up and down, not unlike the way she had done him. Of course, Tally thought with relief, she was fully dressed, so he couldn't see as much. She was very embarrassed about her bony knees and total absence of breasts. The cream she had ordered from *Love Stories* had made her nipples larger from rubbing calluses on them but had not noticeably enlarged her bosom as guaranteed. "Hey, look at you," he finally said, shaking his head a little sadly as he observed the puffed starched sleeves and unbecoming lines of the uniform. "How like my stepsister to clothe the natives in missionary cloth."

Tally wished she knew what he meant by that, but she didn't. "I beg your pardon?"

Cane laughed. "Oh, don't pay any attention to me. I talk in

riddles half the time. Drives my enemies crazy. My friends, too. It's just that I liked you in freckles and honey so much better.'' At Tally's even more puzzled look, he grinned. ''Forget it. Hell, come on in. Let me take those pants off your hands.''

''Thank you,'' Tally said primly. She was sure Miz Lucy wouldn't like her going into Cane's bedroom, but she was unable to will herself to leave. ''This was once my mother's bedroom, you know.''

Cane tossed the pants to a chair and flung himself down to stare at the girl standing there in her prim little maid's uniform. ''Oh, Lord. Of all the insensitive, loutish . . . I'm sorry . . . Tallulah, isn't it?''

''Yes, but folks mostly call me Tally. Please don't apologize. I'm used to it. I really am. It's harder on my mother. I never lived here, so it's not that bad working in the house for Miz Lucy. I only started this year, when my mother's back got worse. That's why you haven't seen me around before now.''

Cane looked at her thoughtfully, oblivious to the fact that he was crushing the painstakingly pressed pants beneath him. ''But I *have* seen you over the years. You remind me of one of those delicate little shell creatures that pulls back into its hiding place at the slightest threat from a stranger. How have you managed to hide from me so well, Tally Malone? And why?'' The white smile dazzled. ''I'm not a bad fellow.''

Tally wished she did have a shell to retreat into. Cane's way of talking to her as though they were equals, as though she were not a mere child, rattled her in a way she couldn't understand. She changed the subject. ''Did you know my mother in the old days?''

Cane looked at the eager face turned up toward his and smiled a little ruefully. How old the child must think him! ''Well, now, it really strains this old memory, but I seem to remember your mama. She was a real pretty lady. I bet she still is.''

''She sure is! I just wish I looked more like her.''

Cane didn't agree. He liked Tally the way she was. ''I remember when you were born. Everybody was worried about you coming two months early, but you seem to've turned out just fine.''

"My mother nearly died having me," Tally said sadly. "She had a hurt back. Maybe that's why I came early."

Cane was ready to change the subject. "That was an eventful year. Marriage, birth, death—all stages of life were represented here on the island. Justin used to tell me that an island was the best world a man could have— But, hey, you wouldn't remember that old redheaded reprobate. You came along later.''

"I've heard some stories. He and my granddaddy hated each other, Mama says. But sometimes when I look at his picture downstairs, I have a feeling I might have liked him. He died, though, before I was born. My granddaddy died not long after that, too." Tally's face sobered. She wasn't supposed to know that Andre Fontaine had shot himself in this very house. But F'Mollie, who knew everything, had shown Tally the "death chair" in Andre Fontaine's old study, where he had collapsed after putting a gun to his head. "I've often wondered why Miz Lucy kept that old chair in what's Mr. Harm's office now. Not just my granddaddy, but his daddy, too, died in that very chair.''

"My friend Gretchen wonders that same thing. But Lucy has a bizarre turn to her about some things. Look, am I keeping you from something you need to do?''

Tally stiffened. He wanted her to leave! "I'm sorry, Mr. Winslow. I got to jabbering and you still have to get dressed and . . ." She started edging toward the door, mortified that she had overstayed.

"Don't go," Cane said quietly. "I just didn't want you to get in trouble downstairs. I don't know when I've enjoyed talking with anyone this much. You're like the island itself— that sun-buttered voice and skin—hell, I just plain like looking at you and listening to you. You know that this island is magic, don't you? And you, Tally Malone, have that magic all around you.''

They looked at each other in an odd little sizing-up silence. Then a burst of "Habanera" from the bathroom penetrated the strange spell that had fallen between them. "That's Gretchen," Cane said with a forced casualness intended to restore things to normal. "She's borrowing my shower again and fancies herself Risë Stevens when she's in there. Wait and meet her. You'll like Gretchen. Most people do."

Not ole Lucy, Tally thought. "Will you two be getting married?" She didn't know where the question came from.

Cane looked a little surprised, even shocked, before he laughed. "Probably. But not to each other. Is there anything else her royal highness wishes to know about me?"

"Her royal highness?"

"You are the real princess of the island, aren't you?"

Tally had never talked to anyone like this, much less to a man of Cane Winslow's age and experience. She knew she ought to leave but she couldn't bring herself to give up the delicious feeling of being with someone exciting who seemed to be genuinely interested in her. It was a little wicked, too, sitting in a bedroom with a man while a lady whom Tally had not even met was taking a shower. She was storing up lots to tell Reba. "My mama is the real princess. If you'd been on the island in its heyday, you might have danced with her. She was the belle of the ball at all the fancy pavilion parties before the place burned down."

"I'm sure she was." Cane was not interested in talking about Genevieve Fontaine Malone; he was interested in learning more about her daughter. "You have her grace and breeding, it sticks out all over, but you're very different from your mother, Tallulah Malone."

Tally's hand went immediately to her nose, her greatest despair. "It's this—the Fontaine nose. It's so big!"

Cane said with complete solemnity, "It's a wonderful, aristocratic nose that suits you perfectly. I've never trusted people with squishy little no-noses. But, no, little Tally, it is not your Fontaine nose that makes you special." He started to say more, but caught himself up. How could he say things to this twelve-year-old girl that even a twenty-eight-year-old man didn't understand? "Your mother was certainly a vivacious one, from all accounts. Even ole Harm, married as he was to Lucy, used

to sneak a dance or two with her that first spring I came here."
Cane bounced a shiny patent leather shoe in one strong hand
absentmindedly as he talked. The shoe froze in his hand as a
familiar old conjecture with uncomfortable implications struck
him. "But then, your mother had many, many admirers, long
ago and right now. And I'm among them." Cane tossed the
shoe next to its twin and took Tally's chin in his hand, oh-so-
lightly. "And I'm an admirer of her daughter, too—Fontaine
nose and all." He dropped his hand and Tally knew that he'd
felt the same shock from the contact she had. "Will I be seeing
you at dinner?"

Tally looked down at her maid's uniform and said, "Not if
F'Mollie turns up tonight to serve. Miz Lucy prefers that the
Negroes do the serving at the table."

"My stepsister has a real thing about living out her fantasy
of de ole plantation home."

"It takes more than a fantasy to run a house like this the
same way the women did in the old days." Tally looked Cane
squarely in the eye. "And, if you ask me, Miz Lucy will never
even be a shadow of those women back then."

The sound of applause from across the room was accompanied by "bravo." "Amen. And I'll say it again. Amen on that.
Whoever this child is, she has won my heart." Gretchen Lee,
her blond hair still streaming about her bony face and her
angular figure clad in nothing but a scanty robe with blazing
anemones, came over and took Tally by both hands. "Look at
you, a fragile Dorothy taking on the Wicked Witch of the
South. Introduce me to this wonderful child, Cane, and then
go shave or something while she and I get acquainted. And
please fix me a martini."

"Gretchen, meet Tallulah Fontaine Malone. Tally, this is
Gretchen Lee."

Tally loved the woman's rich voice and throaty laugh. She
wasn't exactly pretty, as Miz Lucy had pointed out, but being
in Gretchen's company was like being in the morning sunshine.

"Oh, to be named after the wonderful Tallulah! I'm so
jealous I could die. And such dewy youth. . . !" Gretchen
turned to Cane accusingly. "This young woman was put to

the indignity of ironing your pants? While everyone else was dressing for the ball? The very idea!"

Cane whispered loudly to Tally, "She tends to overdramatize. One of the occupational hazards of her business. But she's damn good at what she does."

"Cane, shut up and fix my drink." While Cane walked over to the small table holding liquor and glasses, Gretchen whispered, "You live on this island with all its secrets about putting off witches. I've heard people even paint the house trim blue to keep them out. What can we do to keep Lucy in her place, do you think? Paint our noses blue?"

Tally thought for a minute, then grinned. "Well, there's this." She fisted her small hand and spread the index and pinky finger so they were pointed in opposite directions. "It's the sign some of the Gullahs use to keep the evil eye and hags, too, away from them."

Gretchen laughed heartily and imitated the gesture. "I love it! We'll give the witch our special 'finger'! It's better than shooting her a bird. All right, Cane," she called out gaily. "Tallulah and I have our special sisterhood sign that will protect us from the evil witch."

Cane just shook his head and, after giving Gretchen her drink, disappeared into the bathroom.

That gave Tally a chance to relax a bit. So when Gretchen asked her about herself, she laughed and talked to her with ease. In fact, Tally felt that Gretchen was already her friend. She told her all about her best friend on the island—Reba Taylor—while she watched Gretchen dress, memorizing every detail of makeup application, hairstyling, underwear—everything. Maybe Gretchen Lee wasn't really pretty like Lauren Bacall or even Miz Lucy, but Tally liked her and could see why she might get her very own TV show, as Gretchen had confided she might—very soon.

"This Reba sounds real nice," Gretchen said when Tally stopped for breath. "And since she already has a boyfriend, I know she's interested in looking pretty. Does she like costume jewelry?"

Tally thought of the palmetto bracelets she and Reba had

woven, pretending they were real. "Does she ever! Oh, she'll just love these." Tally's eyes lit up at the gaily colored set of plastic bangles Gretchen slipped off her wrist onto the younger girl's.

Gretchen smiled at Tally's enthusiasm. "You're a generous-hearted little thing. I'll bet you'd give these to your friend without a thought to keeping them yourself."

"It's just that I have so much and Reba has so little. Well, maybe I don't have much in the way of *things*, but I have a mother. And Reba's never even known a mother, since hers died when she was a baby."

"Well, to reward you for being such a sweet new friend, I want you to have these for that beautiful hair of yours." Gretchen took the two combs from her own hair and handed them to Tally. She laughed at the look on Tally's face. "They aren't real gold, you goose. Go on, take them."

Tally did, and impulsively hugged Gretchen. "I can't wait to get grown so you and I can be real friends."

Gretchen was pleased at the hug. "We're already real friends. Now, maybe you better scoot before ole Lucy throws a hissy fit. I think I heard her hollering for somebody a minute ago."

"Miz Lucy's always hollering at something or somebody," Tally said as she was leaving.

Somehow, though, she found herself lingering outside the closed door, reluctant to leave the aura of jokes and laughter and good smells. She put her cheek against the cool wood of the door, smiling when she heard Cane's deep rumble of laughter from within. His laugh made her happy. Then there was a murmur of his voice, then Gretchen's. More laughter followed. Tally pressed her ear more closely when she heard her name clearly mentioned. She pulled away, her face blazing as she thought about what was happening inside the magic room she had just left.

They were laughing at her. Tally's happiness evaporated like a summer cloud. They were making fun of her!

She took the "gold" combs out of her pocket and looked at them for a long moment before cramming them into a potted fern on the landing. The make-believe gold had already begun peeling away from one of the combs, anyway.

It was going to be hard to serve dinner that night, but Tally never thought for one moment about trying to beg off. She might be an object of ridicule to some people, but she was not one to shirk her responsibilities. Still, she was glad when F'Mollie showed up to take her place serving at table and Tally could work unseen in the kitchen. When Essie Mae sent the girl home early with food and a jar of her sangaree "recipe"— rum, water, cinnamon, sugar—for Genevieve, Tally was still so quiet and flushed that the black woman was worried that she was catching something.

Gretchen Lee fell back on the bed, exhausted from laughter at the sight of Cane in the white duck pants Tally had brought him. "Stop it right now, Cane. You're making my cheeks hurt." She sat up and eyed the comical side creases that Tally had carefully pressed to razor sharpness. The amusement vanished. "The poor kid. Such a proud little thing. I'm sure it would just kill her if she knew we were in here laughing at the job she did. I get the impression she's had enough humiliation already to last her a lifetime."

Cane extricated a pair of Harm's old trousers from the closet and held them up against him. "These will do just fine. I'd say the ole boy's put on a few pounds since he wore these." He walked over to the window to look out, his mood changing from joviality to seriousness as he contemplated Gretchen's remark about Tally. "Plucky little thing, isn't she? Reminds me of myself about that age. My dad had died and it was my mother and me against the world. Or that's how I felt. Then along came Justin Randolph to sweep Mom off her feet and my life changed. I was just getting to the age of puberty at the time and resented it like hell that I wasn't still the man of the family."

"How'd you feel about acquiring Lucy as a stepsister?" Gretchen knew how *she* would have felt.

"Lucy was married by then—and, for all practical purposes, not a threat to me. In fact, she and I hit it off. Maybe because she was eleven years older and could play the big sister, or maybe because she'd had her father to herself like I'd had my mother before those two found each other. Anyway, Lucy's got her faults but she's got spunk and fire and I damn well like her, for whatever reason. And I'm nuts about ole Harm."

"He is sweet, but I get the idea he gets sand kicked in his face." Gretchen put on the nylon gloves she used to don her stockings so her long nails wouldn't cause runs. "So tell me more about this Malone child."

Child? Cane wondered if that was a label that could ever be applied to Tally Malone. He had an idea that she had been born into the world with those same old, wise eyes with which she had regarded him just now. "Daddy Fontaine was tough on his daughter Genevieve when he learned she was pregnant— or so I heard. Kept her locked in her room on nothing but bread and water, some say beat her, till she named the culprit who'd gotten her in a family way. Little Vieve finally pointed the finger at Daniel Malone, who had worshiped her from the time he'd come to the island as a sharecropper. He's not a bad sort—and not bad-looking. Gary Cooper-ish, I'd say. He was in the Army about the same time I was. Anyway, Fontaine needed a son-in-law and needed him right then. Daniel filled the slot, father to the coming baby or not."

Gretchen sighed. "Poor Genevieve, forced into a shotgun wedding with a man several notches beneath her."

Cane reminded her, "Gretchen, you grew up southern, too, even if you do live in Atlanta. Nice girls in this part of the country didn't have babies without husbands back then. Still don't, for that matter."

Gretchen wasn't satisfied. "I think Harm should have married Vieve instead of Lucy in the first place and all this wouldn't have happened."

Cane worked on his tie, peering at Gretchen as he did so. "You called Harm 'sweet' a minute ago. He is a sweet guy, but he loves the luxury he cut his teeth on. His family was flat broke when Lucy and her rich daddy came on the scene down here. Justin Randolph made him a deal he couldn't refuse— and Lucy was part of it."

Gretchen made a face. "I wouldn't trade places with him. Or with poor Tally's mother. How horrible to be a servant in the house your family once owned! And the worst thing about it is that Lucy seems to enjoy rubbing their noses in it."

Cane put up a restraining hand. "Whoa, just a minute. Before you go turning Lucy into a cross between a bridge troll and Cinderella's stepmother, let me say this in her defense. Her daddy was a helluva lot harder on her than Andre Fontaine ever thought of being on his daughter. Justin Randolph worked his way up from a slum childhood to owning a New Jersey factory and stayed mean to the very end. He sure didn't help Lucy much by bringing her down here to live in the summer house he practically stole from a bankrupted 'native' and exposing her to people who treated her like she was trash. People laughed behind his back about him changing his name from 'Prelutsky' to what Justin thought would be an acceptable southern last name, but they didn't bother to hide their contempt from an insecure young girl. Lucy didn't have it easy— ever. Before Justin struck it rich, Lucy was sometimes hard put to find scraps to make soup with. About that same time, Genevieve Fontaine was riding thoroughbreds by day and having a black nanny brush her hair out at night. Andre Fontaine had a special cook flown in from Paris because his wife was dying and craved some of the foods from her native country. Lucy, on the other hand, stayed by her mother's bedside for three solid days and nights and watched her cough up her insides bit by bit, crying the whole time because they couldn't afford a doctor."

Gretchen, fully dressed by now, watched Cane thoughtfully as he passionately laid out the case for justifying Lucy's behavior. Did he have a thing for his stepsister? she wondered. Certainly they were very close. She had observed that all weekend. "Well, your Little Match Girl story is touching, but I still think that young girl who was up here earlier shouldn't be the one to pay for the sins of the mother. She's going to amount to something, Cane. I just know it. There's something about her, something I can't put my finger on quite. . . ."

"Guts," Cane said without hesitation. "Guts and determination. Didn't you see that chin come up every time Lucy's name was mentioned? Those two are going to lock horns one of these days—mark my words.''

''I'd bet on Tally,'' Gretchen said softly.

''What?''

''I wonder if Lucy thinks you and I are sleeping together. By the way, I don't think your stepsister is living a nun's life. Did you see that blond hunk down by the pool today, supposedly pruning the shrubs? I saw her lean over to give him a view that would make a man want to get a warm spoon.''

''He's a German convict, Gretchen.'' Cane was trying hard not to grin at Gretchen's ill-hidden envy. The young Kraut was just her cup of tea. ''Sheriff Waymon Fussell brings a couple of 'em over whenever Lucy needs yardwork done. I think it's slightly illegal, but Waymon seems totally hypnotized by Lucy.''

''Yeah. If it weren't for that lump of chewing tobacco he's never without, and that belly of his overhanging his buckle, I'd suspect Lucy had herself a little regular redneck—'' The term Gretchen used was vulgar but absentminded. He was pretty sure her thoughts were on the bare-chested young German she'd seen at the pool.

''I swear, woman, if you don't beat all.'' Cane imitated the Ducktown sheriff's voice. ''Are you in heat again, woman? What am I going to tell your father, who thinks we're down here planning our wedding? You do, by the way, need to tell him the wedding's off when we get back. I'm not gonna be your cover indefinitely.''

''Just for a little while longer, till Daddy gets settled in his new office and stops keeping tabs on me. But to answer your question: I am in heat, as you so delicately put it. God, it's driving me crazy—this island, I mean. It's filled with the smell of musk, dammit—humid, hot, sweaty, wet musk that gets in every crack and itches like aitch.'' Cane was laughing at her and Gretchen threw her damp towel at him. ''I'm serious! How the hell could a person live on an island like this and not think about sex from puberty on? I've only been here one day and one night and I'm suffering from terminal lust.''

Cane threw the towel back. "Go finish dressing in your own room before I throw you back in that shower."

While he waited for Gretchen, Cane stood, smoking, at the window, thinking about the island's sensual magic and the idea of Tally Malone growing up amid it. He felt a twinge of jealousy that he wouldn't be here to watch. Would the local clods be after her? He was sure they would. Tally Malone had been robbed of her heritage. She was poor, which made her fair game. He just hoped that she would have the good sense to avoid getting involved with some insensitive boy without a pot to pee in. Tally Malone deserved better; he hoped she would be able to see other options and really amount to something. He wanted to be part of that process; maybe he could be. . . .

"Ready?" Gretchen stood at the door, her smile just a little crooked from the double martini she'd quaffed while finishing up her toilette in her room. "I hate to take you away from that window, but I'm definitely starving."

"So am I," Cane said, coming over to offer his arm to Gretchen, who was already just the tiniest bit wobbly. "And if that roast pig tastes anything like it's been smelling for the past two hours, I'll guarantee I can eat you under the table."

"That should give Lucy a good story to go to the Ducktown Ladies' Bridge Club with," Gretchen said with a leering grin.

Cane laughed, glad he had Gretchen along to keep things in a nonserious perspective. His thoughts about young Tally Malone had brought into focus his terrible loneliness, which nobody else, not even Gretchen, knew about.

He wondered if Tally had recognized his loneliness in the direct, tiger-colored gaze that she had fixed him with from the moment of their encounter. Somehow he thought she had. Hers was a soaring spirit, too, and those who chose the high, lonely skies always recognized their kin. On the other hand, maybe he was overestimating her sensitivity. Maybe she was still too young for that depth of recognition.

Well, no matter. Cane was a patient man. He could wait.

3

Summers in the Deep South are always remembered above the other, less remarkable, seasons. Tally Malone's summer of 1952 was important for a number of reasons. She entered the mysterious stage of being a teenaged girl, for one thing. She was beginning to enjoy the pleasures of the world outside Moss Island, for another.

Among the more material pleasures was a small portable radio—a cast-off that Harm had extricated from Lucy's box of odds and ends meant for Goodwill and presented to Tally. That old radio opened up a whole new world of drama for Tally and Reba. They became addicted to the Sunday-night "Heartbeat Theater," for instance, and never uttered a word or even a nervous giggle until the narrator finished the latest heart-stopping tale of terror.

Inspired by their enjoyment of spine-chilling ghost stories, the two girls even, one scary night, carried the battery-operated radio out to the supposedly haunted graveyard. It took all the courage they could muster. Resting the radio on the rusted Old World lych-gate, they nearly jumped out of their skin when a barn owl hooted right over their heads. In the past, pallbearers had rested the coffins under the gate while they awaited the clergyman. Ghosts were everywhere.

The story on "Heartbeat Theater" was about a reappearing ghost-light in a churchyard. Once inside the hallowed area, Tally and Reba sat and squeezed each other's hands in delicious terror while they listened to the ominous voice of the storyteller. They were sure that any minute the "real" ghost-light would appear in their own graveyard. People said that the light came from a candle that one of the old island inhabitants had placed on his wife's grave every night until he, too, died. The dead woman had been afraid of the dark, as the two girls were increasingly becoming.

When Uncle Gibber passed by the fence carrying his lantern

to go set his crab traps, the light made the girls run screaming
back to Tally's house, too scared to go back for their radio
until the next morning.

The deliciousness of being frightened to the point of wetting
their pants was only one benefit of the old radio for the girls.
Through programs like "Your Hit Parade" and "Top Thirty,"
they learned all the newest songs. They competed to see which
one could memorize the most difficult lyrics and Reba almost
always won. But Tally beat her finally by learning and being
able to sing on perfect pitch the complicated "Don't Let the
Stars Get in Your Eyes" and the two girls declared a draw on
singing and went back to memorizing boys.

Jim-Roy Tatum was still Reba's "steady," even though she
constantly made fun of him to Tally. The latter decided that
daydreaming was considerably superior to settling for a boy
you couldn't stand. Her fantasizing was helped substantially
by another unexpected gift: a box of grown-up clothes, hats,
jewelry, and shoes from Gretchen Lee. Tally was pretty sure
it had been sent as a conciliatory gesture, since the blond
woman had found out from Reba on a subsequent visit why
Tally was shunning her and Cane.

All it took for Tally to transcend her everyday world was a
trip out to the beach in the moonlight, wearing her favorite of
the things Gretchen had sent. The outfit she loved the best, the
one that she felt suited her soul most perfectly, was a wispy
voile off-the-shoulder dress that might have been spun from
the clouds, with the pastels of the rainbow mixed in for color.
Because the dress made her think of Gretchen and because
Gretchen made her think of Cane Winslow, Tally never got
very far with expanding her fantasy. It always stopped with
her image of the man she'd met last summer and could still see
as clearly as ever in her mind's eye. . . .

A glimmer of white on the beach caught Tally's attention as
she stood on a dune overlooking the ocean. The wind was
whipping her hair and skirts, making her feel wonderfully
romantic and mysterious and grown up.

Had it been a whitecap she'd glimpsed? No, it was more
than that. There had been the sense of a larger white shape . . .

Tally's heart pounded as she strained her eyes to see if she had imagined the shape of the legendary white stallion.

She had, of course. Dreaming time had blended into reality time. There was no beautiful horse racing along the sand under a full moon. Tally felt some of the magic leave her; Essie Mae said that if you stopped believing things, they didn't happen. Maybe at thirteen, she was beginning to stop believing all the old stories.

Still, it was nice to think of *maybe* seeing the white stallion. Island legend held that a person who saw the pale horse racing on the beach under a full moon had a big, exciting change on the way.

So intense was Tally on her thoughts that she did not hear the man who had been standing watching her from the path for a long time. He approached her now on the dune.

"Tally."

As Tally whirled to face the owner of the voice she'd heard a thousand times in her dreams, the wind tore her shawl from her shoulders, leaving them bare. When she and Cane both bent over to retrieve the wispy fabric, their hands touched, sending a shock of feeling through her.

Tally pulled the scarf away sharply, as though it were in danger of contamination from his flesh. "You! What are you doing here?" She brushed her hair off her face, where it had blown now that she had her back to the sea. She was glad the pounding of the waves hid the audibly fast breathing that accompanied her words.

"So you're princess of the sea and the night as well? I have to get permission to wander out here when I can't sleep up at Lucy's house? It's so damned quiet on this island. I must be getting used to the sound of Atlanta's traffic outside my penthouse window." His tone changed to softness. "Do you know how you looked just then? Like the princess in one of the drawings in a French fairy tale I once read. It was a beautiful story."

"My mother used to read those to me. I remember the one I loved best—about a lost girl who found a white deer in the forest and was led to safety. They became friends and she later

freed him from his enchantment.'' Tally suddenly remembered
she was planning to be cool to the man who had ridiculed her.
''But I don't recall what happened after that.'' She did recall—
very well. The deer had been released from his spell by the
young girl's kiss to become a handsome prince and the two
had married and lived in the magic forest forever after.

''Funny. I remember quite well how 'The Enchanted Deer'
turned out.'' Cane's hair caught the silver of the moonlight as
he smiled at Tally in gentle mockery. He knew perfectly well
that she had not forgotten the story any more than he had. ''It
was her very first kiss and full of magic, as first kisses always
are. I used to think about it, about how lucky the prince was
to have had that very first kiss from his very special princess.''

Tally felt paralyzed, knowing what was about to happen and
knowing just as clearly that she could no more move away than
stop the ocean's waves from their relentless cycle. ''Please
don't,'' she whispered as Cane put his hands on her shoulders
and bent his head to her.

''I must,'' Cane whispered back.

It was Tally's very first kiss. As Cane's lips touched hers,
Tally felt a strange quake throughout her body. Her recurring
fantasy of Cane kissing her like this was no longer a dream. It
was happening. The strong mouth pressing on hers was not
part of a fairy tale. It was real, demanding, exciting, and oh,
so delicious in its moist warmth. As Cane's lips pressed hers
open, Tally felt the inside of her entire being go limp and
moist, like a huge raindrop quivering before its final burst.
She felt melting and soft, helpless in his strong embrace. The
tightening hardness of his arms thrilled her. The increasing
pressure of his lips on hers made her feel close to fainting.
Tally could have stood there under the moonlit canopy of night
forever. A boat's foghorn off the shore sounded and touched
off a warning inside her, making her pull away from the embrace that had momentarily enchanted her.

They stood there staring at each other, Cane as shaken as
the girl he had just kissed. ''I'm sorry. No, I'm not. I mean,
I shouldn't have done that, but I'm glad I did, dammit.'' Cane
laughed, running a still-shaky hand through his hair. ''Hell,

it's just this crazy island, that wild werewolf moon up there. Drives a man crazy. *You* drive a man crazy. You had no right standing out here looking like that.'' Cane gave up trying to explain what had just happened. He didn't understand it himself. He wasn't in the habit of going around kissing underage girls. What was this one—a budding Circe? He was still reeling from the impact of hard young breast buds burrowing in his chest and of the sweetness of a very tasty mouth. . . . ''I don't know what I'm saying,'' he finally let out in desperation.

''I'll say this. You had no business doing that. It was very wrong of you.''

''Not *wrong*, Tally. Impetuous, silly, unguarded—but not wrong. It was your first kiss, wasn't it?'' he asked rather anxiously. *Please tell me it was.* That was important to him for reasons he didn't understand at all.

''Yes,'' Tally admitted reluctantly. ''But I didn't like it one bit,'' she added, affording her nose ample excuse for growing. ''And boys have tried to kiss me before this, you know.''

''I'm sure they have,'' Cane said, feeling jealous. ''But I was the first . . . well, I don't guess you could call me a boy,'' he said, feeling slightly sheepish that all this was so important to him. What would his sophisticated Atlanta friends say if they knew Cane Winslow was making a big deal out of being the first to kiss a girl who was about the age of some of their daughters? Regardless, he couldn't help feeling male smugness at being the first man to provide a real romantic encounter for Tally Malone. And she had responded. Definitely. Cane's blood stirred at the thought.

''No, I don't guess I could,'' Tally agreed scathingly. ''And let me tell you something else, Mr. Winslow. I don't appreciate it one bit that you feel like Miz Lucy's owning the island and working my mama and me half to death gives you the right to do anything you feel like doing. Coming down here, for instance.'' Tally waved her arms. ''I try not to come here, even though my folks did own this land once, far as the eye could see, except when Miz Lucy and her crowd aren't anywhere to be seen. All those tents and cocktails and loud music down here—it'd scare the turtles off from laying if it was their time.'' Tally's eyes were flashing now as she got into her subject. "And Miz Lucy's always tampering with something that's been one way for years till she come along. That sand out there—just look at it. Did you know Miz Lucy had the convicts *raking* it smooth and flat? I ask you, how many turtle eggs you reckon have been messed up just so Miz Lucy's fancy guests can have a nice, smooth place to lie down and burn their skin off?''

Cane said meekly, "I'll ask her about that. She probably just hasn't thought about it. Is there anything else I can do for you before I humbly remove myself from the royal premises, your highness?''

Tally stomped her foot. "Stop calling me that! I hate it when people make fun of me. I just despise it!''

"I wasn't making fun of you, Tally. I really do look on you as the true and deserving monarch of Moss Island.''

"Then if you're supposed to do what I say, please move off the path and let me go home. There's some of us that have to work tomorrow. It's puttin'-in day, you know. The tobacco's ripening faster'n usual this summer and it's gotta be cropped tomorrow and strung up for curing.''

Cane would have traded his newly imported Mercedes sports coupe for one more kiss, but he didn't dare. He let Tally pass stiffly by him, watching her walk away from him and wishing, as he had a thousand times already, that she would hurry up and grow up—for him.

Tally tossed and turned in her lumpy bed long after she had left Cane standing on the path. The feelings that were keeping her awake were hard to describe. One minute she felt burning hot anger at Cane for what he had done and at herself for having allowed it. The next, she felt warm anticipation of the next time she saw him, of what he would say to her.

One thing was sure: She was different at that moment from the way she had been when she walked down to the beach. Her lips felt bee-stung. Tally kept touching them, wondering if they had felt as soft to Cane as they did now to her. She got out of

bed and went over to the clouded mirror over her old dresser.
It was silly, she knew, but she needed to know how her lips
had looked when he bent to kiss her. . . .

She closed her eyes slightly, observing the effect when she
did that and parted her lips slightly at the same time.

"Are you going crazy?" she asked the warped image in the
mirror. "It was just a kiss, and you'd better say your prayers
three times extra tonight for letting him do it." She felt a wave
of guilt when she heard Perrie in the adjoining room reading
the Scripture to her mother, as he always did before they went
to bed. Perrie would think she was awful; her mother would,
too. Maybe Tally should think that, too. It would be all right
if she hadn't liked Cane kissing her and wanted more.

Tally turned away from the mirror and looked for her most
uncomfortable, ugliest, scratchiest old nightgown to replace
the cool baby-doll pajamas Gretchen had sent her. If she had
had a hair shirt available (or had known what one was), that
would have served nicely.

The granny nightgown suffocated most of the rosy tingle
that Tally knew she shouldn't be feeling. But it was so hot,
she still couldn't sleep. A noise in the next room made her
stiffen and lie still. And then it started, the sound she dreaded
more than any other: the measured creaking of bedsprings that
meant Perrie was making love to her mother. Tally covered
her ears and prayed, "Get it over with fast, please. Oh, please,
dear God, don't let him go on and on with it." The horrid part
of overhearing her parents' lovemaking was that she never
heard her mother make a sound. All she heard was Perrie's
increasingly stentorious breathing and the speeded-up action of
the rusty bedsprings as he moved toward whatever it was that
men did to women at the end.

Tonight when it was over and the house was quiet except
for Perrie's snoring, Tally was wider awake than before, this
time from her own disturbing thoughts. She was very confused.
Her knowledge about what happened between a man and a
woman was pretty shaky. Maybe it was time to have a good,
long talk with Reba Taylor. Reba knew all there was to know

about sex—even though she swore she hadn't done "it" yet
(whatever "it") was; Tally fervently hoped it included some
kissing.

With that resolve in place, Tally finally dropped off to sleep.

Morning came too soon for Tally. She had promised Essie
Mae, who was visiting a newly delivered niece in Ducktown,
that she would take care of the jugfuls of ice tea for the field
workers. Here it was almost sunup and she still had that to do,
along with the full day's work of puttin'-in. Tally decided she
wouldn't stay up kissing anymore until she had things pretty
well figured out.

The kitchen at the big house was silent and empty when
Tally quietly let herself in. Wide awake now, she mixed up tea
and sugar in the big pickle jars Essie Mae had left out for her.
She hoped as she worked that Cane Winslow would walk in.
But he was probably sleeping in, like most of the island visitors
did of a Saturday morning. Tally wished she could do that
sometime. . . .

"Well, hello. What are you doing in our kitchen?"

Tally whirled around to see a tall blond boy standing in the
doorway, rubbing his eyes sleepily and looking at her with
interest. "Who are you?" Even before the defensive question
was out, Tally knew who he had to be. Anybody with rat sense
could tell from the blond hair and the blue eyes that he was
Lucy Cantrell's fifteen-year-old son, Nicholas. Lucy had seen
to it that her son didn't grow up "suthren," keeping him off
at summer camps and schools up until now. Tally hadn't seen
more than glimpses of him over the years. "Oh, I guess you're
Miz Lucy's boy. How about screwing this top on for me? You
look pretty strong."

The boy looked pleased as well, and stepped forward to take
the jar from Tally. "There, that should do it." He handed the
jar back to Tally, who put it inside the large basket she was
packing with similar jars. "I guess you're one of the help,"
he offered, looking with interest at Tally's long brown legs,
which seemed to have reached her armpits this summer.

"Guessing's what gets folks into trouble," Tally said mysteriously, not wanting quite yet to be labeled one of the "help" by this handsome blond boy. "Where in the world did you get all those mosquito bites?" she asked, suddenly noticing Nicholas's legs, too. Longer than hers by far, they were covered with red, painful-looking welts that made Tally itch just to look at them.

"At the drive-in movie." Nicholas scratched one of the bites and then another. "My mother got my Uncle Cane to take me last night. It was the last time they were showing *High Noon*, and she thought I might like it. Cane says it'll probably get an Academy Award."

"He doesn't know everything. 'Heartbeat Theater' will probably win over everything." Tally ignored Nicholas's blank look and started working on a couple of the big, tough biscuits Essie Mae had laid out for her breakfast. She hollowed out a hole in each of two biscuits and filled them carefully with butter and syrup so they dribbled over tantalizingly. "Did Gretchen come down with your uncle?" That ought to show him she was more than kitchen "help," she thought, licking the syrup off her finger and enjoying the way the blond boy was beginning to look really hungry.

"No," Nicholas said, his eyes never veering away from the syrup dribbling down the side of the biscuit Tally was eating with deliberate slowness. "She had some kind of show in Atlanta this weekend. You guess I could have one of those?"

Tally shrugged and pointed to the platter of cold biscuits. "Suit yourself. But your mama doesn't think all these starches and sweets are good for people."

"She won't know." Nicholas fell upon the biscuits hungrily, hardly waiting to fill one up with butter and syrup before taking a huge bite. "Umm, umm. She and my uncle stayed up half the night talking after he came in from a walk on the beach. I heard him tell my mother he couldn't sleep for some reason and they sat up drinking brandy and talking and laughing till real late."

The "laughing" part reminded Tally of the unpleasant episode of the previous summer. "How come you know what they were doing?"

"I came down for some hot chocolate." Nicholas was licking some dripping syrup and didn't see the jealous look he was getting from Tally. She was thinking mean thoughts about pale-legged boys who didn't have to work at anything in the summers and spent their nights going to drive-in movies and drinking hot chocolate.

"Let me put some turpentine on those bites of yours," she offered. "It'll fix 'em right up." She got the bottle of raw extract from beneath the sink where Essie Mae kept it right next to her bottle of "medicinal" moonshine. "And don't mind the smell. It won't kill you."

Nicholas hopped around on one foot and then the other after the burning application. His inclination was to holler out loud, but his pride stopped him. Tally, picking up the last of her syrup and biscuit, observed his brave silence, and decided maybe this boy of Miz Lucy's had more to him than she'd first thought. He sure passed the turpentine test with flying colors.

The sound of the conch blowing down by the barn set her to moving. "I gotta go. They're heading out to the field and will be back before you know it with the first sled of tobacco."

"What was that noise?" Nick's mosquito bites stopped itching and he stopped scratching. He didn't want to miss anything. "Sounded like a foghorn, only more mournful-like."

Tally gathered up her basket of ice-tea jugs. "That's the old conch horn. They used to use it back in the days when there were slaves on the island. You can hear it for miles around. Poke—he's the man that drives the ferry and helps out on barn day—likes using it to call people up. Just between you and me, I think it makes him feel kind of powerful."

"You guess anybody would mind if I walked down there with you, kind of looked things over?"

Tally shrugged. "Won't bother me none. But I'm here to tell you, there's a good chance you'll be put to work."

"I wouldn't mind lending a hand," Nick said, grabbing the door before Tally got to it with her burden. "And, here, let me carry that basket for you."

While they were walking down the path toward the barn, Nick took the opportunity to find out as much as he could about the tobacco-harvesting process. He hated the idea of walking into a situation about which he was completely ignorant—and Tally was sympathetic. She filled him in as thoroughly as she could.

Anyone who has ever worked in tobacco will tell you that once the leaves on the stalks start ripening, from the bottom up, it's time to get busy. Everything was still done by hand on this plantation. The "croppers," usually four or five men, would move up and down the rows of tobacco stalks, plucking off the ripened bottom leaves. A mule-pulled sled just wide enough to be hauled between the rows would be filled to the brim, then pulled back to the tobacco barn for unloading onto the waist-high shelves under a porch-like shelter attached to the barn.

Then the work of readying the still-green leaves for curing would begin. Most farmers in the South use the two human stringers—usually women, since the job is akin to sewing and requires some dexterity—who work with two "handers" each—one on each side. The process of stringing is rhythmic; a good stringer can loop the handfuls of tobacco handed her by her two helpers with lightning ease. The stems are tied, handful by handful, until the stick—usually five feet long—is full of leaves hanging down for later curing.

"Stick!" is the call that brings the "stick-boy" running to remove the stick full of hanging leaves from the "horse," which is now ready for a new stick for stringing. The stick-boy's responsibility is to take the stick of hanging tobacco leaves and place it inside the barn, which is filled with carefully placed rafters all the way to the top. Handing the filled sticks up to the person straddling the top rafters in the barn is no easy chore; nor is it unusual to hear of accidental falls from the top rafters.

When Tally reached the barn with her new friend in tow, the sled was just pulling up. Everyone rushed over to help the croppers unload the tobacco and stack it neatly so that the handers could get an easy purchase on the stems. Nicholas stood around watching curiously until Poke Taylor caught sight of him standing idle and put him to work bringing up the splintery sticks from the pile near the barn. Before long, Nick was part of the work force; Poke ordered a black boy to drive the sled, since he was dark enough to withstand the blazing sun (and Nick was not) and gave Nick the job of being stick-boy.

Reba Taylor rewarded Nick with a dazzling smile every time he responded to her cry of "Stick!" and he soon decided that it wasn't such bad work after all. Nicholas soon figured out that Jim-Roy Tatum, who glared at him every time he came in with the sled along with the other croppers, was sweet on the girl and jealous as the devil that Nicholas was there under the cool shelter with her.

Tally, handing to Reba, too, was tight-mouthed about Reba's open flirting with Nick. She loved her best friend but was really aggravated by Reba's acting the way she did. Reba was fast at stringing and was showing off to beat the band. She tied off the end of every stick with a dramatic flourish that made Tally want to throw up. Not only that; her dark head of curls had been pulled up on top so that they dribbled deliciously down on her sweaty neck. This called attention, naturally, to the high-tied cotton top that just barely covered full breasts and bared Reba's slim brown middle down to her battered dungaree cut-offs. Tally wasn't sure which she wanted to do most: stuff a handful of tobacco leaves down Reba's cleavage or smear Nicholas Cantrell's silly grin with her grimy fist.

Jim-Roy Tatum wasn't any happier. When Poke blew the conch for dinnertime, Jim-Roy was there before any of the other croppers, making sneering remarks about the knit shirt and camp shorts his rival was wearing.

Poke Taylor was used to dealing with tobacco-barn tensions; he'd seen plenty of them in his time. He got hold of little Junior, washerwoman Mattie's grandson, to entertain the crew while they were waiting for the dinner buckets to be brought up from the kitchen. "Look at this, city boy," he told Nick. "Bet you ain't never seen no ring shout done like they did it all the way back to Africa. Junior, show your stuff, boy."

Junior jumped up on the cleared bench and "showed his stuff." Everybody clapped hands in rhythm as Junior wiggled

his hips as if he had noodles for bones, his shoulders stiff and
thrust forward, feet flat on the bench and moving with steady
heel-tapping clicks. Nick's own bones hurt as the boy's knees
popped and his neck stretched as he went into the "buzzard
lope" that had been passed down from his ancestors.

> Throw me anywhere
> In that ole field
> Throw me anywhere, Lord,
> In that ole field . . .

"That's the graveyard," Tally whispered to Nick. "The 'ole
field' is really the cemetery. The nigras have a lot of old songs
about the graveyard that came from when they were working
the rice. You ought to see Aunt Monday do some of her dances,
but she doesn't like to do 'em in front of strangers."

Nick wasn't sure he liked being called a "stranger." Didn't
his mother own this place? But he didn't want to make Tally
any madder at him than she already seemed to be for some
reason. "I should've brought down my bongo drums," he
whispered back.

Junior overheard him as he was jumping down off the bench
and looked at Nick nervously before he grabbed one of the tin
buckets that were now being distributed.

"Did I say something to offend him?" Nick asked as he
took the bucket handed him and dug into the fried chicken and
corn on the cob. He was sure he had never tasted anything so
good.

"Nah, not really. It's just that drums weren't allowed
back in the old days. The overseers were scared the nigras
would send secret messages and start uprisings like in Africa.
Anybody caught beating drums got whipped. So when you
mention drums around here, the black folks still get real
nervous."

"I really like it down here," Nick said around a mouthful
of fried chicken. "I wish my mother hadn't had all those crazy
ideas about me being better off in military schools and summer
camps." Actually, what Lucy had told her son to justify keep-

ing him away all these summers was that she "didn't want him
growing up to be an ignoramus like all those island children."
"I really like your friends, too," he added, looking up to catch
Reba watching him and Tally with a pretty pout that made Nick
decide he'd better cross his legs—or be embarrassed. He was
going to have to buy some new shorts. The ones he was wearing
were choking tight.

When Cane ambled up to where the group sat scattered under
the shed, Nick was glad for the distraction. "Hey, there's
Cane! Hi, Unk! Come to help with the puttin'-in?"

Cane looked at Lucy's son all caked with tobacco grime and
made a face. "Smoking the product's enough for me, thanks."
He was unapologetically immaculate in an expensive polo shirt
and a pair of white duck pants that Tally recognized as twin to
the pair she'd once ironed. "Well, it looks like Poke's got the
whole island working today," he said, his smile directed toward Tally.

The girl blushed and hopped off the bench. "Come on, Jim-
Roy. I'll help you move those low sticks up into the high
rafters."

The husky country boy looked startled, then pleased to have
the chance to show Reba Taylor that she wasn't the only girl
in the world who wanted him around.

As she was moving into the barn behind Jim-Roy, Tally
heard Cane murmur something to Reba that made her giggle
before he moved on to talk to Poke about the prices that summer
for top yellow. She whispered out of the corner of her mouth
as she passed the dark-haired girl, "Don't act goo-goo-eyed.
I declare, Reba, you don't have good sense when it comes to
men. He's just making fun of us."

"Well, that's your opinion. And I happen to think he's not
one bit old-looking like you said. He's better-looking than
Tony Curtis and Guy Madison put together."

"Just don't make a fool of yourself like you've been doing
with Nick," Tally whispered. And then she looked up to see
that Cane was watching her with amusement, as though he
knew she was talking about him and was pleased by the knowledge. She glared at him and followed Jim-Roy into the barn.

That turned out to be a serious mistake. Jim-Roy's male ego, already damaged by Reba's flirtation with Nicholas Cantrell, was ripe for restoration at Tally Malone's expense. "You go on up," he whispered, hoisting her onto the bottom rafters with a lingering caress on her calves as he did so. Tally grasped the higher rafters as she straddled the two lower ones, unaware that Jim-Roy had a clear view into the nether regions covered by her loose shorts.

"Okay, hand me those sticks on the bottom row. I'll put 'em on the second tier and then climb up higher." While she was straining to place the heavy stick between the two next-highest rungs, she realized it wasn't going to work. Jim-Roy's ungraceful pass between her stretched thighs made her come close to losing her balance. "Jim-Roy," she said in a tight, soft voice, not wanting those outside to hear, "have you gone slap-dab crazy? What in the world are you doing, grabbing at me like that? I could fall and break my neck. Is that what you're after?"

"No, that ain't what I'm after, Tally," Jim-Roy said in a choked voice, having a full view of her pubic area from the angle at which he was looking up at her. "Tell you what, you come on back down here and let me go up there."

That made sense. Tally wasn't quite strong enough to balance between the two rafters and receive the heavy sticks Jim-Roy was handing up to her. She let Jim-Roy help her down and was shocked when he didn't let go of her once she was on the dirt floor. "What's got into you, Jim-Roy? Did the sun out there plumb bake your brain?"

"I don't know, Tally, I just know I can't he'p myself. There's something about you today, something I ain't never noticed before. Shoot, I ain't never noticed you at all with Reba around, the truth be known. She says you ain't never even let no boy even feel of you. That true, Tally?" As Jim-Roy's voice roughened suggestively, his callused hand was inching its way up under the loose shorts. "Just stay still for a minute, Tally, while I find the place. I know how to find it. Reba showed me the first time I did it to her. You'll like it, I'll promise you that. You'll like it so much I bet you'll want

. . . oh, gosh, you're really wet.'' At that, Jim-Roy lost it, closing his eyes and moistening his lips and really going in earnest about his massage.

For her part, Tally had no desire to move until she decided what she thought about the feelings Jim-Roy was causing in her with his frantic manipulation. Was this what Reba had tried to describe to her, these sensations of having something happening to you that you absolutely had no control over and didn't want to stop? Tally closed her eyes for a minute and let Jim-Roy keep on with what he was so enthusiastically doing. It couldn't hurt anything, could it? A girl couldn't get pregnant from a boy sticking a finger up inside her, could she?

Jim-Roy was getting to a place that Tally was pretty sure there wouldn't be any going back from if she didn't put a stop to it right then. She waited till his finger was poised, ready to plunge again—then grabbed his thumb and bent it backward with the strength of a country girl who'd never been spared heavy chores.

"Oh-ey, oh-ey, oh-ey!" Tears started to roll down Jim-Roy's cheeks, and Tally mercifully loosened up some on his trapped thumb. After all, she reminded herself in honesty, she had not exactly said no to all this.

"You won't try anything else if I let you go?" Tally whispered. "You cross your heart and hope to die?"

"I cain't, you got one of my hands hog-tied. Tally, I swear. You're just the most confusing girl I ever knowed in my whole life. I could've sworn you liked what I was doing. And you was just as juicy as a . . ." The word came out muffled since Tally had her free hand over Jim-Roy's mouth.

"It's just that I don't like boys pawing at me when I don't want 'em to, Jim-Roy. I've known you ever since I was knee-high to a doodlebug, but that doesn't mean I want you taking liberties every time you get the notion to."

"Reba said you was different from the other girls. But I swear, Tally, for a minute there, you was just like her and all the others."

Tally let go of Jim-Roy's thumb. She wasn't afraid of him

trying to do anything, especially since the conch had just been blown for them to get back to work. Jim-Roy was a hard worker and wouldn't shirk what he was set to for anything. "That kind of scares me, Jim-Roy. It does, for sure."

"Well, don't worry about it none, Tally." Jim-Roy nursed his sore finger. "I think you can take care of yourself with any man you run into, and that's a fact."

Nicholas Cantrell chose that moment to stick his head in the door. "You guys get lost or something? I need some help piling up sticks before the sled comes in. And, Jim-Roy, Poke's gone back to the commissary for a nap and wants you to take on his job looking after things here." Nick looked at Tally. "Hey, you all right? You look kind of feverish."

"I'm fine," Tally said shortly, brushing by him. Then she took out the melting Hershey's bar that she had saved from her last trip to the mainland, and, carefully dividing it so that the almonds were equally distributed, she gave Jim-Roy the biggest half.

There was something rewarding about seeing the gratitude on Jim-Roy's face. But that was nothing compared to the secret smug elation Tally felt to see how crestfallen Nicholas Cantrell looked. Tally just wished Cane Winslow had stayed around so he could have suffered, too. Giving away half a Hershey's bar was not something a poor country girl did lightly.

What in the world was she turning into this summer? Tally wondered.

4

In the old days on Moss Island, when the plantation was in the hands of the original owners, late summer was not considered a healthy or pleasant time. Everyone on the coastal islands who could afford it left during so-called dog days with their miasmic heat for cooler climes.

The Cantrells had kept up this practice. Lucy always spent

August in a rented cottage on Lake Lanier, close enough to
Atlanta so that she could enjoy the social life of the city. Harm
stayed in a fishing camp a friend owned in the Florida Keys.

That left Nicholas Cantrell on his own at Camellia Hall, a
situation he had never been able to enjoy before. He loved it.

Since tobacco season had wound down and Lucy was away,
Tally had more time to spend in frivolous activities. She, Reba,
Jim-Roy, and Junior took Nick under their tutelage. There were
always exciting things to do on their island, when time and
freedom from chores permitted, and they set about generously
sharing the island's pleasures with the newcomer.

Thus a pleasant routine was established. Essie Mae would
pack a cold lunch each morning for what she termed her "little
band of pirates" and the foursome would spend all day swimming, crabbing, exploring, or simply loafing in the lagoon or
on the beach. Nick got brown as a berry, just like Reba and
Tally, and had long since traded in his fancy shirts and camp
shorts for faded dungaree cut-offs and no shirt at all.

Tally thought Nick was the handsomest boy she'd ever seen.
She knew he was more attracted to Reba than to her, but that
stopped bothering her. Reba needed somebody like Nick to
keep telling her how pretty she looked and act the gentleman
because Jim-Roy simply didn't know how to.

The enchanted month passed too quickly. It was getting close
to the time for Lucy and Harm to return, and Nick would have
to go back to school. Tally felt a real sadness about his leaving.
She had formed a closeness with Nick over the summer that
amounted almost to a special kinship. He never laughed at her
as the others were always doing. When the four "pirates"
spent the night in the top of the old tabby lighthouse, for
instance, Nick was the only one who didn't pooh-pooh Tally
when she told them she had heard the ghost that night. Nick
had been really interested when she described the footsteps that
had come up the stairs and stopped just short of the last landing.
"It really happened, Nick," she insisted after the others
laughed their heads off at Tally's superstitiousness. "It was

just like people said—the old lighthouse keeper came back to check on the light, since the sea last night was rough and clouded over. He really did!''

Nick was the one who noticed the unusual smell coming from the direction of the quarters where all the blacks lived. When he and Tally investigated, they found that the ancient soup pot, which had been kept steaming during the early days of the dreaded "yellow-jack" fever, had been heated up again.

Junior explained it to them. ''Aunt Monday, the ole swamp lady, sent over a mess of snakeroot and other stuff, she says there's a bad feeling to the air this summer. Not just the regular swamp miasma, neither. She says there's bad air brewing and we better try to head it off.''

''He's probably talking about ole Lucy coming back,'' Tally had whispered to Reba. ''This place smells fine without her on it.''

But Tally deep down didn't like the fact that Aunt Monday, who kept to herself except in serious crises on the island, had set the blacks to brewing the fever pot. She told her mother about it that night while she was filling the old hot-water bottle Vieve slept with against her bad back. ''Nick says I'm always exaggerating things about this island, but I've never known Aunt Monday to be wrong.''

Genevieve reached up to kiss her daughter. ''She's getting pretty old, honey. Let's don't borrow trouble. It's been such a pleasant August. I don't know when I've had a nicer one. That boy of Miss Lucy's is partly to thank. He's been the nicest thing to me, always asking me if he can bring me something from town or go get my medicine.'' Vieve's pretty face was haggard from the pain she suffered almost constantly, but her smile was as loving as ever as she looked at her daughter. ''Daniel says no good'll come of you and Nick seeing so much of each other, but I like seeing my daughter happy around such a nice young man. But, honey, you do know that Miss Lucy's not going to like it one bit when she gets back.''

''I know,'' Tally said. She and Nick had already planned it; they would act as if they couldn't stand each other around Miz

Lucy. "Nick's leaving for school anyway. Reba says he won't write to us like he says he will, but I think he's a boy who does what he says he'll do."

"I think so, too. Honey, I sure hate to be calling on you so much, but would you mind fixin' a plate up for Daniel when he gets in? He's over at that special service tonight." She and Tally looked at each other, both of them fearing the same thing. *One of these nights, Daniel wouldn't be able to come home after a "special" service.*

"Mama, I've been meaning to ask you about why Perrie is so hepped on that crazy church of his. You and I both know that those services with the snake-handling and all have gotten to be more important to him than most anything else. He wasn't like that when you and him married, was he?"

Vieve shook her head sadly. "I guess I'll never understand Daniel no more than you do about that religion he's got. I think it has something to do with what happened to him off in the war. He never was the same after he came home. He had these awful dreams, one night he talked to me about it, after he'd waked up in a cold sweat. Seems one of his closest buddies, a boy from somewhere in Tennessee, got Daniel started thinking about religion. That boy took the bullet meant for Daniel and died. Just before he died, he pulled out his old Bible and made Daniel read him the Scripture about taking up the snakes and drinking poison. Over and over, Daniel read it to that boy, until he said it was just . . . like . . . printed on his eyes. And he couldn't have any rest when he came home till he'd gone over to Ducktown to see if there was any truth to what the boy had told him about the anointment being stronger than anything a man could find in this life."

"That's when Perrie started taking up the snakes?"

Vieve nodded. "I think it's come to be a satisfaction to him. He says the anointment comes on him and he feels like he's bulletproof from the wrath of God, and man, too."

Tally knew Perrie didn't have much of his own in his life. Maybe in the church, handling the snakes, he felt invincible and powerful. "I'll leave the porch light on for him" was all she said. Perrie's religion was a mystery she wasn't anxious to get into.

After her mother had gone to sleep, Tally finished her chores in the kitchen. Then she went out on the porch to listen to the whippoorwills calling to one another in the marshes. She shivered as she saw one of the whippoorwills perched up on the roof of the big house. According to the Gullahs, that was a sure sign of approaching death.

"But to Gullahs, everything you do or see means certain death," Tally murmured on her way to bed.

"For heaven's sake, turn that thing off. I can't stand the sound of that man's voice." Lucy Cantrell flicked off Cane's car radio with a cherry-tipped hand and lit another cigarette. Westbrook Pegler's gloomy newscast telling of the poliomyelitis epidemic was spoiling her pleasant reveries of Atlanta. The reception at Cane's new executive offices at Tri-Com had been a highlight of her stay. Lucy smiled secretly and tucked her head onto her stepbrother's shoulder. "It was sweet of you to drive me back to the island. God knows it's going to be dull after the past few weeks."

"Why don't you just sell the place and move to Atlanta permanently?" Cane's mind was still on the broadcast they'd just heard. He'd also heard through his own news sources about the spreading virus. The count was up to fifty-thousand cases—most of them in crowded cities. Maybe the remoter regions, like the south, would be spared.

"You know I can't do that. Harm would have a fit. Besides," Lucy said, snuggling down and closing her eyes, "I like being mistress of an honest-to-God southern plantation."

"So I've noticed," Cane said, smiling to himself. Lucy had made a point of telling everyone she'd met in Atlanta about the island plantation her daddy had left her. He started to say something else, but Lucy was already fast asleep. The lonesome road was dark and boring; Cane turned the radio back on at low volume. Then he strained to hear the weather update.

There was a storm brewing off the Georgia coast; Cane

frowned when he heard the prediction. He'd better drive faster, or they wouldn't be able to cross on the ferry. Sourmash Sound got really rough in bad weather. . . .

Reba Taylor was "real, real sick." Poke Taylor came and got Genevieve Malone out of bed to find out what he could do to bring the girl's high fever down. Tally was too sleepy to understand everything, but she heard Poke saying something about barely getting Miz Lucy and Mr. Cane back across the sound for the rough water. "I'd take her to the doctor on the mainland, but that water's pure-and-tee too rough. We'll have to wait till the storm hits and the eye passes over."

Genevieve fixed up some of her medicine that she thought might break the fever and instructed Poke about using an alcohol rubdown if the medicine failed. "I'll come with you, Poke. Just let me get a robe and some shoes on."

"No, ma'am, you're already frail enough without catchin' something. I'll git Essie Mae over if it wussens. Maybe this here storm'll just blow by us and I can take her into town tomorrow morning."

Tally joined her mother in the kitchen, alarmed into wakefulness by the building wind outside. "Mama? Is something the matter with Reba? There's a storm coming up? I heard a limb hit the roof and the wind just about tore my window shade off when I looked out."

"Go listen to your radio, Tally, and see if you can get a weather bulletin. I'll get Daniel up to go tell them at the big house that we might be in for it tonight." Vieve looked worried. "We might better go down to the quarters and get everybody over to the big house. Those shanties withstood the last storm but just barely. I just wish we could get word to Aunt Monday. She's got that old shanty built up on matchsticks. . . ."

Tally listened to the crackling radio as her mother worried. "Shh," she said once as the weather caster came on loud and clear: ". . . evacuating Saint Simons and Brunswick. Residents are being warned of the risks of staying in their homes in the path of the hurricane, which is predicted to hit most of the coastal area around midnight. . . ."

"Mama, what if Reba's real bad sick? Maybe I better go see if we can borrow Mr. Harm's motorboat. It's about the only thing that'll make it across the sound."

"All right, you go see Miss Lucy and I'll get Daniel and see if we can get all the nigras gathered up. Tell Lucy to draw up plenty of water in everything she can find. And those windows upstairs would do better left open. When Daddy and I used to get ready for a storm . . ." Vieve stopped, realizing what she was saying. "Maybe you better just quietly get somebody else to do all that. Miss Lucy might not take kindly to my bossing her in her own house."

Tally was off like a shot.

When she reached the big house, she found that Cane was already out in the quarters, trying to round up everybody to bring back to Camellia Hall. Huge tubs of water were sitting in the kitchen, and Essie Mae was filling up the last one. "You better go up and see to Miz Lucy," the black woman said grimly. "She's 'bout hysterical and acting plumb crazy. Says she's getting off this island and ain't nobody gone stop her. Maybe you kin."

Tally ran upstairs and found Lucy closing a suitcase and pulling on a shiny macintosh. Nick stood next to her, pale under his tan. "Tally, talk some sense into my mother. She's bound and determined to take Dad's boat, me with her. The ferry was damaged coming in. If we go, there won't be any way for any of you to get help if you need it."

"Dammit, Nick, you'll do as I say!" Lucy's eyes were glazed with fear—real fear. "I feel trapped on this island! Do you hear me—trapped! I'm leaving, before Cane gets back. And you're coming with me." Lucy threw Nick's macintosh over to him. "Right now, son."

"But what about Cane, Mother?"

"I don't give a damn about Cane. He should have waked me up and told me about this weather mess we were coming back to. I would've stayed on the mainland. He was blathering on just now about my responsibility to these people, about how I might be needed—the hell with that! We're getting out of here. Now."

Tally couldn't believe Lucy's utter selfishness. She could tell that the woman was truly frightened, but what about the rest of them? ''Miz Lucy, if anybody goes in that boat, it needs to be Reba Taylor. She's real bad sick, and if that storm cuts us off for days like's happened in the past, she won't be able to get to a doctor and maybe . . . maybe . . .'' Tally couldn't say the word ''die''; she didn't even want to think it.

''I'll take her over, Tally. Mother, give me the keys to Dad's boat. I'll try to get back before the worst hits and we can talk about what to do then.''

Lucy clasped the boat keys against her chest. ''You'll do no such thing, Nicholas Cantrell. If you don't do as I say, I swear to you I'll see to it that you never set foot on this island again.''

Mother and son stared at each other, their eyes the same blazing blue. Finally, Nick slumped in defeat. He turned to Tally. ''I'll get a doctor over here somehow. Tell Reba I'll do everything I can.''

Then they were gone. Tally said a little prayer for Nick but had a very different one for Lucy. ''If Reba dies, Lucy Cantrell, so help me, I hope you burn in hell.''

The lull before the storm was providential for the Cantrells, since it provided them the time for safe passage across the sound. But Cane Winslow, battering his way back through the needle-sharp rain, guessed that the main onslaught of the hurricane was not an hour away. He had managed to get everyone out of the quarters and safely headed to the house. Poke Taylor had been adamant about refusing to leave with Reba, and Cane, after seeing her condition, had to agree she shouldn't be moved—unless it was to a mainland hospital.

He wished he'd known how sick Reba was; he could have had Nick take her over in Harm's boat while it was still safe to cross. Cane didn't want to think about the implications of Reba's racking chills and fever. The word lurking in the back of his brain was too scary. Right now, he would force himself to concentrate on helping these people survive what was shaping up to be a hurricane of the magnitude of the great 1824 killer storm.

The Malones had been as busy as Cane trying to get the quarters emptied. Cane admired the way Genevieve handled the black children with care and tenderness, and though Daniel had been more concerned with the storm being the Lord's wrath on sinners, he had helped board up the flimsier shanties right along with the other men.

The Malones had gone back to their own house to secure what they could there. Cane ducked just as a dead limb from a live oak crashed right beside him. Suddenly he thought, Tally! Where the hell is she? It dawned on him that he hadn't seen her. The wind was coming up and screaming through the trees, but all Cane could think about was getting to the big house where Tally surely was by now.

Essie Mae was making up huge pots of soup that would carry them through the next day or two. Cane barked at her, "Is Tally here? Is she with Nick and Lucy?"

"They ain't none of 'em here, Mistuh Cane, though most everybody else be downstairs already. Uh-oh. There go the lights." Essie Mae hurriedly lit the kerosene lamps she had all filled and ready. "F'Mollie, she say she saw Miz Lucy and her boy heading out in Mistuh Harm's boat, over to the mainland. And Tally, she was here for a little bit, but I ain't seen her since the storm picked up again."

"Oh, God." Maybe she was with her parents; Cane cursed himself for not stopping there first. They all needed to be over here. Their shotgun house was about as safe as a matchbox. "If you see her, make her stay put, you hear?"

"I sho' will. And don't you yourself be gittin' out there for long. It's 'bout to hit big."

Cane was already out the door by then. He had trouble shutting it behind him, and fighting the wind the short distance to the Malones' house made it seem like miles. Genevieve and Daniel were just locking up when he got there. "Where's Tally?" Cane shouted over the roaring wind and rain.

"She's not over at the big house?" Vieve looked suddenly frightened. "Oh my God—she was worried about Aunt Monday. Daniel, she probably went to get Aunt Monday. We've got to go after her! That swamp is no place to be in a storm."

Cane noticed that Vieve's mouth was pinched with pain; the exertion of clearing the quarters had taken its toll, he was sure. "I'll go after her. She can't have gotten far in this rain. You two go on up to the Hall. We'll get there as soon as we can."

Vieve put her hand on Cane's sleeve and whispered. "Thank you. I'll never forget this."

Cane patted her hand and managed a wet smile. "Leave it to me, I'll find Tally. Hurry, now. It's getting hard to walk out there."

He had trouble walking, too. The rain was coming down in whirling sheets by now. "Tally! Tal-lee!" The wind whipped the words out of his mouth as he stopped to catch his breath in the shelter of the old chapel. It was hard to see the path by the graveyard that Tally would have taken to Aunt Monday's. Cane got his bearings and was off again. As he passed the old graveyard he saw an overlying limb crack and fall to crush one of the flimsy tombstones flat. "Hope that's not an omen," he muttered, building up speed in a slight lull in the rain.

"Hullo! Tally! Tally, where are you?" Cane stumbled along the path, cursing the blinding rain and the screaming darkness, feeling hopeless. He would never find her in this. . . .

Stumbling, he nearly fell over her body lying crumpled on the path. "Tally, Tally, are you conscious?" He knelt and patted the wet cheek. He saw the tree limb lying next to her then, and realized she had been knocked cold. Or he hoped that was all. Cane rose with the limp form in his arms. How the hell could they make it back? He looked around desperately and realized that they were right at the path that cut off by the lagoon and came out at the lighthouse. It was a good twenty minutes' closer—and that twenty minutes could save their lives. Cane struck out with Tally bobbing in his arms like a rag doll.

It seemed to take eons to get there. Cane knew he was on the verge of collapsing from the effort of carrying Tally through the pelting wind and rain, but he saw the lighthouse looming through a break in the weather and new energy infused his aching limbs.

The trail broke open onto the shell path that led down to the beach. Cane could barely glimpse the big house through the heavy rain that was like a dark curtain between him and refuge. Not only that, the space between where he stood and Camellia Hall was impassable. The path that led from the quarters down to the beach was totally obscured. Everywhere he looked, there were downed trees, crisscrossed like fiddlesticks. There were no lights, no sign of life in the tightly shuttered mansion. Everything on it that was not nailed down was flapping and tearing. The storm was a giant beast shaking the house in a fury of tearing teeth. He strained his eyes to see if he could see the cellar door, which he remembered was only a few feet away from the kitchen stoop. In a sudden letup of pelting water, he managed to make out the bolted-flat cellar door. There was a pine tree stuck through it like an arrow.

Getting to the house and getting inside was not possible. It was the lighthouse or nothing. He prayed that the old tabby stone would stand up to one more night of battering. Cane shifted the burden in his arms and swallowed some more rain, cursing when a limb landed at his feet and made him stumble.

Tally started shivering and he could tell she was awake— and probably scared. "It's all right, honey," he said, pitching his voice at a level beneath the screaming wind. "We're going to be safe and warm in just a minute or two. Just hold on." Even though his arms ached, Cane treasured the sweet heaviness of her.

Once they were inside, he collapsed, exhausted, on the floor, the girl still in his arms. "We made it," he said weakly, placing her down gently on the floor and crawling over to get the door closed and locked before the elements blew it from its hinges. He crawled back to Tally and took her back into his arms. Thank God he'd brought his cigarette lighter. He struck it and peered at Tally's face. She was shaking like a leaf, but her eyes were open and clear, with no signs of concussion. "We made it, honey. You okay?" He examined her wet head gently, feeling for cuts. "You've got a pretty big goose egg, but aside from that, I think you'll live."

"I guess that was pretty stupid of me, huh?" Tally felt the lump on her head and winced. "But Aunt Monday has always been so good to me."

"Aunt Monday is probably safer than any of us, deep in that swamp as she is. Besides, she's got all her magic charms to keep her safe. Any blankets around here, you guess? Your teeth are chattering and mine are starting to, too."

"Over there in that old chest. We used 'em to sleep on when we stayed here one night." That crazy night seemed very far away. Tally thought about Nick with a deep sadness. Would they ever have another summer like this one, he, Reba, and Tally? And Jim-Roy, of course. She hoped Jim-Roy and his family were safe somewhere. Nick was gone—probably for good—and Reba was sick, maybe dying.

"Uh-huh. This will do just fine." His lighter flickering, Cane pulled out the mottled Navy-issue blanket that smelled of mold and age, but at least it was wool. An old lantern still held a bit of oil. "And look—the wick still works. There," he said when the blanket was nestled over Tally's shoulders and the lantern was casting a flickering illumination over the room. "Snug as bugs."

"So is ole Lucy by now, I expect—staying at the King and Prince Hotel, probably. Her and Nick, both—though he didn't have much of a choice. He wanted to help Reba, but ole Lucy just thought about herself."

When Cane looked puzzled, Tally described the events prior to the storm. Cane did not condemn his stepsister as Tally had expected he would, but said sadly, "Poor Lucy. She failed at her one chance to be the heroine of her island."

"Well, if you ask me, she failed at her chance to act like a decent human being for once! If Reba dies, I for one will always blame Miz Lucy."

"That's a pretty harsh indictment, Tally. Lucy's always had to fight to survive. Can we blame her for doing that tonight?"

Tally flounced over on her side, pulling the blanket with her. "You're always standing up for her. Sometimes I wonder if you're in love with her."

"I'm not in love with Lucy, but I understand her. Are you

going to let me have a corner of that blanket? I think I'm catching a chill." Tally held up the far half of the blanket and Cane settled in under it, careful not to touch the girl beside him.

"Is my mother all right?" Tally asked after a long silence.

"Better than all right. She really came through tonight, though I could see what an effort it was. What's wrong with your mother's back, Tally? Did she injure it somehow?"

Tally thought about it. "Do you know, I'm not really sure. I asked her once and she just acted like she didn't want to talk about it. I think, though, she might have fallen back when she was carrying me as a baby. Before I was born, I mean. Essie Mae says she had a real hard birthing because of her back."

"Well, she's quite a lady. Do you know, I think it's dying down some out there? Or maybe it's the eye passing over. I haven't heard any more trees crashing down around us." Cane settled down more snugly, wishing he could curve around Tally like a warm spoon. His arms ached to hold her again, but he dared not make that attempt. "Tell me about the lighthouse."

Tally turned to look at him. "Why? What's there to tell?"

"Oh, I don't know. I just have always been fascinated by them—maybe because they're symbols of human loneliness." Actually, Cane didn't want Tally falling asleep on him just yet. This was the first time he'd had her to himself for any length of time and he didn't want it to end.

"Well, if you really want to know—it just so happens that I did an essay on lighthouses last year for history class. It turned out to be pretty interesting. . . ." She told him about how the tabby beacon above them had been patterned after the first "Eddystone light" off Plymouth, in the English Channel and modernized to use the incandescent lamp in the early 1900s. "We're not in the living quarters right here. They're halfway up the tower. This is called the entrance room. Underneath there's the water tank and overhead there are power generators. The lantern's in the top, of course. Reba and me, we used to sneak up there and pretend we were watching for pirates and . . ." Tally stopped and started crying softly. This time she didn't resist when Cane pulled her over and held her tight against his chest. "I'm so worried about her," she said between sobs. "Reba's never been sick a day in her life. I'm so afraid something's bad wrong with her. I knew this summer was too good to last, I just knew it."

"Most summers are," Cane said soothingly, pressing his lips against the damp hair. "When you're as young as you are, your whole life seems like a long, long summer. But then you start growing up and the winters start coming, and that's how it is, Tally. Tally?"

She had fallen asleep, the tears still damp on her cheeks. Cane kissed them away, very gently, and whispered, more to himself than to her, "Tally, my little love. Grow up for me soon, my darling."

And then Cane, too, succumbed to the exhaustion of the day.

Tally woke, at first not knowing where she was. Her neck was stiff and cramped; she realized it was because she was curled up against something and had been sleeping almost sitting up.

The "something" was a warm, hard body from which sounds verging suspiciously on male snoring were emitting. Vague memories of the past evening assailed Tally as she carefully untangled her hair from Cane's fingers and just as carefully extricated herself from the blanket in which she and he were wrapped.

She looked down at his sleeping face for a moment and hardened her heart against the impulse to kiss the lean cheek on which reddish stubble had begun to appear. Red? Was that the color Cane's hair had been meant to be? That was funny, for some reason. "Don't look so innocent, Cane Stephen Foster Winslow. You can lie there looking like you're too weak to say 'boo' to a snake, but I know better." The memory of his carrying her through the storm was fuzzy, but she would never forget the feeling of those strong, hard arms holding her safe from the torrent that had come down on her island.

It was quiet outside. Tally tried unsuccessfully to unbolt the door so she could leave, but the latch was rusty and unyielding. Unwilling to stay and listen to the measured breathing of the man who alternately confused and enchanted her, she made her way upstairs to the lantern room.

The sea was smooth as glass. Tally stood looking out at it, thinking about its resilience. If only humans could withstand the destructive powers as the mighty ocean could and did! She felt a hunger to be that strong, to be able to emerge smooth as glass from the terrors of the world. She lifted her arms, unconsciously, as if in incantation, and closed her eyes. She whispered fervently, "Make me strong. Help me get what I want from life and not ever be helpless against it as so many around me are."

Cane had come up quietly and was watching her, but Tally was unaware of his presence. He was glad; he felt reluctant to intrude on the girl's private moment. Her Junoesque pose made her appear mysteriously larger than life, and Cane, for the first time since he'd met Tally, felt intimidated by her. He desired her, was determined to possess her eventually, but at that moment he wasn't sure he ever could.

Still, his blood stirred at the challenge. Winning the heart, body, and soul of Tallulah Fontaine Malone was something he *would* do. But first she, like any other beautiful living thing, must be given room to breathe and grow into what he knew must one day belong to him.

5

"*L*ook at me, Tally. Just look at this awful brace." Reba Taylor flung herself down on her bed in the little house her father Poke had covered with asbestos shingles after the storm. The summer of '53 was traditionally hot; many of the trees previously shading the houses near the ferry had been torn away by the hurricane. "I wanted to look pretty for Junior's funeral, but how the aitch can a girl look good when she's got something like this attached to her leg?"

"At least you've got a brace," Tally told her. "You ought to be thankful that the Ducktown Missionary Society got it for you. All those other young'uns like Junior that died of polio ain't in braces. They're in coffins." Tally didn't like looking at Reba's shriveled leg any more than Reba liked having it. But at least the girl was still alive, and that was more than you could say for about forty-five other youngsters on the island, Jim-Roy's younger brother and sister among them. "Besides, I already told you, I'm gonna help you get the kind of treatment you'll need."

"How?" Reba put her leg up on Tally's lap for the massage Tally was accustomed to providing whenever she could. "Tally, when it comes to money, you don't have diddly-squat, no more than me."

"Well . . . be that as it may, like Nick said in his letter, there's all kinds of places can help you. Miracles can happen."

Reba sat straight up. "You got a letter from Nick?"

"Right here," Tally said smugly, patting her pocket where she'd been keeping Nick's letter all day until the funeral was over and she could share it with Reba. "He says you ought not to be thinking about how you won't be able to be Miss Georgia like you wanted . . . how'd he put it? 'Tell Reba those beauty contests are for bubble-brains and she's got too much going for her to even think about parading her body.' "

Reba's blush was pink and pleased. Jim-Roy Tatum and some of the other island boys had acted so strained around her lately when they looked at her leg that she was hungry for compliments—even if they weren't directed at her physical attributes, as in the old days. But Nick's encouragement wasn't enough to keep Reba from falling back on the bed, depressed as ever. "You can stop rubbing my leg now. And you can stop trying to cheer me up. I hear you talking about Nick writing to you all the time and look at you all healthy and two-legged, and I just want to crawl off somewheres and cry." A tear slid down Reba's cheek. "It ain't fair, you know. You got your legs and you got Nick and you even got ole Lucy buffaloed so's she steps real careful around you these days." Reba looked at Tally assessingly, as though she were seeing her for the first time. The tears dried up. "It's true. Even my daddy noticed.

Ole Lucy acts like you got something she don't know whether she better mess with or not.''

Tally couldn't laugh off her friend's astute comment. She herself was too aware of Lucy's steady, cautious regard of her when she thought Tally wasn't looking. "It's just that ole Lucy doesn't know what to make of somebody that doesn't fall down on their knees every time she says 'boo.' Reba, I don't specially like talking about Lucy with us just come from Junior's burying, but if we gotta talk about her, let's make it kind of a tribute like to Junior. I mean, remember how him and you and me used to bury goofballs under her bedroom window and all?''

Reba brightened, glad to have something taking her mind off Junior's being dead and herself crippled. "Yeah!" She hunched forward, pulling her good leg up to her chin. "Trouble is, none of the Gullah magic works if white folks try it. Let's think of something we can wish on ole Lucy right now." She giggled. "Hey, you know that funny song we heard on the radio—"

Tally laughed. "I know which one! 'May the Bird of Paradise Fly Up Your Nose.' I gotcha. Okay, here's one, Miz Lucy: May the chicken shit squeeze up between your toes.''

They squinted their eyes shut, thinking of new curses to bring down on the woman they hated, but gave up trying to fit them to the song's lyrics. It was easier just thinking up mean things that could happen to Lucy Cantrell.

"Maybe Miss Jolie over at the beauty parlor could put purple in ole Lucy's hair color.''

"Naw, that's not anything. What if we got a Kodak picture of her 'n' that German convict she does it with in the garden shed?'' At Tally's startled "oo-o," Reba grinned wickedly. "Didn't know about that, did you? Shoot, I watched 'em last time he was over pruning the azaleas and you ain't never seen anything like it. Miz Lucy was going crazy and that Kraut was sucking ever'thing that moved. I told Jim-Roy about it and I think him and some of his friends sneaked over there to watch the next time Miz Lucy and her boyfriend was fucking away.'' Reba didn't notice Tally's scarlet face as she went on describing

Lucy's activities. "Jim-Roy said he saw the convict cut Miz Lucy's bra off with the rose clippers. Boy, wouldn't it surprise Mr. Harm if he knew how ole Lucy loves screwing the help?"

Shocked, Tally was finding it hard to think about Lucy Cantrell having the kind of experiences that Reba described with such relish. "I guess it would. But I sure wouldn't want to hurt him by showing him any pictures. It's not Mr. Harm, you know, it's Lucy we want to get in trouble." The fun had gone out of the "I Hate Lucy" game for Tally. In fact, she felt a momentary touch of pity for the woman who apparently had sexual appetites that didn't bear thinking about. "I think you and Jim-Roy and the rest better stay away from that shed. Miz Lucy sure wouldn't like it, you spying on her and all."

Reba lay back in her bed and tenderly propped her bad leg on the pillow Tally had arranged for her. "Jim-Roy's uncle told him the Nazis liked to bite nipples off the girls in the camps and see which one could spit 'em the furthest. Maybe the German convict'll do that to ole Lucy. . . ."

Tally was privately repulsed by that idea. Whatever happened to Miz Lucy, Tally wanted it to be clean and fitting. "Well, I certainly hope not. And maybe Jim-Roy's uncle would do well to go with Perrie to church. I notice Perrie doesn't go around telling horrible stories about Nazi torturing and stuff, much as he's tormented by nightmares about killing and all. Maybe that church of his, for all its crazy ways about handling snakes and all being part of religion, keeps him from dwelling on the terrible things about the war."

"I'm getting too sleepy to talk about it," Reba said drowsily. "The funeral took it out of me, Tally. I couldn't help thinking the whole time I watched little Junior's grave being covered up with dirt that it could've been me in that coffin. . . ."

"But you're still alive," Tally whispered, leaning down to kiss her friend on the cheek. "And you'll be better than any 'Miss Georgia' one of these days—just you wait and see."

F'Mollie was waiting for Tally outside. "Poke said you was in there with Reba. He said he was spending the night on the cot in the commissary back room, case you decided to stay over with Reba.'' F'Mollie didn't dwell on what had become increasingly obvious: Reba's affliction scared the pea-turkey out of everybody around her. Most of the islanders, including Reba's own father, looked on her as being still contagious. Tally knew better, but there was no convincing some folks. "He gave me some mail to give you.'' The black girl held up a postcard and pretended to be reading it, though she and Tally both knew better. F'Mollie had never been much of a student, dropping out of school after she failed the fourth grade two years in a row. "This'n's got some kind of lighthouse pitcher on it. Now who in the world do you—''

"Never mind,'' Tally said, her heart constricting to think that she might have a postcard from someone who remembered the night in the tabby lighthouse as poignantly as she did. *Cane*. She stuck the postcard inside her blouse, not wanting to read it in front of F'Mollie with all her curiosity. "Who's the other mail from?'' The Malones didn't usually get letters. Tally's recent letter from Nick was the first in a long time. She must have read it a hundred times before she'd finally shared it with Reba. Nick's distress over having been sent straight off to school without even being allowed to come back to the devastated island to say good-bye had been the heart of his earlier letters. Now, Tally was touched by his sincere continuing concern about Reba and the others who had polio, and planned to write him back as soon as she could.

"Just an ole Sears Roebuck catalog.'' F'Mollie sniffed. " 'Member how much Junior liked looking at the women in their underwear?''

Tally did. She planned to put the catalog in the two-holer without even so much as looking at it. It would be sort of a tribute to Junior, who'd always held that the Sears book had softer pages than Montgomery Ward. "F'Mollie, I got to go up to see Miz Lucy. She said to come see her tonight after everybody had settled down over Junior's passing.''

"Well, just be real careful. She's full of piss over ever'body taking off so much work time lately.'' Her restrained curiosity about Tally's other piece of mail emerged. "That card you got—that from Miz Lucy's boy, too?''

Too? Tally grinned, realizing that probably everybody around knew she'd had a new letter from Nicholas Cantrell. She just hoped word hadn't filtered over to Camellia Hall. "Nope. But I got a real nice letter. He asked about you in it, by the way. Nick never got over being real upset about having to take off like that, right in the middle of everything. He didn't say it, but we all know that Miz Lucy was the one to blame. Nick's still sorry he couldn't be around to help with all the troubles on the island and all. He said folks here probably looked on him as being like some of the summer people from the old days who just flew away when any kind of trouble hit Moss Island."

F'Mollie was pleased that Nick had mentioned her. "Well, there was some that talked about how him and Miz Lucy made themselves scarce when they could've been here to help, but me, I always knew it wasn't Mistuh Nick's doings. I sure hope he's all right and will come back sometime soon."

"He's doing fine," Tally said, privately planning to add F'Mollie's positive words about Nick's forced flight to the letter she would write. "He says the school is just fine, though he's still worried about the folks down here—especially Reba and the others who got polio."

"Well, I always liked that boy and wish he'd come back. Whatever he's learnin' off at that school of his'n, he could learn a bunch more comin' down here summers. You tell him I said that, will you?"

"I will." Tally was glad to see F'Mollie give up trying to extract any more gossip from her and go on back home. The postcard from Cane was burning a hole in her chest. As soon as the black girl was out of sight rounding the end house of the quarters, Tally snatched the card out and read it to herself and the few remaining gulls swooping down around her head.

I never see one of these without thinking of you. The picture side was a photo of the famous Eddystone light. Tally held the card to her cheek, dreaming of the man who had sent it. She could just see him, smiling as he picked it out from some revolving display in a drugstore, or maybe in an airport.

"Me, too," she whispered, thinking of her own island lighthouse. "I always think about you, too, Cane."

Tally stuck Cane's postcard inside her blouse where Nick Cantrell's letter was already gathering moisture from her heated skin. Her thoughts turned from Cane to his nephew. She hoped Nick's mother never found out that her son was writing to Tally.

"Well, I suppose it's better late than never." Lucy indicated a hard-backed chair across the room from her little secretary desk where she did the household accounts and dispensed the weekly payroll. "Never mind that the dust on the dining table is an inch deep. At least the emotional needs of the *Negroes* are being taken care of by my staff." Lucy's sarcasm was heavy, but Tally didn't much care. Junior had been her friend. Miz Lucy's dust could pile up to high heaven as far as Tally was concerned. Funerals were more important than housecleaning.

"Junior always wondered if the whites and the coloreds went to the same place after they died. I guess he knows the answer to that by now." Tally felt Cane's postcard poking one of her breasts (which had finally started sticking out this summer) and wondered what Miz Lucy would say if she knew about it.

"I'll leave those deep philosophical questions to the liberals in Washington, who seem to think we don't need affordable help." Miz Lucy's cold eyes probed Tally's face. "And how's poor Reba? Nick asks about her every time he writes or calls and I never know what to tell him."

"She's doing fine," Tally said, knowing Miz Lucy asked only so she could pretend to Nick that she had shown interest in Reba. "She told me you were having her doing some sewing for you, by the way. I really appreciate that, Miz Lucy, and Reba does, too," Tally said. Reba appreciated it, but Tally didn't much like her friend's talent being wasted on hemming endless stacks of Cantrell bed linens. "Being sick and all, she's had to let some of her sewing jobs go by the wayside."

"You know, what really amazes me is that you never caught the virus."

"No, ma'am, I didn't," Tally said. "I guess I just got to stick around and be well so I can look after all I got to look after."

Lucy cleared her throat. Sometimes the direct gaze with which Tally always accompanied her answers made the older woman uncomfortable. It was as if the child saw clearly into a person's soul. "Well, I'm glad someone in your family acknowledges responsibility." Lucy tapped her pencil on the desk. "Let's see, what shall we start with this coming week? I think Mr. Nicholas's room would be a good place for you to start. It needs a complete airing, the mattress turned and the closets treated for mildew. Oh, and you can distribute to the little nigras all those worn-out things Mr. Nicholas wore last summer. He won't be needing them again, I'm sure."

"Yes, ma'am. *Mister* Nicholas says he's grown another half a foot in height and another two inches in width." Tally hated herself for letting it out about her and Nick staying in touch, but that "Mr. Nicholas" bit was too hard to take.

Lucy bit down on the sharp remark Tally was sure the woman had been on the verge of making and said sweetly, "Well, from what I gather, he's popular with all the girls from the nearby finishing school. I haven't heard a word about his wanting to come back here." Lucy's blue eyes glittered. "Of course, what's here for him? He certainly has more ambitious plans than burying himself on this island with all its lazy ways. Speaking of which, I take it your mother has turned over the upstairs cleaning duties to you entirely. Otherwise I would have called her in here tonight instead of you."

It was Tally's turn to bite her tongue. "My mother's back makes it hard for her to tote things up the stairs."

"Well, perhaps Essie Mae's sangaree will work a miracle cure on her one of these days. If sugar water and rum can work miracles, that is." Lucy pretended to overlook Tally's grinding of her teeth. "And your father—poor man. The nigras tell me his nightmares come straight from the devil himself. Or perhaps it's from those snakes he feels compelled to handle in that bizarre cult he calls religion." Lucy leaned forward in a falsely confiding manner. "Tally, what are we going to do about all this? Look at the position I'm in with your family. You're the only one who's completely functional right now. And you're just a chit of a girl. You do good cleaning work, but look at my position."

"All right, here's how I see it. You've got my mama and me for the price of one. And Perrie still sees to the tobacco work. We've got the best crop this summer we've ever had, and I'm sure the books show it." Tally took a deep breath and said coolly, "Next year could be even better. There's some people in Ducktown talking about going to peanuts and sweet potatoes along with tobacco, seeing as there's less risk in under-the-ground crops, what with all the hail damage and all."

Lucy looked surprised, then smiled. "Gracious me, maybe you'll turn out to be the farmer in the family, after all. Now, there's one more thing you can do for me. Remind your father about all that good wood from last summer's storm sitting out there rotting. I asked Daniel over a month ago to see to it that it was cut and stacked for use in the tobacco curing."

"It's already been seen to, Miz Lucy. I got Mr. Johnson over from Ducktown with his chain saw. We might think about investing in one of those, by the way. It'd save bookoodles on the kitchen wood and all, if you think about it." Tally stood up. "Now, will that be all? I need to get back home before my mama starts worrying."

Lucy waved a dismissing hand. "That's all. Stop by the kitchen on your way out, if you like. There are plenty of leftovers to take to your family."

Leftovers. That was all the Malones ever got, Tally thought bitterly. She did stop by the kitchen, however, to blow off a little steam about Lucy Cantrell. Essie Mae, still resplendent in her scarlet satin funeral clothes, just chuckled at Tally's diatribe about the woman she worked for. "Sounds like you been suckin' persimmons, girl, and we all know the suck-ER gets the bellyache 'stid of the suck-EE. Just leave off about Miz Lucy and wrap yourself around some of this chok'lit cake left over from Junior's layin'-in. And if I ain't mistook, there's still a pitcher of that fresh cow's milk Poke brung over from Carter's Dairy."

Tally found it hard to stay grumpy with a big chunk of Essie Mae's famous chocolate cake in front of her. Around mouthfuls of the delicious concoction, she turned the subject to her worries about Reba. "Essie Mae, what if Reba can't walk without her brace ever again? How in the world can she get a job and get by? Poke don't have a pot to pee in, and he's getting pretty old besides."

The big black woman looked sober as she sat down across from Tally and wiped up the crumbs from the oak table. "Honey, I hate it how you take the whole world on your little shoulders lak you do. Cain't you leave some of the worries to them what's got 'em and think about your own self for a change? Your condition ain't exactly in the best, neither."

Tally washed down a mammoth piece of cake with some of the cold milk. "Well, I got two legs, don't I—both of 'em good. And I got some dreams about my own self as well as for Reba. One of these days, I'm going to be living in a place bigger'n this one, you just wait and see. And Reba'll be famous all over the world and—"

"Chile." Essie Mae put both her big hands over the girl's small one. "Don't you be no dreamer like your pore mama. Look where dreamin' got her—married to a pitiful shell of a man like Mistuh Daniel and sad as clouds till even the sangaree don't help much no more."

Tally shook her head. "Essie Mae, you're always pooh-poohing dreams, but where would we be if we didn't have 'em?"

The black woman patted Tally's hand again. "Right on God's ground where we b'longs, like me 'n' Miz Lucy and some others I could name is. Now scoot, young'un, and git this here supper over to your ma 'fore she falls asleep. And never you mind about tryin' to look after the whole world. The Lord Jesus saw to all that when he spread his pore body on the cross. And you quit takin' your precious soup over to Reba ever' night. I be going over there right now with a bowl of clabbered milk with sorghum syrup on it so's she has a full belly to go greet Mistuh Sandman."

Tally shuddered. "Well, if that don't finish her off, nothing else will.'' She picked up the basket Essie Mae had packed, noting that there was another jarful of her "recipe" in it. "Essie Mae, this stuff won't get to hurting Mama, will it?''

Essie Mae shook her head. "More'n life itself? Shoot, there ain't nothing you can take by mouth that hurts you more'n what comes in straight through the heart. Yore mama ain't got nothin' left but you and the sangaree, chile. Don't take away half of what keeps her keepin' on.''

"You worry about the whole world, too, Essie Mae. Reba, Mama, me, all the folks on this island. You don't fool me even one little bit.''

She escaped out the door, barely missing being swatted on the fanny by a giant hand that could be as hard as it could be gentle.

Perrie was waiting for her on the porch of their house. "I wondered where you was at," he said when she came trudging up the steps with her basket. "Your mama was worried that you was off somewheres grieving over Junior's funeral and all.''

"There's no use grieving over 'im anymore, Perrie. He's dead and gone and that's all there is to it.'' She covered the top of the jar of sangaree more carefully. Daniel didn't hold with a woman drinking, though he didn't usually make a fuss about Vieve and her habit of using the "recipe" for her pain. Tally guessed that it was because he felt guilty over not having the money to see to his wife's getting legitimate medical treatment. "You want some supper? There's plenty in here if you want some.''

"No. I ain't hungry. Guess it's these tag-end dog days working on me, or something. I took me a couple of Goody's headache powders and come out to cool off. You been up there talking to Miz Lucy?''

Tally nodded. "I told her about your idea about going into peanuts, or maybe potato planting, along with the tobacco. She thought that was a real good idea.''

Daniel looked at her for a minute, then laughed softly. "My idea, huh? You're something on a stick, you know that? So different from your mama, it tears her up sometime. She was raised in a time when the men looked after the womenfolks, kept 'em up, made sure they had everything they wanted. She keeps looking to me for that, and you know what? I fail 'er every time. But you . . . you're a different story. You try looking after her, after me . . . hell, if you'd been born a man, you'd probably make it to governor and try looking after the whole state of Georgia.'' Daniel looked up at the moon. ''I use to lie in my foxhole and stare up at that moon, thinking how it was maybe the only way out of a big black hole like the one I was in. Maybe it was a hole in the sky, and if I crawled up to it, I could get out. But I kept falling back down. I been falling back down ever since.''

Tally didn't know what to say. Perrie had never talked to her like this. ''Perrie, are you all right?'' Maybe one of the snakes had bitten him and he'd come back to the porch to make a die of it.

''Hell, yeah, long as I got my church and the Lord sees fit to keep sending the blessed gift of anointment.'' He patted Tally awkwardly. ''Go look after your mama. God knows I ain't never been much good at doing it.''

Tally knew she was getting to be grown up in her father's eyes when he asked her to come help him with the tying up of the tobacco bags for auction. She was glad Poke wasn't around, so she and Daniel were in the packhouse by themselves; if the opportunity arose, she had a serious matter to discuss with him.

''Jim-Roy says his folks have started going to the reppsheets, instead of the crokersacking we use,'' she said as they started stacking up the tobacco leaves on the spread-out crokersacks. The stems went to the middle, making a complete fan of the leaves, with a kind of hole in the center.

''That so. Put the trash in the middle like I showed you, Tally. And pack it all down real tight, with the best yellow showing on top.''

''The pinhookers drag out the bottom leaves, don't they?''

''How'd you know about pinhookers? You ain't been to no auction.''

"No, but Jim-Roy's been and he says the pinhookers have pins in their shoes and go along following the auctioneer, dragging leaves off other folks' piles to take down to theirs." Tally obediently stuffed dried stems and tobacco scraps in the middle, a practice commonly used to add to the weight of the high-grade bags. "He said, too, Mr. Varnedore was thrown out last year by the warehouse people for putting an anvil in one of his bags."

Daniel let out one of his rare chuckles. "That do beat all, don't it? Well, maybe we'll get fifty cents a pound this year for most of ours. That would sure make me feel good. Here, you take t'other side and I'll take this'un. This bag's 'bout full enough to tie up."

Daniel looped the two corners of the sheet, washerwoman-style, and gave Tally one end to pull tight. Then, after he'd knotted those two corners, he pulled up the other two, so they had what amounted to a large knapsack filled with tobacco. He grunted and Tally did, too, as they pulled the knot tight. "Guess that'll give Miz Lucy reason to think over selling the acreage."

"I hope so. Perrie, I been thinking. What you reckon the cigar folks will be paying for the old stalks and leavings this year?"

"Not much. Five, six cents a pound, I guess. Why? You thinking of taking up ole Shotgun's place doing that?"

"I was considering it. You reckon Mr. Harm might let me have those old stalks left out in the field if I did the gathering and curing on my own? He hasn't promised 'em to anybody else, has he?"

Daniel stopped and scratched his chin, his light-green eyes thoughtful. "Don't think so. Shotgun was the only one willing to work that dang hard for that little dab of profit." Daniel smiled, and Tally realized why some people still called her father good-looking. His face was weathered from the sun, but Perrie's smile was still nice. Tobacco-chewing had not ruined his teeth, which were still strong and only slightly yellowed. "That old nigger was something, wadn't he? Tickled me how he'd gather up all those ole stalks and leftover crap and cure it

right there in his little shanty where he slept. Ole Shotgun got
cured out much as the tobacco.''

"Still, he came home with some cash money in his overall
pockets after he sold his stuff to the cigar people.''

Daniel stopped what he was doing and looked at Tally really
hard. "What's all this about you trying to earn some money?
For what?''

Tally told him how she wanted to help Reba get off the
island and go, maybe, to Warm Springs, Georgia, for muscle
therapy so she could walk without a brace. "They say they can
work miracles there," she concluded.

Daniel shook his head sadly. "Miracles. Tally, Tally. Girl,
how many times have I tried to git you and your mama to the
church to ask for the things you need? We got the spirit, we
got the gift, we got the healing right there for the asking. Forgit
about puttin' money on Reba's pore leg. Let's have the brothers
and sisters lay their hands on it and draw the devil right out
before your very eyes.'' Daniel's eyes glittered like Coca-Cola
glass in the sunshine. "You ain't been but once, Tally. You
ain't really seen what the spirit can mean to you when your
heart's full of the pain of the devil. You can feel it, that blessed
anointment, just working its way into your toes and burning its
way all up to your mouth, till it just spews out. I ain't never
felt nothing like the anointment, ain't nobody ever felt nothing
like the anointment of Jesus. It's like you're washed down in
the blood, covered all over with the blessed blood of the Lord.
And nothing cain't hurt you, blessed be Jesus, nothing cain't
hurt you—not no bullets, not no Germans, not no sinners. You
got to feel it to know it, blessed be the Lord baby Jesus, you
just got to know what it's like being anointed with the liquid
spirit of Jesus. . . .''

Tally wished she hadn't started this. Perrie was getting really
worked up. "Maybe Reba can get over being afraid of snakes
and go to your service next Sunday.''

Daniel's upper lip was glistening with perspiration. His eyes
still shone with the light of fanaticism. "Afraid? If Reba holds
hands with the Lord, she can hold hands with the snakes and
the devil himself. She got to let him inside her first, though.''

"The snake?" Tally asked weakly, thinking about her friend who jumped hysterically at the sight of even a harmless rat snake.

"No. She got to let Jesus inside her," Daniel shouted. "That comes before anything else in the whole blessed world. The snakes ain't nothing. It's Jesus that counts, and his blessed anointment." Daniel had begun panting and sweating until Tally was afraid he was about to pass out. She tried to calm him down with the decision that she hoped wouldn't make Reba mad.

"Well, we'll ride over with you next Sunday, Perrie." She didn't make it out of the packhouse in time. Daniel had her kneel with him on the splintery floor to pray. Reba's name was peppered, along with Tally's, throughout the very long prayer concerning young sinners who had not yet found their way to the light.

Tally just hoped Reba had gotten over her terrible aversion to snakes.

By the time the three of them arrived at the weathered clapboard church far on the other side of Ducktown, Reba and Tally were both sweated down from the hot ride. Poke had lent his battered Model-A to Daniel for the occasion. "How do I look?" Reba whispered as she pulled her flowered dress over her brace and tried to smooth down her dark hair.

"Real pretty," Tally whispered back, though she secretly wished Reba hadn't worn Persian Melon lipstick and put Maybelline blue on her eyelids. None of the women she saw walking into the old church had on makeup or anything like that.

She and Reba walked behind Daniel, who was stopped at the door by two men struggling with three big flat boxes. "In Jesus's name" was written on them in colored crayon. "Give us a hand with these, Daniel. Preacher wants 'em under the front pew."

Tally quickly led Reba away from the suspiciously noisy boxes. She was beginning to wonder if this had been a good idea. Reba could likely have a heart attack and cancel out all the divine healing in a heartbeat.

Just as the two girls started inside the church, an ear-splitting "Hallelujah!" sounded behind them. "Just praising the Lord," the woman who'd shouted explained. "Have you sisters took the Lord Jesus as your Saviour?"

"Hell, yes," Reba told her. Tally whisked her inside as fast as she could.

They walked down the church aisle feeling self-conscious. None of the other women had "fixed up" for the service, and Tally was glad she'd worn her plainest cotton dress and no lipstick.

"Don't pay any attention," Tally whispered as some of the women in the church stared at Reba and her makeup. "They're just jealous. Just close your eyes and sing real loud and pray to be healed." It might not work, she added silently, but it won't hurt.

She and Reba sang along with everybody else as the little clapboard church swelled with the enthusiastic choruses of "Pull Off Your Shoes, Moses," "Running Down the King's Highway" and "Amazing Grace." Some folks started clapping to the rhythm of the music and soon everybody in the room was clapping and shouting the words to the songs.

"When do they start?" Reba whispered.

Tally knew what Reba was asking. "I don't know. I only came once and they didn't have the snakes that night. Reba, you got to take it all serious. Otherwise, Perrie says it won't work."

Reba put another two decibels into her rendition of the rousing "Beulah Land."

The singing died down, but not the energy in the packed room. Tally could feel it pulsating with anticipation of "the main event." The only quiet time during the whole service came when one of the preachers read from the Scriptures: ". . . in my name shall they cast out devils; they shall speak with new tongues; they shall take up serpents; and if they drink any deadly thing, it shall not hurt them; they shall lay hands on the sick, and they shall recover. . . ." (Mark 16:17–18.)

When the man finished reading, the place went crazy. Someone started playing a guitar, someone else a set of drums, and everywhere the girls looked they saw people in the midst of what Perrie called "receiving the gifts."

Everybody clapped, sang, hollered, laughed, or prayed. Nobody was still. The room swayed with its occupants, and Tally and Reba felt they were swaying along with it. A woman standing near the girls started babbling "in tongues," and when the incomprehensible monologue was finished amid great emotional fervor, she fell to the floor.

Reba looked at the woman who lay in writhing, jerking convulsions, and worried. "Is she having a fit, you guess?"

"Yes, sister, praise be," a girl shouted right in Reba's ear. "She's having the fit of loving Jesus. Join in, sisters! Join in and praise the Lord!" The girl took Reba's and Tally's hands and swung them vigorously to the rhythm of the hymn.

Somebody shouted above the music, "The anointment of the Lord is upon us all, brothers and sisters! The spirit among us is true and can't be denied. It's time, blessed be Jesus's name. It's time!"

"To go home?" Reba asked hopefully.

Tally nudged her in the ribs. "Shh. It's time for the main event, I think. Look up front."

The girls watched with fascinated dread as the first long flat box was slid out from beneath a front pew.

Then the serpents were everywhere.

Reba and Tally stood still as statues, afraid to move. Reba whispered, "Jesus Christ. I think I just wet my pants."

Tally whispered back. "A whole bunch of people moved to the back of the church and are just watching. You can go back there." Tally knew Reba wouldn't. The other girl was as fascinated by the whole procedure as Tally was. A bald-headed man was dancing down the aisle with a total of nine snakes dangling from his hands. Tally nudged Reba. "Look at that. And look at everybody's eyes—glazed over like they're all in a daze. It's the Holy Ghost in 'em, Perrie says."

"Oh my God! There goes your daddy with one! Tally, I can't watch. You tell me if it bites him."

"Perrie's got two of 'em wrapped around him," Tally corrected, surprised at the secret sense of pride her father's fearlessness evoked in her.

"I think I got this thing figured out. Those snakes aren't really snakes. They're made of rubber. Or they've had their fangs pulled out," Reba whispered to Tally, her hand squeezing the latter's arm.

"I hope so, 'cause there's one crawling up this aisle, right toward us."

Reba's yelp was one of pure fear, but the woman next to her, who snatched up the crawling snake, took the cry for a hallelujah of ecstasy. "That's right, sister! Shout out your joy in Jesus and his divine anointment of his chosen servants." Reba edged past the woman with the weaving snake and tattooed herself to the wall at the end of the aisle.

When Tally joined her, she said, "Tally, I don't know about you, but I've enjoyed about as much of this as I can stand."

"Reba, we're already here, and it sure won't hurt to see if we can get you some help. Maybe these folks have got something."

Reba shook her head violently. "Talluluh Malone, if you're talking about me picking up snakes or sticking my head in a fire, you're crazier than they are. I ain't about to."

Tally took her friend's arm. "I wasn't even thinking about that. I'm talking about those people over there that's praying together over somebody's sick young'un. Folks praying over you might do some good. Healing's a strange kind of miracle that sometimes happens if there's enough folks putting their minds to it." Tally did not in fact know anyone who had been cured by the "laying on of hands," but they were already there. Why not give it a shot?

"Is that what that bunch over in the back corner is up to?" Reba pointed at the circle of men and women who were murmuring and swaying around a thin little boy. "At least they're close to the exit. All right, let's go."

The small clutch of healers opened up for the two girls to join their circle. The weeping and praying over the child ceased and he gratefully wiggled through the circle to join the other children outside. "He's got the blood weakness," one of the women told Tally. "Ain't no doctor layin' his hands on my boy. It's up to the Lord if he gits well or don't."

"Amen." "Yes, sister." "Praise his name."

"Now, what be the trouble here?" The healers eyed Reba's braced leg as though it were fresh from hell's blacksmith. "Pore thing, you're all shriveled up."

Reba looked at Tally accusingly. *See what you've got me into?* "Polio. Look, I know there's not anything you can do for me. I don't want to take up the time you could give somebody really in need of your help, so me and my friend here, we'll just leave."

One of the sisters put a beefy hand on Reba's shoulder and pulled her into the middle of the group. "Now, sister, that ain't no way to talk. The spirit's in this room tonight—you seen it with the snake-holding—and it's in us and it's in you. Though it might not be showing up plain through all that Jezebel paint you got on your face."

Reba cast an imploring look in her friend's direction. Tally did her best. "Look, it's too late to help the shortening of the bone and all, but there's a chance the muscles can build back up and—"

"Don't talk no doctor talk to us, sister. This is the Lord's hospital, not Satan's. Brothers and sisters, do you be with me in laying the hands on this sinner's pore leg? It's the mark of her sinning, I don't doubt, but maybe with the hands we can pull the devil right out."

Reba closed her eyes and looked resigned. "Pull away."

The prayers being said over Reba had a lot of references to painted eyelids and harlot's lips, but they were enthusiastic and Tally sent her thoughts upward right along with everybody else.

"Oh, Lord," Tally intoned sincerely. "Help Reba get well." Tally was afraid from the intensity of the prayers and the touching that Reba was stuck for the night.

Reba tried her best to talk her way out of it. "I am mighty grateful to all you folks, and I do believe I'm feeling much better. Tally, tell these good people that thanks to their supplication I'm on my way to being healed of my affliction."

At that moment there was an agonized shout from the front of the church. The healers started rushing forward, but Daniel Malone, his face bleached white under the tan, stopped them. "Stay back, folks, till we get the snakes back in the box. Brother Caleb Bill has been bit, but the Lord will take care of him if you'll all help join in the faith."

Reba whispered to Tally, "I knew it didn't work. I knew it all the time."

The men got the boxes secured and carried their stricken brother into a back room. "Won't they take him to the hospital?" Tally asked the man next to her.

He looked at her as though she'd uttered a blasphemy. "And have the Lord think we'd lost our faith in Him? No, sister, there won't be no doctoring 'cept the kind you witnessed here tonight. The devil and the Lord is in a wrestling match over pore Brother Caleb Bill's mortal body. We're betting on the Lord winning."

Daniel came up to the girls. Tally could smell his sweat and felt sorry for him. "You girls go on and take the truck. I'll git home later. There's a lot of praying to be done in here tonight."

What Tally wanted to say was that she wished Perrie would learn a lesson from this and not handle any more snakes. What she actually said was, "I'm sorry about your friend, Perrie. I hope he makes it."

"It'll be a miracle." Perrie looked wrung out and old. "It was a big bell-boy. Eight rattles. Lots of pizen, but what happens, happens. Now you girls git on home, and tell your ma I'll be there when I git there."

Reba and Tally sat in the truck, the latter behind the wheel, and tried to get themselves together before taking the washboard road home. Finally, Reba said, "I may not be cured of my affliction, but I'm sure as aitch cured of ever settin' foot in a church again."

Tally nodded in agreement. "Still . . . you know, Reba, it was kind of funny how I felt back in there, when it got to be like everybody had a fever, I mean." She looked at the little clapboard church whose sides had bulged in and out from the energy of the earlier music and religious fervor, but now seemed as weary and dingy as Perrie had at the end.

"Not me. All I could think about was gettin' the aitch out before those women tore me to pieces for tampering with the face the Lord saw fit to give me. Some of those ole biddies could sure use a few of the devil's paints."

"You didn't feel nothing, Reba? You really didn't?"

"Nope. And I got it figgered out why. You know how the black folks all paint the trim of their shanties blue to keep the hags out?" She tapped the corner of her mouth. "Well, I think Persian Melon does the same thing for religion."

Tally heard Daniel Malone coming in the house just before dawn and suspected by the heaviness of his footsteps that the all-night vigil had not helped Brother Caleb Bill to survive the rattler's strike.

He confirmed her suspicion the next morning. Brother Caleb Bill was dead, and there was a threat that the church would be shut down by the sheriff for good.

The devil had won the wrestling match hands down.

6

Of all the things she liked about her island, Tally liked the smell of the marshes and swamps best. As she and Jim-Roy made their way down the well-worn path that led to Aunt Monday's shack on the edge of the island swampland, bent on finding out if they could get some help for Reba, she sniffed the brackish odors with pleasure. She didn't put the label "sensuous" to the smell, but the decayed musky odor was very pleasant to her. Newcomers often complained about the smells of the island, saying they were too pungent with salt and sulfur and rotting soil. Tally, though, found the scent of decaying moss and ancient damp strata of mud and roots more exciting

than the delicate aroma of the cultivated gardens at Camellia
Hall.

"Oh, Jim-Roy! Isn't it creepy and wonderful down in here?
I swear, it just never changes a bit."

Jim-Roy was too busy watching out for the treacherous
"mash-mud" areas where a person could be sucked down in
minutes to appreciate the aesthetics. He came from a farming
family that didn't value "worthless" land like swamps and
marshes. "We must be purty close to the old nigger graveyard.
You see how Potlikker's ears went up just now?"

"Where is that dog?" Tally asked, suddenly worried. Potlikker
had been sticking right close to their heels, but wasn't to be
seen now. Just then an eerie howl parted the soft sounds of the
swamp life. "Oh my Lord, that's him. Jim-Roy, he's found
Junior's grave. We gotta go get him. He'll howl himself sick."

Jim-Roy shook his head emphatically. "Uh-uh. I ain't going
in no graveyard for no cotton-pickin' mutt."

"Aw, come on. Dead folks can't hurt you." Tally took the
boy's hand and led him off the path in the direction of Potlikker's howling.

"No, but they can make me hurt myself." But Jim-Roy
allowed himself to be led through the dense clutch of shrubs
and trees that shielded Moss Island's black dead from the
whites and the sunlight.

They parted the palmetto fronds at the low broken fence
surrounding the graveyard. "Look at that," Tally said with
wonder. "There's Potlikker, big as anything, sitting right by
Junior's grave. How do you suppose he knew which one?"

"Probably by the smell. Junior always did have a purty high
smell to 'im." Jim-Roy did not mean any disrespect by this.
He had great regard for boys who held regular bathing as
unhealthy and dangerous, as Junior had in his lifetime. "Lord,
Tally, let's don't go no closer. My goose bumps are getting
goose bumps listening to that dog howl."

"Oh, hush," Tally said, looking around with curiosity. She
had come down with F'Mollie to put flowers on their friend's
grave, but apparently someone had been here more recently

to dress up the spot Gullah-fashion. "Somebody put broken crockery on Junior's resting place and even an old clock. My goodness, it's set on the time Junior passed. Isn't that something?"

"Uh-huh. Tally, we need to be going on our way 'fore it starts gettin' dark. Come on, Potlikker." The little mongrel had stopped howling, but was now settled down across the soft mound of dirt covering Junior's grave, with his head between his front paws. "Come on, feller." Potlikker's stubby tail wagged, but he didn't budge.

"Don't worry about him. Let him visit with Junior while we go see Aunt Monday. We'll get him on our way back." Tally pulled Jim-Roy by the hand, but more gently this time. She knew the dog's actions had hurt her friend's feelings. "He didn't get a chance to tell Junior good-bye, that's all."

"Well, I just hope he don't decide to stay here till Judgment Day." Jim-Roy looked back uneasily as he and Tally left the graveyard, careful not to step on anybody's grave. That was bad luck, just as it was to tamper with any of the broken or cracked ornaments that were scattered on them.

They were both silent for the rest of the way to Aunt Monday's. Tally was the first to speak when they reached the rise lying between the end of the path and the black obeah's pole-supported shanty. "Look at that ramshackle place—how many storms has that thing lived through, you reckon?"

"I dunno, but I know somebody says he came down here one night and saw a white light all around the place—and Aunt Monday sure as aitch don't have electricity out here."

"I heard, too, that she knows where the shark-hook stump is." All the children on Moss Island had at one time or another searched for the legendary stump that was said to have the pirate Blackbeard's own mark—a shark-hook—which was supposed to point to a stash of buried treasure. "But if she's found the gold, she sure hasn't put it to decorating. Lord, what a ragtag conglomeration!"

And ragtag the place was. Every square inch of the shack was covered with something that moved, tinkled, glittered, or glowed. Old pieces of tin, scraps of shell, different forms of bark, whatever could be nailed, stuck, hung, or pasted, obscured the original siding of the shanty. Tinkling pieces of glass hung from nearby trees, playing musical accompaniment to the breezes. But the most bizarre feature of all was the "trim" Aunt Monday had tacked to the front-porch railing.

"Jee-zus H. Christ!" Jim-Roy whistled through his teeth. "Shark skeletons? Man, she must have a zillion of 'em. Where you reckon she got all those?"

"She's friends with all the fishermen hereabouts. They must've given 'em to her. Maybe that's why she stays looking so young. Shark meat's real good for you, folks say."

Jim-Roy screwed up his face. "Yuk. I'd just as soon eat boiled snake meat."

"I've got a mess of that on the stove right now" came an amused voice from somewhere above them. Tally and Jim-Roy both jumped and then looked around for the source of the rich voice. "Stay right where you are, I'm coming down."

With that, Aunt Monday slid down from the huge oak limb, which was a good six feet off the ground, and landed nimbly and silently as a cat right between the two amazed visitors. "What were you doing in the tree?" Tally asked. She didn't know that people as old as Aunt Monday still liked to climb trees.

"Sitting in it," answered the obeah as though that were all the explanation needed. "The old live oak and I have much in common. Like her, I spent the first three hundred years growing, the second three hundred years living—and now I'm on the last third, the dying." The black woman laughed softly at the speculative look on Tally's face. "No, child, I'm not really nine hundred years old—though there are some who think I am. You have not been to visit Aunt Monday for quite some time, Tallulah Malone. How is your sweet mother?"

"*Très bien*," Tally said with a formal little curtsy. She knew that the old black spoke French even better than Genevieve. Tally's grandmother had taught both of them at the same time.

Aunt Monday's large white teeth flashed in a pleased smile. "Ah! So you are still struggling to learn French. *C'est bon*."

"*Un peu*," Tally corrected, holding her thumb and index

finger together with a fraction of space showing to indicate just how little. "Mama has given up trying to teach me the proper accent."

"And this one? Does he speak French also?" There was a sparkle of laughter in Aunt Monday's voice as she directed the question more to Jim-Roy than to Tally.

"No, *ma'am*," Jim-Roy said emphatically, his reaction to the impressive black woman causing him to forget that whites weren't expected to address black women as "ma'am." "I cain't even speak *English*."

Aunt Monday and Tally both laughed. "I like your friend, Tallulah. Why have you not brought him to see me before?"

"Because I figured Lionel would take a bite outta him the way he always does any white boy who comes up to your place."

Aunt Monday laughed again. "My old pet boar never quite forgave the boys who set the dogs on him and cost him a leg. But he's not nearly so ferocious in his old age. Like me. Come in, *chéris*, come in. I will brew some sassafras tea while you tell me what brings you deep into the swamp to see an old woman."

After they were inside the shanty, which was as clean and neat as the exterior was decrepit and cluttered, Aunt Monday left them and went into the tiny kitchen. Tally turned to Jim-Roy and asked him excitedly, "Have you ever seen anybody like her? Didn't I tell you?"

Jim-Roy shook his head. He truly had never seen anybody like Aunt Monday. He sat staring at her unabashedly when she came back to join them, bringing a tray of tea and hickory-nut fudge. She moved with liquid grace as she poured the tea, chattering the while with Tally. Jim-Roy couldn't get over how the old woman's skin was as smooth and glowing as mahogany and her flashing white smile like that of a young girl's. Slender hands with long, sculpted nails accentuated the lively talk that was part French, part impeccable English.

But the feature that absolutely boggled Jim-Roy's mind was Aunt Monday's hair. The shining black strands, mixed with silver, had been braided into at least a hundred tiny ropes, each secured by a glittering shell ornament that made music each time the regal head nodded or turned. The entire magnificent cascade reached to the woman's waist. . . .

Jim-Roy realized the woman had asked him a question and he jerked straight up, blushing at having been caught up in such rude staring. "Ma'am?"

"I was asking you if it is true that people on the island think I'm able to heal afflictions such as your friend Reba has. This disturbs me greatly. I am not a 'hoo-doo' woman. I only use the natural herbs and roots of the swamp the way my mother showed me when I was small."

"You mean you cain't use the hair-combings to make a conjure so's Reba can walk without the brace?"

Aunt Monday looked sadly down into the little box of hair-combings Tally had sneaked from Reba's old dressing table. "I am very sorry you think I can work miracles with voodoo. I cannot help your friend except to send her a potion of my root mixture to ward off the fever should it arise again." At the crestfallen looks on both young faces, the black woman laughed. "Oh, dear. I can see that I should have taken this sad little bunch of hair and mixed it up with some sort of goo and mumbled some unintelligible words over it. You could have taken it back to the Taylor child and convinced her it had magical powers."

"If Reba herself believed it did, wouldn't it work?"

"Did she believe in the healing powers of those at your father's church?" At Tally's negative head shake, Aunt Monday smiled. "And you think she would be more likely to believe in the powers of a crazy black woman living in the swamp than in the ordained preachers in a white church?"

"She's right, Tally," Jim-Roy said. "If Reba knew about us taking her hair-combings and coming out here to get Aunt Monday to fix up a conjure, she'd laugh herself sick."

Tally's shoulders slumped in defeat. It looked as if it was going to be up to her, and her alone, to get Reba out of that brace. Well, she would talk to Harm Cantrell tomorrow.

Aunt Monday read Tally's face accurately and told Jim-Roy softly, "Go outside and wait for your friend while I have a private word with her, child." As soon as the boy had left, she smiled warmly at Tally. "You have a big heart, Tallulah. But most of its strength you must keep for yourself. I read your tea leaves in your cup, and they portend wonderful things are ahead, but hard times as well. But I did not need the tea leaves to tell me that. I know you well. There was a strong bond between your grandmother and me, and you are more like her than like your mother. Strong, generous, a lover of life—you must learn to flow with that life stream instead of struggling so hard against it. And instead of trying to protect Reba from her life, teach her what your grandmother taught me—to accept it with dignity. Dignity in one's life is everything."

"I wish I could have known my grandmother. And I wish Reba could come to know you."

"It is best that she never does that." Aunt Monday looked at Tally for a long moment. Then: "I am about to show you something that I have never shown any living white person." The black woman turned suddenly and dropped her tunic from her shoulders as she did so. Tally gasped with horror as she saw the hideous scars reaching Aunt Monday's waist.

"How did it happen?" Tally cried.

"I was accused by your great-grandfather's overseer of insurrecting an uprising. Before Mr. Fontaine returned from a nearby rice plantation he was visiting, I was whipped and left for dead in the swamp. When your grandmother, then a young girl, found me, she nursed me back to health."

"But didn't my great-grandfather punish the man who did this?" Tally was filled with shock and horror. The Fontaines had always been known for their kindness to those who worked Camellia Plantation—black and white.

"Perhaps he might have done so, if the man had not received his deserved fate at the hands of one more powerful. I like to think it *was* God himself who sent the rabid wild boar with his poison mouth to savage the man who wronged me. It was then, though, that the whispers of my powers grew louder and I was sent to live in the swamp for my own protection. Mr. Fontaine had this house built for me and made me promise to stay here always, where I could live safely."

"So the man who hurt you died of rabies?"

"Eventually." Aunt Monday's smile was a rather terrible one, Tally thought. "They tied him to a tree in the swamp to last out his madness—don't look so shocked! It was the practice to thus protect others from the madness of rabies."

"That was cruel treatment, even for a man like that."

"I thought so, which is the reason I took him food and water each day until he could neither eat nor drink anymore. He begged me to kill him, but that I could not do." Aunt Monday's voice quivered for the first time. "I could not kill the father of my unborn child."

"Oh, Aunt Monday! How terrible for you!"

"To be pregnant by a white man I despised, a man who had beaten me and raped me while I was half-dead from his whip? Yes, it was terrible. I could never look at the child's white— yes, white!—face after she was born. I sent her to a family on the other side of the island, who raised her as their own. No one but they, your grandmother, and I knew the truth, or that she was part black."

Tally's question about how Reba's name had led into these revelations never had to be asked. "That was Reba's mother," she whispered.

Aunt Monday nodded. "My daughter—poor creature. She married Poke Taylor, that simpleminded but good soul. With that and her lameness, your friend Reba has enough crosses to bear without finding out she has a black grandmother."

"It's been whispered about her that she has Negro blood. Wouldn't it be better if she knew it was yours?"

"You are complimenting me, and I thank you. No, it would not be better. And you, my angel child, must never tell her. It is our secret." Aunt Monday's smile was sudden and dispelled the earlier sadness. "And now shall I call in your young man and scare him to death with one of my famous ghost stories?"

Tally's eyes lit up wickedly. "Yes! Tell us about Mary de Searche and see how Jim-Roy's eyes get big as saucers."

So the black woman called Jim-Roy back onto the porch, and while the sun went down and the wind blew the chimes in the trees and curlews screamed in from the sea, she told them spine-tingling ghost stories about the island.

It was all Jim-Roy could do to keep from breaking into a run when he and Tally left Aunt Monday's to take the darkening path back through the swamp. And when they reached the graveyard, the boy jumped and yelled as something touched him on the leg.

"It's just Potlikker," Tally said, hiding her grin and reaching down to pet the tail-wagging mongrel. "He's come back to you."

"That's 'cause he knows which side his cornbread's buttered on," Jim-Roy harrumphed, secretly tickled that Potlikker was going home with him after all.

Tally Malone stood in front of Camellia Hall for a long time, gathering up her courage to go inside and meet with Harm Cantrell. She had always loved the front entrance to the mansion. The giant oleanders that reached to the upper galleries had been planted long before her mother was born. The columns on the wide veranda had been tooled by a sightless black man who had a feel for wood-finishing. She thought maybe the old syrup boilers that held spilling branches of impatiens and verbena might have been brought over on one of the first settling ships. Certainly, the huge brass knocker on the polished oak front door was ancient. It had been a gift from a sea captain to Tally's great-grandfather. It hurt to think about F'Mollie being the one designated to polish that old knocker, instead of her.

It hurt her, too, to think about this beautiful old place belonging to Lucy instead of to Tally's family. It hurt a lot. Camellia Hall was a beautiful old house that had meaning for Tally. She wasn't usually allowed to enter by the front door, but, by George, this time she would. She had a business meeting with Mr. Harmon Cantrell, now didn't she? That wasn't back-door business.

She lifted the big brass knocker and clanged it against the door. F'Mollie opened the door, her hands on her sassy hips, and tried to keep a straight face about inviting Tally in as though she were a real visitor. "Well, now, do come right on in, Miss Tallulah." She put her face right up under Tally's and said, "What you mean, comin' in heah 'stead of by the kitchen? You know how Miz Lucy feels 'bout the he'p using the front door."

Tally smoothed out her best dress, a green voile shirtdress Gretchen had sent her. "I've got an appointment with Mr. Cantrell. He's expecting me." Tally walked into the huge tiled foyer whose marble surface she'd waxed two days before.

"Expectin' you? Expectin' you to do what?"

"F'Mollie, I'd be forevermore grateful if you'd just go tell Mr. Cantrell that I'm here for our appointment."

The black girl looked at Tally as though she had taken leave of her senses. "You been teched by the heat, girl? You go tell 'im yourself. 'Cept he ain't in his study right this minute."

"Well, I'll wait down here for a minute. Don't let me stop you from whatever you call yourself doing."

F'Mollie flounced off with her dustcloth and lemon-oil bucket. "I *call* myself doing what you was s'posed to be doing, only Ma couldn't find you yestiddy. I be cleaning up the upstairs for Miz Lucy's guests, and if you know what's good for you, you won't touch nothin' down here while you waitin' for your *appointment*."

Tally meandered into the living room. She'd always loved this room, with its imitation-silk wallpaper and Chinesebro-cade-covered twin sofas that flanked the marble fireplace like sentinels. Miz Lucy had kept the fine pieces of cranberry lusters that Tally's family had imported from Europe. Their tinkling prisms under the huge portrait of Justin Randolph beckoned her to pause to study the picture that had always fascinated her.

An itinerant portrait artist (one of the old "house-painters," as they were called) had done a magnificent job of bringing Lucy Cantrell's hook-nosed, fiery-haired father to life. Tally thought that any minute now the old factory tycoon would step down into the room with her. He had visible spirit, mean or not, that couldn't be dulled even by the stillness of oil paint.

Tally's next-favorite room was the large dining room. She walked through the free-standing ionic columns that framed the arched entrance, past the wall-long china cabinet, which had been placed inside the house before the walls were closed. It had been too enormous to bring inside a door, her mother had told her.

The Queen Anne table could seat a regiment. Tally touched the gleaming surface that she had buffed with her bare hands and grease a thousand times or more. Then she looked at herself in the mirror facing the one on the other end of the room. Her reflection of her reflection went on ad infinitum, creating dozens of Tallys in diminishing images. . . .

"I'm sorry to keep you waiting, Tally." Harm Cantrell's voice behind her made her jump guiltily. "But you know these afternoon socials on the mainland and how Lucy likes us to stay till the last dog's dead. Admiring yourself, are you? Let's go into my study, where we can get down to business."

Tally, feeling like a little girl again instead of the fantasy mistress of Camellia Hall, followed Harm to the study off the main entrance. She averted her eyes from the "death chair," into which Harm lowered himself, and seated herself primly on a straight chair opposite the desk. "You look very nice," she said politely. Reba's cruel crack about Lucy's husband looking like Howdy Doody in an ice-cream vendor's suit passed fleetingly through her mind. She hoped Harm Cantrell didn't know that people on the mainland made fun of the way he dressed in the white linen suits that Miz Lucy bought for him by the dozens. Her face was carefully implacable as she watched Harm take a large handkerchief from his white linen pocket and wipe his perspiring, freckled face. It was a big face, a broad face. Harm sweated a lot for a man born in hot climes. His handkerchief went limp and soggy back into the pocket.

"Whew. Hot today. Tell you the truth, I'm not much on these white suits, but Lucy likes 'em." Harm chuckled and ran his hand through his thinning faded-red hair. "Feel like Sydney Greenstreet in one of those thriller movies. Now, what can I do for you, little girl?" He looked at Tally's bosom, which was a little too full for Gretchen's hand-me-down dress, and quickly averted his eyes. "Well, I shouldn't be calling you 'little,' now, should I? You're—what? Fourteen?"

"Yes." Tally leaned forward and fixed her earnest gaze on Harm. "I'm old enough to harvest what's left of the tobacco patch, anyway. And that's what I'm here to ask you to let me do. Now that ole Shotgun's not around to do it, I'd like to take it over."

"Gracious, the only reason I let him fool with that mess was to make him feel like he was still some good." Harm wiped his face again and patted his neck. Tally felt hot just watching him. "There was an old nigra woman lived on your grand-daddy's place till she got too old to do diddly-squat. Know what your granddaddy did? He gave Aunt Rose the job of grazing a goose every day. She took that goose out on a leash like, every day, regular as clockwork. Your granddaddy said people ought to be made to feel they had a job to do, no matter how little."

"Well, I know I'm not old, and this job's not easy as goose-grazing, but I'd like to have it if you'll let me."

Harm took his bifocals out of his pocket and spit-polished them before saying kindly, "It's hard work and not worth it. Your mama know about you wanting to do this?"

"She won't care."

Harm looked at Tally thoughtfully. "You need some cash money for something in particular, girl? I get the feeling you aren't just trying to bunch up some money for buying you and your mama a few extra pretties."

"It's not 'pretties' I'm after, Mr. Cantrell, you got that right." Tally told Harm about how she planned to help Reba Taylor get the therapy she needed to be freed of her brace.

Harm Cantrell heard her out without saying anything. Then he cleared his throat and put in what he called his two cents' worth. "Gal, shouldn't you be thinking about bettering your own family, rather than trying to help people that's trash?" He blew his nose on his much-used handkerchief and Tally hoped he wouldn't forget and wipe his face with it again. "I'm not down on poor little Reba, but let's be honest about this. You can't help people like that. Helping 'em turns 'em sorry. Why, my mama once gave an old set of mahogany—mahogany!— bedroom furniture to one of the poor families, feeling sorry for 'em having to sleep on pallets on the floor. Those folks splintered it up one cold winter to use for firewood, with the woods out there chock-full of lighter'd knots just waiting to be picked up and toted to the house. All I'm saying is, you can't help trash. I've tried, your mama's people tried, all those other folks before us tried. Trash is trash. Reba Taylor's a nice-enough girl, but she comes from trash and all you have to do is look at her daddy to know where she'll end up.''

Tally didn't like hearing Harm Cantrell calling Reba trash. It made her madder than a snake hearing that term applied to people like Reba Taylor, who'd never done anything but work hard and try to get on the best they could with what they had. Harm Cantrell had better watch his step, calling her friend trash. Next thing, he'd be calling herself and her mama that, like some other folks had in Tally's hearing. "Well, I don't think Reba wants to take on Poke's job of driving the ferry, but I guess what I'm saying is I'd like to see her get a fair shake at walking again without that heavy ole brace.'' She added mildly, "If you agree to me having the job of clearing out the old patch, I guess it's fair for me to say I can spend the money the way I want to, isn't it?''

Harm looked at her with a glimmer of admiration. "By George, I believe you've got the family spunk. All right, let's talk about percentages, since you've turned into a little business lady. Two percent sound fair enough for my take?''

"Yessir," Tally said, getting up and putting her hand out. She was glad Harm put the soiled handkerchief down before shaking. "I thank you kindly, Mr. Cantrell.''

"Well, it's always pleasant doing business with a pretty woman. Oh . . . I almost forgot. My son said in his last letter to be sure to tell you 'hello' and that he hopes he'll see you Christmas—if his mama lets him come home, that is.''

Tally didn't see any point in telling him that Nick wrote her pretty regularly these days. Harm might feel that he had to pass the information along to his wife. "Well, I hope he can. Thank you again, Mr. Cantrell.''

"Not a bit. Let me see you out.''

As they passed the living room, F'Mollie was in there with

her dustcloth and oil bucket. Tally was embarrassed to observe that the way she was leaning over an end table toward the door, you could see halfway down to her navel.

From the rather silly look on Harm Cantrell's face, Tally was pretty sure that he had not missed the view, either. "Well, so long, Mr. Cantrell. I sure appreciate what you're doing for me, sir."

"Not a bit. Not a bit." Harm was flustered as he opened the door for Tally. The girl grinned on her way out and all the way home. Wouldn't Miz Lucy have a hissy if she knew her puppy-dog husband was sniffing after the black help!

Harm hustled back to the living room, remembering (conveniently) that he'd promised his wife he would have F'Mollie air out his study. Lucy despised the smell of the Havana cigars he was allowed to smoke in his office only. "F'Mollie!" She wasn't in the living room; he bumped into one of the love seats when he heard her call seductively from the dining room.

"I'se in here, Mistuh Harm." F'Mollie was dripping drops of oil on the dining table and grinning over her shoulder. As Harm walked toward her, she looked him up and down with a big smile. "My, aren't you looking swell today. Jest like Arthur Godfrey on TV, only handsomer." Harm's pleased grin spread over his face. Dropping her dustcloth on the floor, F'Mollie bent down to pick it up, and Harm closed his eyes in pain.

"Mother of Jesus—she's not wearing any britches," he said to himself, the ache in his groin reaching the point of anguish.

"They ain't nobody in the house but us two. Don't it seem quiet?" F'Mollie leaned over the end of the long dining table, cloth in tow. "Mistuh Harm, if you'll jest give me a little boost from behind, I can get that spot up from the candle."

With F'Mollie's inviting exterior bent alluringly toward him, Harm groaned and put his hands on the round buttocks. "Can you reach it now?" he asked weakly.

With a dexterity that belied her clumsiness in reaching the table center, F'Mollie reached back and unzipped the white pants. "I think that'll do it," she murmured. The oil on her hands sliding over Harm's penis made him quiver with anticipation. And then she turned over and slid on her back onto the shining expanse of table. With another groan, Harm was on top of her and inside her writhing thighs.

In the throes of ecstasy, F'Mollie pulled Harm's head down to her face and whispered. "Kiss me! Kiss me real good, Mistuh Harm."

Harm was sincerely shocked. "*Kiss* you! Hell's bells, F'Mollie, I shouldn't even be fucking you."

When the amorous encounter had run its predictable course, Harm straightened himself up and put things back in the master-servant perspective. "All right, F'Mollie; you've been a good girl and there'll be an extra box of oranges and grapefruits at your shanty on Christmas. Now be sure you clean up this table good before Miz Lucy comes home."

"Oh, I will, Mistuh Harm." F'Mollie waited till Harm had left the room and she heard him close the door to his study before she took her dustcloth out. The residue on the end of the table—at Miz Lucy's place—was not oil, but F'Mollie rubbed it in, chuckling the while, as though it had been.

"There you go, Miz Lucy. At supper tonight, you'll be eatin' off my juice." The idea of it tickled her to death. She wished Tally hadn't turned into such a little shit-pants lately so she could share the joke with her.

7

"Jim-Roy, watch the aitch what you're doing! Don't pile those scraps up so thick. They need to be spread out real thin to cook up dry like they need to."

Tally Malone had never cured a barn of tobacco all by herself, but she decided it was time she learned how. There wasn't that much to it; the most important part was making sure that the furnace, a wood-burning contraption located at the end of the covered-shed part of the barn, was fed wood all during the first night of curing. Inside the barn the underlying flues would glow red-hot when the furnace was heated up, curing the contents of the barn to the degree desired.

She decided to sleep on the shelf under the shed so she could make sure the fire didn't go out. It would take but one night to cure her measly little crop. Cigar tobacco came out dry and brown and crisp, not soft yellow like the top-grade leaves that brought top dollar. Tally figured the stray oak and lighter'd knots she'd gathered up would do the job quite nicely.

Jim-Roy had been a big help, assisting her in spreading out the crop remnants in random bunches on the lower rafters so they would bake fast. "I saw Reba tonight," he said when they'd finished spreading out on the floor a pile of stems and stalks that wouldn't bear hanging. "She seems a lot better after taking Aunt Monday's tonic. You reckon maybe there is something to that stuff, after all?"

"Hope so."

Jim-Roy was sweating so profusely Tally could smell him all the way across the barn. She had no way of knowing that it was more hormonal than physical activity causing it. Her shorts and halter were way too small and he hadn't missed the way she was filling them out—not one bit. "Tally, you reckon that religion your pa's into is driving him crazy? I know my folks ain't been the same since they started going to those services. Maybe all the time your pa's been going has started taking its toll."

"Jim-Roy, if you've got something to say about Perrie, just spit it out."

"I'm just saying you better start keeping an eye on him. He told the fellers over at the mainland mission house last Saturday night that he had taken to handling snakes on his own, outside the church. Tally, if he ever turns loose any snakes over there with them war vets that already got snakes aplenty in their heads, all hell will break loose."

Tally kept on working, trying not to let Jim-Roy see how much what he was saying worried her. She was aware that Perrie's immersion in his strange religious beliefs was getting the upper hand. "Well, at least he's not drinking that rotgut

Mad Dog that your daddy's taken to using since he lost two of his young'uns to the polio."

Jim-Roy looked so crestfallen at that that Tally felt terrible. "I'm sorry, Jim-Roy. That was mean of me to say that. Look, why don't you just go on home and I'll finish up here by myself."

"I wish you'd think of me once in a while like you think about everybody else in the whole durn world," Jim-Roy said, coming over to look down at Tally, who was down on her knees spreading out the last of the cigar crop. "If it wasn't for Potlikker, I'd think there wasn't anybody in the whole world who cared pea-turkey about whether I lived or died."

Tally sprang up and faced him angrily. "Now if that isn't the silliest thing I ever heard in my life! There's a lot of folks who care about you, Jim-Roy, and you know that good and well."

Jim-Roy moved closer to her. "How about you, Tally? How much do you care about me?" He put his hand on her arm and moved it up the grime-streaked flesh to her bare shoulder. Her hair was falling out of its careless knot; Jim-Roy twined his finger in the amber strands and used it to pull Tally closer. "Remember that time in the barn, right here on this very spot, when you let me touch you and make you feel like you never felt before? . . ."

He was mesmerizing her in spite of herself. Tally let him kiss her and force her mouth open so he could put his tongue in and move it all over hers. Tally wasn't sure she liked it, but it make her feel funny, sort of wet and hot from her mouth on down. Jim-Roy was doing funny things, too, to her bare back, using his knuckles to move up and down her backbone—not unpleasantly. She rather liked that, she decided. But then she realized that he was untying her halter top and that wasn't something she was sure she was ready for.

"Don't do that," she said sharply, pushing him away.

"Tally, I ain't ever asked you for anything, but I'm asking now. If you'll let me have just one quick look at your tits, I'll die happy."

"Well . . . ." Tally was torn between modesty and the desire to show off her newly gained bounty. "Just one quick look. But if you touch 'em or even so much as look like you're going to, I'll use one of those lighter'd knots on your noggin."

"Wow," Jim-Roy breathed a moment later, after Tally had bared her breasts to him in one nervous flash. "Yours are bigger'n Reba's, even."

Tally was secretly pleased to hear that but pretended to be miffed. "I'm not in a contest with Reba or anybody else. And now that you've had your look, you better not go around telling people about it."

"Oh, I wouldn't for anything, Tally. Cross my heart and hope to die. Can I stay down here and help you with the firing and all?"

"No, I want to do it by myself." Tally was feeling strangely grown up tonight. Maybe it was because Jim-Roy had looked at her body the way a man looked at a woman and she could tell what he was thinking. She liked the sense of power she felt over Jim-Roy at that moment. "I may be handling a lot of things around here all by myself from now on, and I might as well start getting used to it."

After the furnace was blazing merrily, Tally went out to the bench farthest away so the heat wouldn't get to her. Lying on her back, she looked up at the full moon. What was it Cane Winslow had called just such a full moon on the night he had kissed her?

"It's that werewolf moon again—and here I find you all alone under its spell again."

Tally rose from the bench, wondering if she had dreamed the voice of Cane Winslow. But, no, he was right there, as handsome and impeccably dressed as though he had stepped off a page in *Collier's*. "Where'd you come from?"

"Up there." He pointed to the balcony overlooking the pool at the big house. "I saw the blaze and thought maybe the barn was on fire."

"It's a brand-new barn, but we have to be careful about the kind of wood we use in this furnace. It doesn't have the right kind of venting, Perrie says. I guess this stuff is boring to you. Essie Mae says you've been traveling all over the world since I saw you.'' Tally looked at the flames, hoping they would account for the warm flush she knew was visible on her face. ''That night in the lighthouse—I guess I never really thanked you for saving me out of the storm. It was stupid of me, running off like that to go warn Aunt Monday.''

''I thought it was pretty brave. How is Aunt Monday, by the way?''

''She's fine. Jim-Roy and I went to see her last week.''

''Would you take me to see her sometime? I've always wanted to visit that place of hers.''

Tally hesitated. ''Aunt Monday doesn't much like white men, I'm afraid.''

''Oh.'' Cane didn't pursue the matter. ''By the way, I heard about Junior. I'm sorry about that. He was a pretty neat kid. But I'm glad your friend Reba seems to be okay now.'' Cane sat down next to Tally on the bench. ''Harm tells me you're undertaking this little enterprise all on your own. I'm impressed. As something of an entrepreneur myself, I find it interesting that someone so young has financial ambitions.''

Tally laughed. ''I don't know what that word you used means, but I don't think you can call me what people call somebody like you.''

''No? It's just a matter of degrees.'' Cane stared into the flames of the furnace. ''The South needs people like you and me, Tally—people who try new things and aren't afraid of hard work or taking risks. Generally speaking, Southerners are tagged as lazy, soft, slovenly, stuck in the traditions of our past and hung up on who we are and where we come from. We can change that image, Tally. You and I are going to be a part of the new South—just watch. Tri-Com is going to make Atlanta as big a media center as New York, make the big-money boys in the East sit up and take notice.''

Tally laughed. ''And what will I be doing? Rolling cigars in the factory over at Waycross?''

Cane turned slowly to look at her, at the way her hair caught the color of the flames, at the excited wideness of her eyes, at the new curves of the sun-bronzed body. "I don't think so. But whatever it is that you decide to do, I hope I'm there to see it."

Tally felt the impact of Cane's seriousness and tried to make light of what he was saying. "Well, I hope there'll be lots of money."

"Is that important to you? Are you bitter about people with money?"

"No. I'm just bitter about not having any myself," Tally answered honestly.

Cane laughed. "There you go. That's the right way to look at it. I'll let you in on a little secret. Very early in whatever enterprise you decide to get involved with, you need to make a choice. You decide which team you want to be part of— management or the workers." He shook his head and got up to throw a piece of wood on the fire. "Lord, what am I doing down here, giving you these Dale Carnegie platitudes? I guess I'm just trying to say to you, Tally Malone, that I'm behind you a hundred percent in anything you decide you want to do." He turned back to look at her. "You're a very special young woman, but I guess you already know that. Gretchen, by the way, wants you to go into the media business with us. Ever think about that?"

"No. All I can think about right now is getting this barn cured so I can have two nickels to rub together in my pocket. How is Gretchen, anyway? She promised me she would come down and stay with me—just me—but I haven't seen hide nor hair of her in I don't know how long."

Cane grinned. "You're not the only one. When Gretchen has a new guy on the hook, she's hard to find."

"She's got another boyfriend?" Tally's grin matched Cane's. She loved hearing about Gretchen's romantic exploits. "Bet it's somebody in baseball. Gretchen really likes baseball players."

"The youngest, hottest first baseman on the Crackers' team. Say, maybe you could come up and stay with her sometime. She'd like that."

"I don't have the money or the clothes," Tally said with

plain directness. "And Miz Lucy isn't about to let me get off for long enough to go to Atlanta."

"She might—if you ask her."

"Yes, and it might snow here on this island in August."

Cane poked at the fire with a tobacco stick. "Tally, why do you hate my stepsister so much? She can be difficult, granted, and she has her private demons as all the rest of us do, but she's not a terrible person. Can't you give her credit for the good things she has done? Learn from her, Tally. Lucy's tough as wire grass, just as you are."

Tally pushed his hand away from her stuck-out chin. "I don't care to learn from her, thank you very much."

Cane laughed. "All right, my little island cactus. Say, why don't you come up and eat with us tonight? Essie Mae's put together one of her famous feasts and everybody's feeling festive up at the big house."

Tally poked at the fire. "I have things to do down here. And I'm sure not dressed for dinner with you and Miz Lucy." Tally didn't add that Lucy Cantrell would sooner have one of Perrie's rattlesnakes coiled up at the same table with her than to have Tally Malone.

"I think you look just great," Cane said softly. "But I respect a person who does what she's gotta do. Can I help you with anything before I leave? Bring some more wood up?" He went over to the pile of pine logs that had the dry brushes still attached.

"Not those," Tally said. "They burn too fast and could cause a problem in this furnace. I'm just using the oak, which won't swoosh up the chimney like the brushier stuff could."

"Whatever you say." Cane piled up a goodly stack of the oak and brushed his hands off. "Will that be all, miss?"

Tally laughed. "You've got your pants all dirty. Would you like for me to wash and iron 'em?"

Cane made a face at her and then quickly left as Essie Mae's dinner bell sounded.

Lucy Cantrell was watching the moon lose itself in the ghostly live oaks when Cane joined her on the balcony. "Beautiful, isn't it? I never come out here without remembering those dreadful nights in the slum where I grew up. Sleeping out on that fire escape, breathing soot and listening to horrid noises, I used to promise myself that someday I would look at the moon from a beautiful balcony.''

Cane lit a cigarette for Lucy and then one for himself. "You're a woman who keeps her promises, Lucy. Sorry, I didn't bring you a brandy. I thought you'd already gone to bed.''

"I wasn't sleepy.'' Lucy craned her neck to peer out at the glow from the tobacco barn. "For heaven's sake, where's that smoke coming from—the commissary? Cane, please get Harm to go see about it. God knows we don't need any more disasters on this plantation.''

"It's not the commissary. It's the tobacco barn fired up for Tally's little crop of weeds.''

"Wh-at?'' Lucy turned slowly to stare at Cane. "Tally's *what?*''

Oh, Lord, Cane thought; he had blown it. He had assumed Harm had asked permission from Lucy—as he always did before he made any decisions involving the property—for Tally to harvest and cure her sad little crop. "Harm gave the child the go-ahead about clearing up the field. Lucy, she's doing you a favor, so don't go jumping on poor ole Harm.''

If Lucy had not turned her face away to stare out at the glow from the barn, Cane would have seen the dangerous look in her eyes. But she was silky-sweet when she said, finally, "My silly, silly husband, always trying to do things for other people. I keep telling him that nourishing dependency in these people is not good for us or them. But does he listen to me? No, he goes ahead and does things like *that.*'' She tossed her cigarette out in an angry, fiery arc toward the barn.

"I like that about Harm,'' Cane said, lifting his brandy to his lips and watching the cigarette Lucy had thrown land precariously near the people down by the pool. "He's a sweet guy and I think you should appreciate him more than you do.''

Lucy turned her attention to the area below, from which the murmur of conversation and laughter drifted up to the pair on

the balcony. "Appreciate him? Like that ass of a rice planter
he's talking to right now does? They're swapping University
of Georgia jokes; I can tell by the way Harm is getting red in
the neck. Look at them. Just look at them down there. My
husband is already drunk as a skunk." Just then, the two men
below looked up and saw the two on the balcony and raised
their glasses in salute. Lucy waved airily back and smiled,
murmuring between her stretched lips, "Assholes."

Cane looked at the waxy, beautiful face of his companion
and shook his head. "If you despise him so much, why don't
you divorce the poor bastard?" He was aware that Lucy had
been secretly seeing a man in Atlanta for some time now. He
didn't know who Harm's rival was—and didn't care.

"Divorce is as trashy as pierced ears, darling. Now, tell
me. You're the J. P. Morgan in the family. Will Little Annie
Rooney realize any profits on this pitiful enterprise she's undertaking?"

"Why do you want to know? Do you have a scheme to
confiscate it or something?"

Lucy gave her tinkling laugh. "From what you tell me, it's
hardly worth the effort. But I'm just curious. How much?"

Cane felt a warning of caution. He sensed that Tally's tiny
stroke toward private independence did not please Lucy Cantrell in the least. He shrugged. "A pittance, I'm sure. Look,
I'm thinking about turning in early. Can I get you something
before I call it a night?"

"You can send F'Mollie to me with a glass of brandy. Yours
looked tempting and I'd like to stay out here a little longer."

"I've never seen that black girl carry anything more delicate
than a milking stool without falling over her feet."

"That's the idea," Lucy said with a careful smile. "It's
time she learned more of the social graces."

"Well, good luck—and good night." Cane gave Lucy's
upturned cheek a brotherly peck and left.

After he left, Lucy stared down at the glowing barn, her
eyes narrowed in increasing anger. Tally Malone's plodding
determination irritated her more than anything else about the
girl. She knew it was irrational, her resentment toward Tally

for going to Harm behind her back, getting his support in what was, truthfully, a ridiculous little venture. But the deeper resentment was born of fear. Lucy saw Tally's attempts at independence as direct threats to her own security. She felt a sudden surge of pure hate for the girl's implacable self-certainty. She, Lucy Cantrell, had never had anyone make things easy for *her!* Every agonizing inch upward out of her hell-pit of earlier years had been done on her own. No one had offered so much as a crooked finger to help *her* crawl out. . . .

Lucy's hate burned deep within, as irrational but as real and deadly as one of the dreaded marsh fires. "She needs taking down a notch or two," she said to herself, her lips set thin and mean. "Tally Malone needs to be put in her place once and for all."

F'Mollie was coming out with the tray of brandy. Lucy barked at the girl for bringing a glass instead of a snifter, then drank down half a glass of the fiery liquid without so much as a shudder. She wasn't much of a drinker, but the brandy tasted like water. "Another glass, F'Mollie. And then there's something I'd like you to do before you go to bed."

F'Mollie griped to herself all the way to the barn where she had been set a task by Miz Lucy, a task that she felt was not only unfair because she had been kept busy all day long but because of the physical work involved. "Looks like Tally could put on the wood herself, since this stupid barn-firing's all her own idea. 'The poor girl's probably sound asleep and lettin' the fire go cold,' " she mocked the older woman. "Shee-it. So why should I have to be the one doin' it?" She grumbled the whole time that she was stacking up the dry pine masses of needles and twigs onto the low-burning logs in the furnace. "And why'd she tell me to make sure I piled on all the branches high as I could? Miz Lucy don't give a rat's ass whether Tally's ole barn gets cured or not."

Still, the black girl had never disobeyed Lucy Cantrell in her life. She was secretly terrified of that biting tongue and those ice-cold eyes. "There," she said, satisfied to see the low flames had started leaping. Suddenly, the furnace chimney produced a loud roaring sound as the bone-dry branches flew up and, lit with fire, popped out onto the roof of the barn. F'Mollie's eyes got big and round and darted from the puffs of fire to Tally's sleeping form on the bench. F'Mollie looked up at the stars and said a little prayer of thanks that Tally was outside and not inside the barn.

"Tally," she whispered nervously when a shooting ball of burning mass fell not far from F'Mollie's foot. The smell of singeing smoke was all around and getting stronger. "Tally, maybe it's time you woke up."

Just then a burst of flames encompassed the far top corner of the barn roof and F'Mollie stopped pussyfooting around the sleeping girl. "It's gone to burn! Tally! Wake up! For Jesus's sake, wake up! The barn's goin'!" She began shaking the girl on the bench. "Lord he'p us, she's goin'! The barn's goin'!"

Tally wondered if she was in the middle of a nightmare as she sat up and stared groggily at the black girl pulling at her and shaking her. "What . . . what's going on?" Tally jumped up when she saw black smoke pouring out from around the tightly closed barn door. "Oh my God, the barn's burning up! F'Mollie, run get somebody! Tell 'em to come quick!"

"It ain't no use," F'Mollie said, starting to cough in the thick smoke that was surrounding them. "We gotta get away from here, Tally. The side could fall on us."

Tally pushed the black girl away roughly. "You go get help while I try to put the fire out inside. There's probably just a bunch of leaves caught on fire inside, on one of the pipes. Now, scoot. Go on!"

"You cain't do nothing, Tally!" F'Mollie wailed. "You cain't go inside that barn! It's bad enough out here. Lord, we're both near 'bout chokin' from the smoke."

"My crop's in there, damn you!" Tally ran to try to open the barn door and jumped back, looking at her scorched hands. They weren't burned badly, but she knew that there was no way she could go inside and save her little crop. She walked slowly over to where F'Mollie was standing safely out of the falling sparks. Watching the burning barn without showing any

emotion, she did not look at F'Mollie until the girl's hysterical
crying had stopped. "She was the one put you up to this,
wasn't she?"

"We wuz just trying to help, Tally! I swear to Jesus! Miz
Lucy said you was down here all tuckered out and the fire pro'ly
needed fixin' and I just . . . I just . . ." F'Mollie dissolved in
a flood of tears and ran off just as Poke and some of the men
from the quarters came up with buckets of water and tried
ineffectively to put out the now-raging inferno. By the time
Daniel Malone had managed to get a firebreak plowed around
the burning building so nearby houses wouldn't catch fire, too,
Tally had melted into the background to watch as her hard-
worked barn of cigar tobacco burned to the ground.

From the balcony on the second story of Camellia Hall, Lucy
Cantrell watched, too. "Too bad about the new barn," she
said to herself softly. But wouldn't this be a good lesson for
Harm? Here he had gone out of his way to help a plantation
dependent—and look what the results had been! The barn was
worth twenty or more times what the sorry crop curing inside
had been worth.

Deep inside the darkest part of her, a secret voice gloated,
It was worth it. Lucy raised her glass of brandy to the dying
red cloud of flames that was waning in intensity. "We'll just
see if the little phoenix can rise from these ashes."

The doors to the balcony burst open so abruptly behind her
that Lucy's glass jumped in her hand and drops of brandy flew
up into her eyes, temporarily blinding her. "Wha— Who's
that?" The quaver of her voice was real. She was really afraid
for a brief moment as a strange image of a huge Valkyrie-like
Tally with her hair and nostrils aflame flashed into her mind.

"The question is, who's *that?*" Cane's voice was harsh and
unaccommodating. "Nero? What, no fiddle, Lucy?"

The stinging brandy had brought the tears pouring down
her cheeks. "Oh, Cane—is it you? Cane, did you see what
happened! I feel so terrible. It was all my fault. I sent that
cretin girl down there to help Tally finish up the curing—and
just look, just look at what happened. I'm to blame, God help
me. Mea culpa. How can I ever forgive myself?" Lucy buried

her face in her hands, letting the tears drip from between her fingers. "What you must think of me . . . oh, Cane, I can't bear to think that you think . . . that there's even a possibility you think that I . . . you don't, do you, darling?" Lucy raised a pitiful face from her hands and begged the man who stood looking at her with angry uncertainty. "Please say you forgive me for being so stupid."

"I'm not the one who should be forgiving anything, Lucy." His hands went onto her shoulders and bit into them, hard. "But I won't forgive you if I find out you did this on purpose."

Lucy's perfect mouth worked to produce the piteous crumpled look that had always worked before. "Oh, Cane . . . do you think it's possible that I did it subconsciously? We were out here talking and I felt jealous of you thinking so highly of Tally and I . . ." Lucy made her eyes widen to blue wells of horror. "Oh my God," she whispered, "if I'm that cruel, that depraved, deep, deep down—Cane, please help me!"

For a moment she thought she had failed. With a moan of sincere terror, she crumpled like a rag doll. Cane caught her. After only the briefest hesitation, he held her tightly. "You poor little bastard," he whispered brokenly as Lucy sobbed uncontrollably, this time with relief that he believed her. "Poor, tormented little bastard."

"Don't ever turn your back on me," Lucy cried, her face muffled against the strong chest. "Cane, you're the only one in the world who understands me."

"That's why I have to leave, Lucy. Otherwise, we'll start fighting each other on your terms and it'll be a bloodbath that I don't have the stomach for."

Lucy, filled with secret triumph, raised a tear-stained face. "But you'll come back, won't you? Cane, please promise me that you'll come back."

Cane stared down into the pretty face that had always softened him as no other's woman's could. His bond with his stepsister was as inexplicable as it was irrevocable. But it was a bond that he could not break. "Not for a while. I can't stand seeing what you do to others, what you do to yourself."

"Oh, Cane, you do care for me," Lucy said weakly, pulling

his head down to hers. She kissed him fervently, and when
he tried to pull away from her, kissed him even more passionately. "Papa once said that if only you had been a little bit
older—"

Cane put his hand on Lucy's mouth. "Don't ever say anything like that to me again—you hear me?—not if you want
to keep our kinship."

"I won't, Cane, I just meant . . . Cane, I don't know what
I'm saying. Just hold me. Hold me tight before you go."

From the shadows below, Tally Malone silently watched the
two dark shapes on the balcony move together. Watching her
barn burn down had made her feel numb. But seeing Cane
Winslow embrace the woman Tally hated with all her heart,
she felt a burning anger that melted the icy numbness.

"Don't you know you're hugging the devil?" she whispered. Cane was Lucy Cantrell's ally, and from all appearances
always would be—no matter what his stepsister did to other
people. As Tally watched the couple embrace, the pain in her
heart hardened into steely determination.

"Don't ever pretend to be my friend again, Cane Stephen
Foster Winslow! And as for you, Miz Lucy Cantrell, one of
these days you'll be sorry you didn't run my mother and me
off this place when you had the chance. You'll get your come-
uppance, you ole hag—and I plan to be the one to give it to
you."

Tally punctuated her prediction with the sign of the "witch
finger" and stomped off, fighting back the tears that she'd held
back all night long.

8

Tally and Nick stowed their picnic basket in the grove near
the cove and took a walk on the beach. She liked this time
of day, just before sunset, because of the way it made her

skin look. Her tan fairly glowed. Sunset made everything look rosier.

Nick, too. She kept stealing sidelong glances at the boy who walked beside her. Nicholas had grown very tall in the three years she'd known him. Handsome, too; he was already suntanned from his few weeks on the island to the point that his blue eyes fairly blazed out when they looked at her. Tally decided he was probably the handsomest boy she'd ever seen. The girls at school were always talking about being in love with somebody or other; Tally turned up her nose at the idea of talking syrupy about some fellow, but right now she was feeling sticky-sweet about the boy at her side.

He was different from the other boys she knew. When he looked at her, his eyes didn't shift away. When he talked to her, he acted as if he really cared about her response to what he said. He listened attentively to her prattle about the tobacco and Reba and events on the island, as though he were really interested. Tally found herself opening up under his intense attentiveness as they worked or lazed around together. Before she knew it, she had told him everything about her concerns for her family, Reba, anything else that was bottled up inside her.

One day, she stopped suddenly in the middle of a monologue and said, "Shoot, Nick. Would you listen to me? Here I am down here on the prettiest beach in the whole world with the handsomest boy in the whole world, and I'm feeling sorry for myself!" She laughed with the joy of being alive and having a picnic with Nicholas Cantrell. "Hey—race you to the cove!"

"Well, you better get a head start. I was second in the track meet last semester. . . ."

"Yeah," Tally said, getting herself poised for a takeoff sprint. "But that was on that ole sissy track. This is real running. Ready? One for the money, two for the show, three to make ready . . ."

Tally was off with a peal of taunting laughter. Her long legs were fast, but not as fast as Nick's. When he passed her with a slap on her rump, she panted, "Reba says it's best to let the boys think they're better."

"Ha!" Nick threw back at her. He was already lying on the spit entering the cove when Tally came huffing and puffing up. "What took you so long?"

Tally dropped down beside him. "I thought I saw Aunt Monday's pet dolphins out there." She jumped up and grabbed Nick's hand, pulling him up. "Come on—let's go for a swim before we eat! I bet the dolphins are in there right now."

Nick let Tally lead him into the water, but he wasn't enthusiastic about going swimming with creatures that looked too much like sharks to suit him. "I'm starving to death, Tally. Can't we go for a swim later?"

Tally was already wading into the cove. "Look, they're already out here! Maya! Inca! God, Nick, look at them jumping!"

Nick's apprehensiveness about the dolphins changed after the first soft nudge from one of the playful creatures. Soon, he, too, was having a wonderful time with them. When the two friendly dolphins left the cove, Nick turned to Tally and said with deep emotion, "I never had this much fun in my life." Spontaneously, he pulled Tally into his arms and kissed her. "God, how I've missed you."

They stood there as the sun went down, feeling that theirs was a special moment isolated from the cares of the rest of the world. When the water lapped more energetically at Tally's feet, she whispered. "Let's go have our supper before the tide comes in."

Cane Winslow's mouth was a thin line of unspoken epithets, none of which was complimentary to his stepsister's handsome son. He watched the young couple through his binoculars as they came slowly around the bend, arm-in-arm, toward their picnic, his attention more closely riveted to the much-changed figure of Tally Malone. "Dear God," he breathed aloud. "She's as ripe and ready as those damn sinful figs in Lucy's garden."

And the boy was in love with her; Cane didn't have to be told that. He hadn't been back at Camellia Hall more than ten minutes before he knew what was happening on the island this summer. F'Mollie, Essie Mae, Harm, even Nicholas himself had dropped hint after hint about the unfolding of a romance between the young Romeo and Juliet of Moss Island heritage.

Cane had a mean thought. He could call Lucy in Atlanta and have her back here in five hours, with fire in her belly. But no; he wouldn't stoop to that. Even though he and his stepsister had made up over the incident of the barn burning, Cane wasn't ready to give Lucy more ammunition with which to hurt Tally Malone. Cane laid down his binoculars and stomped back into the bedroom to shower for dinner. He wasn't particularly looking forward to a meal that would be bereft of feminine company. Harm would want to hear all about Cane's Tri-Com expansion in international territories and Cane was not in the mood to talk business. He was up to his eyebrows in business. What he really wanted was to talk to a woman. No, that wasn't being honest. What he really wanted was to talk to Tally. It had been ages since he'd seen her, for Christ's sake, and here she had gone and turned into a woman without his being around to enjoy watching the metamorphosis. . . .

"What's that, Harm?" When his dinner partner repeated his question, Cane answered shortly, "No, Tri-Com won't be going public for at least five more years—not if I have any say in the matter, which I currently sure as hell do. Now, do you mind if we leave the ticker-tape talk to the boys on the Street for the time being? I'm sick of having people ask me if TV is really gonna take radio's place and maybe even the movies'. What's the crop been like lately?"

Before Harm had halfway launched into a commentary on the price of bright leaf and the newly entered peanut industry, Cane had a sudden thought that made him interrupt rudely, "Harm, you never told me what happened between you and Genevieve Fontaine. Why the hell didn't you marry her instead of Lucy?"

Harm's hand jerked on the thin stem of his wineglass. He turned a dark red. "Damned cheeky question, Cane. Why the hell haven't you married one of those Buckhead pinks that run after you hot and heavy?"

"Don't sidestep me, Harm. I know you were in love with the woman. Hell, who wouldn't be? But you, you had the chance. And you didn't take it. Why not?"

Harm poured himself another glass of wine, not offering to replenish Cane's glass. "None of your damned business. Vieve and I had our private reasons for not marrying, and none of them concern you."

Cane was beginning to enjoy watching Harm squirm. He liked his brother-in-law but was not fond of his habit of avoiding straightforward questions. "All right, then tell me this: That summer I visited for the first time you and Lucy had been married, for several years. I saw for myself the two of you—you and Vieve—playing turtledove every time you got a chance." Cane couldn't stop now; the photo-sharp memory of Nick and Tally walking arm-in-arm like young lovers was pushing a raw button in him that wouldn't turn off. "Did you screw Genevieve that summer, Harm? Was that what pushed her into that shotgun wedding with a man who wasn't even close to being in her social pew? Was Genevieve pregnant with your child instead of Daniel's, as the poor woman's proud SOB daddy let everybody believe?"

Harm jumped up from his seat, spilling the rest of his wine onto the snowy linen cloth. "Dammit, man! I've always liked you, but you're stretching our friendship—I'm warning you." He took a deep breath and said more calmly, though anger had filled his ruddy face with color that threatened to burst through the throbbing vein at his temple, "Southern gentlemen don't discuss their private affairs concerning women. And I'll thank you never to bring up the subject again."

I don't have to, Cane thought to himself; you've told me what I was always half-sure of anyway. "I'm sorry, Harm. This island always brings out the worst in me, I'm afraid. I never come to Moss Island without having the feeling that I'm walking back into a morass of old secrets. This damned place is full of ghosts—and not all of 'em pretty."

Harm's anger vanished, leaving a new expression that was half-sad, half-bitter. "Ghosts?" He picked up his napkin and dabbed at the spreading spot of wine on the table, then looked up at the portrait of Justin Randolph that dominated the room. "Let me tell you about ghosts. How would you like it to have that SOB up there on the wall sharing your bed with you and your wife?" He wiped his forehead with the napkin and said quietly, with an apologetic laugh, "I never said that. Lucy would shoot me if she ever heard me say that about her daddy."

"She won't hear it from me," Cane promised, sincerity overriding the shock he felt at Harm's uncharacteristically divulging his hatred of Lucy's departed father. "Just as I'm sure she won't hear from you about Nicholas being tight as Dick's hatband with that girl down there."

Harm's shoulders slumped as he thought of the fury Lucy would bring down on him if she learned he'd allowed Nicholas to consort with the island "trash" while she was away. "We have to do something about that before she gets back. It won't do. Those kids are in for getting hurt real bad if we don't do something about it."

Harm's eyes met Cane's in a plea that sealed the younger man's suspicion about why "something had to be done" about Nick and Tally. "I guess it's up to me somehow," Cane said resignedly.

He didn't answer Harm's "good night," so intent was he on figuring out how he could stop things from going further than they already had between Tally and Nicholas. He told himself he had only Tally's well-being (even more than his young kinsman's) at heart.

He must do something, even if she hated him for doing it, to keep Tally from heading into the emotional disaster that lay ahead of her if she fell in love with Nick. And he could not betray Harm with Lucy by simply laying open what he now thought to be the truth.

Tally must somehow be prevented from sleeping with Nick.

For some reason, Cane looked up to the portrait of Justin Randolph, his eyes narrowing as they met the blistering oily gaze of his late stepfather. "You bastard!" he said. "You bought poor Harm out from under his true sweetheart's nose for Lucy and now everybody's miserable and it's all your damn fault."

And he, Cane, was right in the middle of the whole mess. He knew how to handle anything that came up in the business world—and relished the challenge. But how the hell was he going to handle this? How was he going to keep Tally and Nick apart without making the girl hate him for the rest of her life?

Cane's mouth tightened. He had to do it; that was all there was to it. Harm was too weak, and Lucy, thank God, was ignorant of the true facts of Tally's parentage. Cane did not relish the challenge of breaking up a blossoming romance, but he had to keep Tally from falling in love with Nicholas Cantrell—who Cane was convinced was her own half-brother.

On the way home from tea with Aunt Monday, during which the black woman had shamelessly flirted with Nicholas and had told him a hilarious "fortune," the boy suddenly pulled Tally to a stop. "You really love this island, don't you? Does it ever bother you that it doesn't belong to your family anymore?"

Tally flung her hair out of her eyes. "Of course it does! How would you feel if Jim-Roy Tatum moved into your bedroom and you found yourself working for his father in the fields?"

Nick's face looked stricken with a sudden thought. "My God, I never thought of how you must feel about me living in Camellia Hall. Tally, do you hate me for being there?"

Tally's hand took Nick's strong one and squeezed softly. "You're not like her, Nick. I could never bear it if you were."

"But I'm her son and heir." Nick's voice hardened. "I love my mother, but sometimes I hate the things she does. I swear, if she ever gives me the place, I'll turn right around and give it to you and your family. Tally, I swear it!"

Tally was so deeply moved, she couldn't speak. Instead, she raised up on tiptoes and kissed Nick on the mouth. It was a spontaneous gesture of gratitude, but when Nick's arms went around her and his mouth started responding to her kiss, it became a lot more.

Tally pushed away the memory of another man's lips, four summers before, and gave herself up to the enjoyment of the moment. Nick's lips were incredibly soft and warm. She made a little kittenish purr of pleasure when he drew away and immediately put his head down to nuzzle her neck. "Umm, that makes me shiver, even hot as it is."

"I'm not shivering one bit," he murmured. "As a matter of fact, I was just thinking what a nice evening it is for a swim in the lagoon."

"I don't have my bathing suit," Tally whispered, her stomach undergoing that funny little feeling that she often felt in Nick's presence.

"I always carry an extra one in my back pocket," Nick whispered back, smiling at her naïveté.

Tally's giggle was not altogether from nervous innocence. It was from the sudden recollection of the trick she and Reba had played on poor Jim-Roy at the lagoon. They'd caught him swimming naked and, hiding in the palmetto bushes on the side of the lagoon, had terrified him with animal noises, imitating Aunt Monday's boar Lionel until the poor boy had run naked from the water, leaving his clothes behind.

"Did you see it?" Reba had asked Tally after their laughter had died down.

"See what?" Tally had responded, knowing perfectly well that Reba was referring to Jim Roy's pecker. She had not only seen it, but she had marveled that such a harmless little contraption could make Reba go into kinds of ecstasies she was always describing to her friend. . . .

"Hey, Earth to Mars. You still there?" Nick was brushing his hand to and fro in front of Tally's face, which immediately turned pink at the idea of where her mind had been. "You won't get into trouble or anything, will you? I mean, I don't know exactly when Mother's due back but I've noticed Essie Mae doesn't make you work up there when there's just us."

"How long is your Uncle Cane staying?" Tally asked suddenly as they picked their way down the path, looking for the shortcut that led to the lagoon.

"I guess till my mother gets back. They're real close, those two." Nick didn't notice Tally's tight-lipped look and went on innocently, "Sometimes I think my mother cares more for Cane than she does for Dad. Hey, here we are. Last one in's a rotten egg!'' Nick started stripping the minute he saw the sparkling, inviting water, and with total lack of self-consciousness flung his naked body into the lagoon.

Tally was more timid. When Nick started needling her from the center of the lagoon, she said shyly, ''I don't know if I can. I've never gone skinny-dipping with anybody but Reba.''

''Don't be silly. I'll close my eyes and once you're in the water, I won't be able to see anything.'' Nick's eyes were sparkling with fun—and something else that, fortunately, Tally was unable to identify. ''Come on in! It's great!'' Nick paddled closer to the edge and splashed water on the girl standing on the bank.

''Well . . . if you cross your heart and promise not to peek.'' Nick did so solemnly, and Tally peeled off her clothes, hesitating when she got down to her panties. Then, with a spurt of devil-may-care bravado, she wiggled out of her step-ins and eased into the water, sitting down quickly so that the water came up to her neck. ''All right, you can open your eyes now.''

Nick looked at her, a lump in his throat coming at the sight of her. ''You look like a beautiful lotus blossom with your hair floating out around your face like that,'' he whispered, sudden emotion making his voice quiver. ''Tally, don't ever be afraid of me. I would never hurt you.''

''I know that,'' she said. Then, boldly, she struck out swimming, knowing her nakedness was not completely hidden from the boy's eyes as she smoothly stroked past him—and not caring. Was she turning into a tramp? she wondered.

Soon they were unselfconsciously racing each other and seeing who could swim under water longer. When Tally suggested a game of ''alligator,'' Nick agreed with the enthusiasm of a little boy, soon having the girl in stitches over his imitation of a fierce alligator coming after tender flesh. On one of these ''attacks'' Tally ducked under water and stayed down so long that Nick lost his clowning look and frantically tried to find her.

When she popped up right in front of him, he grabbed her in relief and said sternly, ''Don't ever scare me like that again,

Tally." They both were aware at the same time that their bodies were touching. In his anxiety, Nick had pulled Tally to him, so that her breasts were brushing the golden down on his chest. "Tally . . . oh my God, Tally. You are so pretty. . . ."

This time Nick's lips were not so soft and tender. When his mouth met Tally's, it became insistent in its claim on hers. Shocked at the sensations she was undergoing, Tally responded in kind until they were both writhing with desire to have more, to feel more. Nick's hands tangled in the girl's wet hair, pulling her head back so that her mouth opened in an "oh" of pain. But Nick did not heed; he used the vulnerable mouth again and again to dampen the hot need that was growing within him. . . .

When his wet hand covered a soft breast, Tally's inner governor braked in alarm. "Nick, you can't do that. . . ."

"I just want to feel you. I won't do anything else, I promise. Just let me hold you for a minute. You're so pretty—so soft and pretty. . . ." Tally swallowed hard when his hands slid to her waist to grasp her and lift her easily from the buoyant water, so that his lips could reach the cherry-sweet tips of her breasts. Tally closed her eyes, wondering what was happening but feeling helpless to stop it from happening as Nick awoke her body to all its mysteries. Was everything in her connected, she wondered dreamily, to everything else? The sensations Nick was causing in one place seemed to reach out in quivery currents to every other part of her. Tally felt herself blending into a new languorous rhythm of feelings that were at once wet and hot and shivery and delicious. . . .

Tally knew at this point that she must call a halt to what was happening before Nick went too far. Reba had warned her that boys sometimes couldn't keep from putting it in when they got to a certain point. "Nick," she whispered, "I have to go." He didn't even hear her, so Tally pulled away from him abruptly, feeling guiltily that she was probably acting like one of the "cock-teases" Jim-Roy was always talking about. "Nick, I'm really sorry, but I can't . . . I mean, I'm still pretty young. I'm sorry." She put her hand on his cheek and looked deeply into his eyes, then left the lagoon.

Nick did not try to stop her. It was at that moment that he realized that he loved Tally Malone too much ever to do anything that might hurt her.

Lucy was enchanted, on her return the following afternoon, not only to have Cane back in her fold as the forgiving and once again loving stepbrother, but also to have him willingly acting as her adviser. "Darling, I love the idea of my precious son going to Europe for school, but you know how he sulks with me every time I open my mouth with advice."

"Lucy, I said I would handle it, if you and Harm will give me your blessing. I'd like to see Nicky using the summers to get groomed for his future, rather than frittering them away down here. God knows, I would've jumped at the opportunity to live in Europe when I was his age. Think what an advantage I'd have in my business if I could have picked up foreign languages and some finesse along the line."

Lucy reached out to run her hand along Cane's jaw. "You have no rough edges whatsoever, darling. But I think your idea is a splendid one. Selling it to Nicky is the rub. He has all those hormones working against him, you know, and being around that island Jezebel certainly doesn't help a lot."

Cane ignored Lucy's casual slur on Tally. "Well, I have noticed that Nick has been spending a good deal of time with the girl. She's not a bad kid, but I have to agree with you that Tally Malone's not the right girl for him. . . ." Cane stopped at the curling smile on Lucy's face as she looked past him to someone standing in her bedroom door.

He spun around to see Tally standing there like a figure of ice that froze him to the bone even before Lucy got the words out, "Well, I wondered if Essie Mae had forgotten to ask you to bring our tea up here at half past the hour." She ignored Cane's look of fury and said sweetly, "Thank you, my dear. And I hope you will refrain from divulging to my son anything you might have overheard just now. As his Uncle Cane was just saying, Nicky needs to be exposed to the finest culture, the best schools, young women of family . . ." When Tally set the tea tray down with a clatter and left without a word,

Lucy threw out her hands and asked Cane with a wide-eyed look of wronged innocence, "Now, what did I do to the girl, I ask you? What, pray, did I say or do?"

"Lucy," Cane said between tight lips, his hands clenched so that he wouldn't break his cardinal rule of never striking a woman no matter how much she deserved it, "I would like to pinch your head off and spit it out to the sharks. You set that up, you little—" He stopped, knowing it was no use, that Lucy would be Lucy until she died, and he either had to live with it or kill her.

"Set it up?" Lucy gave a tinkling laugh. "Darling, all I set up was tea time for us to enjoy together on this happy reunion. You were the one who brought up the business about Nicky and that poor girl."

He could not say anything more, since that was true. But damned if he was going to sit and sip tea with Lucy Cantrell while Tally was off somewhere thinking God knows what about him. "I have to go," he said abruptly, banging down the cup and saucer Lucy had handed him.

"Well, you don't have to shatter my Limoges," Lucy said with a sharp look at Cane's set face. "Darling, you're not doing something stupid like running after that sullen girl to apologize for what is, after all, the truth she needs to hear."

"Lucy, what I'm about to do is none of your goddamned business."

Cane slammed the door behind him and was maliciously gratified to hear the tinkling crash of one of Lucy's precious teacups as it hit the floor in his wake.

He knew where he would find her. The door to the lighthouse obligingly did not creak as he pulled it to behind him. Nor did the winding stairs give off signals to the girl who was crouched upstairs.

He knew she was aware of his standing there and was deliberately ignoring his presence. But Cane would not be put off by her pretense that she didn't see him. "Tally, I'm sorry you heard me say that. Try to understand. It's not right between Nicky and you. You're not right for him; he's not right for you. It won't work. All I was doing was trying to keep both of you from getting hurt."

"Nicky." Tally spat out the word. "He hates for you to call him that." She turned a fierce face around to Cane's. "You treat him like he's still a little boy. You all do! Nick's more man than you are! He always has been."

"Tally, please don't hate me. I can't stand that."

"I don't hate you. I despise you. Miz Lucy has you under her thumb like she has everybody else. Don't pretend you're my friend, or Nick's, either. I know you're not."

"But I am," Cane said in a low voice. "Tally, I am your friend, and Nicky's, too. Please believe that. I don't want to see you get hurt—and you will, if you fall in love with each other."

"Because I'm 'beneath' him?" Tally asked scathingly. "Because Miz Lucy can't stand the thought of her precious son getting involved with island 'trash'?"

"Because . . ." He couldn't tell her. He couldn't. How could she deal with knowing who she really was? At least with Daniel for a "father" she had some kind of certain identity. If Harm Cantrell were a different kind of man, revelation of her true parentage might be a positive thing. But as it was, Cane was sure telling her about Harm and Vieve could only result in Tally's being emotionally skewered. "Because Nick's still immature, and you are, too. Tally, this island has made you grow up fast, but it hasn't made you grow up wise. There's a world out there that you don't know beans about. It's different for Nicky because he's got money and he's been out there. But, you . . . Tally . . . Look at me, dammit!"

She had turned away from him in the middle of his impassioned speech and was hugging her shoulders, staring out at the sea. "You're not the boss of me. I don't have to do what you say."

He went over to her and towered over her in a mixed kind of fury that threatened to fill the small space. His hands on her shoulders were controlled as he shook her so that her head wobbled like a rag doll's. "Yes, you do. There's no one else who gives a rat's ass about whether you make it in this world or sink in one of those goddamn mush-holes out there. Listen to me, and listen to me good. I care about you and I don't want to see you get into something you can't handle. Nicky's not for you—just take my word for it—and don't . . . get . . . involved . . . any more than you already are."

With every word he emphatically shook her. When he realized she was staring up at him as if he'd gone mad, Cane stopped, his hands shaking with the intensity of his feelings. "I mean it, Tally," he said hoarsely, more quietly. "Dammit, why are you looking at me like that, as if I'm some sort of monster?" He was filled with a sudden fury—toward Nicky, toward Lucy, toward Tally herself for making him be the one to do this. His anger was almost uncontrollable; he looked at the lovely girl whom he could break in two with one hand. He wanted to assault her physically. He wanted to rip into the deceptive cocoon of youth that held her in soft imprisonment and drag by force to the surface the woman that lay waiting inside. He wanted to pierce her with his manhood, with his reason, with his words, make her scream to the world that he was right. . . .

As though his wild thoughts had penetrated her daze, Tally let out a little cry that was half-pleading, half-terrified. Hearing it, Cane melted and took her into his arms as though she were the tenderest burden in the universe.

"Tally," he whispered brokenly into her hair, against her cheek, against her damp eyelids. "Tally, don't you understand? I can't let anything happen to you. Not till you're safe and . . ."

She struggled like an animal who has just begun to awaken from the hunter's numbing dart. "Let me go. I'll . . . I'll tell Nick. I'll tell Perrie . . . I swear it, I'll scream, if you don't let me go."

"Then let it be something to scream about." He carefully repositioned her so that she was helpless in his grasp, then slowly, deliberately placed his mouth on hers.

He knew he was scaring her to death, but he knew, too, that she was responding to his kiss. Cane had the fleeting evil thought of making her his forever right there, right then. Her resistance had momentarily melted and his desire urged him to take advantage of the weakness in her that would probably never be shown to him again.

But he couldn't. He wanted her free and clear, and when that time came, he would know a triumph that could never be enjoyed under lesser circumstances. "I'm sorry, Tally—really sorry. I had no right to do that." Cane let her go, one of the hardest actions he'd ever taken in his life. "That's why I'm so afraid for you and Nick. It's hard for any man to be around you without wanting to possess you."

Her mouth was so sweet and vulnerable as she stared at him, Cane thought about kissing her again. But he didn't dare.

Tally saw the way he was looking at her mouth and she scrubbed at it furiously. "I saw today how you and Miz Lucy are conspiring to get Nick off this island, away from me. I saw you that night the barn burned, too. You were thick as thieves that night, too." Tally's voice held bitter ice and Cane knew she was remembering his remarks that she had overheard in Lucy's bedroom. "You're a fine pair, the two of you." She scrubbed her mouth as if ridding it of his earlier touch. "I knew that night I saw you kissing her, the night my barn burned, that you and Miz Lucy were two of a kind and that—"

"Oh my God, you saw me comforting Lucy. . . . Tally, it wasn't what you think! I swear it. Lucy and I just . . . well, we have some special bonds that you could never understand even if I told you about them."

"I'll say you do," Tally said scathingly. "Now, Mr. Winslow, if you'll just stand to one side, I'll be going. My mother's had her supper put back so I could go take your . . . your concubine her precious tea." She had seen that word somewhere in a book and while she wasn't sure what it meant, it seemed to fit.

Cane stood back helplessly as she marched, head held high, past him. When she reached the landing, he called down to her, "You know in your heart that I'm on your side—always, Tally. And while you're busy trying to deny that, think about what you're doing to Nicky, tying him to this island. Nicky needs to be out from under Lucy's domination if he's ever going to amount to a damn thing, and you sure as hell aren't helping him. How is the boy going to get anywhere when he's got two strong women pulling him apart?''

Tally froze halfway down and Cane knew he had struck a chord of truth.

She stopped outside the lighthouse to think about what Cane had said. Was he right? Had her sincere concern for Nick's welfare gotten swallowed up in the fever of her obsession to triumph over Lucy Cantrell in any way she could?

Tally pondered that, and for the first time that summer took a long, hard look at her feelings for Nicholas Cantrell. Was she in love with him? She suspected he was in love with her and would do whatever she asked. Suppose she added her voice to those who were urging him to leave. Would he think she had betrayed him, joining in with the others?

No. Nick knows I really care about him, she thought. Cane's wrong about Nick and me being wrong for each other, but he's right about one thing: Nick needs to get away from Lucy. She'll make his life miserable, and mine, too.

What they had to do, Tally decided, was to let Lucy think she'd convinced Nick that he needed to go away. Tally's heart ached at the idea of Nick's being gone again, but they were both young. They could bear being separated as long as they knew it wasn't forever. And when Nick came back the next time, he would be grown and strong and capable of standing up to ole Lucy about him and Tally. Tally's shoulders squared as her decision was made. She would go find Nick and tell him that he had to do what his mother wanted—for right now.

She found Nick down by the ferry landing, talking to Reba Taylor. "I was just talking to Reba about one of the guys I know who got polio about the same time she did," Nick said, perhaps feeling he needed to explain his presence to Tally. "He learned to walk without braces after a lot of therapy."

"And I was explaining to Nick how things like that cost

money," Reba said shortly. "Here, Tally, take the rest of these crumbs and throw 'em out to the gulls with Nick. I've got some patterns to cut out for Miz Pettigrew."

"Did I run her off?" Tally whispered after Reba had limped away to her house.

"No, of course you didn't. You know how Reba gets upset every time anybody starts talking about polio. It was real hard on her, having to go into that brace." Nick threw the last of the bread crumbs to the swooping gulls. "If I stay here and transfer to some place like the University of Georgia or Emory, I can start helping encourage Reba to get some help."

"That's what I came down here for." Tally took the empty bread sack from Nick and folded it up to take back with her. Essie Mae had drilled into her that sacks never got thrown away. "To tell you that you need to go off somewhere, like Europe, instead of burying yourself in this place."

Nick's face turned toward hers, full of amazement. "Tally, what the devil are you saying?"

"I'm saying that you need to go somewhere else and learn how to be somebody! Nick, I don't often agree with your mother about anything, but this time I agree one hundred percent. Look at the kids that stay here; just think about where they end up! Nowhere—that's where."

"Tally, I can't believe you're talking like this. You just trying to get me out of your hair? Is that it?"

"You know better than that." Tally put her arms around Nick and laid her head on his chest. She could feel his heart beating a mile a minute. She hated to have him think she was against him for even a minute. "Nick, I hate to think about you going more than anything in the world, but I know it's best." She raised her head. "Look at me. What chance have I got to get anywhere? I'm stuck here working for your mother, at least till I figure out what else I can do. But . . . you! Nick, you can do anything, go anywhere, be anything! You stay here, your mama'll have you running the plantation, maybe even get rid of Poke and some of the others she says ain't worth diddly-squat." Tally crossed her fingers behind her back on that one, but she knew Nick needed some convincing.

"You really think I ought to go?" Nick held Tally so tight she couldn't breathe. "It scares me leaving you here. Some other man'll come along and . . ."

"No, he won't," Tally said, fiercely shaking her head. "I'll wait for you and nobody else can ever take me away from you. Nick, that's a promise! Cross my heart and hope to die!"

"Don't even say that," Nick said with emotion. He kissed Tally hard and when her mouth opened to his and he felt the dampness of her tears that had rolled down her cheeks, he said hotly, "I'll leave, but I'll come back. And when I do, Tally Malone, you will be my woman, mine alone, and the whole world will know it." Nick raised his head and looked down at the girl in his arms. "Tally, prove that you really love me and aren't just trying to get rid of me."

Tally went rigid. "Nick, what are you saying?"

Nick was pale under his tan. "I'm saying that if we belong to each other—really belong, I mean—we'll both be true no matter how long I'm gone."

"No, Nick." Tally pulled away, angrier at Nick than she had ever been before. "If I let you make love to me, what does that prove? Maybe you do need to go off and do some growing up!"

"Well, maybe I do—and you sure as hell could stand a little growing up, too! I heard about how all the mainland boys have been sniffing around over here the minute I leave!"

"And I heard about all those dances off at school that you were 'forced' to go to!"

"I'm glad I'm getting out of this damned stinkhole!"

"Not as glad as I am!"

They stood there glaring at each other and when Nick finally whirled away and stalked off, Tally fought the urge to run after him and beg him to stay with her on the island. But it was really better this way. Nick's anger would cool. They would start writing each other and their love would have a chance to strengthen so that when the time came, they could stand up to Lucy together.

A gull swooped down on her, and with it, new doubts. It was going to be mighty lonesome on this island with Nicholas

Cantrell gone. And what if he met somebody else? Tally wondered if she was crazy, adding her voice to Lucy Cantrell's. Maybe Nick would never come back to the island. . . .

When a lingering gull dived for the empty bread wrapper in her hand, she threw it at him. "Oh, go catch a fish, you stupid gull!"

That's what she was, Tally told herself despondently on the way home—a stupid "gull." She had just sent off the boy she loved—maybe forever.

9

To celebrate Nick's minor victory over his mother, Nick and Jim-Roy went to the small carnival that had set up at the fairgrounds on the mainland. It hadn't been much of a victory, Nick admitted to Jim-Roy as they wandered around the cheap carny grounds together, but at least he wouldn't be going to school in Europe.

"Hell, MIT's still too far away from Tally, but at least it's far away from my mother, too. All my other college credits will transfer, which means I could graduate and be completely away from her in two years. I've got plans that would give my mother heart failure if she knew about 'em. For one thing, I'm secretly taking flying lessons. Cane says once I solo, he'll get me checked out on the Tri-Com helicopter, too." Nick's face glowed with excitement as he talked about his plans. It wasn't easy to outsmart his mother; his success was heady. "My ROTC commander says I'll be able to join the Army and probably work on some sort of special force, what with the flying training and the kind of engineering program I'm going out for. They're always anxious for officers with cartography and surveying-engineering backgrounds. And having some helicopter experience . . ." Nick's imagination began to take off, and he saw himself being a decorated hero adored by Tally Malone.

Jim-Roy pulled at Nick's sleeve, his eyes bugged out at the

spectacle being unveiled at the next tent. "Man, forget this rigged-up game and look at what's over there. Whooo-ee. Hot damn."

Nick put down the tinny gun to look at what Jim-Roy was pointing to. " 'Dee-light and Her Deadly Darlings.' Oh, Jim-Roy, it's just another big con."

"Hell, no, Nick, that's a pitcher of a snake up there in that painting. She does it with a snake, can you believe it? Come on, man, we gotta see this."

Nick was already pretty drunk from the beer he and Jim-Roy had been drinking since early afternoon, but he wasn't too drunk to know that he had no desire to watch a sleazy carny woman put a snake up her . . . "I've about had it, Jim-Roy. I gotta pack tonight and get up pretty early in the morning. Hey, what's going on?"

The women who had come out on stage in skimpy costumes to lure customers stopped their gyrating as a bearded man came out and took one of them—apparently "Dee-light"—by the arm and whispered something to her.

"Hey," Jim-Roy said, turning to Nick, who was feeling slightly sick from eating cotton candy on top of all the beer. "Did you hear that? Somebody stole their big snake. Took it right out of the cage back in their tent."

"Stole their snake?" Nick laughed, then hiccupped. "Hello, Sheriff Waymon? I'd like to report a very important theft. My pet rattler is missing."

"It ain't funny, Nick. What they took wadn't no rattler. It was a cobra."

"Probably Dee-light herself did it. Jim-Roy, let's go home. I'm sick of this place."

In fact, Nick thought, after he and Jim-Roy had parted at the ferry landing, he was just plain sick of everything and everybody. Not only had Cane and Harm taken his mother's side about his going off to some faraway fancy school, Tally had taken her side, too. That was a real burr in his belly. And the way she had recoiled from him when he told her he wanted them to make love to show their commitment to each other! The memory of her look made him mad all over again. He wasn't some jerk from the mainland who just wanted some island pussy. He loved Tally Malone, and *damn* her for not knowing that!

"Who's taking you to the airport in the morning?" Jim-Roy wanted to ask Nick why he wasn't spending his last night on the island with Tally, but he figured that wasn't his business.

"My mother. She plans to fly up with me and then go back down to New York for some shopping after I get settled."

The wind blowing off the ferry sobered both boys up, but they didn't do much talking. Jim-Roy was thinking about the missing cobra and trying hard not to give credence to a suspicion he had.

Nick, of course, was thinking about Tally. He had lain awake till dawn thinking about how unfairly she had acted. As though he were some two-bit Don Juan! "Reba wouldn't act like that. She'd give a man she loved a proper send-off."

"What?" Jim-Roy threw the landing rope over and jumped off to the landing.

"Nothing."

After the boys had exchanged solemn good-byes, Nick walked down to the beach. He kicked at the sand, so that the phosphorous cochinas sparkled under his feet like ground-up diamonds. "Damn it all to hell. I'm eighteen years old—old enough to go to war, and I'm still a fucking virgin!" The irony of what he'd just said made him laugh. "Fucking! Hell, I don't even know if I can!"

He must have had a hundred wet dreams after that time in the lagoon. They'd come very close to going all the way that day. Nick's crotch got tight at the thought. But his fury at Tally didn't dissipate. "Reba wouldn't back off like that from a guy, after she'd gone and gotten him all hot and bothered."

By now he was at the little spit of beach near the cove where he and Tally had lain in the sun so many times. He felt more alone than he'd ever felt in his life.

"Nick, what are you doing down here? I thought you were leaving in the morning."

Nick whirled to see Reba limping toward him. "Hey, girl! I was just thinking about you."

Reba laughed softly as she came close to him. "Sure you were." She looked up at the stars. "It's a real pretty night, isn't it?"

Nick was feeling a little funny about Reba. He couldn't keep his eyes off her. He knew that was why she wouldn't look at him. She knew something had changed about him. "You guess they'll be that big and pretty up in Massachusetts?"

"I reckon they will be. Some things are the same wherever you go." She put her hand on Nick's shoulder and reached down to unstrap her brace. "Hold me up while I take this off. I like the feeling of the water without this mess on."

He became her crutch as they waded out a little. Nick didn't pay any attention to his pants getting wet to the knees. Everything that Reba did seemed incredibly sensual, from the way she moved to the way she tossed her hair back off her face. When the big wave came up, Nick was watching Reba instead of the water. They both went under and came up soaked and laughing.

"Help me up," Reba told him, holding her hand out. "I feel like a baby, not being able to get up by myself."

"You don't look like one," Nick said in a choked voice as he pulled Reba up and held her. Her thin blouse was clinging to her breasts, her skirt to shapely thighs. Nick knew his desire was as evident to her when she lost her balance and fell against him. "I never saw anybody who looked more like a woman than you, Reba."

He picked her up in his arms and carried her to the beach. "I came to get the blanket I left down here this afternoon," Reba whispered. "It's over there by the last dune."

Nick carried her there and laid her down very gently. "This has nothing to do with Tally," Reba whispered as she pulled Nick down beside her. "She's my best friend and I'll love her till I die. Can you understand that?"

Nick nodded, pulling his wet shirt and jeans off. He was amazed that he felt no shyness at being naked. His heart constricted with gratitude at the gift Reba was offering him. "I can. Don't do that." Reba was about to pull off her wet blouse. "Not just yet." He bent over her and put his mouth over the thinly covered nipple, tasting the salt of the seawater at the same time that he felt her harden against his lips. "You're so beautiful," he said when he could speak. Reba's body was incredibly sexy, the breasts as large and full as he'd heard they were. He peeled the wet cotton away from her, marveling at the golden smoothness of her skin, the narrowness of her waist as he pulled her skirt down over her legs.

And then they were both naked under the stars and Nick knew that this would be a night he would never forget. Reba Taylor was the most generous girl he'd ever known, he decided as she gently led him into the right moves to keep him from betraying his sexual gaucheness. "Don't rush things," she whispered to him as she stroked him until he felt that all of the liquid in his body was on the verge of bursting forth. "Let's make this a night that both of us can remember."

He moaned in bliss when she gave him the gift of her breasts, letting him use them as he wanted and not even crying out when he became too rough. "It's all right," she told him, when he pulled away in horror that he might have hurt her. "I'm not as fragile as you think. I like seeing you get carried away like that." She bit him on the neck. "See? I can be rough, too." Nick took in a deep breath when she guided his hand to the wet velvet between her thighs. "And soft at the same time," she whispered.

He knew he could not hold back anymore. He wanted to be inside her, wanted to feel his manhood throb to its natural conclusion. And then he wanted to start all over again. He was glad they were doing it on the beach, under the canopy of stars. He felt bigger than life, swollen to giant size, capable of anything. . . .

The premature explosion shocked him. So did Reba's soft little laugh when Nick murmured a stumbling apology. "Don't be embarrassed. It happens to most boys their first time. Next time, just count to ten when you're almost there and don't move."

The next time was wonderful. Nick lay next to Reba, still breathing hard, and tried to think of how he could tell her how great she had made him feel. He finally told her. "Reba, I don't know how to say this, except just to say it right out. I'll never forget you for this. You knew without me telling you that it was my first time, didn't you?'' He couldn't see her smile in the dark. ''Well, I'll tell you this—I'm really proud my first time was with you.''

''I wish it had been mine, too,'' Reba said a little sadly. She was being honest. The things that island boys still said about her sometimes hurt her to the quick. She wasn't a ''tramp'' like some people said. She just loved life and the feelings to be enjoyed from it. ''Nick, you know now that this is all there's gonna be to this.''

Nick put his hand on hers and squeezed. ''I know that, Reba. It's funny, though. Even loving Tally like I do and planning for us to have a life together, I know I'll always think about you in a special way.''

''I hope so. Now, hadn't you better get going? Miz Lucy'll be sending out a search squad if you don't get on up there.''

''Tell Tally when you see her that I'm sorry we fussed. I'll write her. You, too.''

''You don't have to do that,'' Reba told him with a sad little smile. ''But I would appreciate it if you'd bring that brace over here and help me strap it on.''

Nick did so, handling Reba's afflicted leg with the gentleness that was her favorite thing about him. ''I wish I weren't leaving. This is sort of a screw and run, isn't it?''

Reba grinned. ''You'll have some other chances up there in that school. And don't turn them down. Making love is like making waffles. The first two or three are just practice.''

Nick put his hand on Reba's dusky cheek. ''Not in my case,'' he said softly. ''This was the real thing.''

But already he was thinking about how it would be with Tally the first time. Nick wasn't a callous young man. He was just young.

Perrie had been acting very strange. Tally watched him walking up from the swamp where he had taken to visiting almost every evening nowadays. She knew he was upset about his church's having been closed down by the law for the snake-handling incident that had ended in Caleb Bill's death. She hoped he wasn't trying to start up something on his own, but his secretiveness about his swamp excursions bothered her.

That wasn't all that was bothering her. Nick had finally written her from MIT, saying how sorry he was they had ended the summer on such an unsatisfying note. He loved her more than ever, he wrote, and knew that her wanting him to get away from the island had been an unselfish wish for his best interest.

Tally wasn't so sure about that unselfish bit. Looking back, she could kick herself for prompting his leave-taking. She missed him like crazy. Everything on the island reminded her in some way of Nick and their wonderful times together. She performed her chores for Lucy Cantrell with grim efficiency, looking forward to the day that Nick would stand up to his mother and she would know she had lost him to Tally.

Then came the night when Tally discovered what Perrie had been up to in the swamp.

Tally knew when she set supper out that night that something was going on with Perrie that boded ill. As he sat at the table eating the fried chicken and roasting ears of white corn she'd fixed, his eyes were so bright and full of a secret that Tally knew something was on his mind. No doubt, it had to do with the box he'd brought back that evening. She'd seen it in the corner of the bedroom earlier and felt sick inside, afraid to think what its contents might be.

Her dread congealed in her stomach, making the fresh fried chicken, whose neck Essie Mae had wrung only two hours before, turn to cold lumps of grease. Daniel Malone had never before brought one of the serpents into the house. She tried hard to think of a subject that might get his mind off what was in that box. War. That was it. He hated war so much that once he started in on it, there was no stopping him.

"Jim-Roy says he's thinking about joining the Army. 'Course something like Korea could come along, and then he'd really see some action!" Jim-Roy didn't betray Nick's plans, but he couldn't resist trying to impress Tally by talking about running off to join the service.

Perrie's eyes lit on hers with contempt. "You young'un's

don't know nothing about war—not enough to be talking about it. Not till you've been there. Tell Jim-Roy he needs to go find out for himself what it's like, see for himself his buddies dying right next to him in some godforsaken slime-hole that's already swimming with guts and blood. Tell him to sign up and go find out for himself what fighting's all about. Let him shoot some kid that ain't even started shaving yet or watch a grenade splatter somebody into a bunch of goo and then let him come back and talk to me about whether our boys are gonna go fight for something in some furrin' country that don't mean shit to the folks back home.''

"Daniel.'' Vieve put her chicken wing, which she had been nibbling delicately, back on the plate. "We're eating.''

"Yeah. I ate dog mixed with noodles—dog schnitzel, they called it—in a little village outside Berlin one time close to the time it was all over. I hadn't had nothing but C rations mixed with a little water for six weeks up till then, and you know what?''

Vieve put her napkin to her lips and looked over at Tally, begging her for help. "I don't think I want to hear any more.''

"Perrie . . .'' Tally pushed back her own plate.

Daniel ignored them both. "It tasted wonderful. It tasted just goddamn' wonderful—that's what.''

"I'll clear up,'' Tally said, getting up quickly and reaching for the platter of uneaten chicken.

Daniel reached out to trap her wrist. "You just do that and then you come on into the back room where your mama and I'll be. It's time I helped you learn the ways to the Lord.''

"She reads the Bible with me every morning,'' Vieve said meekly, a muscle at the side of her jaw twitching slightly. "Tally and me are going to services every Sunday morning nowadays, aren't we, Tally?''

Tally nodded. "Regular as clockwork. Perrie, how about I get you a nice cup of coffee and you can take it out on the porch and have a smoke on this pretty evening?''

"The only smoke I'm interested in is that boiling up from hell, where we're all headed if we don't do something to get ourselves right with the Lord.''

Daniel's eyes were burning fanatically across the table at her, but Tally bravely ventured anyway, "Perrie, it's not for everybody, that stuff about handling rattlers and drinking strychnine and all. You gotta see that."

"Tallulah," Daniel said, his voice dangerously soft in the unusual pronunciation of her full name, "you're a right smart girl, smarter'n some men twict your size, but there's some things you don't know pea-turkey about—and this is one of 'em. Now get them dishes cleared right quick and come on back where your ma and I'll be waiting."

"Perrie, I don't want to! Mama doesn't, either!" Tally defiantly pulled her wrist free.

Daniel leaned across the table and grabbed her by both arms, knocking over one of her mother's favorite Blue Onion bowls with a crash. He paid no attention to the sharp little cry from Vieve's direction, but whispered hoarsely into his daughter's face, which was less than two inches from his. "You do what I tell you, girl. 'Honor thy father and thy mother.' "

"How can I, when you're crazy as a coot," Tally said, knowing even as the words came out that she'd gone too far.

"You're a daughter of Satan!" Daniel yelled at her. He slapped her across one cheek, and then brought his hand backward across the other cheek. Tally felt her teeth rattle at the brutal blow. "You're a little slut, just like—"

"Daniel!" Vieve's cry was full of anguish and successfully held back the next blow that would have followed the first two. Daniel let his hand fall slowly back to his side but his eyes stayed bright and warning on Tally's face, where the marks of his hand were reddening visibly. "You've spoiled her, Vieve, with your fancy lies and dreams. She needs bringing down some with the help of the Lord. She needs purifying."

Tally grabbed up some of the dishes, her eyes still locked with her father's, and backed away from him, stumbling when her shoulder struck the kitchen doorjamb. Then she hurried into the small room, shaking so much as she unloaded her burden into the sink that the dishes rattled precariously. "Dear God," she whispered, taking a dishrag and wetting it and

putting it to her stinging cheek and then to her forehead, which
was burning hot. "Jim-Roy was right. He's gone over the
edge. I got to think of what to do, so he won't kill himself or
Mama or me or all of us."

Then she thought about the gun that Daniel had, in happier
days, taken out and shown to her and Reba, bragging about how
he had taken it off a dead German in the first few days of the war.
"It's a Luger," he'd told them proudly. "Real valuable, the
gunsmith over in Brunswick told me when I showed it to 'im.
Got the original firing pin and all the same numbered parts. But
just hold this baby. See how good it feels to your hand."

Perrie was capable of anything tonight. He was going to
bring that snake out tonight. Tally was sure of it. She had to
have something to kill it with. There would be no anointment
tonight. Perrie was too far gone, too angry. They could all
wind up bitten by some desperate rattler.

Tally took the gun carefully out of the little oak box that also
held a few pieces of her family's cherished silver flatware. She
fitted the gun into one hand, marveling at the shiny coolness
of the gray metal. Daniel took it out often and cleaned it
lovingly; she knew he kept it in good firing condition.

He'd shown her how to load and unload it, telling her the
while, "Always take it for granted a gun's loaded, girl. Nothing
more useless than an unloaded firearm, though. That's why
this baby's always ready and loaded for bear. . . ."

It was loaded now. Tally hefted the gun with two hands,
trying to remember all the things Perrie had directed her to do
as she'd shot at the tin cans he'd set up in a row for practice.
"God help us," she prayed fervently, her eyes tightly closed
for a long moment before she wrapped the gun in a dish towel
and went out of the kitchen to face whatever was in store for
her that night. She would get as close as she could and shoot
the snake before it hurt any of them.

He didn't even notice her as she slipped into the bedroom
where her mother was crouched still and scared on the corner
of the bed. Easing down beside Vieve, Tally put the towel-
wrapped gun between them, her hand creeping from it to cover

the cold fingers of her mother. "It's all right, Mama. Try not to make him mad and just be real still."

Daniel, who was reading aloud the Scripture that formed the core of the cult's beliefs, was hardly aware of anyone else in the room. As he read from the worn Bible, Tally's eyes went to the crate that rested at Daniel's feet. It worried her that there was no telltale rattle from inside, only a slithering sound that sent chills down her spine. Jim-Roy had confided in her that the carnival folks had gone to the sheriff about their missing cobra. Tally prayed that the box did not hold that deadly reptile. Daniel had only handled rattlers and coppermouths. The cobra was a heathen snake from a heathen country. How could it be expected to share Daniel's religion?

Her mother had dropped her hand from Tally's and felt the presence of the cold metal between them. Slowly she turned to her daughter to search her face with scared, questioning eyes. Under the rising tempo of Daniel's reading, Tally whispered, "Don't move, Mama. Whatever you do, don't make any sudden moves."

Daniel's eyes were becoming glazed and unseeing. "You see? You see? It's the anointment coming on me. It's the anointment, praise the Lord." He babbled the Scripture over and over, his face glistening with sweat and his eyes fixed on something in the room neither of the others could see. Then he reached down and with a choked "It's time. The Lord says it's time," he opened the crate and stood back as the hooded head of the cobra rose from the box. Everyone, including Daniel, was transfixed as the snake gracefully began undulating in a rhythmic pattern.

Daniel's voice held ecstasy as he whispered, "It's the granddaddy of them all. I been keeping her in the swamp, in a box, feeding her live rats from the corncrib, and we've come to know the Almighty together. Brother Allgood said I couldn't bring her in the church, that the law would get us for sure. But I kept 'er, and she's got the spirit of the Lord in 'er. See how I can just reach right out and have her wrap around my arm."

Tally's hand tightened on the gun and she managed a soft "shh" to her mother's little gasp. They were both paralyzed with fear, watching the cobra's sinuous motion to and fro as Daniel slowly stretched his hand down into the crate.

"*No!*" Vieve's scream was like a jagged bolt of lightning in the mesmerized mood of the room.

"You fool!" Daniel screamed back at her. "You've spoiled it! You've broken the anointment!" Tally watched in horror as the snake, quicker than the eye could see, darted back and forth, leaving a spot of crimson on Daniel's arm each time the lightning motion was made. Tally felt faintness threaten and fought it with all her being. If the snake got out of the crate, they were all done for.

The gunshot cracked through the room. Tally stared at the writhing snake on the floor and then at the openmouthed visage of Daniel, whose eyes were blanked with death. She stepped backward as he lurched toward her a couple of steps, then caught him as he fell into her arms. Under his weight she staggered backwards, and hit the apple-crate bed table.

She had heard of people collapsing after the ordeal of the anointment and the handling. Tally looked beseechingly across at her mother who was, she knew, going into shock. "Mama, you've got to help me. Mama, Perrie's like deadweight. Help me!"

"I don't think the snake's dead. It's still twitching. Oh my, I hope it is. I never could stand a snake in the house. Papa says I'm not very brave for a little girl raised up on an island full of every kind of creature under the skies."

Something about her mother's tone made Tally's head jerk toward her. Why was Vieve talking in that little-girl voice? What was wrong with her that she just stood there smiling as though this were not really happening? "Mama, did you hear me? I can't do anything to help him. He's so heavy." As Tally spoke, the strength left in her arms gave way entirely and Daniel slid like a crumpled sack to her feet. He made no sound and Tally looked down at the front of her old shirt with horror, as unable as Daniel to utter a sound. But her voice's paralysis was from a different cause.

Vieve looked at Tally and said sternly, "Whatever am I going to do with you? Putting on your prettiest dress just this morning, and just look at you! Such a mess all over, and what in the world is that dreadful stain? Have you been into cook's strawberry punch that she made for our guests?''

''Mama,'' Tally whispered. ''It's blood. It's Perrie's blood. Mama, I think he's dead.'' She looked down and saw the spreading stain of crimson that was seeping out from beneath Daniel's limp form. ''Mama, Perrie's dead. The snake bit him.'' But Tally could tell from the amount of blood that Perrie had been shot, too. Maybe he was already dead when the bullet hit him. She hoped so. Out of some sort of automatic response, Tally pulled off her stained shirt and tossed it on the floor. Vieve's robe was on the bed; she pulled that on, shivering.

Vieve looked distressed and then her face took on a look of half-serious reproach that chilled Tally's blood. ''Shouldn't have done that, you know. Papa says guns are for men to use, not pretty girls.''

Tally fought back a wave of impatience. Something was wrong with her mother but there was a lot more wrong with Perrie. ''Mama, you've got to help me with Perrie. I can't do it by myself.''

''Oh, the big tease. He's had too much port, as usual. Just leave him there. He'll be all right by morning.''

Tally looked down at the lifeless form and thought, *I don't think so, Mama*. Then she saw the snake coiling near Perrie's limp foot and felt a surge of hysteria. *It'll kill us, after all!* She reached blindly for the nearest object, the kerosene lamp on the bedside table, and hit the loathsome reptile as hard as she could with its brass base. The snake lay limp, dead at last, and Tally turned back to see what must be done next. She stared at her mother, at Perrie's limp body, and thought about the stolen cobra, about the bullet hole. Each would raise a thousand questions.

He was dead, after all, his soul probably already on its way to wherever it was bound.

Her mind settling on the only solution open to her, Tally got the kitchen matches that were always kept on the table next to the lamp she'd just broken. The spill of kerosene took only one tiny torch to ignite it. Tally stood for a brief moment watching the flames lick at the worn chenille spread, then gather momentum as they found the cornshuck mattress. By then she realized it was time for action. Thank God the window had only the primitive wooden shutter, already open, and no screen. Just before she bundled her mother out, Tally spied the Luger lying there in the middle of the floor. It would not burn, she thought with sudden clarity, and it wouldn't do to be found in the ashes along with Perrie's burned-up body.

She held it by the barrel and tossed it out the window into a palmetto clump where she could retrieve it later. Then she got her mother out the window, Vieve giggling the while about what sport it was outwitting Papa this way.

It wouldn't take the little house long to burn down, Tally knew. She led Vieve to a safe place, the tabby chapel, and waited, her arms tight around her mother. Minutes later, she tiptoed out to see that the Malone dwelling was completely in flames. She said a prayer for Perrie and went back to her mother.

Part Two

Spring 1956

10

Tally Malone and her mother had been living in the old lighthouse since Daniel's death and the fire that destroyed their house. Tally was now seventeen. She stood at the searchlight window atop old "Tabby" and thought about how old she was getting to be.

"I'm getting as old as those old turtles that waddle up down there on the beach to lay their eggs." She sighed and looked out at the familiar view of her island. From up here she could look all the way across the compound to where the settled part of the island melted into the marshes.

After she and Nick had made up by way of letters, she had written to him about how much she loved living in the lighthouse. ". . . I can look out on a clear day and see as far as Aunt Monday's place. Those trinkets she has dangling all around catch the light and twinkle like crazy. I can even see all the way to the cove. . . . Remember how we swam with the dolphins? Nick, you were so scared at first. . . ."

Tally leaned her chin on her hands and smiled, feeling not quite so lonesome when she thought about Nick. She wished he could be up there with her at night, her favorite time to sneak up to the searchlight room and dream. He would laugh at her for acting as if she could see the famous slave ship, *The Wanderer*, out in the ocean, coming up on the island in dark secrecy. "It's true," she whispered as though Nick were there, teasing her. "I can even hear their chains rattling as they're herded off the boat like animals. I can!"

At night she could hear the wind whistling through the ancient live oaks and imagine she heard moans and whispers from the "Hainted Oak."

Tally laughed out loud at herself. "Me and my ghosts!" She thought about how she and Reba had spent all those hours in the old graveyard listening to "Heartbeat Theater."

Tally's smile disappeared. Now that Perrie's charred remains were part of that graveyard, she avoided it as much as possible. She avoided, too, walking near the ruined foundation that was all that was left of the Malone house. Talk about ghosts!

The house fire had been far worse than the barn burning. Tally had been left with all of the explanations and no support from her mother. Lucy had grimly listened to the story about Daniel's being bitten by the cobra and had had surprisingly little to say beyond a sharp comment about the insurance being inadequate to cover human carelessness. For some reason, her silence had worried Tally more than the harshest recriminations would have. Tally also worried about the way Lucy would stare at her and Vieve with speculative eyes and then make some cryptic comment about "grief-stricken widows and children." Did she suspect something? Tally wondered.

Tally had gone back two days after the fire, when the embers had finally stopped smoldering, and searched the palmetto clump for the Luger.

The gun was gone. Tally was uneasy, but reminded herself that every black on the island, in typical Gullah pack-rat fashion, had been plundering the ashes for bits and pieces of household shrapnel. Daniel's gun was, no doubt, safely hidden in some secret cache down in the quarters—or already sold to the shady pawnshop dealer on the mainland.

The disappearance of the gun was a worry, but not as pressing as the situation in which Tally found herself after the fire. At least the dreadful secret involving the death of Daniel Malone was not a daily concern. Genevieve Malone was. Her retreat into a private world had been complete and apparently permanent. Vieve was like a child these days, locked away in her girlish fantasies. It appeared she would never grow older than she was at the time of her happiest memories—when she was a young woman, courted by all the eligible young men, beloved by her father.

The doctor Harm Cantrell insisted on bringing out to see Vieve told Tally that he could not do anything for her mother, except sign the papers for a commitment to the State Mental Hospital in Milledgeville. Tally reacted in horror to that idea. Vieve had been through hell already; her daughter would never agree to send her to "the snake pit."

Dr. Paulk was sympathetic, agreeing that Vieve would be better off at home. "It's not that she's dangerous to herself or anyone else. She's in more of what's known as a fugue-state, best I can determine, Tallulah. Trauma of your daddy's death, I reckon, and the fire and all. I could give her some Thorazine or some sort of sedative, but truth is, she don't seem unhappy or anxious."

In fact, Tally's mother seemed actually happier than she had ever been before in her daughter's recollection. When they moved into the lighthouse, she ran excitedly up to the search-light room and called down gaily every time she saw anything moving on the horizon. Tally, busy trying to arrange the scraps and bits of furniture Ducktown residents had contributed to the bereaved family, had not been resentful of her mother's playfulness. Indeed, she encouraged it. She even managed to cadge an ancient pair of binoculars from Harm Cantrell so that her mother could watch for ships and dolphins hours on end.

It wasn't easy, though, taking over the bulk of the chores around Camellia Hall. Vieve couldn't function in that area, so all her chores at the big house fell to Tally. F'Mollie had gone crazy over some new boy, so most of the work was left to Tally and Essie Mae. Lucy hired Lem Tarver, an overseer to take Daniel's place. But since he commuted back and forth from his own place outside Ducktown, he did not become an integral part of Tally's life.

She still helped out in the busy stages of tobacco growing. So did Jim-Roy Tatum, when he could spare the time from his job at the pulpwood mill. When it was time that first spring after

Daniel's death to apply poison to the young tobacco plants, he
had patiently helped Tally tack small cans to stick handles,
puncture the bottoms with holes, and fill the homemade appara-
tus with the powdery insect poison. "God, how could anybody
smoke who'd ever been around this stuff," they both grumbled
as they moved up and down the rows sprinkling small dollops
of the powder on each plant. They missed Reba, who was
spending a lot of time at Warm Springs, Georgia, getting therapy, thanks to Harm Cantrell's sponsorship.

Now as Tally stood in the searchlight room looking out on
the island's vistas, the image of Cane Winslow came into her
thoughts. She got an occasional postcard from him, but she
didn't need a reminder to think about Cane. A wink of a plane
tip in the clouds, a glimmer of a gamboling dolphin, a flash of
moonlight on the waves—almost anything triggered the image
of Cane Winslow. Tally always thrust the impression away, just
as she thrust away memories of the night Daniel had died. . . .

The fact was, Tally's sexuality was coming to a full awakening. The lonely nights in which she fantasized alternately about
Cane and Nick left her feeling ashamed, but the distressful
images still came. An incident in the new barn had not helped
the situation. She had found herself trapped in the rafters during
a sizzling encounter between F'Mollie and her latest boyfriend
on the dirt floor below.

The two had not known of Tally's presence and had gotten
into their enthusiastic enjoyment of each other's bodies before
the girl above could do anything but stay hidden from view.

Tally had tried not to watch or listen, but it was very hard
not to. F'Mollie's enthusiastic reaction to every thrust from the
man lying atop her resounded throughout the barn—and her
partner wasn't much quieter. Tally's face burned with embar-
rassment as the moans and groans got more frenzied and the
slipslopping sounds of F'Mollie's lover trying to satisfy her
filled the air.

She had to hold on to keep from falling or she would have
plugged her ears with her fingers when the union reached its
climax. Tally was downright shocked at some of the things she
heard the two say to each other about what had just occurred.

At the same time, she was aware of a peculiar sensation in the pit of her stomach that stayed with her long after the copulating couple had left the barn.

Since her nights were lonely, she had trouble keeping from conjuring up images of herself in a man's arms. Cane Winslow was taboo; she could, however, think more innocently about Nicholas Cantrell. . . .

She was thinking about Nick again as she looked down at the beach where they had so often walked together.

Oh, just stop it. He's probably got a girlfriend, she thought morosely in her perch above her island world. After all, he's probably more handsome than ever. The infrequent letters had hinted at activities at nearby girls' schools, activities that were as foreign to Tally's experience as the funny-sounding phrases Nick sometimes used in his letters, as though he expected her to understand them. Besides, he forgot my birthday last time. He could've at least sent me a card.

It was at that zenith of Tally's self-pity when Poke Taylor appeared on the stairs bearing a package. "Tally? You up there? You got yourself something here come all the way from Massatoosetts."

Poke beamed as Tally ripped off the parcel wrapping and then waited for her to unwrap the beribboned package that was revealed. Tally looked at him with a smile and said softly, "I'd kind of like to just look at it for a while like this, Poke. If you don't mind."

Poke obtusely ignored the hint that Tally wanted to unwrap Nick's present all by herself. "It pro'ly cost a whole lot, but I made sure Miz Lucy didn't catch sight of me bringing it up."

"I appreciate that, Poke." Tally waited for her visitor to leave. But Poke was fishing around in his pockets for something, his face screwed up with the concentration to remember which pocket held the object he'd obviously just remembered to produce.

"Oh, here it is." He held out a minuscule package, actually an envelope folded into a square for mailing. "Plumb forgot, what with that big fancy 'un, that you got something else here."

Tally's heart lurched when she saw the familiar handwriting. She'd kept all of the postcards from Cane and couldn't mistake that scrawling, distinctive script. She snatched the tiny parcel from Poke's grubby hand. "It's probably a little something from Reba. She said she was sending me a surprise."

"That ain't my girl's writing. Reba writes in little-bitty squiggles just like—"

"Poke," Tally said with an edge of impatience, "I thank you for bringing up my mail and all, but I really need to get on with seeing to Mama's supper."

When he was gone, Tally sat down with the package from Nick on her lap. Tearing its wrappings off slowly, she found herself wondering more about the contents of the package from Cane. But a stubborn loyalty made her open the larger box first.

Nick had sent her a daring two-piece swimsuit, which only the boldest mainland girls had taken to wearing on the beaches. Tally blushed as she held up the skimpy suit to her body. "Why, that rascal. If he thinks I'd go out with nothing but this on me, he's got another think coming. . . ." But she smiled at the card that said only, "I'm coming home in May and I want you to meet me at the dock wearing this."

May! Nick was coming home in May! At last! Tally touched her burning cheeks with the silky scraps of material, blushing at the thoughts of Nick seeing her in such a revealing costume. Then her eyes lit on the tiny package from Atlanta.

The gift from Cane was an exquisite gold charm on a long delicate chain—a mermaid with a princess's crown on her flowing hair. Tally sat holding it for a long time, admiring the sculpted fishtail and jeweled eyes. Then she fastened it around her neck and shivered as the cold metal slipped down between her breasts. The goose bumps on her matured bosom came from the sensation of having been kissed by the ghostly lips of the gift giver. "What's happening to me?" she whispered. "Am I getting to be like Reba? All I can think about is some man?"

To calm herself, she fished out the card from inside the

ripped envelope. It was not signed and said simply, "To the princess of my island."

She sat there for a long time, dreamily gazing out at the sea, until the impact of the message hit her.

"*His* island!" she growled. "*His* island! Cane Winslow, this island will never belong to you, no more than it really belongs to Miz Lucy."

But for the rest of the day, as she went about her chores, she was aware of the sensual feel of metal next to her flesh and could never quite lose the feeling that Cane knew, even from far away, that she was now wearing his gift between her breasts.

That night, lying in her round bower whose windows' only curtains were the April-washed night and stray moonbeams, she clasped the golden mermaid and closed her eyes. Pushing from her mind forbidden images of the man who had given it to her, she thought of Nick and of how his eyes would sparkle when he saw her again.

Would he think she was pretty? Tally felt her Fontaine nose and let her fingers trail down to the mouth. Why did her mouth have to be so big, too?

She wondered if Nick would try that French-kissing business on her again. This time she might not mind it. She blushed again and realized she was burning up in the small room. When the nightgown came off, there was only the cold presence of the charm, and Tally had to start all over again taking her mind off things that she had no business thinking about.

Still, it was hard to get to sleep after the exciting news that Nick would soon be coming back to Moss Island. He would find a lot of changes, including the ones that had happened in Tally's life. He would find her a lot older, too, Tally thought suddenly. Plenty of girls that she'd grown up with, only a few years older than her, already had kids getting ready to go off to school. One of them, Sallie Fay Murdoch, had visited Tally recently, bringing her newest baby, and had sat there running her mouth off like crazy while her little walleyed baby sucked noisily on a brown-tipped nipple.

Tally had avoided acknowledging the spectacle until finally

she couldn't help bursting out with "Doesn't that . . . well, *hurt?*"

Sallie Fay had giggled before whispering conspiratorially, "Now, honey, don't tell me you've never had your tit sucked before. It don't feel exactly *good*, but then it don't feel so bad, neither. . . ."

Tally sat up in her moon-striped bed and looked down at her breasts as though she were seeing them for the first time. Would Nick want to do things like that, things he almost had done that day in the lagoon? Would he close his eyes so he couldn't see the Fontaine nose and oversized mouth and just do things to the parts of her that she was beginning to realize had a mind of their own? Even now, her breasts felt tight and full to the point of bursting and there was a peculiar achiness between her thighs that moved from the depth of her triangle to the pit of her stomach and back again every time she imagined Nick looking at her and touching her like this, all naked.

Her hand had crept down unconsciously to soothe the uncomfortable ache. Now, when Tally jerked her hand away and touched her cheek to cool it she felt the moistness, and shame washed over her like a wave of salty sea. Jim-Roy had told her that if boys did things to their peckers, they got warts and could eventually go blind. What happened to girls? she wondered. Nobody ever talked about that.

Tally, thoroughly disgusted with herself and the whole notion of sex, turned over on her side and tucked her miscreant hand under her pillow. Then she looked down to see that her breasts had squeezed together, trapping the cold metal of Cane's charm, and everything in her started up all over again. Only this time she had to do *something*, for God's sake, if she was ever going to get to sleep.

Anyway, nobody had ever said anything about it being wrong for *girls* to do it—had they? Surely one time wouldn't make her go blind. And she could live with warts.

Maybe it was because Nick was coming home, or maybe it was just that Tally was older and maturer, but whatever the reason, she found that this year's spring cleaning was less of a drudgery than usual; it was rather a soul-satisfying challenge. Tally helped Essie Mae supervise the team of Ducktown women who came in to scrub down walls and porches and woodwork until every square inch of Camellia Hall was sparkling clean and smelling of lemon oil. Silver was polished to a gleaming finish, and every chandelier was lowered and painstakingly washed with ammonia till the prisms caught fire with transparent light. Rugs were hauled outside and hung on lines and beaten clean, while every curtain was washed and ironed to crisp newness. The activity was just as brisk outside. With Poke's help, Tally had barrel after barrel of fresh shells brought over from the Ducktown oyster cannery and spread out with rakes over the paths around the compound. Lucy Cantrell called in an old chit with the local sheriff and had him bring over his convicts to prune, trim, and manicure the gardens. Reba Taylor, now home from Warm Springs, and Tally both secretly enjoyed the catcalls of the bare-chested men—some young and not unattractive—every time they walked past the hardworking crew. The girls were careful not to respond, though. Lucy made it clear that the chain gang was there to work and not to ogle.

Essie Mae gave over the cleaning supervision to her young assistant two days before Nick was due in and dedicated herself to the preparations in the kitchen. F'Mollie confided to Tally that Essie Mae had decided to make her famous boneless turkey dinner for the big night. Though the two cajoled and begged, Essie Mae was adamant about not allowing an audience when she performed the magical rites of preparing the turkey that would appear at table in perfect original shape, browned to golden perfection, tender to a fault—but miraculously without a single bone to hamper marauding appetites.

The famous turkey preparation took place as it had over the years of Essie Mae's rule over the kitchen, and her mother's and grandmother's before her. A sheet was placed over the kitchen door, through which none dared enter or peek, and over a period of several hours of total isolation, Essie Mae performed her mysterious machinations with the unfortunate bird. At the hour before dinner was to be served, the perfectly

formed cooked turkey would be brought triumphantly through
the service doors and placed on the buffet, to be carved only
after all who were to be served were in place to admire the feat
of a magnificently intact turkey with no bones.

In the meantime, Tally scrambled to get herself cleaned up
and ready to meet Nick at the ferry. She and Reba had made a
pasteboard placard with the neatly lettered greeting "Welcome
home, Nick!" only slightly askew on its tobacco-stick base.
Reba had acted a little funny when Tally had invited her to
take part in the welcoming ceremony, but had finally agreed
to be there on the dock when the ferry, with Nick aboard,
pulled up.

Tally thought it was probably because her friend felt awkward around boys these days. But she had enough to worry
about without worrying about Reba, too. She had to find something in her sparse wardrobe so she would look pretty on Nick's
first night home. There would be no starched maid's uniform
tonight, thank goodness. Miz Lucy had reluctantly agreed to
Essie Mae's stipulation that this one night, and this one night
only, Tally Malone would not be pressed into service at the
big table and would even be allowed to join the second seating
at dinner. Traditionally, the second seating included middle-
tier household help such as Vieve, Poke and Reba, Essie Mae
and old washerwoman Mattie, and sometimes the sheriff and
a deputy or two.

Tally brought out her best dress, an off-the-shoulder cotton
sundress that Reba had helped her fashion from the prettiest
cotton yard goods they could find. She looked at herself in the
wavy mirror in Vieve's bedroom and decided that the dress
was fine but her hair looked downright countrified.

Vieve came in from her walk on the beach, an activity she
had taken up on a regular basis, and clucked over Tally's
appearance. "Oh, dear, that won't do at all, nòt at all. Papa's
guests are very important. He won't like it, your wearing one
of your day dresses to meet all his important friends."

Tally sighed, wishing her mother had not chosen this moment to come home. Now she would be late meeting Nick at
the ferry, maybe would miss him altogether, since Vieve would

spend interminable time going through an imaginary array of party wear for something "more suitable for Papa's little girl to wear" and then insist on putting Tally's hair up in elaborate ringlets and curls "that would make those horrid Bovanne girls cringe with envy."

"Mama, I don't have time to change. Here, let's help you get bathed and dressed. Essie Mae says she has a special treat for you at dinner—a dish of her sherry Jell-O, made specially the way you like it."

The ruse worked. Vieve's eyes lit up. "Oh! Mama's secret recipe!" She danced off to start her bath and Tally breathed a sigh of relief. Later, she would have to hang up the worn dresses donated to Vieve after the fire, but at least she would have time now to finish dressing and sneak off to the dock. Tally quickly touched a spot of powder to her nose and applied a brief brush of twenty-nine-cent Tangee natural lipstick to her full lips, deciding after a glance in the mirror that rouge would be redundant. The thoughts of seeing Nick again had brought a healthy color to her cheeks that cosmetics could not improve upon.

Her hair was hopeless, as always. Tally lifted the heavy mass experimentally, looking at the effect of pinning it atop her head, then let it drop with a sigh. Why couldn't she have curly hair like Reba?

An early gardenia bush was blooming near the chapel. Tally picked up a couple of bobby pins and called out to her mother, "I'm leaving, Mama. Is there anything you need me to help you with?"

"No, precious. You mustn't keep Papa's guests waiting. Did Sukey put up your hair?"

"Yes, Mama," Tally said, crossing her fingers. Sukey had been dead for twenty-five years but had been revived in Vieve's selective memory. "She even put flowers in it."

"Oh, lovely," Vieve sang out gaily. "Do have her put a pitcher of sangaree in my dressing room so I might have a sip while I'm getting ready. Goodness gracious, it's getting warm!"

Tally obediently put a pitcher in her mother's room and

tiptoed out. She had thoughtfully added a plate of cucumber sandwiches so that her mother would not go hungry. She would bring the sherry Jell-O later.

Genevieve Malone had not set foot inside Camellia Hall since the night of Daniel's death and would not do so tonight, though in her mind she would have a "marvelous, marvelous evening with Papa's friends making so much over her."

Tally had learned the scenario well and had, after much despair, accepted it as the only way her mother could continue to face her life. . . .

Reba and Tally waited together at the ferry landing, their skirts and hair whipping in the breeze from the mainland. Now and then, Tally stole sidelong looks at her friend, marveling at how much prettier Reba had become over the past year. The girl's dusky skin was olive-smooth, touched with damask-rose; her tousled hair was black and shiny, her eyes sparkling bright. With her special genius for sewing, she had transformed an ill-fitting dress from Goodwill into a flowing creation that flattered her lush figure. Tally could easily have been jealous of Reba's looks.

She wasn't, though. Her compliment was from the heart. "Reba, I declare you get prettier every day that goes by."

Reba turned, her face beaming with pleasure at the unexpected compliment. "Why, that's just real nice of you to say that, Tally." The friendship between the two girls had been strained during the months following Daniel's death, for reasons that—as only Reba understood—had at their root their feelings toward Nicholas Cantrell. The older girl looked at Tally with a long, appraising look. Then, sensing the genuineness of her friend's admiration, she leaned over and kissed Tally on the cheek. "You, too. You're the prettiest thing on this island. Why, Nick, he's gonna die when he catches sight of you."

A gull swooped down between them just then, breaking the odd little assessing silence, and Tally laughed and waved off the attack. "Maybe we should've brought some crumbs to feed the gulls."

"What about the boys? Shouldn't you throw them some crumbs, too?" Reba and Tally laughed together over the years-old joke.

"There you two are, giggling just like always."

The sound of Nicholas Cantrell's voice behind her made Tally whirl and Reba gave a little squeal of surprise. "Nick! But how . . . where . . . ?" Tally looked at the empty landing, then back at the tall blond young man standing there looking at her. "Where's Poke? He was supposed to fetch you."

"He was so slow getting there, I went ahead and rented a motorboat and came over by myself. Well, are you girls just going to stand there, or do I get a real down-home welcome?"

Tally held up the sign they'd made and Nick laughed, then staggered under the weight of Reba, who'd rushed forward and flung herself into Nick's arms. "Whoa! You're pretty enough to knock a guy off his feet, but don't overdo it." Over Reba's curly head, Nick's eyes sought Tally's and she felt her stomach lurch at the look he was giving her. "Hi, beautiful," he whispered, hardly noticing that Reba had grown still in his arms, nor trying to stop her from slipping from him and limping away to lean against a dock-post.

"Hi, yourself," Tally replied, all the fancy words of welcome she'd planned leaving her mind like scattered quail. The moment for an innocent hug and kiss had passed; the two stood there looking at each other, not noticing when Reba, forgotten in the shadows, left them alone on the landing. "Did . . . did you have a nice trip?"

"You're beautiful," Nick said again, his eyes going hungrily from Tally's face to her streaming hair and over the length of her slender body. "You've gone and grown up on me," he said shakily. He moved toward her slowly, then stopped, remembering. "Oh, God. I'm really sorry I couldn't make it to the funeral. I kept trying to call you, but they said you were looking after your poor mother."

"I got your wire. And the flowers. Those meant the world to me, Nick. And I understand about you not coming home for the funeral. I really do. That scholarship is too important to you."

"But I missed being here. You. Everybody on the island. Your mother—how's your mother?"

"She's fine." Tally felt herself moving forward, overcoming a strange paralysis. "She's just fine."

He was almost there. With considerable effort to concentrate on anything but the emotion he was feeling, Nick managed, "And Reba—where'd she go?" Nick looked a little worried that Reba had slipped away without so much as a good night. He hoped she wasn't mad at him for not writing all this time. "She looks great, too. Is she really okay?"

Tally nodded.

When the interminable distance between them had been reduced to an infinitesimal space of separation, the shrill cry of joy from someone on the path from the main house splintered them apart again.

"Nicky! Nicky, they said they heard you motor up—Nicky! Nicky, where in the world are you?"

Nick's eyes stayed unwaveringly on Tally's face as he said with the new conviction of a boy-turned-man, "She'll never come between us again, Tally. I swear it." He took a deep breath and, slinging his duffel bag over his shoulder, walked off the landing to greet his mother on the path.

Tally listened to the fading sounds of Lucy's excited chatter and Nick's low-voiced replies as mother and son walked back to the house together. Then she heard the lonesome call of a whippoorwill, a sound that usually filled her with sadness at her own loneliness.

But tonight she felt no sadness—only joy—at the mournful sound. And when an answering "whip-poor-will" came out of the marshes, Tally laughed out loud, sure her lonely days and nights were over.

She and Nick were in love, they had their beautiful island, and the summer stretched ahead in warm, golden endlessness.

11

Lucy Cantrell had never been truly accepted into Atlanta society, so when she received an invitation to be part of a week-long whirl of festivities centered around the membership drive for the soon-to-be-opened Cherokee Country Club, she eagerly accepted. It had always stuck in her craw that the old-guard Piedmont Driving Club members had snubbed her father's application.

But then she worried aloud to Harm, "Nicky refuses to go with me. You'll have to stay behind and keep an eye on him. I've arranged for all kinds of invitations to mainland galas, but Nick is acting very peculiar this summer. And you know how that Malone girl operates. She'll have him all to herself. God knows what that could lead into."

Harm pointed out mildly, "The boy's a grown man, Lucy. Besides, I'm not much of a chaperon. Get Cane down here to keep an eye on 'im. He always seems to be able to influence Nick when nobody else can."

"Cane's in Tokyo negotiating some kind of deal for his company. That awful Gretchen went with him. Cane said she's doing a series of tapes for their Tokyo affiliate, but I expect she's just out for another cheap adventure." Lucy touched perfume to the back of her neck and wrists. "It's up to you to look after Nick, darling."

Harm Cantrell sighed. "I'll do my best, my dear. But I think you worry too much." He patted his wife on the shoulder, secretly relieved that he was not being pressed into attending the round of boring social events in Atlanta. "Have a good time, my love. Buy yourself some new dresses and knock those Junior Leaguers' socks off."

Lucy Cantrell intended to do just that and did not need her husband's patronizing advice about adding to her wardrobe. She already had six new gowns on order at Froshin's and had made arrangements for Mr. Charles to come to her suite at the

Georgian Terrace each morning at ten to do her face and hair. Nor did she lack for a suitable escort for each of the parties. "The only socks those women would be caught dead wearing are those with the little pink balls on them that they wear to the market after their tennis matches."

"I hope you'll have a wonderful time up there, Lucy," Harm said again, filled with gratitude that he had several days' worth of deep-sea fishing to look forward to in his wife's absence.

"Oh, I shall," Lucy said with a little smile as she thought about her own secret plans. "I certainly shall . . ."

Tally and Nick couldn't believe their good fortune, Tally especially. "Are you serious? Do you mean to tell me that your mother is leaving you all alone on this island with me, the Venus's-flytrap?" Tally shook the bucket of cochinas she had been gathering as she and Nick walked on the beach. There still weren't enough for the stew she planned, but she had the whole afternoon free—now. With Lucy gone, the work at the big house always slacked off. And the bottom leaves on the tobacco stalks wouldn't be ripening for several more weeks. "It's a trick," Tally said darkly. "She plans to come back tomorrow and catch us at something."

Nick laughed and lifted his eyebrow in a comic leer. "Well, let's not disappoint her. Why are you walking so far away from me? I like holding hands."

Tally shifted the handle of her bucket and smiled at him a little shyly. She still couldn't get used to how big and handsome Nick had gotten. Now that he'd added a healthy, glowing tan, he was almost too good-looking to be true. Tally was sure he had every girl within seeing range of his college madly in love with him. But for right now, it was their time, their beach, their summer. Tally tucked her hand into Nick's happily. "Just another half hour and I should have enough cochinas gathered. Then you want to go with me to take 'em to Aunt Monday? She promised me she'd show me how to make up her special soup that not even Essie Mae knows the secret recipe to."

"I'd like that a lot. But this time I'd just as soon we didn't have any fortune-telling." Nick turned Tally's hand over in his and traced the broken heart line in the girl's palm. "I'd just as soon let things happen the way they're gonna happen—and not know about 'em ahead of time."

"Me, too," Tally agreed, enjoying the shivery sensation that she felt when Nick's nail moved lightly over her bare palm. "I wish I had soft, pretty hands," she said, suddenly aware of her stubby nails and rough calluses.

Nick lifted the object in question to his lips, pulling Tally to a stop beside him as he lingeringly kissed each fingertip one by one. "They're the most beautiful hands in the world and they belong to the most beautiful girl in the world."

Tally felt beautiful when she was with Nick. She stood on her tiptoes to kiss him, when over his shoulder she glimpsed a flash of color in the dunes. It was Reba coming down to the beach. Tally and Nick dropped hands and waited for the girl to catch up to them, both aware that Reba had seen them holding hands but not wanting to flaunt their new closeness in front of her. "Hi! Come help us gather up the rest of supper." Tally was well aware that she had been neglecting Reba since Nick's arrival.

"Can't. Pa's got me wrappin' pole beans and I gotta finish up 'fore supper. Just came down to tell Tally her mama won't be needing her tonight. Miz Fisher over at the cannery come and got her to play the piano for Brother Joseph's tent meeting tonight and tomorrow night. Regular piano player got sick and they thought of Miz Vieve. She seemed real tickled, said her papa making her take them lessons all them years finally paid off."

Tally didn't dare look at Nick. She could feel his thoughts as clearly as though he'd spoken them aloud. *We'll be all alone. No Vieve. No Lucy.* Tally's heart gave a few staccato beats as she tried to ask naturally, "They know that Mama's . . . well, not quite herself, don't they? I wouldn't want anything to happen to make her feel embarrassed or have someone say something."

Reba shook her head. "Miz Fisher brung up two water-head babies herself. Ain't a kinder, sweeter person on this island. Your mama will be just fine. Matter of fact, I think it's just swell that she's gettin' away from this place for a little while. That lighthouse can get mighty lonesome.'' Reba's eyes brightened. ''Say, you want me to come spend the night with you? I could fix Pa's supper early and you and me could maybe listen to a show on the radio like we used to.''

Tally could feel Nick looking at her and she knew she was making a conscious choice when she said, ''Reba, I don't mind being by myself. Matter of fact, I kind of need to be alone for a change. Mama's sweet and I love her to death, but she keeps me plumb tired out with her talking most all the time I'm with her.''

''Oh . . .'' Reba's eyes darted to Nick's face and back to Tally's before she lowered her gaze. ''Sure. I don't blame you for that. It's the same for me when Pa spends the night off. Nothing but the hoot-owls and blessed quiet. Well, I'll be going. I just wanted to tell you about your mama since they couldn't find you to tell you their own selves.''

''Thanks, Reba,'' Tally said warmly. ''I wish you didn't have to work so you could spend some time with us on the beach.''

''The summer ain't over yet,'' Reba said with a crooked little smile in Nick's direction.

''What do you reckon is making Reba act so standoffish lately?'' Tally demanded of Nick after the girl had limped off.

''I expect she's a little jealous,'' Nick said with deliberate ambivalence.

''Jealous. . . ? Oh, of you and me being together all the time, 'stead of her and me the way it used to be.''

''Maybe we could wait till she's through with the beans and take her with us to Aunt Monday's?''

Tally hid her alarm at that. Aunt Monday would never forgive her! ''Oh, no. Reba's . . . scared of that graveyard we have to go by. And besides, Aunt Monday doesn't like surprises.''

''Well, you're the boss of the island. At least for the next few days.'' And then they looked at each other and grinned with the perfect happiness of knowing that they could spend as much time together now as they wanted for the next forty-eight hours.

It was almost too good to be true. They held hands again and walked down the beach together with a new awareness of each other that started at their fingertips and moved like flames into their bodies.

Several thousand miles away, Cane Winslow was getting dressed for a breakfast meeting with the Japanese businessmen whom he had finally pinned down to talk business. "These people exasperate the hell out of me," he confided to Gretchen Lee, who had taken the room adjoining Cane's. "They consult every five minutes during a meeting, then take forever to come to a decision."

"They sound almost southern, don't they, boss?" Gretchen had come in to borrow Cane's razor before she left for the dubbing session at WPDQ's sister station. "I wish you'd see me on these tapes they're making. It looks so funny to have Japanese coming out of my mouth." She held up the razor. "I promise I'll clean this off before I return it."

"I've never understood why women don't buy their own razors," Cane grumbled. "And another thing—if I get raw fish for breakfast, I may throw up all over that soft-spoken group of little bastards."

Gretchen stuck her head back in the door at that. "Are you sure I can't go along to watch?"

"I guarantee you that there will be no women at a Japanese business meeting—not in our lifetime. Only in America, kid—only in America."

"Whee—lucky, lucky me."

Cane had learned very quickly that Japan was no place to exhibit his sense of humor. When one of the Japanese businessmen asked Cane about his background and Cane conveyed through his translator that he was from the Deep South, the question came back, via the intermediary, "Do you live in a place like Tara in *Gone With the Wind?*"

"Of course," Cane said with a laugh. "We all grew up like that in the South."

The interpreter passed this along and Mr. Shikato, the questioner, listened seriously, then called his compatriots off for another consultation. Cane leaned his forehead on his hand and groaned. Breakfast could lead into dinner at the rate they were moving.

The translator came back and said quite seriously, "And your family had slaves—many of them?"

Cane decided, since he was already into it up past his wing-tips, that he might as well go whole hog with the southern shit. "Oh, yes—three hundred or more." Okay, Hirohito, he said silently to the huddle of Japanese, put that in your pipes and *talk* to me about radio and TV.

The gathering dispersed and came back to the round, low table which, by now, held sweet rolls and pots of tea. Cane was relieved, though he had been prepared to eat raw fish if it was necessary to save face for his host. The interpreter waited until tea had been poured all around before saying to Cane, "My employers are now ready for you to talk about the ideas you have for mutual expansion in the area of transistors."

Cane was on firm ground now. "Well, you can tell Mr. Shikato that my proposal is a boilerplate version of a simple mutual-expansion plan. You got that so far?" At the man's nod, Cane went on. "Your associate, Mr. Asani, still holds the license from our AT&T to produce pocket-sized radio transistors. It is our understanding that your company has managed to cut down the cost of six dollars per transistor to something like a fraction of a dollar. We won't worry about yen value at this point. My concern is getting a good solid corner on this market for my Tri-Com investors. I see the transistor radio business taking off like gangbusters, given a healthy shot of American money in the old production and marketing arm."

"Gangbusters?" the translator murmured with a twitch to his lips as he went back to huddle with his compatriots. He came back after a brief consultation. "Mr. Shikato wonders why his respected friend, Mr. Winslow, has elected to investigate the radio-transistor markets instead of the color television possibilities. Is not, he asks, Tri-Com calling itself the leader of the wave of the future—television?''

Cane lit a cigarette and, seeing the Japanese men looking longingly at his pack of Viceroys, passed the pack along. ''Good question,'' he said after everybody had lit up and was puffing away. ''I just have it from good sources that the American public won't be ready to buy color televisions until the cost gets a lot lower. That's according to my market research, mind you, and it could be off. But what Tri-Com needs is a bread-and-butter subsidiary electronics line, and from what I gather, what Asani Productions needs is U.S. money and export channels to the mighty American public's dollar. I think we both got ourselves the solution to our problems in this transistor thing.''

While the interpreter went back to the consulting table, Cane puffed at his cigarette and looked around the room. The old Imperial Hotel was undergoing the face-lift to which Japanese property owners were subjecting all their buildings now that Western influence was having its dubious effect on them. He wished people would leave the old buildings alone. He liked the frescoes of fugi dogs and the cracked vases that had age and timelessness written all over them, and he abhorred the tendency to redecorate with modern cubes and abstracts. . . .

''Mr. Winslow? Mr. Shikato says he will consult with Mr. Asani about your proposal and give you their decision by the end of the month.''

''The end of the week,'' Cane said firmly. ''I'm leaving Saturday morning and I need something in writing to take back to my board.'' He knew that the decision-making and consulting would go on for another six months if he didn't act tough. The Japanese were nice folks once they signed the dotted line, but getting them to that point was an exercise in extreme patience. ''I am, by the way, considering a deal with the Musaki people about the hearing-aid-transistor business, if this doesn't work out.''

The interpreter bowed and went back to report to his clients. He came back with a big smile on his face. ''Mr. Shikato says he is honored to say that it is highly probable that he and his associates will come to terms with you on this transaction. The papers will be drawn up for your signature before you leave on Saturday morning.''

Cane repressed the desire to give a rebel yell right there in one of the Imperial's poshest meeting rooms. "That sounds mighty fine to me." He bowed to everyone in the room and they returned the bows, everyone smiling and talking in Japanese except Cane. To join in the affable conversation that he could not understand, he asked out of range of hearing for the interpreter, "One thing I've always wondered about you guys was why did your kamikaze pilots wear crash helmets?"

They all smiled and clinked their cups of sake, which had replaced the tea. Mr. Shikato alone was unsmiling, then he looked at Cane very hard before he broke into peals of laughter.

Why, that sneaky SOB, Cane thought, as he clinked his cup of warm rice wine against the one Mr. Shikato held out. The oriental man had understood every word Cane had said. "Harvard?" he asked softly as he and Shikato stood together, away from the others.

"No. Southern California University." Mr. Shikato laughed. "It can be very convenient being in a business meeting in which you are assumed to be ignorant of the other language being spoken."

"I'll remember that the next time I have a meeting up in New York," Cane said.

Nick and Tally laughed their heads off at Aunt Monday's screwed-up face as she launched finally into one of her Gullah stories, after much cajoling from her audience. "Aunt Monday can talk old Gullah with the best of 'em," Tally had told Nick proudly when they'd sat down in the black woman's big room to sip sassafras tea. "Except for Uncle Gibber, who's famous for his Brer Fox and Brer Rabbit tales, she's the best I've ever heard."

"I thought Joel Chandler Harris of *Uncle Remus* fame was the one who made up the Brer Rabbit tales," Nick had whispered.

"Where do you think he got 'em? They've been telling those

stories ever since the slaves came over from Africa,'' Tally
whispered back. ''Now, shh. Aunt Monday's in a story-telling
frame of mind.''

''But first go hot the water and out the light. The sun de red
for down.''

''Sunset,'' Tally whispered as she ran off to boil more water
and turn out the kitchen stove light. ''Daybreak is 'day clean'
in Gullah.''

When she got back, Aunt Monday was starting another
story—the one about the buzzard and the hawk.

''. . . Now the buzzard always was a nice educated animal,
you know. Um-hum. 'E take 'e time—just like he done with
the hawk. Um-hum. Well, him and de hawk was sitting on the
limb one day, and 'e and the hawk had a consolation.

'' 'E say, 'I'm very hungry.'

''Hawk say, 'I'm hungry, too,' rubbing his stomach. 'Lord
o' lord, I too hungry!'

''The buzzard say—patiently—'Wait on the Lord,' and 'e
look up—nothing for dead, you know, not nothing—and he
look up to the sky and say with exasperation, 'Man! Ain't
nothing dead! Nothing!'

''The hawk say, 'I can't wait no longer.' So when 'e look,
a little sparrow come along. And the hawk get up and fly at
the sparrow and hit a tree—uh-huh! And the buzzard sit on the
limb and look at the hawk, look at the hawk hit the tree.
Buzzard say, 'I tell you wait on the Lord. Now I gone eat you
now!' ''

Aunt Monday ended her story with a comical buzzard-neck-
guzzling pantomime, sending Nick and Tally into hoots of
laughter.

''Now, children,'' Aunt Monday said in her normal voice
after they had quieted down, ''I am chasing you home before
it gets too dark and Mary de Searche can lure you off the path
with her pitiful cries.''

''Did Mary de Searche really die for her lover?'' Nick asked,
eager to leave and be alone with Tally but still intrigued by the
black obeah.

''Who can say? Is a ghost dead?''

Tally shuddered. "Let's go, Nick." She kissed Aunt Monday's smooth cheek. "I loved the cochina stew. Thanks for helping me make it. Is Lionel still sleeping, or do we need to pen him up again so he won't chase us?"

"Lionel is snoring happily away. I think he's getting too old to chase people nowadays." Aunt Monday looked at Nick and suddenly became deadly serious. "You will take care of this one," she said, her arm surrounding Tally's shoulders. "You will not let harm befall her."

"You can count on that," Nick said, holding his hand out to the black woman. "Thank you for a most enjoyable afternoon. Won't you come pay us a visit sometime?"

Aunt Monday smiled. "And why should I do that? Don't trouble trouble and it won't trouble you. Me leaving this place is asking for trouble."

"Good-bye!"

They did not see or hear Mary de Searche on their way home, but they did hear something as they passed the black graveyard. It was only after they nearly burst their sides running for home that Tally drew up short, remembering the keening wail that she had first heard at Junior's wake. "It's old Mattie. For gosh sakes, Nick, I plumb forgot. Today's Junior's birthday! Old Mattie's in there keening for him on his birthday."

"Well, just so long as it's something human. What about that up ahead?" Nick stopped short, staring at the Hainted Oak, his arm protecting Tally from moving ahead of him. "Tally, do you see what I see?"

When they got up closer to the big tree and saw the long, dangling beards of moss, Tally giggled. "There's your ghost with long arms. Funny, isn't it, what the imagination can do to a person."

"And I can't believe what my imagination is doing to me right now," Nick said, stopping in the path and turning Tally toward him. "I'm imagining you in my arms and imagining that I'm kissing you—like this—and I'm imagining that there's nobody on this island to come between us. . . ."

"That's not your imagination," Tally finally said shakily. "There's nobody between us right now, Nick."

They looked into each other's eyes for a long time, then Nick took a deep breath and said slowly, "I want to make love to you, Tally. Tonight. In your bed, in your lighthouse."

For answer, Tally kissed Nick on the lips. "Then what are we standing around here for?" she whispered.

Gretchen poked her head inside the adjoining door as she was dressing for her lunch date with one of the hottest disc jockeys in Tokyo. "How'd it go?"

"Okay." Cane hung up the phone after trying unsuccessfully to reach Lucy. "Wonder what's going on at the plantation? I've been trying to get Lucy for two days. Nobody seems to be home."

"I can't believe you're all the way over here worrying about what's going on back in Georgia. Cane, when did you forget how to relax?"

"When I signed my first million-dollar note." Cane looped his robe tie around his waist, wishing he didn't have this uneasy feeling about needing to check in with the home folks. Why was it that he worried when he didn't hear from Lucy for long periods at a time? "I wish you weren't going out. You could give me one of your hundred-dollar massages."

"I can do better than that," Gretchen said, her eyes getting an impish light. "There is the most gorgeous masseuse downstairs next door to the salon. She'll fix you right up."

"Gretchen, for Chrissakes, I don't want—"

"Hello? Opal-Lei?" Gretchen held out her hands and admired the manicure she'd treated herself to that morning. "I was wondering if you could bring your stuff up to room four thirty-seven . . . no, not me, love—my boss." Gretchen smiled and winked at Cane. "Yeah, that's the one. I know. All the girls back home say the same thing. Ten minutes? Great. I'm sure he'll be ready—loaded for bear, in fact." Gretchen's mouth twitched as she listened. "No, that's not what it means. Opal-Lei, just come up, will you? And have room service send up some really good champagne. Lots of ice, honey. On the side."

Cane sat on the edge of the bed, his arms folded and a stern

look on his face. "Since when did you start handling my
personal needs?"

"Since you stopped doing anything about 'em yourself. Oh,
come on, Cane—loosen up. Have some fun! When's the last
time you had a nice romp in the hay? I've been really worried
about you recently. Are you practicing for monkhood or something?" Gretchen went over to Cane and patted him on both
cheeks gently. "If I didn't know you better, I'd say you're
pining away for unrequited love."

Cane pushed her away. "You don't know me half as well
as you think."

"I hope not. Bye." Gretchen blew him a kiss and disappeared just as there came a knock on the door.

Tally put on the scratchy 78 records she'd bought at a junk
shop as soon as she and Nick were inside the lighthouse. The
old Victrola she'd found was on its last legs, but it worked.

Suddenly, she was overcome with shyness at the realization
of being alone with Nick—truly alone. "Do you want a glass
of ice tea?" she asked nervously as Jo Stafford's mellow ren-
dering of "You Belong to Me" filled the room.

"No, I've got all I want right here." Nick pulled Tally into
his arms and started leading her in a slow fox-trot.

"I never really learned how to dance," Tally whispered as
Nick's lips sought the warm spot dangerously close to her ear.
"I'm not very good at it."

"You're as smooth as silk. I like that song, don't you?
You've already got your 'tropic isle,' but someday I'll take
you to see the pyramids."

"I'd like that," Tally said, her nervousness evaporating in
the magic of the music, the night, of being in Nick's strong
arms. She'd never felt so safe. No one's arms had enveloped
her in a long, long time. She felt soft and feminine, protected
from the world and its problems. "I'd like to see everything
in the world. I've never been further than the mainland." She
burrowed her cheek in Nick's chest. "What if your mother
finds out about this? What will she do to you?"

"My mother doesn't know everything about me." Nick's

arms stiffened around Tally. "Besides, she's not going to be able to tell me what to do much longer."

Tally twisted her head around in alarm. "Nick, I hope you're not thinking about joining the Army or something. Everybody knows we could have another Korea—or even worse, go to war with Russia. Don't do something crazy just to spite your mother."

"I'm not planning to do anything crazy. Now, will you relax and stop talking about things that we don't need to be thinking about right now?"

Tally wished she hadn't mentioned anything about war. It made her think about Perrie. She headed off Nick's kiss, feeling shy all of a sudden. "There's some sangaree mixed up in the icebox. Want some?"

Nick's eyes lit up. "Yeah! But it needs some *real* punch. I'll go over and sneak out some of Harm's vodka. I know right where he keeps it. We'll have ourselves a real party." He grabbed Tally and swung her around as she headed for the little kitchen. "Oh, baby, are we going to have a good time tonight."

Tally stood at the kitchen sink and drank a full tumbler of the sangaree without stopping. She drew a deep shuddering breath afterward, wiped her mouth with a dry dishcloth, and marched unsteadily back into the main room, the pitcher of sangaree held shakily in both hands.

By the time Nick got back with the vodka, Tally was feeling pretty good. "Listen to that," she said, as "Jailhouse Rock" filled the room. "If that Elvis isn't something, I don't know who is."

"I like this better," Nick said, when the softer strains of "White Sport Coat—and a Pink Carnation" filled the room. Mellowed by the vodka-strengthened sangaree, they melted into each other's arms as they danced. "Oh, Tally," Nick said, closing his eyes and sinking his head into the sweet area between her head and shoulder, "I don't want this to ever end."

"You mean the song?" Tally wondered if all the funny feelings she was experiencing were from the punch, or Nick, or both. Whatever they were, she didn't want them to end, either.

"No, not the song. This. The way we feel right this moment. It's before everything that's gonna happen between us actually happens. I keep thinking about it, about how it's gonna happen and how I want it to happen, but . . ." Nick pulled back and looked at Tally, his eyes a little glazed from the vodka. "Hell, Tally, I won't lie to you. I'm scared. I've been worrying about how to do it ever since the song started. What do I do? Start trying to yank your shirt off to get at your tits? Or run my hands up your skirt and start making a move on you that way? Dammit, Tally, I want it to be right between us the first time. I want it to be everything we've both dreamed about."

Tally reached up and kissed Nick softly on the lips. "I feel that way, too," she whispered. "And I think I know how we can make it perfect. There is a beautiful little alcove up on the next floor. Mama lies up there at night sometimes on the daybed I got for her and just looks out at the stars and the moonlight on the ocean. . . ." Tally wished she hadn't thought about her mama just then and added hastily, "Sometimes I lie up there, too, and dream about all kinds of things."

"Of me?" Nick moved his hand so that it went up under the back of her shirt and caused goose bumps. "You ever go up there and think about me . . . about me doing this. . . ?" He put his lips on the shivery place where her neck went into her shoulder. "Or this. . . ?" His lips moved up to the corner of her mouth and she felt the tip of his tongue tracing it. He was gaining confidence in what he was doing and getting bolder with his hands. Tally caught her breath as she felt them tracing the outline of her breasts as his mouth moved tantalizingly along hers. "Tally," he whispered. "I want you so much— and I can feel you wanting me, too. Remember that time in the lagoon? You made me stop, but I knew you didn't want me to any more than I did."

"I won't make you stop this time, Nick," Tally told him softly. She took his hand and led him toward the circular stairs. When they reached the little room looking out over the island, she lay down on the bed and looked at him. "Do you like this place?" she whispered.

Nick nodded, unable to speak for the passion that was filling him. He had been so afraid that Tally would think he was taking advantage of her. Looking at her, at the way she watched him with half-closed eyes, at the way she moved her body sensuously, he realized she was as ready for their union as he. "You look very beautiful dressed in moonlight."

Without speaking, Tally smiled and unbuttoned her blouse very slowly. Nick lay beside her and pressed his lips against her breasts as they were revealed to him. "God, how many times I've dreamed of this, Tally! Of this . . ." He dragged his tongue slowly over the peak of one breast and felt it harden. Male triumph over arousing her filled him with boldness. He eagerly applied himself to the other breast. Then, while its sweetness filled his mouth, he moved his hand to take possession of the silky triangle between her thighs. It thrilled him that the soft hair was damp and sticky. Nick covered the mound with his fingers and moved gently until he heard Tally's sigh.

"Please don't do any more of that," she whispered, her eyes still closed, her lashes fluttering. Nick ignored her and she was soon heaving beneath him, her slender hips arching as he relentlessly explored the depths of her woman's quick. At the sharp intake of breath that let him know she was ready for him—really ready—he plunged inside her, closing his eyes in ecstasy for a moment before moving again. "You are so soft . . . so sweet . . . Tally, I love you."

She could not speak because he was piercing the innermost part of her. One sharp little gasp, then he was united with her, moving inside her with increasing vigor.

Tally's legs wound around her lover as she felt herself fitting into a satisfying rhythm. She was a passionate person, she realized in surprise. But hadn't she always known she was? Wouldn't Nick be surprised if he knew about all those nights she had lain up here after her mother was sleeping, and allowed the moonbeams to play over her naked body? She gave a muffled little laugh and Nick covered her mouth with his,

mistaking the sound for a moan of pleasure . . . which it soon
became.

"It's open. Come on in." Cane was pouring himself a healthy
snort of bourbon when he heard the light tap at his door. He
could have cheerfully strangled Gretchen (if she hadn't run off)
for putting him in the position of having to eject the hotel's
masseuse from his suite. He would give her a big tip to make
her happy and pretend that he was too tired for the rubdown
and . . . "Come in, dammit." He despised the way these
people padded around and had absolutely no assertiveness,
even that required to open a client's hotel door. "I told you,
the door's . . . open." The last trailed off as the door opened
and he saw the woman standing there.

"Mr. Winslow?" The girl moved forward, smiling as Cane
took two steps backward and stared as if he were in a trance.
"I am Opal-Lei." She pulled behind her a rolling cart stocked
with towels, jars of creams, and oil. Before Cane could get his
breath, she had snapped into place a massage table attached to
the cart. "I'm sorry I was so slow coming in, but my equipment
is quite cumbersome. You would have been much better served
to have come downstairs to my salon."

"You . . . you speak English quite well," he said, stunned.
When she first walked in the girl had looked so much like Tally
Malone his heart almost stopped.

"I should." The girl bent over next to the bedside table and
plugged in a pot that held suspicious-looking oil. *Oh no*, Cane
thought. He'd heard about the oriental massage. "I grew up in
Seattle and have worked as a translator since I moved here,"
she said as she moved over to the table and smoothed out a
cover on it. "You like it hot?"

"What? Oh, the oil. No, thanks. Lukewarm will do nicely."
Cane took off his robe, draped the towel she handed him
around his waist, and laid facedown on the table. "You sound
American."

"I am. My mother was a red-haired Irish-American." She
lifted her long straight auburn hair and let it fall so that it

brushed Cane's bare shoulders, sending a shiver through him. He was fantasizing like crazy. "She was disowned for marrying my Japanese father. You're very tight. Does that feel good?"

Cane closed his eyes as the strong hands kneaded the muscles near his neck. "Umm. You say you're a translator. Why are you doing this?"

"My other work isn't regular. I like making money. I guess it's the American in me." Her hand moved down into the small of his back and Cane felt the warmth of the oil she was rubbing in and shuddered. His fantasy of her being Tally Malone was so strong he could almost smell the island. "Would you like me to pour some of the champagne your friend ordered up for you?"

"I'll do that—if you'll join me." Cane rose up to a sitting position on the table. He took the pot of massaging oil from the girl's hands and set it beside him, then hopped off and got the champagne. He felt giddy already, even before he had opened the bottle and poured himself and the girl a glass each. "I feel as if I already know you," he said softly. He reached out and stroked the girl's long hair. "You have beautiful hair." He lay back on the table and luxuriated in the feel of the long, strong fingers stroking, stroking. . . . The girl's long hair drifted across Cane's naked chest and he caught his breath.

"That feels good?" The girl's voice held a hint of laughter as she dribbled the hot oil onto Cane's body. "You are very tense, Mr. Winslow."

Certain parts of him were beyond tense, Cane thought wryly. The magical massage and the champagne were fast having a physical effect on him. He felt the girl's hands slide to the underside of his neck and opened his eyes to see Opal-Lei's full mouth parted above his. It was too tempting. Cane pulled her down and kissed her, his mind seeing another girl in Opal-Lei's place.

Her robe was easily undone. Soon she was naked atop him and the oil was all that was between their bodies. Cane let the girl think she was in control for a moment, enjoying her assertiveness, then he rose up. Without a word, he took her to his bed and covered her, feeling her passion mount with his own. Before he entered her, he whispered a secret name inside his head.

He let her come before he did, watching her face as she writhed beneath his strong body. He drove into her as she peaked, not letting up, even when she gasped for mercy, watching her eyes close at the moment of release. . . .

"Did you like that?" Cane asked after the girl lay still, her body covered with the dew of perspiration—and some of the oil.

"Yes, very much," she told him, smiling and wriggling up close to him. "You're a wonderful lover. Not many men know that a woman likes to have a man moving inside her right at that special moment." She touched his face. "But I didn't make you happy. I'm sorry."

"When's your next appointment?"

Opal-Lei's smile broadened. "After lunch."

"You've just made me happy." Cane poured them both more champagne. "We have another two hours." He pulled her over to him and started teasing one of her nipples with his tongue.

12

To the delight of the two young lovers, Lucy Cantrell extended her stay in Atlanta. Since Harm had taken to inviting Vieve along with him on his day-long fishing trips, there was a kind of unspoken conspiracy between him and his son.

Tally was a little concerned about her mother's spending so much time with Lucy's husband, but when she and Nick joined the fishing expedition on one occasion, she lost all anxiety. Harm treated Vieve with the gentleness a father bestows on a daughter. The innocent delight he took in ensuring Vieve's pleasure and comfort was touching. When Tally thanked Harm at the end of their excursion, he said simply, "It's so good to be able to make a woman happy with just the small things, like baiting her hook and bringing pillows for her chair. Don't thank me, girl! It's I who should thank you for letting me have one of the most enjoyable weeks of my life.''

Nick confided that his mother had called him and tried subtly to find out how much time he was spending with Tally. Apparently whatever Nick had responded had satisfied her, for she changed the subject to Cane Winslow. ''He's visiting some of his Far East contacts,'' Nick reported to Tally later on their way to the lagoon for a late-afternoon swim. ''Mom always manages to keep up with Uncle Cane, even when nobody else can.''

Tally still hadn't forgiven Cane for acting as if she weren't good enough for Nick. ''I'm surprised he didn't get her stirred up about you and me the way he did the last time,'' she said with a sniff.

''He tried,'' Nick said with a grimace. ''He told my mother that if she had any sense at all, she'd have me sent over to him so he could start teaching me the business. He's still pissed that I didn't go to school in Europe.'' Nick spread his shorts and shirt over a palmetto bush and snapped the elastic band of his trunks. He was feeling his oats nowadays, Tally couldn't help noticing with some amusement, and she was pretty sure why. Nick did not disguise the pride he felt in being the first man in Tally's sexual life. ''I told her that I'm through letting anybody send me anywhere, unless I damn well want to go. Look, are you ever going to put on that swimsuit I sent you, or not?''

Tally blushed and slipped out of her shorts and top. ''I've got it on right now.''

Nick let out a wolf whistle when she stood before him clad only in the skimpy suit. ''Wow,'' he breathed finally. ''Honey, you look beautiful—even sexier than when you don't have anything on.''

Tally dived into the water and splashed Nick thoroughly for being so sassy. And soon they were playing their usual games in the lagoon with childish abandon.

''Nick, what in the world do you think you're doing?'' Tally whispered when the sunset mood of the lagoon had set in,

changing their mood of playfulness into something more serious. "You can't do that underwater!"

Nick laughed at her shocked tone. "Wanna bet?" He suc-
ceeded in the tricky feat of removing the bikini bottom with
one hand while he kept Tally from swimming away from him
with the other. "Oh, Tally," he said, kissing her while he
explored the delights of her. "I just wish this summer would
last forever. I could do this with you all day—and all night—
from now till doomsday."

"Well, be careful not to get carried away." Tally whispered
something in Nick's ear and he looked surprised.

"No kidding? A girl can get pregnant just from being in the
water where a guy . . . aw, come on! Reba's just pulling your
leg. Come here. Let me see if your breasts have gotten even
more beautiful since the last time I saw 'em."

"Nick, you're impossible," Tally said, laughing and trying
to squirm away from him. She popped him across the cheek
when he grabbed her top and snapped her back to him. "Will
you stop that? You're going to tear my new suit."

"I'll buy you another one," Nick growled into the breasts
he had just freed at peril to the strapless top. "How long can
you hold your breath? I want to make love under the water like
a couple of guppies."

"Oh, you." Tally stopped slapping at him, her breath coming a little short at the reactions she was undergoing at Nick's
playful but relentless hands. "You know what we talked about
that first night, about you not having to use anything, you
know?" She still felt shy talking about such things as birth
control to Nick, but Reba had insisted that she needed to discuss
the matter with her partner. "Well, Reba gave me one of her
old . . .. uh, you know . . ."

"Diaphragms," Nick supplied helpfully. "Isn't that a little
bit like using somebody's toothbrush?"

"I scalded it really good." Tally felt her hated blush start
again. "Reba gave it to me for a joke on my sixteenth birthday.
I bet she'd die if she knew I kept it and am using it for real."

Nick laughed a little uncomfortably. He hoped Tally was
keeping her promise and not confiding in Reba about her new

intimacy with him. But it excited him to think that Tally was taking their new relationship so seriously. "So, little girl, do you happen to be equipped with said safety device at this very moment?" He laughed softly at the giveaway look on Tally's face. "Uh-huh. So you came to this lagoon with more on your mind than a Girl Scout swim." He could hardly keep his hands off her, she was so adorable, but he finished solemnly, "Tell me, Miz Expert, just how safe is this device of yours?"

"Reba told me once that nothing's really safe except not doing it. Look, Nick, I don't really like talking about this stuff. Could we maybe get back to something romantic like how pretty the sun is going down like that, or how sweet your dad's been to Mama the last few days, or . . ."

"This? Or . . . this?" Nick didn't need urging to get back to the loving part. He figured that maybe, if he lived to be a hundred and ten, he might get enough of Tally Malone. "And how . . . about . . . this. . . ?"

Tally's affair with Nick made her feel very grown up. At the same time, it made her a little sad to know that she would never be the same girl she was before she and Nick made love. Long ago her mother had told her a fairy tale about a princess and a unicorn. Only virgins could see unicorns, the story revealed, and the princess lost her precious pet when she lost her virginity.

A world without unicorns: Tally Malone's romantic side mourned the passing of innocence. Reba would have said to her, had she been privy to Tally's confidences about Nick, "Once a guy's got your cherry, you better be sure you don't end up with the pit. With most fellows, when the cherry goes, the romance goes."

But for Tally, romance was still in full swing. Having a handsome lover was exciting. She and Nick were together constantly—for swims, for picnics, for long walks on the beach. Nick introduced Tally to his favorite poetry, that of John Keats. He loved to read it aloud to her, loved to drawl out the sensuous passages and linger over the passionate imagery. Tally pretended to be offended when Nick nicknamed her

the Beautiful Lady Without Pity, but secretly she loved it. She
was never happier than when Nick was treating her as though
she were as well-schooled as he.

To surprise him, she learned "The Eve of St. Agnes" by
heart and recited it dramatically while they were alone at their
special spot near the cove. When she finished, Nick sat staring
at her in amazement. "You never fail to astonish me, Tally,"
he said then. "That was wonderful, just wonderful." His kisses
were as passionate as those in the poem. When they made love,
he whispered snatches of poetry into her ear, dwelling over the
sensuous words whenever passion was at a height.

Tally decided that Nick was as close to being the perfect
lover as a man could get. He was awakening her body, all
right, but he was also awakening her thirst for knowing about
things outside her usual ken, like poetry. He introduced her to
the less literary aspects of boy-girl activities, too. He took her
to her very first drive-in movie.

He was very serious about this event. "Probably the most
important actions that take place in young America take place
in this parking lot," he told her deadpan as they captured their
spot and affixed the speaker to the car window. "You see that
movie up there on the screen?" It was *On the Beach*. "Ava
Gardner's gonna die. The young guy and his wife and their
little baby are gonna die. The sports-car fellow—"

"Fred Astaire. I thought he just danced in the movies,"
Tally said, getting interested in the screen in spite of the distraction from her companion.

"He's not gonna make it, either. Nobody is. They're all
doomed. The big boom has taken everybody else in the world
out and now the few left are going out, too. And do you
think anybody out there thinks that's real?" Nick fastened a
phosphorous mosquito burner to the dash of the '57 Chevy
Harm had bought him the week before. He held up the burning
match after he'd lit the repellent's tip. "Just look around and
see how many heads you see above the seats." He blew out
the light. "They know that what's happening out here is the
real thing and that"—Nick jabbed his finger in the direction
of the big screen—"that isn't."

"But something like that could happen." Tally shuddered as she watched the desperate attempts of the final survivors in the movie to find life anywhere else in the world. If there were another Korea, Nick could be called up. She wished tonight's offering had been a Doris Day movie instead. Or that Nick had not gotten into this funny mood and that they had started smooching right off the bat, as everybody else was doing. "God, it was just a Coca-Cola bottle. What they thought was a sign of human life was just a Coke that had been caught in the venetian blind and was tapping on the telegraph."

Nick pulled Tally over to him and kissed her. "It's just Hollywood cashing in on mushroom-cloud mania. Don't fall for it." He adjusted her so that he could get at her blouse. "Fall for me instead." When Tally kept watching the movie, Nick put his hands on her cheeks and asked with mock shock, "Hey, are you crazy or something? You're trying to watch the movie at the *drive-in?*"

Tally was secretly embarrassed that she really was interested in watching. "I just feel funny about being out in the open like this." Doing it out in the open was what she meant. "People can just walk by and look in the car and see us."

Nick laughed at her, but did not pursue his undressing of her front. "Honestly, you do beat all, as Poke would say. Sometimes I think I got myself a real hot woman who can't get enough and other times I think I've got Miss Prissy. Which one *are* you tonight?"

"I'm a little bit of both." Tally snuggled back into Nick's arms and positioned his hands comfortably beneath her breasts. She knew that wasn't a safe arrangement but she knew, too, that Nick was not going to move until she was ready. "I've decided I want to watch this movie again. Why don't you go get us some popcorn and a real cold drink and we'll just pretend that it's the first time either of us even thought about getting hot?"

Nick loved the idea. When he got back he made a big deal about working around Tally's underwear and pretending to discover each new delight as though it had been invented at the drive-in movie.

Tally Malone returned home that night with a new opinion
about the appeal of outdoor theaters. Maybe, she thought wickedly, Lucy's dragged somebody off up in Atlanta and had
herself a good time. She hoped so. She, Nick, and Harm were
all dreading that lady's imminent return to Moss Island.

Lucy Cantrell's fury was of a magnitude that surprised even
Nick. She learned very quickly upon her return that her son
had not only failed to show up at any of the debutante parties
at the Cloister—he had also spurned a leading socialite's
daughter, one of the season "catches."

Nick waited for the sputtering tantrum to come to a lull. He
wondered at that moment if he loved his mother as much as he
hated her. "Mother, I despise the Bulloch girl and all the rest
of those silly, spoiled socialites, and I only told you I was
going to their stupid parties so you'd stay off my back."

Lucy flounced over and sat down in the death chair. She
looked like a Fury with her blazing eyes and tight mouth.
"Well, it sounds to me as if that little slut down there didn't
stay off hers! Nelia Pomeroy said it was all over town that you
and Tally have been close as sardines ever since I left!"

Nick defended. "I enjoy Tally's company more than any
other girl's. I always have, Mother. When are you going to
accept the fact that I'm old enough to choose my own friends?
I don't give a shit about those girls you're always trying to
push on me. I do care about Tally, and you might as well get
used to that."

"Don't say anything that you can't take back, son. If you've
got some fool notion about marrying that girl, you'd better get
rid of it right now. I've got every nickel that's coming to you
tied up in a trust fund that God himself couldn't break open."
Lucy's words came through her teeth like bullets. "But that
girl has you acting so stupid, you probably don't care about
that. All right, let me get to something that might matter to
you. I'll make it short and simple. Either you leave tomorrow
on that backpacking trip to Europe you've talked about taking,
or Tally and her mother leave forever."

"Good God, Mother! What are you saying?"

"I'm saying that your precious Malones are here by my charity. That's what I'm saying."

"Charity, hell! You've worked them like white niggers!"

Lucy raised her eyebrows. "How vulgar. I hope you don't talk like that in front of the servants."

Nick exploded. "Ask the servants on this island who's the most bigoted person here! You don't give a damn about anybody but yourself, not anybody, and everybody on Moss Island knows it. I can't believe you're threatening the Malones with eviction. My God, after all they've been through, how could you even think about it? Eviction!"

"Well, not exactly eviction. Let's call it relocation." Lucy patted her newly platinumed French twist in place. "I have a new friend with a lovely place on West Pace's Ferry Road. She has a little house on the place and has agreed to take Tally on as housekeeper."

"That's great!" Nick fought his rising rage. His mother had been thinking about getting rid of Tally all along. It made him feel sick, especially since he knew he was to blame. Lucy Cantrell would not be trying to get rid of Tally if she didn't suspect Nick was involved with her. "That's really great. Mother, just what have you got against Tally? She's never done anything to you."

Lucy's eyes spat liquid fire. "Just what do you know about what people have done to me? You've been off in your safe little Ivy League world, having everything fall in your lap because you were born to it. Not like some of us who . . ." Lucy got up, walked toward Nick and, leaning over him, said with calm venom, "I just hope it's not too late, that you haven't caught some venereal disease from her."

It was the last straw for Nick. He struck her across the cheek. He looked at the red mark on her face and then down at his hand, not believing he had actually hit his mother. He was not sorry, but he was shocked.

"I didn't mean to do that," he said slowly. "But you shouldn't say such terrible things. I'm your son and Tally is the girl I love. You can't say things like that to me about her."

Lucy gave him a terrible smile. "I could say worse things,

but I won't, since I have no desire to be abused further. I will say, though, that you are no longer welcome in this house. I'll wire Cane and he'll set you up with friends in Frankfurt for your backpacking trip in Europe. And we'll keep this little . . . skirmish to ourselves, if you don't mind. Your father gets upset when you and I fight.'' Her lips curled. ''I can't imagine what he'd say if he knew you'd bashed me. Probably he'd agree with me finally that you're under the wrong influence on this island.''

''I'll keep quiet, you know I will. Dad is as stymied as I am about your crazy notion that Tally Malone is contagious or something. But I won't stand still for your following through on your threat about evicting the Malones. That's cruel and unfair and I'll fight you to the death on it if I have to.''

''You won't have to. If you leave quietly after a nice little dinner with your father and me, there'll be nothing more said about the parasite Malones leaving.'' Lucy ignored Nick's instant bristle at the word ''parasite.'' ''Well? Do we have a truce?''

Nick laughed, a sneering laugh. ''Dinner? You, Dad, and me, sitting around the table like in 'Ozzie and Harriet,' eh?'' His smile stretched and he shook his head slowly. ''You never cease to amaze me, Mother. But I'll be there.'' He started toward the door, pausing at his mother's chair on his way. He reached out and touched the red imprint of his hand on her cheek. ''You forced me to do that, you know. I've never struck a woman before in my life.''

Lucy pushed Nick's hand away. She would not soon forgive Nick for the slap. They both knew that. ''Too bad you started with me. I can think of other women who need knocking around more than I do.''

Nick knew that if he pursued the matter his mother would soon have herself martyred and him groveling for forgiveness. Well, he wouldn't give her that satisfaction. This time she had gone too far. ''This is going nowhere, Mother. I'll see you at dinner, but don't expect me to be sociable.''

Lucy said sarcastically, ''Considering your recent behavior, why should I? Don't drag out your good-byes with Tally too long, Nicholas. Your father drinks too much if dinner's late.''

"Maybe tonight I'll join him. I sure as hell don't have any appetite.''

"Nick, I can't believe you did that.''

"Hit my mother to make her stop saying those nasty things about the girl I love?'' Nick pulled Tally back into his arms. He hadn't told her all of what Lucy had said but she could read between the lines. "Maybe I should have done it a long time ago.''

"No, no—fighting Lucy on her own terms isn't any way to beat her. Let her think you're giving in. Go to Europe and have a wonderful time. You've got your degree now. We'll stay close somehow. And one day soon you'll be on your own, and we can decide then what we want—together.''

Nick squeezed her. He looked around the spit of beach that had come to be his and Tally's special place. "God, I'll miss being here with you. I'll miss you. Oh, Tally!'' Nick kissed Tally's face passionately, the eyes, the lips, the cheeks, and then the lips again. "I'll leave, but, damn it, I won't go on that stupid preppie trip she's planned for me. Look, I didn't tell you about this, because I wasn't sure how it would turn out, but it looks like I'm going into the Army. The real Army.''

"Why, Nick? Why? What about you and me?''

Nick was as gentle as he could be, but his conviction was firm that he had to make his break with Lucy Cantrell now or never. "I've been in ROTC for four years now. You know that. I have my obligations to the military. Besides . . .'' His passion broke through the calm reason. "Tally, goddammit, I have to get out from under my mother's control once and for all. Can't you see that? I can never lead my own life until I've proved I'm my own man. When I've done that, I'll come back and claim you, and the hell with my mother!''

"You've been planning this for a long time.'' Tally fought back the resentful tears. Couldn't Nick put her feelings ahead of his obsession to escape Lucy's domination? "It sounds to me as if you've already made up your mind."

"My commanding officer made it up for me. They need me in a special unit, Tally. I'll be starting intensive basic training as soon as I get my orders, then go straight into copter training." He felt guilty at the sadness on Tally's face. "Don't look so worried. I've flown helicopters on my own for almost two years now. The training will be a snap. Besides, it's peacetime overseas now." That wasn't what Nick's commander had hinted to him, but Nick saw no need to tell Tally that military advisers were being sent all over Southeast Asia. "I'll be doing dull things like surveying and mapmaking in some jungle where the worst danger is getting eaten by gnats."

"And flying helicopters! You don't fool me. I know that's the most dangerous kind of flying." She tried to make the best of what she was hearing in spite of her dismay at the fact that Nick had kept his plans from her. "But you'll be stateside for at least six months."

Nick shook his head slowly. "I'm sorry, honey. It won't be eight weeks, if that. I'm trying to explain to you—this is a special unit. We've had a lot of training already."

Nick took Tally's shoulders and looked down into her eyes, which were filling with tears. "Oh, honey, don't cry. I'll send you the money to come to Fort Stewart the first weekend you can. And then, when I'm at Rucker, you can come there, too, to see me off." He pulled her against him. "Tally, sweetheart, don't cry. Please."

"Off?" Tally's voice was muffled against his chest. "Off to where? Nick, where will they send you?"

"Honey, I have no idea. Wherever I'm needed, I guess."

Tally pulled back and stared up into Nick's face. "You're . . . you're excited about going, aren't you?"

"Not about leaving the island. Not about leaving you. It's just that . . . hell, sweetheart. This is the first real decision I've ever made about my own life. Can you understand that? I can learn to be my own man. Look at my father. Do you want me to be like him—under my mother's thumb for the rest of my life?"

"You're not like Harm. You never will be."

"I could be if I don't start taking control of my own life."
Nick pulled Tally back to him and stroked her stiff back as he
spoke softly, comfortingly. "I'll come back to you. We'll have
a life together, a wonderful life. You'll be proud of me, I
promise that."

Tally felt numb. She didn't feel the kisses Nick was raining
on her. "Lucy will blame me. You know she will."

"No, she won't. I'll write her as soon as it's all settled and
she can't do anything to stop me. Tally, Tally. Please don't be
unhappy. This isn't the end of our love. It's just the beginning."

Over Nick's shoulder, Tally saw the shrimp boats coming
home. Usually the sight pleased her. Now the nets spread out
like wounded wings made her feel incredibly sad.

"I always hated for summer to end," she whispered. She
knew, no matter what Nick promised, that there would never
be another summer like this one.

13

Lucy Cantrell's shock at learning her son had left, as promised, but not on the trip to Europe, turned into cool accep-
tance once she discovered her control of her son had transferred
to that of the U.S. Army. "At least," she told Cane when he
called to see why Nick had not appeared at his friend's place
in Frankfurt as planned, "he's away from that dreadful girl's
influence. And, who knows, this could be the best thing for
him, getting his military service out of the way and learning to
be a man."

Cane, back in Atlanta after an exhausting trip, hoped that
Lucy wasn't aware of the hazards of being a helicopter pilot
these days when there were special missions to Southeast Asia.
But he wasn't about to bring this to her attention. As a newsman
he had learned things few people knew or spoke about. "I'm
surprised you didn't pull your usual strings and get him some
cushy stateside assignment."

"It was out of my hands. Damn him, he planned it deliberately, so I wouldn't be able to do anything. But, Cane, at least he's away from *her!*"

Cane secretly exulted in that, for his own mixed reasons. "How's Tally handling it? If she's as dead set as you say on trapping the guy, I should think she'd be trying to see as much of him as she can before he leaves Fort Stewart."

Lucy chuckled evilly. "You'd be proud of me. I didn't have to interfere at all. The first time she tried to leave on the bus for a visit, it broke down just outside Midway. And by the time she got to the camp, Nick was already on a practice maneuver over at Fort Rucker. Then her mother got sick just before the next planned tryst. . . ."

Cane couldn't help a sympathetic "Poor kids. They don't have just you, me, and the Army working to keep them apart — now, they've got God." He wished he could see Tally, try to comfort her in some way, but he knew that would be a disaster. They would just end up in some kind of misunderstanding. Besides, he couldn't leave Atlanta right now with the negotiations for a model TV station underway. "So you did keep your word to Nick about not running Tally and her mother off the place. I'm glad to hear that."

"I'm sure you are," Lucy said with a sharp edge. "I don't know how you run that business you have, being so soft on people. When are you coming to see me?"

"Not for a while. But at least I'm back in the good ole U.S. of A. I'll call you first chance I see to break away for a visit. Lucy . . ." Cane's voice changed. "Don't blame the girl for what Nick's gotten himself into. It's time you started giving your son credit for taking responsibility for himself."

"Cane," Lucy said sweetly, "I hope when you finally get around to being a parent, I may be allowed to give you advice like you've always given me."

Cane laughed. "You'll be too old by then, Lucy. So long, now. Keep me up on things."

"You're the communications mogul. Keep up on them yourself."

* * *

"It's those blackberries I ate," Tally told herself the first time she got sick and threw up after she and Reba had been out ravaging the thickest brier patch close to the compound. "Or maybe because I'm so worried about Nick." She was glad Reba had left before she started retching and heaving till her stomach was empty.

The letter from Nick didn't help. After she read it, Tally went up to the searchlight room of Old Tabby and just sat, staring out at the sea. "He sounds happy," she said out loud to the room in dull moroseness. "How can he sound so happy, going so far away from me and not knowing what kind of mess he's getting into over there in some foreign country?"

After the second week straight of throwing up before breakfast, Tally started getting worried. Even Vieve had commented on Tally's wan appearance, saying, "Honey, are you working too hard? Papa says a little lady shouldn't be out in that hot sun at midday. Are you wearing your hat when you go out, darling?"

"I don't think my hat would do much good," Tally replied miserably, but Vieve was already back in her private world, leaving her daughter to face alone what she was beginning to suspect was the truth of her situation.

Aunt Monday faced it with her realistically. "You're pregnant, child," she said bluntly after Tally had been only ten minutes into her visit at the obeah's shanty. "It's the Cantrell boy's, of course. What do you plan to do?"

"I don't know," Tally said miserably. "Isn't there something . . . don't you have something that . . ."

Aunt Monday smiled and finished for her, "Something that can make you discharge the child that's growing inside you?" She shook her head slowly. "Do you think I would not have used such a miracle cure on myself had I had that option when I was burdened with an egg fertilized by a man I loathed? No, my child. I have no such power, nor want such. At least there's love between you and that young man. Let him know what he has left you to bear alone. He's a good young person. He will not turn his back on you."

"Oh, Aunt Monday, this was not my planning! Miz Lucy—think what Miz Lucy will say about me! And how can I face people when they learn that I'm . . . that I'm . . . pregnant." She finally managed to get the word out in a whisper.

"You could go away secretly, have the child, and let some good family take it to raise as their own. As I did."

Tally looked up in horror. "Nick's baby? Oh no, Aunt Monday! How could I give away his baby with him being so far away and not even knowing about it?" She encircled her belly with two protective hands. "No. No, I couldn't do that. Nick will want our baby," she said with a sudden surge of certainty. "He'll want it as much as I do. He'll get leave, come home; we'll get married and live here, Nick, me, and the baby. . . ."

"And Grandmother Lucy?" Aunt Monday interjected into the fairy tale softly.

"Yes!" Tally said, her eyes glowing defiantly. "It's her blood, too. She can't deny that. She'll love it, too. I know she will. She may hate me, but she can't hate a baby that's her own flesh and blood after it's come."

"Write the boy first, before you make any decisions," Aunt Monday said quietly. "You need to find out if he's willing to take the responsibility for being the father to your child."

"Why shouldn't he?" Tally asked. "It's his child. His and mine."

"Write to him," Aunt Monday said again, before she went off to fetch them both a bowl of her nourishing gumbo. "He has a right to know that he's going to be a father. And you have the right to know how he feels about it."

So Tally wrote to Nick about her plight. The letter took hours to compose, with Tally alternately sweating and undergoing chills as she tried to put the words to paper.

Accompanying the arduous task of breaking the news to Nick were guilty doubts about her own role in this situation. Had she been deliberately careless about their intimacy? Had she wanted this to happen? The device she'd used hadn't been one hundred percent safe; she'd known that from the beginning, yet had taken the risk without hesitation.

Was she, as Lucy Cantrell would believe, a manipulator who wanted to trick a rich young man into marriage?

It was a sobering self-examination that she put herself through, one that resulted in her letter being far from demanding.

> *And so, darling Nick, I'm ending this letter with a sincere plea to you that you follow your heart in what you want to do. I could not bear it if you felt that my having our baby is a way to trap you into something that you don't want as much as I do. We never talked about marriage. I don't even know if you've ever thought about me as someday being your wife. But I know this much—whatever you decide is right for you, I will accept it as best I can. If you want to make our life together, the three of us, I'll do my best to be a good wife to you and the best mother to our child that I can be. And, Nick, I will make you so happy! I'll make myself so happy!*
>
> *Please let me hear from you as soon as you can. You must know how hard it is for me waiting back here, not knowing what I can do, not knowing if you'll be happy about our baby or feel trapped into something you don't want. . . .*

Tally sealed the letter with a tear or two and gave it to Poke Taylor to mail when he made the daily run to the mainland.

Lucy Cantrell was Poke's only passenger on the ferry that day. She was off to attend a mainland fashion show and do various errands, including a trip to the post office.

She saw the letter addressed to Nick sticking out of the ferryman's pocket as they pulled into the ferry slip. "Is that something for mailing? I can take it with my letter."

Poke Taylor wasn't totally stupid. He muttered something

about having other letters to mail and offered to take Lucy's letter along with the other mail. But short of being obdurate, he had no choice in the end but to relinquish Tally's letter to Lucy.

Tally pestered Poke about the mail every day from then on, to the point that Poke stopped his usual teasing of the girl and all "them lovesick boyfriends."

Finally the letter from Nick arrived. Tally restrained herself from ripping into it until she was out of sight of the ferry.

A short time later, she was in her room sobbing, the crumpled letter from Nick held loosely in her hands as she hugged her knees against her thickening waist. "How could he?" she moaned with heartbreaking sorrow. "How could he act so unconcerned about it, like it's just something that happens and doesn't really matter? And he didn't say anything—not anything—about us maybe getting married!"

In fact, Nick had responded to Tally's earlier letter, one in which she had mentioned Reba's disillusionment with her new job at the new dress factory. So she thought his carefully sympathetic reaction was to her news about the baby.

The letter she had written to him was in Lucy Cantrell's jewelry case, but all Tally knew was that Nick Cantrell was extremely blithe about the fact that she was carrying his baby.

It was too late to try to find one of the back-street doctors in Savannah who performed illegal abortions, she learned. They didn't like working on girls over two months gone. Tally was despondent, feeling like a zombie as she moved from chore to chore, from barn to kitchen to field and home again, day after never-ending day. Her breasts swelled along with her tummy. In a desperate attempt to hide her secret, she took to wearing some old, faded, loose shirts that she found packed in a box in the lighthouse.

Nobody said anything, though F'Mollie came the closest to addressing the situation directly. "You—uh—stoutening up a little, aintcha?" the black girl said one afternoon when the two were engaged in canning tomatoes. Tally was busy pulling off the boiled skins from the piping-hot pulps and plopping the bared products into mason jars. Sweat rolled off her brow and she brushed lanky hair off her forehead from time to time. The baby was taking its vitamins from her hair, she decided; it was either that or the teeth, she heard, so she was just as glad.

"None of your beeswax," she told F'Mollie fiercely. "You're one to talk, with that fanny of yours that looks like two boys wrestling under a blanket when you walk."

F'Mollie's bottom lip stuck out all the way to town with that, and the two finished their canning chores in silence. In the end, Tally was ashamed enough to say, as they put the final jars in the pressure cooker, "I didn't mean to hurt your feelings, F'Mollie. Hope you know that. Fact is, Jim-Roy says you got the cutest butt this side of Savannah."

F'Mollie's pout vanished in a flash of teeth. "He say that, did he? Lord, what a little devil that boy be." Friendly again, she nudged Tally conspiratorially. "You know what I think? That boy'll marry you in a minute iffen you tell 'im about that bun you got going for 'im in that oven of yourn. Jim-Roy, he's crazy about young'uns."

"But he's not . . ." Tally stopped on the verge of correcting F'Mollie about her mistaken assumption that Jim-Roy was responsible for her "stoutening up." Maybe it was safer to let the gossipy black girl go on thinking that Jim-Roy Tatum had been the one to "knock her up." "He's not ready to take on a wife till that job of his gets to be full-time. F'Mollie, I'd just as soon you didn't go around telling folks about this." It was blowing in the wind, Tally knew, but at least the black girl wouldn't be bringing Nick's name into her gossipy assumptions.

"My lips is sealed," F'Mollie said with a dramatic show of zipping up her very considerable mouth.

Poke Taylor took his responsibility as liaison to the world outside Moss Island quite seriously. When the telegraph office on the mainland called him to say there was a wire for the Cantrell family, he locked up his little commissary and immediately went to fetch it.

He knew the wire was important. He carried it up to the big

house and handed it to Lucy Cantrell and waited on the veranda while she opened the windowed envelope.

"Miz Lucy?" he asked with concern when she lifted her eyes from the yellow paper and stared at him, her eyes big blue marbles. "Miz Lucy, is it bad news?" Poke knew it was bad news, not just from Lucy's stricken face but from tradition. Nobody ever sent telegrams with good news. "You want I should get Mr. Harm or somebody?"

She looked at him and her melon-orange mouth made a gasping "O" without any sound coming out. She held out the telegram with a shaking hand. "It's not true," she gasped out, her other hand going up to clasp her throat as though she were forcing the words out. "Read it and tell me. It's not true. Nicky's not dead. There's some mistake."

Poke moved his lips as he painstakingly read the message from Washington. "No, ma'am, it don't say he's for sure dead." Lucy's eyes locked on his finger eagerly as it traced the black-typed words. "It says here he's missing, that his hee-leo-copter went down in Indochina somewheres and . . ."

Lucy's scream ripped through the island peacefulness. She tore the wire from Poke's hand and slammed the door almost on his hand. Poke stood there, stunned, then decided he'd better move fast, before Tally Malone got the news about her sweetheart from the wrong source. . . .

Essie Mae, her heart heavy with the dread of the news she must impart to her beloved chile, went to the pantry where Tally was labeling the canning jars. "Honey, come on in here in de kitchen and let's have ourselves a little Luzianne. I got something to tell you, and it ain't the best news in the world."

Tally got down off the little three-step ladder very carefully. She was clumsy as the devil these days. "Essie Mae, if it's something to do with F'Mollie getting in trouble again, I don't want to hear it. I love that girl of yours, but I swear if she don't—" Tally stopped at the sight of Essie Mae taking the Lydia Pinkham pint from under the sink and pouring a healthy dollop in each cup of coffee. The black woman's medicinal cure was offered for only the most dire disasters. "Oh my lord." Tally sat down at the table and waited in dread. "It's something to do with Reba. She got hung up in one of those giant sewing machines at the factory.''

''No, chile.'' Essie Mae looked at Tally and the big hollows under the anxious eyes and wept inside. ''It ain't F'Mollie and it ain't Reba. It's some'n else, some'n you love in a different way from F'Mollie and Reba.''

''Mama,'' Tally whispered, her heart clutched with dread.

''It's yore Nick, honey. He done gone down over one of them places in one of them heathen countries where nobody nebber comes back from. Indy-China or some such. Oh, honey, it's just breakin' my heart lookin' at your little face. It ain't the end of the world, sweet darlin'. You young. Ain't like you and Nick was married to each other or nothin'.''

It *was* the end of the world. Before the real pain set in, all Tally could think about was Sammie Sue Bagley, who had been pregnant by a boy killed in Korea. Sammie Sue had been pointed at, chastised, and otherwise made miserable by every so-called Christian on Moss Island. Finally, the fact that the baby was born with a birthmark on its face had satisfied the girl's moral monitors, who said it was a fitting symbol of sin. But suddenly the immediate pain of what Essie Mae was saying hit her. ''Oh, Essie Mae—Nick's gone! I knew he wouldn't come back to me. I just knew it! I can't stand it, Essie Mae. Nick not ever coming back to the island. Essie Mae—help me!'' Tally got up and ran around the table to throw herself sobbing on the black woman's bosom.

Essie Mae let her cry her heart out, patting her and saying ''There, there'' until Tally's well of tears had run dry. The sobs subsided, and then the hiccups, and then Tally was wiping her eyes on the black woman's apron and pulling herself together with a few sniffles.

''I don't know what I'm going to do, Essie Mae. It hurts so much, knowing I won't ever see Nick again.''

''I know, honey. I know.'' Essie Mae rocked Tally in her arms. ''It's hard bein' born into this world, but that ain't nothin' to what it is livin' in it. Things go thissaway for a while, then they go thattaway, and a body gets dizzy tryin' to keep up.''

The black woman's rocking was making Tally dizzy and she

felt the Luzianne mixture coming up in her throat. "Essie Mae, I'm real sorry but I got to . . . throw . . . up."

She barely made it out to the back stoop. When she came back in, pale as flour and looking close to collapse, Essie Mae looked at her long and appraisingly.

"Oh, baby chile. Oh, baby girl. Is that what you got making those big ole eyes look like they's seen the end of the world tonight? Is that what it is?" She hugged Tally so tight the girl was afraid she might throw up again, but she didn't. It was wonderful having someone's arms holding her. Someone caring what was happening to her. Someone who knew that the world had just come to an end for her.

"Essie Mae, I've lost Nick and I can't stand bringing his child into the world having no daddy. Think what's gonna happen to me. The baby, too. Why don't I just go climb up on top of that lighthouse and jump off and save us both all the grief ahead?"

Essie Mae looked serious. She knew the child was distraught and didn't need any nickel-plated psychology. "Cain't shake a good egg loose—don't you know that? Woman back in my time, she jump off the barn, try to bring that baby out beforetimes. Broke her legs, that woman, but de baby? He come out strong and nine pounds big five months later."

Tally started weeping. "But Essie Mae, what am I going to do? Nick's gone, you know what it's like with Mama. Who's going to help me?"

"We all will, darlin' baby girl. We all will." Essie Mae suddenly pushed Tally back from her enveloping arms so she could search her face. "You sure it be the Cantrell boy's baby? You sure 'bout that?"

"Oh, Essie Mae—of course I am. What do you think I am?"

"Pregnant, with no daddy to point to. Now, here's what, and don't you get one bit stubborn on me 'bout what I got to say. Pregnant girls cain't afford no stubborn business. If you're abso-lu-tootly sure that baby you got in the basket is a Cantrell, we got somethin' to work with. Miz Lucy, she just lost her boy, only one she's got or likely to have ever in this world.

What you think she'd do if she knowed there was a little Cantrell ready to make his way out come the first of the year? She'd be crazy with joy, that's what she'd be.''

"You want me to tell Miz Lucy I'm pregnant with Nick's baby?" Tally asked, her eyes wide and scared.

"Seems to me you ain't got much choice," Essie Mae said with a grim smile. "But I'd wait till I got myself all ordered like and ready to deal. You got somethin' she wants, chile. That's what I calls holdin' all the aces. Oh, Lord, you're lookin' green like you need to go call for your Uncle Roark agin. I'll open the door and you do the rest. Praise be, there won't be no wake for Mistuh Nick. You'd never make it past the ham and potato salad.''

Tally felt the rising gorge and ran for the back stoop, Essie Mae in close pursuit. It was going to be a long night.

Tally and Reba cried together for hours over the tragedy of Nick. At the tiny prayer service Lucy arranged in the tabby chapel, the two girls sat together and wept while Brother Thomas from the mainland Methodist church conducted the simple service.

Lucy Cantrell sat stiffly alone on the front bench, her blond head wreathed in veiling so that no one could see if she cried. Harm Cantrell wept unashamedly, as did all the blacks who attended the little service. Jim-Roy, dressed in a too-small dark suit, his hair slicked back to the new longish ducktail young men were wearing, blew his nose a time or two and watched Tally with great concern. The girl looked sick to him; he was afraid at any minute she would faint away.

Cane Winslow, trapped by an air strike at London's Gatwick Airport, sent telegrams to both Lucy and Tally. That crumpled piece of yellow paper was clutched in Tally's hand as she sobbed through Nick's service. She wished Cane were here. He'd loved Nick. It would have made Tally's grief easier if Cane had been there.

Lucy stopped at Tally's side after the service was over. "It's time you and I had a talk," she said coldly, looking contemptuously at Tally's red-rimmed eyes and trembling mouth. "I'll be resting in my room until four. Please bring my tea at that time. And for God's sake, stop that sniveling."

Tally had never dreaded an interview so much as she did this one. But how had it happened that Lucy was the one to say they "had to talk"?

Did Nick's mother suspect something?

Tally was nervous when she went to Lucy's darkened room at exactly four. She had put for herself a cold glass of goat's milk on the tray to settle her queasy stomach.

"Good Lord, what's that?" Lucy said when Tally set down the tray. Her long nail pointed at the glass of milk.

"I'm pregnant," Tally burst out, the long preamble to her news that she had planned flying out of her head in the same moment she realized she had a kind of power over this woman for the first time in her life. "With Nick's baby."

Lucy leisurely poured her tea, stirred in two lumps of sugar and a dollop of cream before she raised her eyes to Tally's. "Really." She sipped her tea so slowly Tally wanted to scream, then said with the same maddening calm, "I know."

Tally was aghast. "Nick told you?"

"Of course," Lucy lied. "He wrote to me about it. He felt bad, naturally, that you apparently assumed he would marry you, but since it was out of the question . . ."

Tally felt as though she were going to fly into a million pieces. Nick had betrayed her like that to his *mother!* To Tally's deadliest enemy! Her face scarlet with the rush of emotion, she managed, "I didn't say he had to marry me. I left that up to him." She choked back a sob. "What . . . what else did he say?"

"He asked me to see to any . . . arrangements you might agree to." Lucy spread her hands delicately. "Abortion, adoption—but now, of course, that's all changed. You'll have the child—privately, far away from here—and I'll see to its upbringing."

Tally's nails bit into her hands, drawing blood. "The hell you say," she said through gritted teeth. "It's my baby. I'll have it and raise it myself, on my own."

Lucy's laugh was brittle. "Raise it yourself? My dear, look at you! You have nothing to offer a child—nothing! And even if you did, think of the disgrace. Darling, surely you know the stigma of a young unmarried woman attempting to raise a child without a husband, without a father. And if the stigma of it doesn't bother you, think about the child. What would become of it? How would you support it? Clothe it? Educate it?"

Tally had no answer except an emotional one. "I'll think of something!"

"Fine. And in the meantime, let me make a proposal to you." Lucy walked over to the window and looked out. "This is a beautiful place for a child to grow up. Nick's child would have every advantage of growing up a Cantrell. The nannies, the pony carts, the birthday parties, the pretty clothes—" She turned back to Tally. "All the things you should have had and were denied. Think of it, Tally. You can give your little girl all those things you wanted . . . why are you looking at me like that?"

Tally was staring at Lucy, her anger distracted for a moment. "Why do you assume it will be a daughter?"

Lucy's eyes widened and then a look of sincere happiness spread over her face. "I don't know! I swear I don't know why I . . . it's just that I've always wanted a little girl to bring up sweet and feminine and pretty and . . ." The dreamy look vanished. "You don't have long to decide. What are you—four months along? You'll start showing any day now and people will start to talk, if they haven't already."

"F'Mollie has," Tally said grimly.

"No, she hasn't. I've already spoken to her. The story will be that you are ill with mononucleosis and will be spending several months with your relatives in Savannah. Essie Mae, of course, won't say a word, and your friend Reba is the only possible leak. . . ."

"Reba doesn't suspect, and even if she does, she won't say anything. But you're talking like it's all settled. Why should I agree to having my baby and then just giving it to you?"

"Because," Lucy said carefully, looking at her nails, "I hold all the cards, starting with the black Queen of Spades."

She raised her glittering eyes slowly to Tally's. "You remember when your father, poor man, burned to death after that holy-terror debacle he pulled on you and your mother?"

"Of course I remember!" Tally cried out. "What do you think I am?"

"We're about to touch on that," Lucy said softly. She looked at her nails again, worried one with a tiny snag delicately, as though that were the most important issue in the world. "Well, there's a part to that night's scenario that you don't know about."

Tally was staring in honest-to-God shock by this time. "What in the world are you talking about?" But her heart beat faster with fear whose reason only she knew. Lucy Cantrell had an unerring gut instinct for weak spots and her prodding was getting too close for comfort. "Are you saying you don't believe things happened that night the way I told you? Is that what you're saying?"

"That's exactly what I'm saying," Lucy replied calmly. "I *saw* what happened, Tally."

Tally's heart froze in terror. It was not she who held all the aces, as Essie Mae had put it, but Lucy Cantrell. "What do you mean?" she whispered, barely able to get the words past the lump of fear in her throat. "You weren't there. And when I saw you after the fire, you didn't say anything. You're bluffing! Damn you, you're bluffing so I'll agree to what you want me to do!"

"I never bluff," Lucy said softly. "I only bided my time until I needed something to use against you when there was no other choice. If Nicky had not gone away when he did, a certain person would be in Sheriff Waymon's custody right now, awaiting trial for the murder of Daniel Malone. You see, I kept the coroner's office out of the matter, so that your poor father's charred remains did not undergo close investigation."

"You're a monster!" Tally cried out. "Look at what you did. If you hadn't tormented poor Nick about me, he'd be here today!"

Lucy came over and looked at Tally, her face not inches

away and full of fury. "Don't . . . you . . . ever . . . say . . .
that . . . again!" she screeched, almost spitting in Tally's face.
"My son was the only thing in the world that meant anything
to me after my father died. I only wanted the best for him. The
best! You hear me? The best. And now I will have that for his
child, and not you, not God, not anyone can stop me from
seeing to it that Nicky's baby will be brought up right here,
like I say!"

"You said you saw what happened. How? Were you spying
on us that night that Perrie died?"

"In fact I was. Sheriff Waymon had come to me about
Daniel, saying he'd heard that the fellow was going over the
edge about that snake-handling business. He said there was
some pressure from people around the community to outlaw
the practice forever, even to the point of prosecution of prac-
titioners. He also said he had reason to suspect that Daniel was
the one who stole the cobra from the carnival. Somebody had
seen him lugging a crate up from the swamp that very day."

"So why didn't the sheriff come talk to Perrie? He should
have, if he was all that worried."

"Because I asked him to let me handle it. Daniel was my
foreman. I didn't want him going to jail and leaving me high
and dry with no supervisor for the plantation." Lucy walked
over and looked out the window. Tally knew she was relishing
the thought of the next part of her revelation. "So I went over
that night to talk to your father, see if I could talk him into
giving up his ridiculous . . . hobby and make Camellia the
productive plantation I want it to be."

Tally held her breath and closed her eyes. At first she'd
thought Lucy was lying but now she wasn't so sure.

Lucy turned around. "The front door of your house was
latched. I knocked, but nobody came. I knew you were still up
because I could hear Daniel's voice from back in the bedroom."

"He was reading from the Scripture," Tally whispered.

"Well, I knew if I didn't do something, Waymon would be
out the next morning to arrest your father and I would be out

an overseer. So I went around to the back and tapped on your parents' bedroom window. Nobody heard—and no wonder! I have never witnessed such a dreadful scene in my life! Daniel was practically frothing at the mouth, and there sat you and your poor mother watching in as much horror as I felt." Lucy's eyes riveted to Tally's. "And then I saw the Luger being pointed at . . . the snake? Or Daniel?" She shrugged. "As a witness, it's difficult to say. I mean, when the gun went off, your father collapsed. . . ."

Tally screamed, "Stop! Goddamn you, stop!" She jumped up and ran to Lucy's wastebasket and retched until she was gasping for breath. Then she raised a ravaged face to her tormentor. "You win. I'll give you the child."

"Good." Lucy whipped out a tissue from the container by her chair and handed it to Tally. "Clean yourself up and we'll go over the conditions. I don't want you to think I'm being unfair." At the look Tally gave her, Lucy had the grace to blush. "Well, at any rate, I don't want you to think I'm not going to provide ample remuneration for your . . . uh, sacrifice."

Tally waited. She felt empty inside, as though the baby had already been taken away. "Just say what you want to say," she said dully.

"All right," Lucy said almost cheerfully. "Oh, dear, this splendid tea you brought has gone cold. No, no, don't fret yourself." This was said sarcastically, since Lucy knew that Tally would not have fetched Lucy anything at that moment. "I'll be having cocktails soon—some very strong ones. I just lost my son, you know." She stared at Tally as though she really weren't seeing her. "That's the worst part, you know. Not having anything of him to say good-bye to, knowing he's scattered over some godforsaken jungle." Lucy almost lost control then, but regained it. "Maybe that's why the child means so much to me. Maybe it's a spiritual trade-off. Nick's gone but he left me his child."

Left ME his child! Tally wanted to scream but didn't. "I have the feeling you're working up to the real bargain," she said with more calmness than she'd mustered during the entire dreadful interview. "What do you want from me?"

"Besides the child? Nothing else, really, except your promise that you won't try to interfere or raise maternal claims later on. In return, I'll make your life sweet. Oh, it won't be a lark for you, but I'll try to see that you're at the best place available. Vieve will be taken care of in this perfectly wonderful place not far out of Atlanta. It's a sanitarium that specializes in the vague sort of mental illnesses like hers." Lucy said with emphasis and significantly, "She will be watched constantly. Her every need will be taken care of, as will yours."

"And when I turn the baby over to you. Then what?"

Lucy smiled in an almost friendly fashion. "Smart girl! So you're looking ahead to what happens after that—the most important phase for you, if you ask me. I'll send you to a top-notch girls' school—Stevens—for two years. They specialize in silk-purse miracles." Lucy held up her hand at Tally's start of indignation. "Don't blow up at me! I'm telling it like it is. Then I'll pay your way through the best secretarial school in the country. Katharine Gibbs. Top executives fight for those graduates. You can call your own shots, pick your own city, name your own salary. Well, almost."

Tally felt a pang in her womb. It was as if the child knew it was being bargained for. She felt a wave of sickness that had nothing to do with pregnancy. In the period of less than one week she had lost Nick and his baby. What did she have left? Herself. "I'll want all of this in writing."

Lucy nodded. "Of course. I'll have the agreement drawn up. Discreetly, of course. But in the meantime, shall we shake on it?" She held out her hand.

Tally ignored it. "How will you explain it, coming home with a brand-new baby? Plenty of women your age have babies. But won't people ask questions? Wonder a little bit?"

Lucy's hand dropped to her side. "Oh, I expect something will turn up to take care of that fuzzy bit of detail. It usually does. It's my experience that when you know what you want and go after it, things usually work out."

Tally picked up the tray and looked Lucy square in the eye. Then she made a deep, mocking curtsy. "Will that be all, ma'am?"

Lucy laughed a little uncertainly. "Goodness, what's all that about?"

"I just want you to listen to the way I said that 'ma'am' and remember how I just now bowed to you. I want you to look at this tray in my hands. And I want you to know that this will be the last time you'll ever hear 'ma'am' from my lips again, or see a tray of your dirty dishes in my hands again."

"Fair enough," Lucy said with a curling smile and a look that was just short of admiring.

14

"Tally, for heaven's sake, try to look more cheerful when we get to the home. I've talked with the director and she assures me that's important, that you try to be as cheerful as possible. After all, you won't be the only girl there who got herself into the fix you're in. There are probably sixty others in the same boat—or worse." Lucy Cantrell turned on the Cadillac's windshield wipers. The slight drizzle of rain that had accompanied their drive from Moss Island had turned into a pelting downpour on the outskirts of sprawled-out Savannah. "At least you've got a future to look forward to. Think of some of these other poor unfortunate girls who don't have anything ahead of them."

Tally didn't want to think about those other girls. Didn't she have enough problems of her own to think about? She tugged at the new maternity top that Lucy had bought her. She hated the way she looked right now, hated the rain, hated Lucy's new cheerfulness. "I didn't like leaving my mother at that place outside Atlanta. And I didn't like fooling her about me going to stay with her cousins in Savannah. We both know what a big fat lie that is."

"Don't be ridiculous," Lucy said sharply, looking for the turn into the driveway she was seeking. "She'll have the best of care at Autumn Oaks. I've arranged for that, as well as any medical care, even surgery for her back if it proves necessary. Your mother's in better hands than she's ever been in. As for your going away for a while, I think your mother was relieved. She was worried about your being by yourself in the lighthouse while she was gone." Lucy's mouth curled a little. "She said her papa didn't like for his little girl to stay by herself. Tally, face it. Your mother was as thrilled as I've ever seen her to be going into that place back there."

Part of Tally's grouchiness came from her reluctant agreement with Lucy's observations about Vieve. Tally felt just the teeniest bit hurt that her mother had blossomed happily under the attention of the staff who had welcomed her into the pleasant sanitarium Lucy had chosen for her. It was housed in an impressive mansion on a large estate. Tally had to admit it was obvious her mother enjoyed telling everybody there about her daddy's plantation and all the pony carts and special treats of the island. The nurses had, according to their training, accepted Vieve's usual confusion of her "daughter" with herself at Tally's age.

"You haven't told me much about this place I'm going to. Will it be filled with girls lying around weeping and wailing about what they've got themselves into? I couldn't stand that."

Lucy chose to ignore that. "Isn't Victory Drive a lovely old street? Ah, there's the park, just as Miss Wayne said. Not far now. Don't forget, now, there are ground rules for you to follow that will make your stay at the McIntosh Home much pleasanter. First of all, don't make friends with any of these girls. And if you run into one of them later on, for God's sake, don't let on. Most of the young women are here in total secrecy and plan to resume their normal lives after . . . well, afterward. After all, discretion is the very purpose of this kind of home. Privacy is part and parcel of that. There'll be some curiosity, of course. Miss Wayne says the 'old' girls always exhibit curiosity about a new girl. Just act friendly, do what you're supposed to—and keep your distance."

"That shouldn't be hard with this shelf I'm growing," Tally said, making her first joke since leaving the island.

Lucy glanced over at Tally's abdomen anxiously. "It doesn't seem to me you're all that large. Are you still taking those vitamins I had made up for you?"

Tally rolled her eyes. "Those and all this 'motherly' concern are making me want to throw up."

"They're both for my son's child," Lucy said coldly—and truthfully. "I expect you to take good care of yourself for the next few months so that the baby will be born strong and healthy. It's part of our bargain, after all."

Tally put her hand on her abdomen, amazed as always to feel the strong pelting of motion inside her. "It's part of God's bargain, not yours. I don't think I could do anything to keep my baby from coming out healthy and strong. Lord knows, it's taking plenty of vitamins from me." Tally held out a strand of stringy hair, looking at it despondently. "Especially from my hair. Do you suppose she'll be auburn-haired, too?" Since Lucy ignored that, Tally sighed and asked, "Does Miss Wayne expect me to cook and scrub? Somehow I don't see myself having breakfast in bed every morning."

Lucy smiled. "Sorry. It is, as you've guessed already, a working kind of place. You'll have some assigned chores, along with the other girls. But Miss Wayne assures me that's to keep her young women from getting bored and too heavy from no exercise. This is the best we can do, Tally. Make the best of it, please."

Tally leaned forward when they pulled up into a circular driveway and stopped at the entrance to a large gingerbread house. "My God," she breathed, suddenly frightened at the lonely experience ahead. "It's too pretty. There's probably a witch waiting in there to fatten me up for the giant's dinner. Lord, look at all those faces in the windows! I think I want to go home."

Lucy, with unaccustomed charity, did not point out that Tally no longer had a home. "Miss Wayne said the girls like to see if they can recognize the license tags when the new girls come in. It's sort of a game with them. Shall we?"

Tally took another deep breath and gathered up the raincoat Lucy had bought her—the first raincoat she had ever possessed.

"Are you coming in with me?" She hoped not. She had had about as much of Lucy Cantrell as she could stand.

"No. I was just going to get your bag out for you. Miss Wayne says it's best if the girl faces this experience on her own." She pulled up the brake and looked over at Tally's strained face. "Besides, I'm not your mother. No one but direct kin is allowed to accompany a girl into Miss Wayne's establishment on her first night. They don't want their girls to be 'put out' by some immoral boyfriend or the like as if they were unwanted bitches being dumped at the pound."

"Well?" They stared at each other in the ensuing silence. "This is good-bye, I suppose," Tally said then, her hand on the car-door handle. "At least until the big day. Have you thought any more about that, about how you're going to explain coming home with a teeny baby and raising it like it's yours?"

Lucy looked a little smug. "I didn't tell you, did I? We're letting the fields at Camellia Plantation lie fallow the next planting year while I look for a new overseer. Lem has given notice."

"But the baby—how will you explain to people about the baby?"

Lucy smiled. "I have no intentions of explaining anything to anyone. I'll take my child home with me to Camellia Hall and people can think what they will."

"You're not going to let them think it's yours, are you?" Tally felt sick.

"They're holding the door open for you up there," Lucy pointed out calmly. "Did I give you enough money? I'll send more, of course."

Tally got out awkwardly. She still wasn't comfortable with the thickening of her middle. "Somebody's holding a door open for you, too. Only it's not one I'd want to go through, since it leads straight down to hell."

Lucy smiled coolly before shifting into gear. "That sounds like something I would say, Tally. You're learning to get tough. Good! You'll need to be tough in the life ahead for you. Good-bye—and good luck."

Tally stood there watching as Lucy Cantrell drove off leaving her with her bag, an unborn baby, and a house full of strangers.

* * *

Life at McIntosh Home was not unpleasant, Tally soon discovered. Routine was important, but not intolerable. Most of the girls were given their choice of chores, so the work, for an island girl used to more grueling tasks, was relatively easy. Tally picked the downstairs cleaning detail and had no trouble at all handling her assignment, cleaning the director's, Miss Wayne's, quarters on a daily basis, with a once-a-week thorough go-through, to her supervisor's satisfaction.

She was rather shocked to learn that the group of mothers-to-be included one fourteen-year-old and one forty-year-old woman. But Tally adapted quickly to her new life. Her roommate, Betty T., was about as silly a girl as Tally had ever met and she was not surprised in the least when she found out that the girl was sneaking out at least twice a week to meet the boyfriend who'd gotten her pregnant.

"How can you do that?" she finally asked the rotund blond girl who seemed to think that what she was doing was quite all right. "How can you go on seeing a boy who's told you right up front that he doesn't give a flip what happens to the baby?"

"He didn't want me to come here," Betty T. told Tally. "It was my mother—that bitch—who made me do this. Jake says he loves me and wants to marry me one of these days, but we just can't start off having a baby. We'll get it back one of these days, when we're married and he's got a good job."

Tally was exasperated at that. "What about the adopting parents? Don't you even think about them? You can't just go up one day, when Jake says he's ready, and tell those people, 'Well, we're ready to settle down now. We want our baby back.' "

"Well, maybe we'll just have another one and forget about this one."

Forget? Tally shook her head to that, and ignored Betty T.'s request to borrow her newest maternity top to wear out to meet Jake at the Huddle House.

Over the months, Vieve's letters were vague but cheerful. Tally had made an agreement with Lucy to send her own letters in manila envelopes to the director of Autumn Oaks, for direct delivery to her mother. It wasn't likely that Vieve would be astute enough to track her daughter to the unwed mothers' home, but Lucy didn't want Tally to take the chance.

Vieve was occasionally ecstatic about Tally's being in a big city. The guilt that Tally felt when she encountered her mother's enthusiasm about her "broadening experiences" (ha—broadening, indeed, thought Tally when she ran across that) was not permanent. The real guilt she felt was about depriving her mother of her only grandchild. How would Vieve react if she knew that Lucy Cantrell, not she, would know the joy of Tally's first child?

Tally consoled herself with the assurance that Vieve would never, never learn of the deception she was carrying out with their mutual enemy. . . .

Reba Taylor was delighted to have a phone call from Tally. "When are you coming home?" she asked at the end of their hurried conversation, after a hundred questions about how she liked life off the island, about the boys she'd met, about the clothes women wore in Savannah—questions that, fortunately, she didn't give Tally a chance to answer. "Jim-Roy's been pestering the fire out of me about it. Essie Mae, too. Oh, guess what?" Reba giggled. "F'Mollie got herself knocked up. Some handsome high yaller from the mainland that cut and run the minute F'Mollie started puffing up. She's gonna keep the baby; Miz Lucy says she'll help."

Oh, Lord, Tally thought. *What's she up to?* Lucy was not a charitable person. No doubt she had some kind of exchange in mind—an exchange that Tally had a pretty good suspicion about. "When's F'Mollie due?"

" 'Long about the end of February."

Tally felt a pang. Of course. F'Mollie would be the wet nurse for Tally's child. For some reason that hurt a lot. . . .

So did the first real contraction that Tally felt while she was bending over her ceramics project. She was working on a mug for her mother when the pain went through her like a shock wave. A somewhat older woman, LaTrelle, who was glazing a silly-looking Goofy figurine, responded at once. "Tally? Tally, is it time? Are you going into contractions?"

"Yes," Tally gasped when the wave had ceased. "Start timing it, LaTrelle. Miss Wayne says we need to wait till it's sure."

" 'Sure,' hell." Betty T. elbowed her way up to Tally's side and took over. "Those people would like for us to wait till the baby's nose is sticking out our twat 'fore they fool with us. I'm getting Wayne right now, and if she don't see her way to getting you to the doctor pronto, I'm calling Jake."

Tally forgot about her own plight. "Jake! Betty, you can't have your boyfriend driving up here big as anything! Why, you'll be kicked out of this place so fast, it'll make your head swim."

"That's neither here nor there. You hold tight for a second while I go find Miss Wayne. Just don't be jumping up and down or nothing."

Tally grinned. "I thought I might practice the shag steps you taught me last week."

"Atta girl," Betty whispered approvingly, patting Tally on the shoulder. "That's the ole spirit. I'll be right back."

She was, too—and Miss Wayne was right there with her. If Tally had known about the sizable contribution Lucy Cantrell was making to the McIntosh Home for Unwed Mothers, she might not have been surprised at the immediate attention she received.

Tally woke up at one time during the delivery, when it felt as if something was ripping half her insides out, and tried to climb over the railing of the bed she was on. A very mean-looking nurse, with blue-blazing Lucy eyes, said authoritatively, *"Get back in that bed, right now!"* To the doctor, the nurse said, "We didn't give her enough anesthesia. Should I give her another shot?"

That was the last thing Tally was aware of until she woke up. She was empty. "My baby," she said to the nurse who came in when she pressed the little button next to her bed. "My baby. Is it all right?"

"It's fine, Tally. And you did just fine during the delivery. You'll be getting out of here soon. Going to college, I hear. Won't that be a great thing."

Tally wasn't interested in college at the moment. She'd just given birth to a child, for God's sake. "Can I see it?"

"Her," the nurse said with a smile. "Your baby is a beautiful little girl."

"Can I see her?"

Miss Wayne came in just then with Lucy Cantrell, and the nurse, her smile turning uncertain, quickly left. "It's best you don't see the child," Miss Wayne said as soon as the three principals were alone. "This moment is always very hard for my girls, but I can attest to how much better it is if there's no contact with the baby. Not if it's being adopted out. Tally, don't cry. You know it's for the best."

Tally wiped away the tears she had allowed to fall over the unseen daughter and looked straight at Lucy Cantrell. "I hope you know," she said with a quavering voice, "that this would never have taken place if Nick had lived." The ache of giving up her baby was compounded by thoughts of its father. *Nick, Nick! If only you had come home to me.* A fat tear rolled down Tally's cheek.

"But Nick's dead, which makes a very big case for what you're doing," Lucy said, looking straight back. "Tally, we've been through all this before. Think how much better a life my Nick's little girl will have living with me."

"God," Tally said, closing her eyes. "I didn't know—I really didn't know how this would feel. To give up my daughter to you to raise! What have I done? God help me, what have I done?"

"The right thing," Lucy said. "The best thing you could do for your baby girl." Lucy came close to the bed and looked down at Tally, her eyes filled with tears. Tears! Tally realized that she had never before seen Lucy Cantrell on the verge of weeping. "I will do everything for her, Tally. Everything. That child will want for nothing."

"Can't I just see her?" Tally begged. "Just once?"

Miss Wayne would have said something, but Lucy stopped her with a gesture. "No, Tally. It's harder that way, believe me. Can't you take comfort in knowing your child will have the best of everything?"

"Except mothers," Tally said in almost a moan. "You know you're not the best of mothers, Lucy."

"Would you be a better one?" Lucy asked softly.

Tally burst into tears.

Tally had a hired driver to take her back to the Home for her things. After that she would be driven to Vieve at Autumn Oaks, where she would be staying for the interim before summer school at the guest house on the sanitarium grounds. Lucy had arranged for a tutor for some of the classes Tally would be taking at Stevens College the approaching quarter. She had also paid for ceramic classes, since Tally had laconically confessed to having some interest in that particular craft.

At least Lucy Cantrell was keeping her word about paying for every conceivable cost of Tally's and her mother's comfort. She had even arranged with the sanitarium to have a rented car available for Tally and Vieve while the girl was visiting. Tally admitted to herself that she was looking forward to her visit.

Tally was given the traditional farewell as she left the Home, her bags in tow. She even managed to smile over her roommate's weepiness when Tally gave her the warped ceramic mug she'd been working on the night of her birthing. "Keep it," she told the girl softly, a big lump in her throat. It wasn't much of a legacy, that mug, but it meant something to Tally somehow. "But more important, keep your head high and those legs together."

Lucy had Tally's baby, but not her future. Let it begin, she said with a final wave back at the girls of the Home. She felt the tears start in earnest. It was as though she were saying good-bye to Nick, too—forever. But it was time to get on with her life, her new life without the baby she and Nick would have loved so much. . . .

Tally jabbed at the tears on her cheeks and said out loud, fiercely, "Let it begin, and let it be better. And, so help me, if Lucy Cantrell ever tries to take anything away from me again, I'll kill her!"

Part Three

Summer 1961

15

Cane Winslow stood back in the crowd of happy parents and boyfriends who were waiting to envelop their special Katharine Gibbs graduates as soon as they filed off the stage with their diplomas.

He had picked Tally out at the beginning of the ceremony and had not heard one word of the speaker's address. His attention was on her glowing face which, in his opinion, had grown even more beautiful since he'd seen it at the Stevens commencement two years before.

"Tally, please look my way—please. Just once." But Tally Malone seemed intent on the speaker's words, watching her only with those deep amber eyes. Tally's full mouth parted in smiles at the slightest witticism; her graceful hands moved to join in the applause at the end.

And then Tally filed out with the others, coming so close to him as she passed that he could have reached out and touched her—which he almost did.

The golden freckles were still there on the Fontaine nose, he noticed, glad that some of the young Tally was still visible in the proud young woman striding past him. He put his hand in his pocket to make sure the small package was still there after his visit to Tiffany's. Too late, he wished he'd bought something less extravagant to give her, something more along the lines of the simple golden mermaid he'd sent her long ago.

He followed in the crush of well-wishers who crowded out onto the quadrangle to seek out the graduates.

"I can't accept this, Cane." Tally looked up from the topaz ring nestling in its velvet box. She had shed her graduation garb and was dressed in a yellow linen sheath that set off her hair and eyes. "You know I can't, even though it's the most beautiful thing I've ever seen." Carefully, she tucked the ring back into its box and handed it across the table to him. They were sitting in the restaurant at the Copley Plaza, where Cane had rented a suite with hopes that he was no longer sure about.

He didn't argue, just took the gift back and silently cursed himself for going overboard when he should have gone the understated route. "I want to do something for you, Tally. For you, for me, for Nick. God, can't I give you something? Anything?"

"Yes. I want a job with Tri-Com. Mama's close to Atlanta, you know. I want to work there."

Cane was pleased. "Tally, that's terrific! I can't think of anything I'd like better than having you work with us at Tri-Com. Are you serious?" He could think of a few things he'd like better, but they might scare her off. "When are you leaving? When can we have dinner again to talk about it? When can you—"

"Cane, slow down. Let's have dinner now and talk about it. That waiter's been circling us for thirty minutes. Order something and let's get down to business." Tally was having trouble sounding like the poised woman graduate. Her heart was leaping with excitement at seeing Cane again. All her old feelings for him were back, stronger than ever, but she knew she had to control them, especially now. It was up to her to make a life for herself before she could give in to the luxury of passion or emotional dependence on any man. "Now, sir, what can you offer me at Tri-Com?"

Cane ordered for both of them while he thought about what he could do for this young woman who was making him feel like an awkward teenager on his first date. Once the waiter had taken their order and left, Cane made his pitch. "I can offer you a management-trainee position at my new model TV station. We're looking for women who want to work up beyond the limited job levels that females have been held to in the past. Do you think you qualify?''

Tally's eagerness lit up her whole face. For a moment she forgot about her attraction to Cane and felt only gratitude toward him for giving her a chance at a real career. "Do I! Cane, if you only knew how much I want to get somewhere in a company like Tri-Com. . . ! I look at my mother and the women like her who've never given themselves any options in life and I'm more determined than ever to achieve something— on my own.'' Tally looked at Cane with a little grin. "Don't get me wrong. I know what you're doing for me is helping me get several rungs up the ladder without proving myself beforehand. But I'm not too proud to accept that help.''

"Good! Then it's settled. I came up in my private plane. We'll fly down together tomorrow and . . .''

Tally fought hard to keep her emotional equilibrium in Cane's heady presence. She wanted the job at Tri-Com as much as anything she'd ever wanted in her life, but she had to establish the professional boundaries that would help her succeed on her own. "I can't do that. I have my own car, and besides . . .''

Cane wished he'd thought of buying Tally a car instead of the extravagant ring. Harm had beaten him to it. "I'll have someone drive it down.''

Tally stood firm. "Cane, we've got to get something straight right now. If I'm going to work at Tri-Com, I don't want to appear there as your pet. Just think about how it would look, me flying in with the big boss and going to work at three notches above the usual starting place! No, I'll drive down as I planned, visit Mama, then stay with Gretchen till I find a place. I thank you very much for offering me a job, but let's be all business for a while, till I get my feet on the ground. I can't succeed if people are saying I'm getting special treatment from the boss.''

Cane put his hand on Tally's and gazed into her eyes. "Are you trying to tell me that I can't see you except at work? Tally Malone, you are crazy as hell. I can't . . .''

Tally withdrew her hand, which was tingling at Cane's touch. "I'm not talking about forever—just six months or so. By then I'll know if I can cut it on my own and . . . well, let's just see. After six months, we can take a look at where I am and . . ." Tally sipped her wine nervously, wishing Cane wouldn't look at her like that. "I've had a terrific offer from a corporate law firm in Chicago. If you don't agree to what I'm asking, I can always take another job."

Cane Winslow growled about it before he finally agreed. He even let Tally eat her steak in peace, without pushing further. But, he decided, as he went up to his suite (alone) after a very unsatisfying handshake on their deal, at least he would be able to see her.

Still, six months seemed like an eternity.

Tally sang along with the new Bob Dylan song, "Blowin' in the Wind," as she turned her new Mustang into the grounds of Autumn Oaks convalescence wing. Lucy had not balked at the additional cost of Vieve's move to a less restrictive caretaking arrangement, but she had hit the roof when she heard that Harm had given Tally a new car on her graduation.

Tally chuckled now, thinking about what Reba had told her. "Lucy was spitting nails, I don't mind telling you, and poor ole Harm was dodging for all he was worth. But you'd be proud to know, he never backed down for one minute. He said you was his son's sweetheart and that he wasn't doing it for you as much as he was doing it for Nick. He said that fifty-seven Chevy had sat out in the garage for four years now, and he'd thought about giving that to you. But he just couldn't. Nick loved that car. Harm just couldn't give it up."

Tally stopped laughing and drew in her breath at that bit of poignant memory. She was glad Harm had not followed that plan. The new Mustang didn't carry the imprint of Nicholas Cantrell. . . .

Tally was eager that her mother's stay in her new quarters would be a short one. "I want her with me. I'm through school now and able to look after my mother myself. The people at the sanitarium told me she's gentle and totally nonviolent and ready for rehabilitation.''

Helen Cagle, director of Autumn Oaks, looked at Tally sympathetically. ''Your mother's fugue-state has never caused problems to anyone else. Sometimes these post-traumatic hysterical neuroses even resolve themselves, leaving the victim as she was when she left reality. But right now your mother is not at all ready to resume a normal life outside.'' She quickly brought realism to bear on Tally's fantasy concerning Genevieve Malone. ''My dear, how could you possibly assume full-time care of your mother, especially if you take the job you mentioned?''

''But you told me she has little or no pain with her back after the last surgery. Mrs. Cagle, I really want to have my mother with me after I find an apartment in Atlanta.''

''Tally, I know you think, as all devoted children do, that you can do a better job of looking after a parent than we can. But what if she decides to take a bath at two in the afternoon when you're not around—and dozes off in the tub with the water still running? Or leaves the flame on high under a pot of soup and forgets it? Or invites a stranger in for tea?'' At Tally's look, Mrs. Cagle added gently, ''Yes, your mother has done all those things—more than once. If an aide had not been around at the time, Genevieve could have harmed herself.''

Reluctantly Tally conceded that she would not be able to look after her mother and hold down a demanding job. ''But I can take her out for drives every weekend now that I have a car.''

Mrs. Cagle agreed that regular visits and occasional jaunts in Tally's new Mustang would be very pleasant for Genevieve Malone. Disappointed, but reconciled to the idea of leaving her mother where she was comfortable and well-cared for, Tally returned to Atlanta.

''Celebration?'' Tally heard Gretchen laughing from the kitchen as she popped the cork on a bottle of champagne. When she reappeared with two glasses of the bubbling liquid, Tally repeated her question. "Celebration? Of what? You sent me all those balloons when I graduated from Katharine Gibbs. You're letting me stay with you until I get settled. Heck, I should be the one buying you champagne."

"You'll have opportunity. I believe in celebrating everything that comes along that doesn't knock you off your slats." Gretchen handed Tally a glass of champagne and settled back with her own. "So, tell me. How does it feel to be going to work for the biggest communications conglomerate in the South?"

"Just how big is it? Gretchen, I wish you'd tell me all you can about Cane's company. I hate going in there without knowing more about Tri-Com."

"Wel-l-l, let me see. At last count, there are now seven radio stations, two VHF TV units, and forty-seven newspapers under the big umbrella. I just got a copy of the director's report in my mail stack last week, so I can impress you with some figures. The newspapers are still the biggest part of Tri-Com, with something like sixteen thousand people involved nationally, but TV's coming up fast as a big priority. The other communication units have about a hundred forty people in lower-level management. We're not just region-based in that area now, not anymore. Cane even has a dream of founding a worldwide newspaper, but that's way, way off."

"It sounds like Tri-Com's getting ready to go into more TV business."

"Astute of you, my dear. Yes, it is. TV's the new frontier and Tri-Com intends to be the up-front scout." Gretchen's eyes sparkled. "Which has something to do with my reason for celebrating. But let me keep you in suspense a little longer about that. Anything else you want to know about the company? Like where the bodies are buried?"

Tally nodded. "Give me a quick rundown on the people I'll be working with."

Gretchen ticked off on her fingers, "Well, there's your direct boss, Bob Frazier. He's on-air and off-air talent, but I kinda think he's a little poor in the latter area."

"Gretchen, don't talk in buzz words. I don't know what you mean."

"Well, I mean that Bob has two jobs. He's emcee of a TV news commentary spot and he's also vice-president for programming. He's more efficient on-air than he is off-air. I suspect that you're being brought in to be groomed for the programming spot. Cane is really gung-ho on getting more women ready for management positions. I guarantee you, he's one of the few men in this town who feel that way."

"Who else?"

"Well, there's the general manager, Speck Dodson, who's over the station manager, Grady Lunt, who's over all the VPs in the TV station. Both of those guys are hardworking, low-profile, generally okay. Then there's Pepper Cole, VP for sales—you'll find out about him soon enough—and Bob, of course. Jack Polfax you won't ever see—he's engineering VP. Then there's Parnell Jones, VP for news. You two'll have some contact, mostly through Bob. The operations VP you won't see too much. He keeps things running so smooth, there's never any reason to talk to him. I doubt seriously that you'll ever have much contact with the VPs in the field—newspaper and TV—but they're pleasant-enough blokes when they come for regional confabs. The biggies, the ones you want to keep happy, besides Cane, of course, are the senior vice-presidents. You'll know who they are after your first week or two."

"You haven't mentioned any women. You said Cane is interested in getting women involved in upper-level management, but I haven't heard a single woman's name mentioned."

"Well, there's me, of course. I was station manager of the radio part of PDQ until last week, along with doing my show, but that's changed now." Gretchen's smile was big and bright. "More champagne?"

Tally laughed. "You're still not going to let me in on whatever it is that brings out the Cheshire-cat grin every other word. But I'll wait. Tell me about the other women I'll be working with."

"There's Rachel Parmenter. Not an exciting person, but real

salt of the earth. She's executive secretary to Bob Frazier. Plain little thing, but a real whiz at the typewriter. Then there's Eden Thorpe. You'll like Eden. She's sharp, gorgeous, ambitious. Women aren't doing too well in the male-dominated newscast area, but when they do break through, you can look for Eden in the first wave.''

"Cane seems very fond of his secretary. Tell me about her.'' Tally hoped she wasn't young and beautiful.

"Marsha Perkins? You'll love her. She's loyal, smart. Cane adores her.'' Gretchen added with a twinkle, "Marsha's fifty-eight, happily married, and has three grown sons.''

Tally blushed. "You little ole mind reader, you. Now tell me your news before you bust wide open.''

"Get ready for the toast.'' Gretchen refilled their glasses and touched hers to Tally's. "You're now looking at the star of WPDQ-TV's fall-premiering show. From radio's 'Grits and Gretchen' to—ta-da—TV's soon-to-be-syndicated 'Woman Alive!' ''

"Syndicated!'' Tally let out a rebel yell and hugged Gretchen, spilling champagne over both of them. "That's wonderful! Gretchen, I'm so proud of you! You'll be a national star.''

"Wel-l-l, not for a while anyway. Our network will carry the show, of course, but it could be some time before the big boys pick it up. In the meantime, though, I plan to knock that Lovey Carmichael on Channel Ten out of the air. And I'll make that damned executioner Blake Edenfield eat his own shit.''

Tally felt a chill go down her spine. She sat down and put her champagne on the coffee table. "Executioner? Gretchen, are you talking about someone who works at Tri-Com? You didn't mention Blake Edenfield before.''

"That's because I try not to think about him. I don't like him and he doesn't like me. He tried to keep me from getting my own TV show. Somebody told me he said on the 'hill' that I have a big mouth and dinky tits—and would never make it on television.''

"How nasty.''

"He makes it a profession being nasty. He got his nickname

honestly. Blake goes into every property Tri-Com acquires and trims out the deadwood and cuts and shapes to company specifications. You could call him Cane's hatchet man, a lot of people call him worse names than that. But I personally think 'the executioner' suits him best. When Blake Edenfield looks at you, you feel like you've got an invisible X on your neck.''

Tally shuddered. ''He doesn't sound like a very nice man.''

''That's what Cane pays him a big salary for—not to be nice. Sometimes, Cane's looked on as an SOB, too, but he's a *lovable* SOB. Blake Edenfield is not, to put it mildly. Watch your step with him.''

''You're beginning to scare me.''

''That's what makes being in the business world—especially ours—exciting.'' Gretchen's elan was returning and she did a soft-shoe dance around the coffee table, drinking her champagne the while. ''I've got a new show—my very own show! And Blake can go screw himself. Mark my words, women are going to control the airwaves one of these days. I think it's kind of an omen that Lucille Ball is coming back with 'The Lucy Show' this fall, just when 'Woman Alive!' is making its debut. They said she'd never be back again, and Blake, bless 'im, said I'd never get there in the first place.'' Gretchen, not realizing the demons she'd raised with the mention of ''Lucy,'' any Lucy, asked suspiciously, ''Say, you *do* watch television, don't you?''

''Not very much,'' Tally admitted. ''Mama likes 'Ben Casey' and 'Ed Sullivan,' and I've watched those a few times. Maybe I should start watching more, huh?''

Gretchen pondered that. ''I don't know. Maybe not. Cane still likes his newspapers and radios better than the boob tube, even though he realizes it's the wave of the future. He'll never favor television over his precious newspapers.''

''Maybe that's because he started out with them. Like your father did. Gretchen, I don't know about you, but I'm bushed. Will you wake me when you get up?'' Tally stood up and stretched, yawning, then picked up the dirty glasses and now-empty bottle. ''You coming to bed now?''

"Not yet. I want to savor the evening a little longer, maybe top it off with a little brandy." Gretchen moved over to the glass-topped bar that held several elegant decanters. "Sure you won't join me?"

Tally shook her head. "I'll have a glass of milk while I'm setting up the morning coffee." Her head was starting to pound a little from the champagne. "And maybe a couple of aspirin."

She filled the coffeepot and took her milk with her back into the bedroom, along with the classified section of *The Atlanta Constitution*. It was time she started looking for a place of her own. Life around Gretchen was fun and exciting, but could be exhausting.

Maybe Gretchen was used to getting up with a hangover every morning, but Tally wasn't.

The next morning Gretchen was indeed hung over but came to life when Tally asked her advice about what to wear on her first day at Tri-Com. "The black-and-white-check job—the long-jacket thing, yeah, that one—and your black-and-white spectators. Oh, yes. Perfect. Get one of the rosebuds off the patio. Um-hmm. Terrific. No, not the prissy little pearl earrings—the heavy gold loops. You're looking at a glamour job! No Bobbie Brooks or Peter Pan collars—but not too much flash, either." Gretchen groaned as Tally turned on the overhead light so she could check her stockings in the long mirror on the bedroom door. "God! For heaven's sake, get yourself a supply of the seamless nylons. Seams are sexy as hell, but out, out, out!"

"I'll bring you a cup of coffee," Tally said, grateful to her friend for her fashion advice. She felt Gretchen's taste was unerring. When she was back with a steaming mug of coffee, she asked hesitantly, "I know you're getting tired of baby-sitting me through every little thing, but I don't have the slightest idea where Tri-Com's offices are located. Should I take my car?"

"You'd do better catching the bus. It's quicker and easier. When you pass through Big Five Points, watch for Peachtree and Mitchell. Tri-Com's in the tall building right across from the Chamber of Commerce, just up on the left from the Henry Grady Hotel.''

"Darn it, I wish they still had the trolleys. Mama told me how much fun she used to have riding those when she came to Atlanta.'' Gretchen was lying so still Tally leaned down to pull a lock of hair off her face and ask, ''Hey, are you okay? I could run down to the Huddle House for some breakfast and bring it back up before I . . .''

Gretchen groaned and pulled the cover over her head. Her muffled response gave Tally the idea that breakfast was not the ideal suggestion at the moment.

A few minutes later, Tally was aboard the bus and on her way to—what, she wondered?

Personnel had a stack of forms for Tally to fill out. By the time she finished those and was ushered into the office of the man for whom she would be working, the influence of Cane Stephen Foster Winslow was evident. Gretchen's contention that he stayed out of the nitty-gritty details of Tri-Com might very well be true once she started working, but Tally was pretty sure he was behind the warmth with which she was treated by everyone she met.

Still, as Gretchen had pointed out, why not take advantage of having a friend in the castle? And starting at the lowest rung of the career ladder might have been more noble, but it sure as hell wasn't very smart, not if you had a chance to start a few rungs up as she had.

The secretaries she met were carefully friendly. Gretchen had already warned her that the local grapevine was electronically efficient. Tally smiled back at Rachel Parmenter, Bob Frazier's on-air super secretary, when she brought her a cup of coffee. A woman in her late thirties, Rachel was the color of a wren and about as timid. ''Mr. Frazier won't be but a minute. He says to make yourself comfortable. You're getting the full tour, I hope you know.''

Tally suspected that wasn't usual for a brand-new young employee. But Cane had made it clear to her that he expected her to learn her job fast. ''You're going to set the standards

for women in the Tri-Com industry, Tally. Women are going
to start moving up in this kind of business, and I want you to
be right up at the head of the legion.'' Tally sipped her coffee
contentedly as she recalled those words. She liked the picture
of herself scaling the heights previously ordained for men. She
liked the idea of proving herself to the industry, to Lucy Cantrell, to the world—and, above all, to the man who was giving
her the opportunity. She was pretty sure Cane was allowing
her all the rope she needed to either reach her potential—or to
hang herself.

"Miss Malone?" Bob Frazier was there in front of her then.
"I'm sure you've seen my mug on television enough to know
who I am.'' He ran his hand through the mop of white hair that
Gretchen had said was one of his biggest assets. Viewers
trusted broadcasters with silver hair and brown ("dooky-col-
ored,'' as Gretchen had described them) eyes.

Actually, Tally had only watched "Newpoint'' a couple of
times. Gretchen had brought home the three tapes sent in by
the final job candidates so Tally could get an idea of the requi-
sites for becoming a Tri-Com on-air commentator. "Of the
three, Frazier was way out in front. See this one? Too smooth,
like oatmeal. Uses smiles like commas. Not a smidgen of Joe
Pyne. . . . Okay, after Mr. Oatmeal, here's the Good Ole Boy.
Just listen to that south Georgia drawl! Atlanta would murder
us in the ADI ratings if we used this guy. They want Snuffy
Smif on the late-night used-car sales circuit, but not delivering
news commentaries. . . . Now, see how Frazier comes across?
He's abrasive, like Paul Harvey, but creates the intimacy of an
FDR fireside chat. And I happen to know he's stupid as hell,
but his researcher has made him look smart, even using words
you might hear from a Bill Buckley. . . .''

Tally had been fascinated with the "lesson" and was even
more fascinated now that she was with the successful on-air
candidate.

Bob Frazier was smooth as silk, but Tally hadn't been in
his company more than ten minutes before she realized that
Gretchen's estimate of his intellect was too high. She soon met
the person who made the newscaster look good. Eden Thorpe,

Bob's research assistant, was everything Gretchen had said she was—only more so. In addition to being blond, blue-eyed, gorgeous, and stacked like a *Playboy* bunny, she also had a sense of humor.

When Bob introduced Eden to Tally, saying she was the one working up a piece on Princess Grace's new little kingdom, "Morocco," Eden with a wink at Tally mouthed *Monaco.* "That's right, boss. And we're going to let you wear a scarlet-and-black tasseled fez to fit in with the place. How are you?" Eden said with a dazzling smile for Tally. "Glad to have you aboard. Gretchen says you're looking for a place to live. I'll be glad to help you out with that—I used to be in real estate."

Bob Frazier made some kind of crack about all the women in Atlanta being in real estate, but Eden took it good-naturedly. "Don't worry. Once you start doing all his work for him, he'll stop with the suburban-wife jokes. We'll have lunch sometime soon, okay?"

"Great." Tally followed Bob out the door. "She's really nice. Everybody is." She even liked Bob Frazier, for all his bad jokes. The feeling was apparently mutual, for Frazier was soon telling her all about his wife, Kay, and their daughter Jeanne and how much they liked living in the South.

She enjoyed the whirlwind tour Frazier took her on, too. ". . . and here's the control room. Heart of the studio." He tapped on the glass through which Tally could see rows of screens. "Top's for monitoring, bottom's for effect." He rushed her along, then pulled her into another room where he let her listen for a moment to off-camera directions, look at different camera angles, and hear his whispered opinion of which was the most effective angle. "That's our biggest bread-and-butter account. We like to give it our best shot."

"Bread-and-butter?"

"Sponsor ad. Where our bread's buttered. Hey, 'Exercise with Judy' is on its bye-bye. Next week, you'll get to see Gretchen's pilot. She's good, damned good; I don't care what Blake says about her getting too old."

Tally laughed heartily. "Too old? *Gretchen?* Are you kidding me?"

"Honey, you've got a lot to learn about this business. There's the Eric Sevareid kind of old and there's the other kind. And Gretchen will tell you as quick as I can that women aren't allowed to age on television." He dropped his voice to a confidential level. "Maybe she better watch the booze. Blake's out for her ass and if she doesn't cut down on the sauce, he'll have her out so fast she won't know what hit her."

"Cane—Mr. Winslow would never let that happen," Tally said with a hint of indignation.

"Oh no? Cane's all business when it comes to his wallet. And don't let anybody tell you different, Blake Edenfield's sharp as a tack. Cane depends on him, too. There's a story around here that he owes Blake for getting that Texas broad to sell out her interest in Winslow's very first TV acquisition. Just watch your step with the executioner. He's lean and mean— and has the boss behind him almost every time."

Tally was uneasy every time she heard the term "the executioner." She changed the subject. "Is that Judy right over there? Could I meet her and tell her how much I like her show?"

"Best not to bother her. She's busy cussing out a cameraman." Bob laughed. "It's a kick, isn't it, how we on-air folks can be assholes one minute, yelling at the technical director during the bread-and-butters and then stepping out on camera oozing charm all over the place."

Tally watched for a minute as Judy did just that. "I could never do that—not in a million years."

"That's good to hear. I'd hate to think the boss put you to working for me so you could take my job."

Tally shook her head. "I'm still not quite sure what your job is—or mine, for that matter. Could we sit and talk for a while about that?"

"You got it." Bob took her arm and hurried her back to his office. Tally decided that the pace around the station was always going to be dead heat. But she already loved the vibrancy of the place, the feeling of being in the middle of something exciting happening every minute.

"Now . . ." Bob indicated the seat across from his desk

and grinned at her. "About my job. Actually, I wear two hats. I'm the anchor on 'Newpoint,' as you've already seen. In addition to that, I'm vice-president for programming here. Rachel and Eden take care of the first part, you'll be my assistant in my VP part. You know the setup of the station?"

"Not as well as I should. I know this is the model station for the Tri-Com network of five units and that it's part of Tri-Com."

"Right. Now let me explain the programming part. The on-air job doesn't concern you and you've already said you aren't that interested."

"I didn't mean I wasn't interested, I just meant that I—"

"Tallulah—Tally? I want you to know that I have had it up to my eyebrows with fresh young college graduates coming in and pretending they want to do the work they're hired for— the programming work I'm going to tell you about, for instance—when all the while they're just sticking around to be discovered on TV. I've worked with a string of those kids and, believe me, your telling me you don't give a rat's ass about being on-air is the best thing you could've said. I love ya already. Now . . . where was I?"

"You were describing your job as programming vice-president."

"I'm getting to that. My job, simply put, is taking care of purchasing or arranging for all the programs on our station. Seventy percent are network, about thirty percent we buy or produce. It's our job to keep up with first-run syndication, off-network reruns, et cetera, et cetera. You're looking at the guy who's in charge of the air talent, the producers, and the writers—but only to an administrative degree. Actually, I've found out that those people, for the most part, do better running themselves."

Maybe, Tally decided, Bob Frazier was not stupid at all. He had obviously figured out, as she had, that Cane Winslow had deliberately put her in an administrative apprenticeship under him—and wasn't unhappy at the thought. She had an idea that Bob would very gladly relinquish the "second-hat" position if his more glamorous on-air job turned into what he wanted.

By the end of the day, Tally felt as if she had been at work a month. She was the last one in the office simply because she felt the need to catch her breath before she went home to all of Gretchen's questions.

The phone on Rachel's desk rang and Tally hesitated before answering it. Well, hell, I work here, don't I? she thought. "Hello. This is Bob Frazier's office, Tally Malone speaking."

"I hoped you'd still be here. I didn't want to break your damn rule, but I haven't been able to concentrate all day for thinking about you being six floors beneath my office. Do you think it would bother anyone if you came up to my office and gave me a personal report of your first day on the job? I am president of the company, after all, and I like to keep up with things outside my ivory tower."

Tally laughed softly. "I'm sure you do this with all your new employees, Mr. Winslow. Very well, I really would like to thank you in person for giving me the job. Where's your ivory tower?"

Cane's laugh could barely contain his joy. He had almost expected Tally to say no. "Take the elevator just down the hall from you, go to seven, and hang a right. Mine's the office at the end of the hall." Maybe he could talk her into dinner since it was her first day, Cane thought happily. "Marsha?" His secretary stuck her well-groomed head in his office. "You can finish that report tomorrow. Go home and cook George a big dinner for a change." He was always teasing Marsha about the way her husband pampered her.

"George is out of town and I'm waiting for Gretchen to call. She wants me to meet her for a drink to celebrate her show."

"Gretchen and her celebrating," Cane said with a grin. At the sound of the elevator door opening and shutting, he said, "Marsha, in about two seconds you are going to lay eyes on Tallulah Fontaine Malone, the princess of Moss Island that I told you about."

Marsha raised her eyebrow. She had never seen Cane look quite so boyishly happy. "I've heard already that Programming's crazy about her."

So am I, Cane thought. Then he was looking at Tally and

everything he'd planned to say went right out of his head. He was glad it was Marsha who was witnessing his first meeting with Tally since her graduation night. His secretary might be surprised at the way Cane was acting, but she would never say anything to anyone about it.

"God, you look wonderful," he said finally. "Isn't she beautiful, Marsha? And smart—this girl carried a three point eight all the way through college, I want you to know."

"No wonder Cane is so thrilled to have you here," Marsha said with a smile, holding out her hand to Tally. "Marsha Perkins, Tally. Welcome to Tri-Com. Sometime when Gretchen and I are lunching, you'll have to join us."

"I'd like that very much." Tally turned back to Cane, not knowing quite what to do next. The way he was looking at her made her think he might hug her, and she wasn't sure she could keep her resolve about staying cool if he did.

The phone rang and Marsha excused herself to answer it. Cane asked Tally softly, "So how do you like us so far?"

Tally's eyes shone. Her enthusiasm was sincere. "Oh, Cane, I love it already. How can I ever thank you for giving me a job at Tri-Com?" She blushed as soon as the words were out.

Cane's satanic eyebrow lifted. "Perhaps in six months or so I might be able to think of something."

"Tally." Marsha covered the telephone mouth. "Gretchen wants you to join us. We're having drinks and maybe dinner at the Top o' the Mart. She says it's a good way for you to get a view of our wonderful city at night."

"Why . . ." Tally wondered if it was politic to dine with the boss's secretary the first day on a job. She thought back to her office-protocol class. *The most direct line to a powerful executive is through his secretary*. Tally could remember the dictum word for word. "I'd love it."

While Marsha was busy reporting back to Gretchen, Cane said a little grumpily, "I thought you came up here to see me."

"Eden Thorpe is joining us, too," Marsha reported cheerfully after she'd hung up. "She just rang up at Gretchen's to see if you were home yet, Tally. She says she thinks she's got a place for you—on Ponce de Leon, across from Caruso's. It's in an old house, but Eden says she thinks you'll love it. We'll run by there and look at it after dinner.''

Cane shook his head and looked at Tally. "Are you sure you've only been here since this morning?"

Tally laughed, happy about everything. Even Cane's obvious pique at not having her to himself was titillating. She told him, "It feels like six months."

Tally thanked Eden the next day for her lead about a place to live. She described it to Rachel Parmenter, "I love it! It's got three huge rooms and the funniest old-fashioned tub you ever saw. If I can find the right kind of stuff to furnish it with, it'll be charming."

Eden promised to help her scour the secondhand stores, saying she would drive Tally out to Kimbrough's in Buckhead the first time they could take a lunch hour together.

By the end of her second week at WPDQ, Tally was in the Ponce de Leon apartment. She had Gretchen and Eden over for dinner and showed her new digs off with great pride. The mix of Victorian pieces that she had bought for next to nothing blended beautifully with the worn orientals and high, ornate ceilings of the old apartment, as did the scarred round oak table and painted captain's chairs she'd picked up. A miraculously intact set of Blue Onion china made the simple meal of spaghetti festive; Gretchen had brought along a large jug of Chianti.

By the time her guests had left, Tally was in a state of happy exhaustion. After she'd cleared the dishes and made herself a cup of Ovaltine, she went to the window seat overlooking busy Ponce, which was already her favorite sitting place.

All in all, it had been a great two weeks. Bob had shown very quickly that he was all too ready to turn over the administrative part of his job to someone capable. Discovering that Tally was a fast study, he very quickly left as many details as he could to his new assistant. Since Eden and Rachel were both too busy with their on-air responsibilities to do more than lend moral support, Tally soon found herself learning on her own.

And learn she did. She picked everybody's brains, starting

with Speck Dodson, the general manager and friendly Saint Bernard of a man, who took a great liking to Tally. Through him, she got to be friends with Grady Lunt, the station manager, who provided as much patient advice as actual help in Tally's first few weeks.

She quickly wrote off Pepper Cole, head of sales, as a fanny-pincher whose reputation for sleeping with female time-buyers was well-known. Parnell Jones, the news director, was too kinetic and busy trying to beat deadlines to be bothered with a new trainee, as was Robin Harris, who ran the physical operations of the station.

Tally watched Bob Frazier in action, listened to everybody she could, and then gradually began taking over her boss's programming duties. She opened his mail, answered letters from viewers or routed them to the proper person. She gave orders on new programs, tentatively at first, and then, as she learned scheduling procedures, more confidently. Phone calls from viewers came in incessantly. Rachel began turning over the more delicate ones to Tally. Eden explained to Tally over lunch one day that was because Rachel had had a very religious, strict upbringing and still wasn't used to some of the language.

Bob happily spent his freed-up time trying to upgrade his show. He was worried about it. Tally was made aware of her value to him when he came to her with his problem. After flinging himself down in a chair across from Tally's desk, he started in glumly. "All right. Let's have it. What's wrong? The ratings have plateaued after that first giant leap right after I took over the show. I know you never miss my show and watch it like a hawk. The executioner's already sent me one of his famous little 'Can we talk?' memos and I may be in deep shit."

"You won't get mad if I tell you what I really think's wrong?" At Bob's gloomy head shake, she leaned forward eagerly. "I think 'Newpoint' ought to have its own separate impact—not be so much a local recap of the news people have already heard from the big guys."

"I don't know what you mean. 'Separate impact'?"

"I mean that you ought to take a local issue that relates to the national issues—like that Mrs. Doughty from Marietta who's going over to China to try to get her missing son back—and milk it for every ounce of its emotional impact. You've got the soapers watching you. They love any kind of drama. They love to cry.''

"Hear, hear" came a dry voice from the doorway. "You're full of good ideas, little lady. You told Gretchen that Atlanta was ready to talk openly about birth control, and it worked. Biggest ADI rating after that show we've had this year.''

Tally turned slowly to see a tall man with the coldest gray eyes she had ever seen. It was her first glimpse of Blake Edenfield, Tri-Com's executive vice-president, otherwise known as the executioner.

16

Tally's initial encounter with Blake Edenfield was, she was certain, responsible for some of the positive reports she got through the grapevine. It seemed that Edenfield had been impressed for some reason and was quietly smoothing the way for her progress. Bob Frazier's dependence on her had already made her intense concentration on learning her job a necessity. Now that became a plus as more and more calls from the Hill were directed to Tally instead of to her boss.

Bob was good-natured about it. He brought up the subject over lunch at Herrin's, where Tally had taken him for his National Boss Week freebie lunch. "Honey, I hear the rumbles and they're all saying your name. Word is that the big guy has been keeping up with you like a duck on a june bug, and that even ole Blake thinks you're hot shit.''

Tally made a face at her stuffed avocado. "Thanks—I think. But let's be honest. Now that 'Newpoint' has taken off like gangbusters, any fool can plainly see that you don't have time for much else.''

"Yeah." Bob wiped his chin and beamed over at two women who were obviously from out of town and had recognized him.

They were nudging each other and giggling like schoolgirls. "That idea I had for doing a whole series on Mrs. Doughty and other mothers of sons missing in Asia who are trying to get their boys back really took off. Blake says I may come out with some kind of award at the ADDY convention next spring."

Tally hid a smile behind her napkin. Let Bob Frazier have his fantasy of being the one to have come up with the idea of the Doughty story. She was perfectly content adding to his success in that area—so he would leave her alone to wrestle with the job she really wanted. "Wouldn't surprise me. But, Bob, that idea you had for a program on the unwed mothers of Georgia . . ." Tally's eyes met her boss's with clear innocence, though she was lying in her teeth. "Eden and I did some preliminary stuff and it's no-go. Seems we could get our pants sued if we did it, even with the mothers' faces blacked out on the show."

Bob's beaming smile dimmed. "Aww. I had a lot of ideas for that show. We coulda followed up with one on the birth-control clinic in New Haven they closed down. Think of the fire and brimstone we would've stirred up on that one around here! But oh, the mileage I could've got from a story about poor, pitiful, pregnant girls toughing it out in the unwed mothers' home. Couldn't you just see 'em, all crying every time I asked 'em anything about what it felt like to give up a baby or even if I looked at 'em straight?"

"It's not a feasible idea," Tally said with a menacing softness that Bob was too self-engrossed to notice. "Besides the legal risks of invasion of privacy, there's another problem. One of our biggest sponsors is on the board out at the Home, and he says 'nix.' Too emotional an issue. It could backfire on the folks that have worked hard to keep discretion and privacy a big part of the unwed mothers' program in Georgia."

"You have a way of taking the fun out of things for me. Are you springing for dessert, or is that all I can have?"

"Tri-Com is not paying me one-third as much as you get," Tally said, gathering up the check and her bag. *Not yet*, she thought fiendishly. "Even though I do six times the work."

"Awww, come off it, Malone. You know good and well that my ulcers from that damned show make up for . . ." Bob followed her out, bickering, but stopped at the table of his admirers to bestow silvery thanks for their gushing compliments. Tally watched him from the check-out register, her face wearing a careful smile that concealed what she was thinking about the inequities of life.

But she was not bitter about the fact that her salary was paltry next to her boss's, even though she performed most of his programming VP duties and many of his other related jobs. One of these days he would give up the programming and she would be running the show—and at a hefty salary, too.

One of the perks that the on-air personalities enjoyed was one that Blake Edenfield had implemented at the beginning of his career with Tri-Com. Everyone heading a television program was required to take at least a three-day vacation from the air every six months. Bob Frazier did not consider this "uncivilized" practice a benefit. He groaned to Rachel, Eden, and Tally when he was winding up his day prior to spending a long weekend at West Palm Beach, Florida. "That cold-eyed bastard does this to keep us humble and make us realize we're replaceable. I hate coming back to a cold audience."

"But you'll come back fresh and suntanned," Eden sang out.

"There's something about a suntan in January that's obscene," Bob grumbled. "Who's my replacement, anyway? That turd from the weather forecast?"

Tally and Eden exchanged grins. "Nope," Tally said cheerfully. "It's Eden."

"Eden!" Bob's sunny visage took on the aspects of a thunderhead. "What the hell does Winslow think he's doing?"

"According to all reports," Rachel Parmenter piped up, "he's real interested in bringing women into the fore in the industry." She rolled a new sheet of paper into her typewriter and started typing. "Could be that they'll have me out there doing the sportscast next. Ever taken a look at that 'Coach Thursday' they've got doing the predicts for all the games on WTNT?"

"You don't have the legs for it," Bob growled, glaring at all of them as he closed his briefcase and tossed his London Fog over his arm. "Well, I'll be back in my office Thursday. That is, if I have an office when I get back," he said, looking straight at Tally Malone.

The three women waited until Bob was gone before bursting into laughter. "Boy, did we have him going!" Eden touched her carefully made-up eyes and patted the blond chignon that never had a hair out of place. Tally had videotaped her the week before, allegedly running her through a dummy broadcast of the weekend 'Newpoint' show. In fact, Tally had had a deeper motive behind the taping. "Can you imagine *me* going on the show for ole Bob?" Eden said.

"Oh, yes," Tally said with a smile. "In fact, it wasn't a joke on 'ole Bob.' Cane Winslow approved the substitution two days ago. Blake Edenfield came to me and asked who I thought should sub for Bob and I told him that you were a natural."

Eden stared at Tally, the color draining from her face, the pale blue eyes big as saucers. "You told him *what?* Tally, you've got to be kidding! Why, I'll shit in my drawers right in front of all those people."

"No, you won't," Tally told her calmly. "You'll stand up there and use those spooky pale eyes of yours to hypnotize everybody in the audience. I've watched Pauline Fredericks a zillion times. By the way, why not copy her diamond-horseshoe-pin bit and wear your mother's cameo? You've got that same classy presence she's got. Don't turn your back on this, Eden. They've hidden your bushel under a stack of old research for way too long, and I, for one, think it's time you broke out."

Eden's shoulders under the tailored navy suit (that never, Tally had noticed, hid the fact that the blond girl was really stacked) straightened. "I think you mixed a couple of metaphors there, Tally. But hell, what do I care? You really think I can handle it?"

"Cane does, too," Tally said with a smile. "My vote doesn't mean much, but damned if his doesn't carry some weight."

"Rachel?"

The secretary didn't look up from her smoking typewriter but said, "You'll put the Ipana Kid in the shade. Will one of you get that phone while I get the other one?"

Tally fielded the one from an irate viewer who said that the collarbone exposed by Gretchen Lee on "Woman Alive!" had been offensive. Eden whispered, after Tally's creamy voice had finally said good-bye, "My God, how do you keep from telling those assholes where to go?"

"Their uncles could be FCC regulators," Tally told her unperturbedly. The caller had wound up calling Tally a "cunt with a crack that a Mack truck could probably turn around in," which made her have strong doubts that the collarbone exposure had been a serious problem for him. "Is that one for me, too?" she asked Rachel, who was waiting for the end of the exchange between the other two women.

"It's Marsha Perkins," Rachel mouthed, holding her hand over the receiver. "Wanta take it in there? The big boss's secretary doesn't go for conference calls."

Tally nodded and retreated into Bob Frazier's office to take the call from Marsha. Cane's executive secretary and Tally had not had much time to develop a social relationship beyond the occasional friendly lunch or drink after work. Still, they liked each other and stayed in touch.

From the first moment of conversation, Tally knew Marsha had something more on her mind than inviting her for a drink. There was the usual polite southern ritual of exchange, which warmed up when Marsha mentioned a sale of eclectic junk she'd heard about. She knew Tally was always on the prowl for new ways to liven up her apartment. Then Marsha congratulated Tally on the contract she had signed at the end of her trial six-month period of employment. "Cane has heard very good things about you, my dear; I hope you know that. And Gretchen was by here today. Goodness gracious, how long has it been since we've all gotten together?"

"Too long. We'll have to do something about that. Soon." Tally waited.

"Well, we will. We just will. But right now there's something else I need to ask you about."

Tally knew that. She held her breath until Marsha said in her Wesleyan College, soft southern voice, "Cane has asked me to ask a favor of you for this weekend. He wonders if you would take my place as his official hostess at the dinner he's having at his new house." At Tally's silence, Marsha added hurriedly, "But, Tally, if you've already made plans . . ."

"I haven't really," Tally lied. She would think of some excuse for Mrs. Cagle at Autumn Oaks to pass on to Genevieve Malone. Surely Tally didn't have to sacrifice every weekend to making sure that her mother was well-cared for and happy. "Well, nothing that's founded in concrete. What's the deal?"

"There's a conference in town that some very important newspaper publishers are attending—a few whose papers are negotiating with Tri-Com. And there are at least three state senators and one Washington biggie expected to come to the party." Marsha's voice became even more confidential. "You know how hard Cane tries to work at keeping those folks on our side."

"I've heard." In fact, Tally had heard that Cane Winslow had provided the oil to smooth out several squeaks in the political wheel. "I've heard, too, about what great parties the boss gives. Why aren't you going yourself?"

"Oh, I would, of course, but my son's flying in from Texas for just that night. The dear is in helicopter school out there, and I worry day and night about him. They say it's so dangerous, and, of course . . ."

Tally didn't hear the rest of what Marsha said. Her mind was tripping over the painful memory of Nick Cantrell. And as a matter of course, that thought triggered images of their daughter being raised by the woman she hated most in the world. "I'll call you in the morning, Marsha, to get more details—about what to wear and everything. I have to go now."

Pepper Cole stuck his head in to ask her about the available local time spots and Tally snapped at him, "Why didn't you get to Bob on that before he left? I'm sick to death of everybody protecting him from the shit around here and dumping it on me instead!'' With that, she got her bag and new leather jacket and left for home, after only the briefest good-nights to the girls in the office.

"What's with her?" Pepper asked Eden Thorpe. "Did I say something?"

"You never have, to my knowledge," Eden replied, not looking up from the notes she was making on the idea she and Bob had been working on for the weekend show. Now that she would be doing it, she had decided on a few changes. "Maybe she didn't want to be trapped by a known sex maniac."

"Cute. Say, did either of you guys hear the one about the . . ."

"Pepper." Eden stuck her pencil behind her ear and her formidable bust in front of the sales manager's nose. "You know how they're always tearing up Peachtree Street and there are those signs that say 'Men Working'? Well, substitute the word 'women' and move the sign mentally to right here." Eden clicked the glass window with a long nail at the same time that she opened the outside door with a flourish. "Don't let us keep you from your futile efforts at selling a little time on our local spots."

The protesting sales manager was evicted and Eden came back brushing her hands dramatically. She asked Rachel, "Did you hear anything?"

The secretary smiled and nodded. "Every word. That was Marsha, the boss's secretary, talking to her. Tally's gonna be on show Saturday at Jade Tree."

Eden's face lit up. "She's made it! Do you know what that means?"

"It means one of two things. He's after her body—or he's seriously planning to groom her for Bungling Bob's job as VP for Programming, which she already does anyhow."

"Or maybe both. Oooo! I'm so excited about everything around here right now! Things are sure looking up for the womenfolks for a change." Eden hugged herself expressively, squeezed her bountiful bosom, while Rachel looked on enviously. "I have a feeling our Tallulah is on the move. Up."

Tally let herself be talked into having Mister Craig, one of Atlanta's foremost hairdressers, do her hair for Cane's party. After he had finished dressing Tally's long thick locks (amid much oohing and aahing over their texture), she took one look in the mirror and nearly burst out laughing. The huge, teased, lacquered mess made her look as though she were wearing a dried hornet's nest on her head. Very solemnly, she paid her bill and caught a taxi outside on the busy Peachtree corner.

She looked at her watch. She would have just time enough to wash out the mess and get dressed before she was expected at the house on Habersham Road.

Cane Winslow's home was not at all what Tally had expected. She knew that he had moved from his penthouse to a place he'd had custom-built, but she had assumed it would be one of the white-columned "Tara" look-alikes that abounded in Atlanta's finger-bowl district.

Jade Tree, as Tally learned the estate was called, was as far from the typical southern-mogul dwelling as any residence could be. It was a pentagon cluster of separate glass-and-stone units linked by gardens, walkways, bridges, decks, and pools. Tally had never seen anything like it.

Blake Edenfield joined her as she stood on an arched bridge that crossed one of the many little pools. The bronze fountain statue in the middle looked very old. "It is old," Blake said, when Tally commented on the piece. "I asked Cane about it at the housewarming he had when he first moved in here. You wouldn't believe how patient he was negotiating for that art. Cane's determination about getting what he wants is legendary. So is his good taste." At this, Blake's attention was switched from the statue to the woman beside him.

Tally could feel Blake's gaze sweeping over her like a cold gray searchlight. She pulled her coat around her, and knew it wasn't only because of the sudden chill in the air. "Yes, Mr.

Winslow does have exquisite taste. Look . . . do you suppose
that's the jade tree?'' Tally pointed at the beautiful shrub whose
natural sculpture was marked by sharp green thorny limbs. She
turned to the man beside her, not giving him time to respond.
''I gather you've been here many times. Does it surprise you
that I'm here at Cane's party?''

Blake's thin lips emulated a smile. ''I notice you dropped
the rather pompous 'Mr. Winslow' bit. Good for you. Everyone
knows how far you go back with the Man. Too far to refer to
him by his last name.''

He lit a cigarette, cupping the light against the cool April
breeze that had sprung up and eyeing his companion in the
reflection. ''Let's go in—the weather's changing.'' He took
her elbow and led her through the entrance hall. ''Thank God
you have the good sense not to wear your hair in those ridiculous wasp nests or whatever they're called. And whoever made
that dress you're wearing should be given a designer's award.''
In fact, Reba had copied the simple black dress with its collar
of rhinestones from a *Vogue* cutout Tally had sent her along
with the material and money. ''You're very beautiful, Tallulah
Fontaine Malone. A number of people have speculated about
how far you will go in your job.''

The innuendo made color rise to Tally's cheeks, and she
didn't notice the surprising use of her middle name. ''As far
as hard work and devotion to the company will take me, Mr.
Edenfield.''

''Blake, are you harassing this beautiful girl?'' The silver-
haired man who joined them flagged down a servant with a
tray of champagne. ''Cane sent me to fetch you two. He was
getting worried that you might be bogged down in business
talk.''

Cane was waiting for her when they entered the central
module of the complex. ''Well, at last! Two of my most indispensable cogs in the Tri-Com wheel.''

''I'm a very little one,'' Tally reminded him with a smile.

''But you've got Tri-Com stock, don't you, pretty girl?''
Judson Dole, the silver-haired president of one of the largest
insurance companies in the country, winked at Tally. ''The

rumor's been going around that the stock could split two for one most any day now."

Cane took Tally's half-filled glass and placed it on a table. She decided that was her signal to pay close attention to what was being said. Two other important-looking men had wandered up and Tally was pretty sure it wasn't just to look down the front of her dress. "Now, Judson, don't be spreading stories like that. Hell, Tri-Com didn't go public till last year," Cane said.

"Yeah," said the latest newcomer, a chubby-faced man whom Tally recognized from the business section of *The Atlanta Constitution*. Darwin Redwine was rumored to be negotiating for the Milwaukee Braves and to have his finger in every financial pie in the Southeast. "What is it you own now? Fifty newspapers in sixteen towns, six radio stations . . ."

"Fifty-two newspapers," Tally corrected him firmly. "And seven radio stations. But still only *two* VHF stations."

"Tell 'im, Tallulah," Blake murmured as all eyes turned to her with surprise, including Cane's.

"What's this I hear—a voice in the newspaper-and-radio wilderness?"

Tally squared her shoulders and waded in. "Everybody at Tri-Com knows that the newspaper side of the business has your heart, with radio next in line. They know darned good and well that you feel WPDQ is your Bible in the whorehouse, so to speak." Tally acknowledged the ripple of male laughter with a ladylike smile. "But a lot of us at the station think you're making a big mistake ignoring the impact of television, especially in the South. Look at the opportunity you've got in Atlanta. For the first time since Reconstruction, we've got a shot at beating New York to something big. TV is going to take the place of all the other media in *everything*—news, entertainment, advertising, the whole ball of wax. Why not let the South, for once, be the leader of the pack?"

"Hear, hear," someone with a Southern drawl said softly. "The little lady's got something there. Color TV's gonna be where it's at as sure as shootin'."

Cane's eyes were steady on Tally's face. She noticed that he hadn't offered a yea or nay on what she had said, in fact, had not even opened his mouth since she'd opened hers to give her opinion. Maybe she'd put her new I. Magnins in her mouth on this one. . . .

Gretchen came up just then and all the men graciously paid homage to Atlanta's new local talk-show hostess. Only Darwin Redwine didn't lose his thoughtful contemplation of the young woman in black who'd spoken her piece in a group of combined centuries of business acumen. Finally, he asked her softly, "You a poor relation to Winslow? That where that feisty spirit of yours comes from?"

"Not exactly—I'm poor, but not related." Tally looked down at herself and then back at the immaculate millionaire with a rueful laugh. "Golly, does it stick out all that much? I thought I cleaned up for this shindig pretty nice."

Darwin Redwine's eyes twinkled. "You don't fool a cracker from scuffletown—not much, you don't. I just forked over three thousand big ones for the original of that dress you're wearing—for my wife, mind you, and it come straight from Paris, France."

"Uh-oh," Tally clucked sympathetically.

"What I mean to say is, a woman don't copy an original dress 'less she's trying real hard to cover up that she don't have the money for the original. So you're looking to get rich at Tri-Com."

"Yes," Tally said, not beating around the bush. "I'm putting every penny I can put my hands on into profit-sharing—employee stock options."

"Smart girl, but you'll be older'n Moses 'fore you realize any real profit, 'less you put a heap more in before the first split. It's like Coca-Cola. Everybody's grandma and grandpa in Georgia, to hear people tell it, had a chance once to invest in Coca-Cola stock and be millionaires. Well, you're in on the ground floor with this Tri-Com deal."

"But I don't have much money, as you've already noticed."

"Get it." At Tally's look of chagrin, the man smiled. "You got to have it to get it, that's what you think—right?" At Tally's nod, Darwin Redwine shook his head. "Wrong. You can buy undeveloped property without a pot to pee in. Now, how'd you feel about acting as my agent and partner in a little deal that could make us both a bunch of money?''

Tally shook her head, not knowing whether she was being teased or if he was on the level. She and Darwin Redwine were off by themselves now and she caught Cane Winslow watching her with the older man, his eyes full of amused curiosity. "Why would you pick me for something like that?"

"Because you're a smart little cookie and I like you. Besides, I'm on Cane's board and I like to know what's going on in that place. You strike me as being someone I could call up now and again to find out what's happening at Tri-Com—I mean, belowstairs where the real shit happens.''

"Mr. Redwine, I don't think I—''

"I ain't asking you to be a spy or anything like that. Hell, no. I just like having a little inside edge in the companies I invest in.''

Tally thought hard. She looked up and met Cane's gaze from across the room, and at his almost imperceptible nod, cleared her throat and said to Darwin Redwine, "All right. What is it you want me to do?"

The future baseball-team owner picked off a couple of drinks from a passing tray before he told her.

"Can I give you a lift home?" Blake Edenfield was one of the last of the Tri-Com executives to leave. Tally was pretty sure he had been waiting around until she was alone so he could offer her a ride. He didn't know that she had her car.

"I'm sorry, Blake, but there's a job I have for you to do before you can go home." Cane appeared at Tally's elbow just a moment after Blake did. "I'll see to it that Tally gets home tonight. Will you excuse Blake and me for a moment, Tally?"

Tally walked over to study the painting over the fireplace. Someone had said earlier that it was a Matisse or a Gauguin, she wasn't sure, but it meant nothing to her. Maybe it was time she took one of those art courses that the High Museum offered people like herself. . . .

"Like it?" Cane had come up and stood beside her. "It cost me a fortune, but it's worth it.''

Tally wasn't interested in discussing Cane's art acquisition. She was more interested in the underlying bidding levels that had been part of the evening's currents. "What on earth could you have the executioner doing for you this time of night?"

Cane poured them both a brandy from the decanter on the bar behind the sofa. "So you've heard Blake's nickname. He's amused by it—likes it, as a matter of fact." He handed her a snifter and took his own around and sat on the sofa. "He's doing me a rather nefarious favor, one I couldn't ask just anyone to take care of for me. Blake's an SOB, but a discreet one. He'll get that case of Jack Daniel's smuggled into a certain legislator's room at the Grady with nary a trace back to me or Tri-Com."

Tally was shocked. She sat down next to Cane, her knees together as prim as a little girl's. "You're bribing one of the state legislators? For God's sake, Cane, that's illegal. Immoral, too."

Cane shrugged. "Nobody's asking him for anything. We just want him to be happy when he votes on the branch-banking issue. One of our board members who backs Tri-Com's local acquisitions doesn't want the national big boys coming in and swallowing up his statewide banks—that's all." He laughed. "Now, it's your turn. What was Redwine bending your ear about?"

"You gave me the idea that you wanted me to go along with whatever he wanted me to do," Tally told him. Maybe she had misconstrued Cane's signal.

"I did. Darwin is one of those board members who enjoy snooping around the company and think they're pulling things over on me. I trust you to handle him and feed him the right 'scoops.' "

"Honestly! You're worse than he is. Why is everyone at Tri-Com suddenly zeroing in on me, Girl-Nothing?"

Cane reached over and touched a lock of hair that had fallen across one bare shoulder. "Because you're so adorable when you're serious about what you're saying . . . so, tell me, what did Darwin want from you? Besides a few inside tidbits from time to time and maybe a crack at that gorgeous body?"

Tally tossed back her hair away from his hand. Her back

went up at the "adorable" bit and the insinuation that Darwin
Redwine might have been out to get in her pants. "It sounds
legal, but I still don't know why he would pick me to do this
piece of business for him." Tally told Cane what the financier
had proposed and he listened intently before he responded,
with all former levity gone from his voice.

"He's right about that tract out near Roswell Road being a
gold mine when the new interstate plat hits the drawing board.
As for it going cheap at the auction Saturday and the sealed
bid you're making for him locking up the deal . . ." Cane
shook his head thoughtfully. "I don't know. Those bids are
supposed to be on the up and up. But I'd bet on Darwin being
ten bucks over the high one. Hell, he owns half of downtown
Atlanta and most of Sandy Springs. I say, go for it! What sort
of deal did he cut you?"

"He offered me thirty percent commission when the resale
goes through." Tally couldn't see any flaws in the deal but she
was still unsure about Darwin Redwine's motives.

Cane reassured her. "He's too well-known, Tally, that's
why he's using a shill like you. It's like Nick the Greek getting
an Albuquerque housewife to place a bet for him in Vegas. If
word got out about Redwine or one of his known associates
showing up at that auction Saturday, the smell of money would
draw every real estate entrepreneur in the state. He's apparently
oiled some cogs to keep the sale low-keyed—and when you
outbid the highest bidder, plus have the sealed bid in the bag
. . ." Cane made a circle of approval with his forefinger and
thumb. Then he looked at Tally speculatively. "You can come
out with a stash, honey. What do you plan to do with all that
money? Buy yourself a mansion?"

Tally just smiled. "Oh, I don't know—maybe so."

She knew very well what she would do with her cut of this
deal once it was actually in her bank account. She would buy
Tri-Com stock as if it were going out of style. She stood up,
feeling suddenly very excited. "Cane, I really ought to go
now. Unless you have something else for me to do."

Cane looked at her without smiling at her little joke. "I'm
not ready for you to leave yet," he said.

"Cane, it's getting awfully late," Tally said, her heart starting to beat furiously.

"You're damn right it is," Cane said, getting up and walking toward her. "Don't you know what tonight is? It's your six-month anniversary. And I have very special plans for how we'll celebrate it."

"Marsha Perkins set me up," Tally said, her voice accusing, but her heart not in the accusation. "She probably doesn't even have a son coming in from Texas."

"Oh yes, she does," Cane said with a diabolical smile. "I happen to be a good friend of the commander at the Lackland base. Marsha was so thrilled when she found out her boy was flying into Atlanta unexpectedly that she was just too flustered to think who to get to take her place tonight."

"But you had a couple of suggestions," Tally said weakly.

"One," Cane told her softly. "And now I'm about to make another one."

17

"You look surprised," Cane said as he expertly folded over the omelet he was making for them in his perfectly equipped kitchen. "Surprised because you thought I was going to attack you—and didn't—or because I'm a great cook?"

"That's a can't-win-either-way kind of question, Mr. Winslow. I choose the 'great cook' option. If your eggs are anything near as delicious as your coffee, I'll totally overlook any other misbegotten intentions on your part." Tally took a deep, satisfying sip of her Luzianne and closed her eyes in contentment. It was almost like being back at Camellia Hall in the good-smelling kitchen where Essie Mae ruled with a cinnamon scepter. She was feeling terribly sentimental and just the teeniest bit tipsy. "How'd you know I've been craving a pot of home-brewed chicory coffee ever since I got to Atlanta?"

Cane put two pieces of bread in the toaster and went back to his omelet. "Don't even think about it, Socrates," he warned his Great Dane, who was eyeing the toaster as though it were a geyser expected to erupt bones at any second. "I got to liking chicory myself with all those visits down to Moss." He brought out two plates and deftly divided the omelet, then buttered the toast. "Want to eat here in the kitchen, or shall I impress you with the formal dining room?"

"I'd like it right here," Tally told him. She dived into the food with an appetite that she had no idea she had; he *was* a good cook!

"More ripple, ma'am?"

Tally laughed. "I've been off to the silver-spoon schools, remember. That cracker jive don't cut it with me." She held out her glass for Cane to refill with the Pouilly-Fuissé that was, she recognized from the label, a very, very good year. "Don't mind if I do."

They didn't talk until the omelet had been devoured along with the wine and two more cups of coffee each, then Cane said, as Tally started gathering up the dishes, "Leave those. There's so much you and I need to talk about. Let's go back to the fire and have a brandy. And then I want to know what you think about Lucy's adopted daughter, about how Vieve is doing out at that nursing home—and why the hell you haven't been back to the island since you left for Savannah and then school."

That was a lot to cover, Tally decided after she had her brandy and was settled in front of the painting. "Should you hang it over the fireplace like that? I mean, it being such a valuable painting and all?" she asked into the silence that had fallen between them. "Matisse, someone said."

"Not Matisse—Gauguin," Cane said a little impatiently. "He couldn't get the women of his island out of his system any more than I can. Maybe that's why I had to have that piece of work." He got up and poked at the fire, then turned to poke at Tally. "All right, enough hedging, enough beating around the bush about everything in the world except what's on both of our minds. Tally, I want the whole story—about what happened between you and Lucy. What could happen so terrible that neither of you could bear to be on the same island together

again?'' He sat down by her, his eyes drilling into her like
holes burning a blanket. "Was it Nick? Did she blame you for
him going off like that and getting himself shot down in never-
never land? Was that it? Or was it Harm? He always had a soft
spot for your mom, then for you. He bought you that car. Was
there something there that Lucy couldn't stomach? Dammit,
girl, talk. I'm not kin to you, but I'm family, and I know
something's been eating at you for years now. Something that
has a lot to do with Lucy, Nick, or some damn body on that
island you called home and now won't even visit.''

Tally was paralyzed with a pain of the homesickness she had
denied so long she hadn't known it existed. "I keep in touch
with Reba. Jim-Roy, too, though he hates writing letters. But
he did write to me that Potlikker died of old age and that he
buried him right next to Junior. Reba says F'Mollie's little girl
is the same age as Lucy's Amalie and that they play together
just like Reba and I used to growing up.''

Cane could tell that she was on the verge of tears. He said
more softly, "For all her faults, Lucy loved that boy of hers.
And now—they say she dotes on that little girl, whoever she
is.''

He got up, fortunately missing Tally's reaction to his words
and having no way of knowing those words had turned a knife
in her heart. "She sent some pictures—a birthday party or
something.'' When he came back, he was holding out the
pictures, and Tally had to battle the paralysis before putting
out her hand to take the photos. It took great effort to look at
a smiling Lucy with Tally's own child, aged four.

"She's . . . beautiful. She's just beautiful,'' she managed,
her eyes soaking up the image of her daughter and imprinting
it on her mind forever. She knew Cane was watching her with
odd intentness, but she didn't care. She could have sat there
gazing at the face of her beautiful little girl forever. "Essie
Mae told me when I talked to her a month ago that she's as
smart as a whip, that she's already reading better than the
second graders, and that she can swim like a fish.'' Her voice
cracked. "Wherever Lucy got her, she's a little doll.''

"Tally, surely you can't look at that picture and not admit the truth that's obvious to anybody who knows the family."

Tally's heart beat a terrified tattoo. *How could Cane know? Had Lucy told him?* "The truth?" she stammered.

"Yes, the truth. Anybody with rat sense could look at this picture and know whose kid it is." His brown finger jabbed at the photo. "Look at that poochy little mouth—just like Lucy's. Look at those baby-blue eyes—Lucy's, all over again. And look at the chin. If that's not Lucy's chin, I'll eat my hat. But it's the hair that clinches it. Look at those curls. Reddish-gold all over, like somebody scrambled the sun and set it on that child's head—Justin Randolph's hair. Lucy's father wouldn't've taken two seconds to put a claim on this one as his grand-young'un, I'll guarantee you." Cane snatched the photos from under Tally's stunned gaze and started striding around the room. "But who was the father? Lucy's had her peccadilloes, but none of 'em with men I know of she'd let father a child."

"Somebody said there was a cousin or something in Seattle that died in childbirth. Lucy rescued the baby, said she'd take it and raise it as her very own."

Cane's snort of derision cut short that string of nonsense. "That's a lot of crap. The only cousin Lucy has in Seattle is a sixty-five-year-old spinster with a terminal case of cobwebs between her thighs. Come on, kid—out with it. What's going on with you and Lucy? Do you know the secret behind this baby of hers—is that why you haven't been home since little Amalie came to Moss Island to be its new princess?"

Tally barely managed to whisper, "It's my mother more than anything else. She still gets upset about everything that happened. And now, in her mind, the big house still belongs to our family. I wouldn't dare try to take her back there. Jim-Roy went by to visit her last month and she thought he was his granddaddy, who used to train my granddaddy's horses. It was sad."

"Do you think it would upset your mother if I went out to see her sometime?" Cane put on another piece of wood and

Tally reconciled herself to an extension of the uncomfortable dialogue. "I was always fond of Vieve. Harm tells me that she's quite content living in the past and that the pain from her back is pretty much under control now that she's had several operations." He sat back down beside her. "What was that from anyway, that damage to her—spine, was it?"

"Vertebrae." Tally met Cane's gaze fully, candidly. "It wasn't from Perrie, if that's what you're thinking. Perrie never struck my mother, not once. I'll go to my grave saying that, even when I curse 'im for some of the other hurts that weren't to her body."

"A fall maybe? Harm said she was fond of riding ponies when she was little."

He was picking at her, and she felt sore from his probing. It was as if he wanted to know everything in her mind, everything that had ever had anything to do with her or anyone close to her. "Would you stop it, please? I don't want you to ask me any more questions."

"Only one more. And think carefully about this one before you answer it. If Nicholas Cantrell walked through that door this very moment, would you still be in love with him and want to marry him?"

Tally gasped in horror. "What the hell kind of question is that?"

"I'm sorry," Cane said quietly. "I guess I never could accept it—the business with you and Nick, I mean. He was just so totally wrong for you. I hated it that you couldn't see that."

"What gave you the right to be the judge and jury of that? What gave you the goddamn right to decide who was the right man for me?"

"This." Cane reached over and pulled Tally into his arms, his eyes blazing on hers before he pressed his mouth on hers in a crushing, ungentle kiss. "This," he whispered hoarsely as he dragged his hands through her hair and held it like a rope by which he kept her lips at his mercy. "Tally," he whispered an eternity later, after their mouths parted. "I want you so much. Why are our feelings for each other so complicated? They always have been, you know."

Tally pulled away from him, more shaken by the embrace than she cared to reveal. "Complicated" was a simplistic term for what lay between her and Cane. She tried to explain that. "I can't work for Tri-Com and be mistress to its president. You have everything you want. . . ."

"Not everything," Cane whispered, "not yet, by a long shot."

"I don't know how to say this except to just say it. I've always been attracted to you, Cane. I'd be a fool to lie about that, and you're not fool enough not to know it." Tally got up and walked around the room, spreading her arms to encompass all of the luxury, the expensiveness, the rightness of every object, every touch of exquisiteness. She stopped in front of a pedestal holding a valuable oriental vase, highlighted subtly by a perfectly focused light. "I found a lamp at the Salvation Army resale place last week. Spent half of last weekend rewiring it with a three-dollar-and-ninety-five-cent do-it-yourself kit. My bookcases are painted concrete blocks with boards I got at the lumberyard for next to nothing," she said, looking at the magnificent teak bookcase that held a grouping of objets d'art and the first editions Cane collected from rare-book sellers all over the world.

"So? Gretchen says your place is charming."

"Charming." Tally turned to look at Cane. "Like the feed-sack dresses I wore as a little girl? Like the corncob dolls Essie Mae used to make me for Christmas when all the mainland girls got Shirley Temple dolls? Like the fillings I got at the dental clinic without benefit of Novocain because I was a charity patient?"

Cane grimaced. "Your family's had some tough times, all right. But it's not like you to whine, Tally. Look at you now. Educated, beautiful, on your way up." He held his arms out. "Do you have to be intense on my last night in town for a while? I turned down a chance to go cavort with the legislators at Copa Atlanta just to have this time alone with you."

That broke the intensity. Tally was glad. "The Copa? Where Patti White the ex-schoolteacher is doing her reelin', writhin', and rhythmic tricks? *Cane*. I didn't know that you were that kind of guy."

"I'm not. The only woman I want to look at is standing in front of me—but she's much too far away. Come here."

She wouldn't, so he went and got her. A long, breathless time later, she pulled away and expressed her delayed reaction to what he'd said earlier. "Last night in town?" She pushed back the hair that had intrigued Cane's hands while they were kissing. "Are you off again on what Blake calls one of your Clark Kent capers?"

"He says that, does he?" Cane laughed softly and pulled her back into his arms, nuzzling the top of her head while they looked at the dying fire. "Well, I've never made it a secret that the newspapers are where my heart lies. Do you know how hard it is for me to keep out of the field when a big story's breaking? I want to be everywhere at once—Oxford, Mississippi, Saigon, West Berlin . . ." He kissed her. "But this will do fine, right here with you in front of the fire, thank you very much."

She wanted him to keep talking like that. Until a man told you his deepest dreams, you could not really understand him. Tally wanted very much to understand Cane Winslow. "I hear that you have a very big dream, that someday you want to have an international newspaper, one that spans the globe and brings the whole world together in a single publication."

Cane laughed a little self-consciously. "God, who told you about that? Whoever did should have added that my critics think that is probably the most far-out, ridiculous idea I've ever come up with. What does Winslow think he is, they say— God? A literary tower of Babel with about as much chance of getting there, they say."

"But you're establishing outposts for Tri-Com," Tally said loyally.

"Oh, yes. Guam and the Philippines will be my first stab at establishing an outer-limits flagpole. I happen to think Tri-Com needs newspapers there. That's still a strategic area, getting a foot in the publishing door there is a strategic move. The Philippines is important to our country, always has been. I want Tri-Com to represent the U.S. in every area that's important to our country. We'll support autonomy on the papers, of course, but think of the influence we can have in an outpost traditionally important to our national security. . . .'' Cane cut himself off with a soft curse. His arms had shifted during his excited talk about international possibilities so that the undersides of Tally's breasts were pressed against them. "Would you listen to me? I can't believe this. I'm sitting here in front of a perfect fire with the most beautiful girl in the world—and I talk about depressing things. Let's talk about something that really depresses me, the difference in our ages.''

He looked at her, trying to make a joke of what Tally suspected was an important issue to him. "Our generations are even different. You're a fifties girl, for God's sake, and they're totally different from the ones I grew up with.''

Tally couldn't help laughing. "Baloney! As for the difference in our ages—you should hear how some of the young receptionists talk about you. They think you're a . . . uh . . . doll.'' Actually the word the young women used to refer to their handsome President was "stud,'' but Tally had no wish to pass it along. "It's really not fair, you know. Gretchen's not even as old as you and Blake's always making cracks about her age. Can't you say something to him about her, about how far you two go back together?'' Even before Cane's long pause before answering, Tally regretted bringing Gretchen's name up. Cane probably thought Gretchen had put her up to it, knowing that Tally would probably be staying after the party to clean up, as Marsha always did.

"I'm sorry,'' Cane said coolly. "I never intervene in major on-air personnel decisions. That's Blake's exclusive bailiwick.''

"Bullshit!'' Tally picked up a sofa pillow and, changing her mind, tossed it harmlessly back into its corner. "You sure as hell intervened in my case! Cane, I didn't just come in on the turpentine wagon. I know good and well that I'm one of maybe three women in Tri-Com who are in true management-trainee positions.''

"But you're not on-the-air talent, which is best controlled without too many hands on the control stick." A devil lurked in Cane's eyes as he murmured, too softly for Tally to claim safely that she was meant to hear, "Come to think of it, you're not even between-the-sheets talent. Whatever happened to the good old days of bosses chasing women around the desk and trading raises for a little hot, juicy nooky . . .''

This time the sofa pillow found a successful target. "That does it. I'm going home, Mr. Boss Man." Actually, Tally was enjoying this side of Cane that she had never seen before. He really did have a silly streak that surprised and rather delighted her. "You and Socrates can walk me to the car."

"We'll be glad to." Cane got Tally's coat and whistled up the Great Dane. "Oh, my," he said with innocent surprise as they opened the door and Socrates bounded out, skidding on all fours when he hit the walkway. "The Atlanta weathermen have been caught with their pants down. Look at that!"

Everywhere they looked the ice was forming. Slender trees were bending down with the weight of unaccustomed burdens. Bushes were frost-white. And the road—! Tally looked at the winding driveway back down to Habersham (equally winding) and at her Mustang crouched on frozen haunches in the parking space halfway down the hill. "I can't believe it. God, Cane, there I was sitting and talking to you while all this was happening." She turned suspiciously to the man who was watching his dog carefully pick his way back through the unusual accumulation of snow to where they stood. Socrates lifted each paw as gingerly as though it had been planted in flypaper. "You have all these newspapers, radio and TV stations, and even *you* didn't know this was coming?"

Cane's face held the expression of an Abel as he lied happily, "Not a clue. Did you? Hell, did anybody in Atlanta predict this? I'm going to have to have a talk with my weather crew," he added sternly.

"Well, I'd better get started." Tally took a tentative step

out in her high-heeled sandals, knowing after the second step that it was hopeless. She would never get down that hill in these shoes. And even if she did . . . As punctuation to her misgivings, a car with squealing brakes turned sideways as it crept down Habersham and landed in someone's icy yard.

"Maybe you'd better stay here tonight." Cane reached out a hand to Tally and helped her back to the point where she'd started. "Don't give *me* that look, give it to the man upstairs. He's the one who's responsible for this little overnight arrangement—not me!"

By the time they were in front of the TV with steaming cups of hot chocolate, the incredulous weather bulletins were all over the air, interrupting every program. WPIC's popular Channel 10 forecaster was making self-deprecating jokes that made Cane curse, "Damned weather comics. I'm glad they're working for the competition. Let's see what our crowd is doing with this mess." When he switched to Tri-Com's TV weather report, he groaned to see Eden Thorpe filling in for the regular, Graham Conyers. "Oh, God, if that dame makes one joke about the weather-forecast dart board, she's history. Gone." He looked at the blond woman pinpointing part of the projected map and frowned. Suddenly, he realized what was happening. "What the hell is Eden Thorpe doing on the air anyway?" He looked at Tally with suspicion. "Do you know about this?"

"Only that Eden did a great fill-in for Bob Frazier and Blake's trying her out for some other spots—including weather. They've never had a woman do that before in Atlanta. Besides, she lives off Peachtree Battle and wouldn't have as much trouble getting to the station as Graham."

Cane was silent as Eden launched into some of the power-failure reports that were coming in faster than she could chalk them in on her map. Then he said grudgingly, "She's damned good. And the big boobs won't hurt our ADI ratings one bit."

Tally smiled and gave Socrates the rest of her popcorn. Eden owed her for this one. She had put the bug in Blake's ear, right after the great sub job the blonde had done on "Newpoint," that WPDQ ought to get in on the ground floor with female

weather casters, before the more popular Channel 10 beat them
to it.

The inevitable moment of bedtime decisions arrived. Even
Socrates was yawning, bored with watching the incredible pan-
orama of changing weather outside. He finally gave one last
Cerberean yawn and, with a don't-you-humans-need-sleep-
along-with-us-dogs look at his master, lumbered off to his pad
in the kitchen. Tally watched him go with the ambivalent
trepidations of a girl losing the protection of her duenna.
"Umm, uh—where are your extra sheets and stuff? I can bunk
down right here on this very comfortable sofa in front of that
wonderful fire."

"You'll do no such thing." Cane pulled her to her feet
and firmly led the way through the enclosed walkway to his
bedroom. "And don't act so stiff-lipped. You knew as well as
I did what could happen if you and I, by some crazy miracle,
found ourselves alone again without outside interference." Inside the bedroom, before he turned on the lights, Cane pulled
Tally into his arms. "Tell me you don't want this as much as
I do. Tell me you aren't glad the gods upstairs got tired of
blocking the natural course of Cane and Tally's attraction to
each other and created this night just for us. Tell me one
goddamn reason why we can't make love the way I've dreamed
about since the first night I met you. And tell me very quickly,
because I'm fast running out of patience."

He switched on the light and Tally searched in panic for
some focus other than Cane's direct gaze. "What a beautiful
room," she said inanely. "Just look at those oriental screens!
And your artwork. Cane, I had no idea you loved beautiful
things so much."

Cane let her walk away from him, unable to stop the rush
of desire that was threatening his control. "I don't know how
you could miss that about me."

The gasp from Tally made him smile. He wondered how
long it would take her to find the central treasure of his room,
the priceless objet d'art that had kept his heart alive with desire
and love for the one woman he really wanted for eternity.

"Cane!" Tally whirled to face him with accusing eyes. "How did you get this? And why's it so huge? It was just a little snapshot that . . ." She stopped, confused memories rushing in about hers and Nick's last summer.

"The snapshot that Nick took of you just before he went away. They sent his things back and Lucy couldn't bear looking through them. I found this and I couldn't let it go. I'm sorry, Tally, but one thing that you've never accepted is that my love for you has always been greater than Nick's."

Tally looked at the beautifully framed blowup of the picture of her kneeling on the beach with a large shell held up to her ear. Her hair was pulled up in a loose Psyche knot and most of it had dribbled down to her neck, causing a halo where the sun shone through the gleaming strands. The wispy summer dress, one of Reba's cheap creations, was somehow classic-looking, like the dress that a provocative Aphrodite might wear while listening to the sea through its shell product. "It makes me feel funny, knowing you've had this all these years."

"It shouldn't. Tally . . ."

The lights went out. Atlanta, "The City Too Busy to Hate," had also been too busy to prepare for any sort of weather emergency of this magnitude.

"Don't worry. I've got a flashlight here somewhere. Stay right where you are. Don't move." Cane fumbled his way to his bedside table and found the flashlight. "There. Now to light a few candles." As he did this, he reassured her, "It could get pretty cold, so I'll light the fire in here. We've got plenty of blankets . . ."

"What about Socrates? Won't he freeze?"

Cane laughed. "No, Socrates will be here in"—he beamed his flashlight down on his watch—"two more minutes."

Tally laughed, too, because precisely one minute later, the Great Dane was scratching at the door. When Cane let him in, Socrates went directly to the fireplace and curled up on the rug in front of it. "You see?" Cane pulled open the draperies so they could see the phantasmagoric miracle of the landscape outside. Atlanta was experiencing its first major ice storm in half a century, and Cane Winslow wasn't about to let its romance be overlooked during the night that lay bewitchingly before him. . . .

18

The silence awakened Cane. For a panicky moment he was afraid Tally was gone from his side; then a delicate little snore rippled gently along his shoulder and he grinned—more relaxed and happier than he had ever been in his life.

Socrates let out an echoing snore of contentment, making his master's grin widen. The Great Dane had discreetly snoozed through the noisy human excesses of the previous evening. To reward him, Cane very carefully got out of bed and resurrected the almost-dead fire. He was thanked with a canine groan and a sleepy tail wag.

Still tiptoeing, Cane checked the outdoors, carefully cracking the draperies only enough for a private view.

The view was of a crystal fairyland with every tree and shrub limb or twig encased in ice, every surface insulated with Mother Nature's own refrigeration process. The unusual silence came from the dearth of traffic on the usually heavy-trafficked Habersham below the house. That silence was broken after Cane tiptoed to the opposite window, which held a view of the main road. Ecstatic kids, some of whom had probably never even seen a snowflake, were out having a ball on the big hill over which no cars dared travel. Dishpans, pasteboard boxes, plastic chair cushions—every conceivable sliding object had been converted into makeshift sleds. There were a few adults out there, too, already hard at work on amateurish snowmen. Since there was more ice than snow, that was not an easy feat.

Cane let the curtains fall back on the Vermontesque scene outside and went back to the scenery he was even more interested in admiring.

The chair made a slight scraping sound as he moved it closer toward the bed so he could enjoy the sight of Tally sleeping.

She stirred slightly and Cane held his breath, hoping he had not awakened her. He just sat looking at every contour, every curve, every sweet part of the lovely body. She seemed so vulnerable, lying with one leg out of the covers, the other pulled up almost under her chin. Neglected eye makeup was a smudge of erratic color, but the slightly parted, full mouth was bereft of any artifice. Its bruised nudity reminded him that last night's passionate kisses had been those of a man long-starved for a particular brand of honey. Cane had found it in Tally's kisses.

He saw a red mark on the slender neck—a teenager's "hickey," he thought with a grin. He longed to kiss it tenderly, but was afraid Tally would wake up before he had a chance to savor the sweet memories of last night's dream.

A dream it had been, too, from the first moment Cane had lifted Tally in his arms and carefully laid her on his bed. . . .

"I'm afraid that at any moment Socrates will pull at the covers and wake me up and I'll find out this isn't really happening." His whispers were in awe of that possibility; every touch, every kiss was part of his longtime fantasy of holding Tally in his arms, of making love to her throughout a long, magical night.

"I feel that way, too," Tally whispered back. She was scared, too; he could feel her trembling as he removed the high-necked gown that was keeping him from charming treasures he longed to exploit. "Cane, this wasn't meant to happen."

"This night has been charted in the heavens since the first time we saw each other, and you know it." He took a deep breath as his success with the back zipper of her dress allowed an encounter with the warm silk of her skin. He trailed his fingers down the furrow of her back leading to the delightful cleft of her buttocks. "You've got goose bumps," he murmured.

She was breathing unevenly but made a game try at damming the flood that was sweeping them both away. "Making love isn't going to change anything, Cane. It won't make our problems go away."

Cane buried his mouth in the hollow of a sweet shoulder.

"Somehow, holding you like this makes all my problems non-existent. Tally, don't tamper with the magic of tonight. Whichever god is in control of destiny has gone to a helluva lot of trouble to get us together at last. Don't bring the real world into this bedroom. I just want you and me in it." He moved his lips up the column of her throat, thinking that if he was very methodical, he could, by the end of the night, have kissed every square inch of the world's most beautiful body. "And Socrates, of course, who seems to share his master's obsession with you."

Socrates's tail thumped against his warm spot by the fire and Tally and Cane laughed. Then Tally turned serious again. "Oh, Cane, I've dreamed of this moment so many times. I won't lie to you about that. But now that it's here, I'm scared. Why do I feel like I'm doing something wrong?" She caught her breath. "Cane, don't *do* that! I'm trying very hard to have a serious conversation."

Cane lifted his head and looked as solemn as a man could under the delicious circumstances. "I find it hard to think of anything more serious than what is happening right now, but go ahead. What do you mean, you feel like you're doing something wrong? Tally, you're not a little girl anymore." Cane took a moment to check that out for himself until Tally made him behave. "How could two people finally being together after years of longing be wrong?"

There was Nick in between those years, Tally thought. She had never felt Nick's presence more strongly than she did right now. Maybe it was because of the photo Cane had taken for his own, as he was taking Tally for his own. Uneasiness was mixed with her desire. Yet she was reluctant to bring Nick's name up. It wasn't fair to Cane. "I know it's silly, but I keep thinking somebody is going to come tearing up here, maybe the police, the sirens screaming, and I'll be the subject of Brother Thomas's sermons for years to come."

Cane hugged her and lifted her hair away from her neck so he could nuzzle. "Nobody's going to come tearing up here tonight, unless they're driving a snowmobile. You funny little thing—you funny, sweet, little adorable thing. It's Nick, isn't it? You're thinking about Nick and what might have happened between you two if he hadn't gone off and turned up missing.''

It did happen between us, Tally thought. But she was glad Cane didn't know how close she and Nick had gotten that summer. She knew it would be painful for him, since he had done everything to keep them apart. "Not anymore," Tally whispered. "To tell you the truth, it's getting hard to think about anything right at this moment—except you." Tally ached with desire for Cane to make the dream real. She felt as though every part of her was on fire. There had not been another man for her since Nick. Tally's thoughts were wanton; her body followed suit.

Cane had deftly managed to shed his own clothes in the process of removing hers. For all his confidence, he felt the momentary insecurity of a new lover exposing himself for the first time to a woman he passionately desired. A glance in the mirror that reflected him and Tally together reassured him. He pulled her up to look with him at the reflection. "Look at us, Tally. We're great together. Made for each other. No, don't turn away, darling. There's nothing wrong with knowing we're beautiful.''

Tally delighted him by turning in his arms so that he could feel her nipples hardening against his chest. Cane closed his eyes when she slipped her hands over his shoulders and up to the sides of his face so she could bring it close for a soft kiss. "It's the wrong word to use for a man as masculine and handsome as you, but you *are* beautiful." She let her hands slip down to touch the red-gold wisps on his chest. "Was this the color your hair once was?"

"Sort of. Why? Do you think my hair makes me look old?" Cane had never felt younger in this life than he did at that moment.

"No, no." Tally's hands went to his head and mussed the crisp curls that Cane's hairstylist had allowed to grow longer and fuller with the current trends. "I love the way you look. I always have, from the first time I ever laid eyes on you."

Cane lay back down on the bed and pulled Tally on top of him. He was so full of joy at having her this close to becoming his that he wanted to put the night on hold forever. "I'll never forget that time you delivered my freshly ironed pants. You took such a long inventory of me with those serious big eyes, I was afraid to ask if I'd passed muster." He looked down at Tally's breasts, longing to taste their sweetness again, but not wanting to interrupt the equally sweet confrontation of old, old feelings. "Did I?" The question held a tinge of anxiousness.

"Not only did you pass, you made an A-plus. I don't think I'll ever forget the first time I saw you. I was in a daze the whole time you were talking to me. You must have thought I was mentally retarded."

Cane kissed her, his voice holding emotion when he said, "I thought you were the most wonderful girl I had ever met in my life and I can't tell you how much I wanted you to grow up." He held her face between his hands, no longer smiling as he looked at the six golden freckles on the Fontaine nose, at the full, ripe mouth, into the amber eyes. "And now look at you, Tallulah Fontaine Malone. You're all grown up and beautiful and smart and educated and you're going to be all mine. I still can't believe it. I've wanted this for so long that I'm scared as hell that it isn't really happening, that I'm just fantasizing."

Tally took one of Cane's hands from her cheek and kissed the palm softly before nipping a brown finger with her teeth. "Did you fantasize that?" she whispered. "This?"

"You're driving me totally crazy," Cane whispered back. "And I think maybe you aren't far behind me." Cane was not unaware that his continual caressing of Tally's thighs was having its effect. When his fingers gingerly parted the down-covered opening between, her readiness for him thrilled him. "Oh, Tally," he whispered, turning her on her back so he could get at her better, "if you only knew how proud you make me, going moist at my touch, letting me know you want me, too."

Her breasts were enchanting and he could no longer resist setting upon them like the hungry man he was. Feeling somewhat fearful of his urge to suck the last vestige of resistance from her, he waited until she was too breathless to respond before asking her if he was hurting her.

The surprise of finding himself inside her made him gasp. Cane wanted to shout with elation that it was Tally who had guided him, she who clasped her legs about him so tightly that they were soon as one, intimately joined for the mount to ecstasy.

He was relentless in seeing that she reached the heights before him, and carefully moved inside her when her peak was attained. Only later, when the bursting need inside his own body could no longer be contained, did he let go, forgetting Tally, the world, everything but the tumultuous joy of releasing his years-old passion. . . .

"Cane, stop that," Tally said sleepily, not opening her eyes but smiling at the wet kiss on her cheek. "Unless you've got some coffee and a good hot fire ready, I'm not budging out of this bed."

The repetition of a kiss was more like a wet lick this time. Tally opened her eyes and found herself on a nose-to-nose level with Socrates. She sat up with a jerk. "Socrates, what the devil has your master put you up to doing? What is this?" There was a yellow rose (from the party last night, Tally realized) stuck in the Great Dane's collar, along with a note with her name on the outside.

"Okay, boy. Let's see what he's up to." Tally opened the note and read,

> My darling, I hope you still respect me though you had your way with me mercilessly last night. . . . I sat and stared at you for two hours, willing you to wake up so there could be a repeat performance. And now, dammit, the world has caught up with me again. A glitch in the Guam negotiations has called me away, through snow, sleet, and untold reluctance at leaving you.
>
> They sent out a salt truck and Habersham is pretty

clear. Not the other roads, so don't try to drive. I'm being picked up by the only mobile vehicle in our Tri-Com fleet. Call my driver, Frank Hennis, later if you need to go home for anything. (I wish you'd stay.. I like thinking of you there in my bed while I'm gone.)

Frank dropped my maid Vanessa off when he came by. She's fixing your breakfast, and coffee's already hot in the kitchen. Reba called and is stranded at the Greyhound station. Maybe you and Frank can fetch her. (Did you know she was coming?) I won't be back in time for the First Wednesday meeting, dammit, dammit, dammit. I was really looking forward to you and me being in a meeting together for the first time, trying to act normal. I feel anything but after last night.

I'll call you tomorrow night. Socrates was instructed to look after you. I'm jealous. With passion, love, friendship, whipped cream—whatever your precious heart desires, I'm your—Cane.

Tally hugged her knees, smiling, thinking about the previous night. Wouldn't Cane have been surprised to know that she had not once thought about Nick while she was in Cane's arms? She reached over and scratched Socrates's oversized head. "Thanks for the kiss, fellow, but I would prefer it from the man himself. No hard feelings?"

And then it struck her what else Cane had mentioned in his note. "Oh my God—Reba! What in heaven's name is she doing here?" Tally swung her legs over and frowned. "Jesus! I hope to God she's not pregnant." She got up and put on Cane's silk robe, which he'd thoughtfully left her. "And what's this about me being invited to a First Wednesday? Nobody but Tri-Com execs and visiting board members and Marsha Perkins get to those inner-circle confabs."

She padded to the door, Socrates right behind her.

Tally laughed, feeling suddenly happy. Lord, it would be great seeing Reba! Maybe the two of them would find a sled somewhere and goof off like a couple of kids. There were some great hills off Ponce de Leon.

"Come on, Soc. I could kill for a cup of coffee."

Tally went off toward the good smell of fresh-brewed coffee, stopping to admire the magical landscape from the walkway linking the bedroom and kitchen modules, and whistling "Zip-a-dee-doo-dah."

It was a "zip-a-dee-doo-dah" day, all right, for a south Georgia girl who had the world by the tail. As for the night she had spent in Cane's arms—well, Walt Disney's theme songs wouldn't cover *that*.

Reba Taylor looked wonderful and Tally told her so all the way home from the Greyhound station. "And your brace is gone! Reba, that's great!" She hadn't gotten Reba's letter about an Atlanta visit, but was thrilled to see her old friend.

"I have this special-built shoe," Reba said, showing her the subtly disguised buildup on her attractive wedge-heeled pumps. "I couldn't have done it, though, without the help you gave me. Tally, are you really making a lot of money?"

They were slipping and sliding a little on Ponce de Leon, so Tally held her breath, waiting till Frank Hennis had righted the car before answering, "Not yet. But I could, any day now. I'll tell you about it when we get to my place."

Reba wasn't in any hurry to get anywhere. She was enjoying being driven around in a chauffeured limousine as if she were someone important and was fascinated by her first sight of snow. "God, Tally, I can't get over how great all this is. And it's great seeing you." She turned from ogling the sights outside the car window and examined Tally's unusual attire for a snowy morning, but decided not to ask questions. Except, "How far's your apartment?"

"It's right here on Ponce de Leon, pretty close to downtown. I love the area, though it's getting a little seedy now that so many of the rich people have given up their big homes to move out to West Pace's Ferry or Peachtree Battle. See, up there on that little hill, the house with the steep driveway? That's it, that's my place. There are three separate units, but I hardly ever see the other tenants. Everybody in Atlanta has a job. Frank, just let us out by the sidewalk. There's no way on earth you can make it up that hill.''

Frank swiveled his head around and grinned at Reba. "Don't let Malone get you into any trouble, pretty girl. If you know what's good for you, you'll forget about moving up here and go back to that island of yours.''

"Frank, I'll look after Reba. Come on—and watch the ice. Bye, Frank!''

Reba loved Tally's apartment and poked her head into every nook and cranny while the other girl made coffee. "This is just the kind of place I want when I move up here.''

Tally brought their coffee out to the living room. "Then you were serious back there in the car? You're really going to move up here?'' She sat down hard and pulled the other girl down next to her. "All right, let's have it. The last I heard from you, you were making beaucoups sewing up prom dresses for the little darlings of the mainland. Are you serious? Do you plan to get a job in town? Do you want to live with me?''

"Yes, yes, no. I am serious, I do plan to try to get a job in Rich's Bridal Salon and, no, I won't impose on you.''

"It wouldn't be imposing, but I know how you feel. I was the same way about staying with Gretchen.''

Reba asked around a mouthful of Triscuit and cheese, "How is Gretchen, by the way? I saw her show right after it got started. She's so skinny! I can't get over how you and I used to think she was the most glamorous thing this side of Hollywood." Reba coughed as the scratchy cracker went down her throat. "Tally, she's looking *old*. There are these terrible *bags* under her eyes.''

Tally wished Reba hadn't said that. "Well, she's not old. TV just exaggerates things. Look, we're not going to be able to go out tonight or anything, but Caruso's is just across the street. Want to go there for Italian tonight?''

"Anything. Tally, when in the world are you going to ask me about the island? I can't believe we've been together for almost an hour and you haven't asked one question! Your mother was the same way that time I went by to see her. It's like you two just erased Moss Island and all its memories right out of your heads.''

Tally saw no reason to confess to her friend that she had been dying to ask about little Amalie but was afraid to let herself in for even more of the heartache than she'd encountered when Cane had talked about "Lucy's child." But since Reba had offered the opening, she asked as casually as she could, ''Is little Amalie still as happy as everybody seems to think she is?''

''Oh, my goodness—*happy!* That young'un leads the life of a little princess. Lucy dotes on her, I declare she does.'' Reba looked at Tally speculatively. ''You know, I'm ashamed to say for the longest time I suspected you might be the one that child belonged to, but not anymore.'' Tally waited, and sure enough Reba explained, ''Not only did it come to me that I was being silly—you wouldn't give up a baby, not you, I just know it in my heart—but it's so dad-blame obvious. That little girl's the spitting image of old Lucy! I mean, nobody could doubt for one minute that she's her close kin.''

But what about Nick? Tally wanted to yell. *Amalie could have Nick's eyes and coloring since she's his kid.* But her lips were still bound to silence and the yell died in her throat. ''How's Essie Mae? And F'Mollie? Isn't her little girl about the same age as Amalie?''

''She is, but what a difference. They play together like Junior and the rest of us did as kids, but even little Amalie is right careful with poor Jolamine. F'Mollie took up with that fellow that everybody knew was her first cousin and you know how that can turn the blood, it being too thick and close and all.''

''You mean she's retarded? Poor F'Mollie. And poor little Jolamine.''

''Don't feel too sorry for that little girl. She's got as much spunk as her mother did at her age. And there's something—well, I don't know what to call it—special, I guess.''

''Still, it surprises me that Lucy lets her precious Amalie

have a steady playmate who's slow.'' *And black*, Tally added to herself. Lucy Cantrell was not famous for her equal-right attitudes.

"Honey, she doesn't have a whole heap to say about it Amalie Cantrell has got a mind of her own. If she decide she wants to play with Jolamine, not Lucy, not the Georgi Bulldogs, not a ten-mile-high barbwire fence could keep he from it." Reba grinned and finished off the last of the Triscuits "That child's got determination like you wouldn't believe."

Tally felt so happy again she was barely able to contain herself. "You know what," she said, "if this big money dea comes through for me, I'm gonna help you set up in a littl shop right down on Tenth Street. It's getting to be like Green wich Village, and the rent's not bad at all. I think you'd lov it. The beatniks are pretty much gone, but there are still som interesting shops and coffeehouses."

"Coffeehouses?" Reba, for all her new refined way of talk ing since she'd been to the Sears Roebuck Six Weeks Finish ing Seminar for Young Ladies, sounded so much like Poke Tally fought the urge to laugh. "What the aitch is a coffee house?"

"It's a juke joint, only without the beer and Redman spi cans and guys in pickups. No knife fights, either. Everybod talks real soft while somebody plays a guitar real, real quiet and sings about war and taxes and rioting in Africa and famines.'

"Well, I'd just as soon listen to Loretta Lynn sing abou divorce and despair, but it don't sound too bad. Let's go jukin one night real soon."

"We will," Tally promised. "I'll take you to the Golde Horn one night next week after I get off from work."

"Shoot. I'm ready to go right now."

"Can't. Even if the roads weren't so bad, there's a blue lav in Atlanta. Can't get liquor on Sundays."

Reba was incredulous. "You mean to tell me you can get drink on Sunday in Ducktown, Georgia—and you can't ge one in Atlanta, Gee-A?"

"I mean to tell you."

"But this Horn place, you said it just sells you coffee."

Tally laughed somewhere between amusement and consternation. "Reba, would you please just shut up and get us a beer out of the icebox while I tune in the news? I want to see if I can get to work tomorrow without calling Deadeye Hennis to the rescue."

Too late, as Reba was getting the beer and Tally was dialing the knob to Channel 5, she realized that she'd called the refrigerator an "icebox." Another few days with Reba and she'd be back where she started.

"But, hell, what's wrong with being a country girl?" she told herself with a grin, kicking her shoes off and wiggling her manicured toes. When she and Reba were on their third beer (each) and the sportscaster gave the Georgia Tech basketball-team rating, she let out with a rebel yell that would have cleared Sourmash Sound of every varmint for miles.

The melting of Atlanta was pretty well complete by Wednesday, when Tally finally made it to the office under her own steam. She was fed up, along with a lot of other Atlantans, with the chortles of northern and midwestern transplants like Pepper Cole who said that nobody south of the Mason/Dixon line had the slightest inkling of what to do in bad winter weather. "Frankly, my dear," she told Cole when she got in late Wednesday after skidding all over the parking lot, "I don't give a damn about you and your precious snowplows and Snow-Day Plans back in Minnie-Mouse-Apolis. If God had meant us to have this kind of weather more than once a half century, he'd have given us all big red ears and W. C. Fields noses like yours."

"Well!" Pepper Cole stopped bugging her after that.

Marsha Perkins caught her between calls and congratulated her on the reports she'd had of the big party. "And what an end to the evening!" She chuckled. "I'm jealous, I admit. I never got snowed in with the big boss before. But, Tally, before we get into more chitchat, you've got to put this on your calendar. It comes straight down from the Hill. You're to be at the First Wednesday meeting, which's been postponed till next week, thanks to the bad weather. And I don't have to tell you, it's a real honor to be invited. Even the general manager doesn't get to go to those.''

Tally was very much aware that the Wednesdays were comprised of ''hill'' executives and visiting regionals only. ''Then why me? Why not Lucas, our new station manager, or Bob, the VP of this outfit?''

''Well, can I be straight? They are looking at women moving up in Tri-Com. And TV's been slighted for years, you know about that. Tally, dammit, don't ask questions, just be up here at two next Wednesday. And I suggest you wear your best power suit. People will be watching you.''

''I'll be there with bells on,'' Tally said. She was glad that she would have the weekend in between to take care of Darwin Redwine's proxy bid and get her own money invested before the First Wednesday meeting. It would make her feel more secure to know she owned a respectable amount of stock in Tri-Com when she attended its first insiders-only kind of meeting.

Tally followed Marsha's advice and wore her gray silk shantung suit to the Wednesday meeting. She was glad she looked especially professional. When she took a seat at the large conference table in the directors' room on the sixth floor, she realized that she was one of only two women in the room.

The buzz of excitement in the room increased when Blake Edenfield entered, bearing a tray of slides, and made a motion to have the room darkened.

''Mr. Winslow has asked me to preside over this meeting,'' he said, handing the tray to the projectionist, ''and to welcome each and every one of you to this regular monthly confab. I hope you'll all have plenty to say after this little show—and I hope you'll share the joy Mr. Winslow expressed over the phone from Washington this morning when I called him to report on a real exciting development at Tri-Com.'' *Washington?* Tally frowned. Hadn't Cane's note said he was off to Guam? Well, maybe he had some political axes to grind in getting the new acquisition underway. . . . Tally turned her attention back to the man at the front of the room. It wasn't hard. Blake was a showman. He let the suspense build while he fiddled with the contrast and focus on the slide projector, ignoring the boy who had been delegated to take care of it. "It seems, ladies and gentlemen, that Tri-Com has split two for one."

Tally sat numbly through the applause, waiting until the slides were being shown before allowing it to sink in. The money she'd collected as her commission on the Roswell Road–future I-75 sale had been invested in Tri-Com only the day before.

She was rich! Not the kind of Lucy Cantrell–rich or even close to anybody-in-this-room-rich, but she was rich by her standards!

Tally sat completely fascinated by the slides showing Tri-Com's scattered news bureaus (three now, in significant capitals) at work. The organization of volumes of information to be dispensed regionally was impressive. So were the graphs on profitability percentages, credit ratios, and dividend payouts, which came on next. Tally leaned forward, concentrating on the side of Tri-Com that she had not been privy to before now.

Her background in the economic framework of her company was scanty, she realized. If she was going to prove herself at Tri-Com, she needed to round out her education. She would check into the offerings at the university branch downtown. Perhaps there were some courses in marketing and economics that she could take at night. If she and Cane were going to be seeing each other more from now on, she wanted to be able to discuss Tri-Com business intelligently. And she wanted to be ready for her big opportunity when it came.

Besides, wasn't she a Tri-Com investor now? What was good for the company was good for Tally Malone.

19

Someone nudged Tally and she realized that Blake was staring right at her as he talked. She got her mind quickly redirected to what he was saying: ". . . and not only the seven-percent lineage gain was terrific for Tri-Com—credit to ad sales, of course—but we've had some more exciting changes lately. My hat's off, along with that of your president in absentia, to the ad department's VP, Pepper Cole, who came up with the super idea of offering subscribers group-wide market coverage. I've been working on licenses now for three new bureaus to spread out some of the work. Now it's your turn. Questions, anybody?''

A hand went up. ''Why isn't our TV station showing up better in the profitability reports?''

Blake frowned. ''I'm not sure that's a question that should be addressed in a general-media meeting like this, but what the hell.'' Blake's eyes sought out Tally. ''Speck Dodson isn't here to field that question, but there's someone else here today who probably can. Tally?'' As all eyes turned to the woman thus pinpointed, Blake said with only the slightest patronizing tone, ''Miss Malone is one of the fastest-rising women in the business. Someone with our major affiliate told me that Tally is tougher than most men when it comes to keeping the network from encroaching on local time—where, of course, we make our best money. But I'll let Tally herself tackle the profitability issue.''

Tally stood up and nodded coolly toward the man who had introduced her so condescendingly. ''Mr. Edenfield is putting me on the spot, since I don't have any figures prepared to illustrate the problems we have with network preempts. But off the top of my head, here's what's going on. We fight like hell at WPDQ for the precious three-to-five-thirty local spots, but at the same time, we fight to hold a fine line with the networks. According to Speck, who should be talking to you about this instead of me, it's difficult—damned difficult!— to negotiate the twenty-to-twenty-five-percent backing of the hourly rate that the affiliates provide their shows. But I'm learning from him how important it is to get delay-time-videoed network movies. This gives us more prime time for high-paying preempts. In other words, we're doing what we can to increase station profits, but it's a balancing act, and the networks sure as heck have more weight on their end.''

Another hand shot up. "What's the bottom line on low percentages from the network?"

Tally smiled. "Boy, everybody's trying to put me on the spot today. Okay, let me think." Tally flipped back through her mental files to the report she'd help Speck write up for the Hill. "Five percent," she said crisply. "Remember, too many preempted network spots can get us in financial trouble. Too few can get us in Dutch with the networks. But I'm happy to say we've never hit that five-percent low. Thanks to Speck's expert finesse, which he is teaching me to use in dealing with the affiliates, we're actually in better shape than some of the profitability reports indicate. Remember, this is Atlanta—not New York. WPDQ charges reasonably for local advertising. We're not supporting the Madison Avenue boys' three-martini lunches."

Tally sat down amid the ripples of laughter. She was pretty pleased with the way she had handled herself at her very first First Wednesday. She just wished Cane could have been there to see her.

Later that day, Blake caught her as she was on her way into the office elevator. "Nice going, Tally. Congratulations to you and PDQ for the Atlanta Ad Federation Topaz Awards, by the way. I hear you had a winner in the public-relations category for the Pony Express ad."

"Thanks. I'll pass the kudos along to Eden Thorpe. She worked her tail off on that spot and deserves a Clio for it." Tally smiled cordially at Blake and got on the elevator. "Sorry," she murmured to the people who had been holding the door for her as Blake talked to her. "Anybody else going down?" she asked before pressing 2 for Gretchen's office.

Someone laughed. "From the looks of things in that meeting, you ain't going anywhere but up, sweetheart."

"I hope so," Tally said with a grin as she got off the elevator.

Tally's grin vanished when she walked into Gretchen's office and found her staring gloomily out the window. "Hey, what's with you? 'Woman Alive!'s been going great guns. Hasn't it?''

Gretchen swiveled her chair back around and Tally could tell she'd been crying. "I don't know. You tell me." Gretchen pulled open her bottom desk drawer and hauled out a half-full bottle of vodka. "At least you've got something to celebrate. I hear you wowed the boys on the top floor. Here." She poured a coffee mug full of vodka and held it out to Tally.

The latter shook her head. "All I did was survive an attempt by the executioner to nail me to the barn door." She watched as Gretchen took a big swig from the mug. "Gretchen, do you think you ought to keep liquor in your desk? You know how word gets out about things like that."

"This isn't just liquor, it's Dr. Smirnoff. He's a good guy. Has nice breath, no aftertaste, and, most important of all, he's around the next morning when you need him."

"Oh." Tally sank into the chair opposite. "Is it a new man? Is that what's been going on with you lately? Eden says you've turned her down for dinner every time she's asked you. And when I invited you to join Reba and me last night, you were just short of rude. Gretchen, what's wrong?"

"There's always a new man," Gretchen said gloomily, "but that's not the problem. I watched myself on TV this morning— that's the problem. You can see these damned wrinkles from the last row in the audience. And these pits and scars from all the nervous breakouts I've had in the past year. . . ." Gretchen pressed her hands to her cheeks and rubbed so hard, her flesh was dragged down into a distorted shape. She laughed harshly. "I overheard the makeup girl telling someone they use less pancake on Vampira for her Madame Blood show than on me."

"Oh, Gretchen, why do you put yourself down like this? If being on television is putting too much pressure on you, go back to radio! You *loved* that—and it loved you!"

"Boy, wouldn't Lovey Carmichael enjoy that!" Lovey was Gretchen's counterpart at a competing station. They were always fighting for the highest rating and Gretchen was currently on top. She poured more vodka into the cup, which had around its rim the slogan "Behind every woman who succeeds there's a man who tried to stop her." "Tell you what, though, you could send out Lovey's tape to some of the stations up north." Sending out tapes of the competition to larger stations in distant, more lucrative sections of the country was a common practice. Strong TV personalities were sometimes "taped out" several times in a season. The rumor was that Bob Frazier was being taped out to stations as far away as Seattle.

"Better than that, why don't I discreetly tape you out? Chicago's been interested in you for a year—but of course you wouldn't have to take the job. Just letting people around here know how valuable you are would take off some of the pressure."

"Chicago hired Jingle Hardy. Remember, she was that really sharp-looking black woman in Nashville who stirred up a fuss at last year's Addy award banquet."

"Yeah, I remember." When the talented Jingle Hardy had walked off with a top Addy award, more than one disgruntled competitor had jealously grumbled about the black woman's recognition coming more from her first-black-woman-in-a-major-on-air-spot status than from expertise. "Gretchen, I don't like seeing you like this. The last time you got this way, you went on that stupid grapefruit diet and wound up in the hospital."

Gretchen wasn't even listening. She said musingly, "I wonder if that plastic surgeon I had on my show last month would do something?"

"Plastic surgery at your age?" Tally was getting really alarmed. "Gretchen, for God's sake, you don't need that! Lay off the booze and get more sleep and go to a dermatologist for your skin if it really bothers you, but for heaven's sake, don't go having your face worked on thinking it will change your whole life."

Gretchen looked at Tally with a crooked little smile. "Thank you, Dr. Norman Vincent Peale. It's interesting how women who are born beautiful don't seem to think the rest of us ought to do anything to improve our looks." She added less sharply, "Don't worry, little Miss Worry-Wart. I'm not going to do

something crazy. If you see Eden, tell her I'm having everybody to my place for spaghetti Sunday night. Now, scoot! I've
got a show to put together.''

Tally was glad to see that Gretchen put the vodka back in
the drawer and closed it firmly.

"Reba, honey, it's not as if I'm handing you the world on a
silver platter. You'll be doing all the work. All I'm proposing
is that you let me take care of the lease for the first six months,
which will give you time to get the shop going without draining
every cent you make.'' Tally walked over and flipped off the
TV, which Reba watched nonstop when she was at Tally's
apartment.

Tally was still tense from her worry about Gretchen. Besides,
Cane hadn't called and Tally was getting really edgy, wondering if their night together had meant as much to him as it had
to her.

"Why can't I just take that job at the bridal salon at Rich's?
The pay may not be hot, but it is regular.'' Reba started to put
her peanuts in her Pepsi and remembered just in time that Tally
had told her that it was considered really gross.

"Reba, you'll *hate* that job. And, anyway, why would somebody with all the talent you've got want to keep on doing
alterations and tooky little sewing jobs?'' Tally sat down right
next to Reba. She knew she was bullying her friend, but it had
to be done if Reba was going to amount to anything. "Look,
it's like I told you. I've got the money, Tenth Street is booming,
and that little shop we found is just perfect for a custom-design
shop.''

"How could I make enough dresses to make it pay off? You
know how slow I am doing the actual work.''

"That's because you do everything yourself now—including
the basic cutting, basting, and seam-stitching that any moron
could do. Here's what you'll do—you lease three or four sewing machines, hire two full-time seamstresses at minimum
wage and one part-time. You deal with the customers yourself,
showing them your book of original designs, help 'em pick out

colors and all that—and sock it to 'em when they ask how much.''

"Customers. Now you've hit on the real snag. *What* customers? Nobody's ever heard of me or my designs. Why would they come to my shop?''

"Because," Tally said, not letting her exasperation show, "they will have heard about you. Are you forgetting that I know every media person in this town? I can get you mentioned in everything from *Creative Loafing* to *Atlanta* magazine. In fact, I saw Jim Townsend Friday and he loved the idea of a series on small-town girls who come to the big city. I told him all about you and he says yours will be the kickoff piece.''

"The polio business has to be brought into it, doesn't it.'' Reba looked down at her leg and back at Tally ruefully. "I don't know, Tally—''

"Come on, Reba! What's wrong with a little pathos to get you some really good publicity? Besides, think about the people out there who could be inspired by you.'' Tally saw a little tear ooze from the corner of Reba's eye and was immediately appalled at herself for bulldozing her friend, without once thinking of Reba's feelings. She knelt down and hugged the girl. "I'm sorry, Reba. I just got carried away. It's just that I want so badly for both of us to be successful. I want it for you even more than I want it for me.'' Her voice softened. "Remember how you and I used to cut out those stupid paper dolls and all those clothes with little tabs on 'em?''

Reba smiled. "Essie Mae would fuss at us for ruining the Sears Roebuck catalog. Gee, we did have some pretty good times together, didn't we?''

"Yes, we did, but the point I'm making is that while I just cut out the dresses like they were in the book, you always managed to add things—a ruffle here, a scarf there, a new neckline or such, so that they looked really great. Reba, we don't have to do that piece in *Atlanta*. We can just pay for an ad in the newspaper, but please, please let me help you make something of that wonderful talent of yours.''

Reba hugged her. "Okay. And I don't mind about the article

coming out in *Atlanta*. I'll even wear one of my new designs.
It's this long skirt that goes over shorts, if you can believe
it. . . ."

"See? Think about how many women would never dream
up having a skirt match their shorts. And think how many will
see your design and want one for themselves!"

Reba, now that she had accepted Tally's plan, was content
to move to another subject. "Tally, do you ever dream about
being rich and famous and going back so Lucy can see you
like that?"

"You bet I do! I can see myself right now, getting out of
my big ole Cadillac limousine—no, a Rolls-Royce!—pulled
right up in front of the house. And I can see myself showing
Lucy the deed with my name on it for the house and all the
land the Fontaines once owned. And then . . ." Tally stopped,
because it was at this point that she would think about how
little Amalie would look when her real mother showed up and
revealed herself. "Dreams come true if you keep them in your
head long enough."

"Well, you're making 'em come true right and left for everybody. Essie Mae said you sending the money for her to pay
off her back taxes was like a dream come true."

Tally bristled at the reminder of how coldhearted Lucy had
been in that matter. "Would you believe that Lucy was planning to buy that little house at the tax auction and charge Essie
Mae rent to live in it?"

"Nothing that witch does surprises me. Say, now that I've
got my future settled, why don't we go over to Manuel's?"
Reba cradled the peanut hulls in her skirt and got up to dump
them on the last fire of the season. "I wouldn't mind us having
a pitcher of beer."

"What you really mean is, you get a kick out of all those
Georgia Tech fellas coming over and hanging all over you,
trying to get you to go out with 'em." Tally looked at the silent
phone and thought about Cane. Well, one night in bed and
some whispered endearments did not a commitment make. She
didn't find the Tech boys as exciting as Reba seemed to, but
maybe some plain old flirting would do her good. "If I hear

one more guy tell you how much you look like Sophia Loren,
I may upchuck my beer.''

Actually, it tickled Tally to death that Reba had the boys hot
after her again these days. As for Tally, the college boys
found her attractive but sensed (accurately) that she found them
incredibly young and immature.

The two young women had not been gone more than five
minutes when the phone in the apartment started ringing.

Cane stared at the receiver in his hand, cursing the repeated
rings on the other end. He was pretty sure Tally would be hurt
and confused by his not phoning her. He hated the fact that
he'd had to lie in his farewell note. Well, the part about the
Guam emergency had been true; it was just that the business
in Washington, all very secretive, had had to be put first.

The secret trip he'd made with Lucy had been a success, but
what lousy timing! Here he and Tally had finally gotten to the
point he'd been trying to get them to for years and—boom!
Everything hit at once, just as the ice storm in Atlanta had hit.

''Lucy should have let me tell Tally what was going on,''
Cane said, cursing as he hung up the receiver and picking up
the dime that came clattering back out. ''Damn her eyes, and
damn those stiff-shirts who insisted on no phone calls and damn
this rotten ice storm!'' Unlike the one in Atlanta that had
brought him and Tally together, this one was keeping them
apart. ''No more takeoffs till later,'' he grumbled, mocking
the airport officials. Well, he had had to let his small private
plane take Lucy and her very special cargo. If it weren't for
that noble gesture, Cane himself could be in Atlanta where
they probably were by now.

When the bartender at the Washington Pump brought the
Jack Daniel's double Cane had ordered, he pushed a bill at
him. ''Keep the change except for a dime.'' Grabbing his coat
from the adjoining stool, he went back to the phone.

He closed his eyes and prayed as he heard the phone start
ringing again in Tally's apartment. *Be there. And don't talk to
anyone until I have time to explain.*

''Mr. Winslow?'' The uniformed man who came up to Cane

was, he recognized, an aide to the high-ranking Army officer he'd spoken with at the landing. "Major General Litzenberg has asked me to invite you to his suite at Senators Towers for a private conference."

Cane hung up the phone slowly. Tally still wasn't home. "I've got a plane to catch."

"Sir, the major general says to tell you it's a matter of the utmost importance, in fact, one which might be a matter of national security."

Cane wasn't impressed by that catchall phrase, but he was by the next one. "Lieutenant Colonel Mayer will be there, sir."

The U.S. Army psychiatrist, Cane knew, had controversial inside information on current troop-indoctrination programs that Brigadier General Marshall had done his best to dispute. What a story Cane could get once all this was declassified!

Cane hung up the receiver and went out with the aide to a waiting car. He would charter a plane after this meeting and be at Tally's side with a dozen roses and breakfast when she woke up the next morning. In the meantime, he was a newspaperman who was being handed a story that could turn into Pulitzer Prize material for Tri-Com Newspaper Enterprises. . . .

The old-fashioned lock on Tally's apartment had given her trouble from day one. Now she cursed as she inserted the six-inch key and wriggled it to no avail as the phone inside rang insistently. "Damn." The door was open, finally, but of course the phone stopped ringing just before she reached it. Maybe it was Cane, she thought despondently. She had left Reba drinking beer with two Tech men, not in the mood for the second pitcher or the initial stages of pickup that Reba had been enjoying tremendously. "Well, he'll call back." She looked at her watch. No, it was almost twelve. She had missed him.

She put on some milk to heat for Ovaltine and got into pajamas, then scrunched down in front of the TV to watch the news. Too late for that, too, she realized as Jack Paar came on to do his puckish cynic number on nervous-looking guests. She would give Reba twenty minutes to get home, then she was packing it in for the night. It was time to stop feeling responsible for her old friend. Leaving Reba at Manuel's to deal with the Georgia Tech guys had been a first step in that direction. Besides, Reba might have a weak leg, but she'd always known how to deal with men. . . .

The doorbell made her jump. Ha. So Reba had decided to come home already. "I'm coming, I'm coming," Tally called, as she ran the last few steps to the door, afraid that the persistent ring would arouse and upset the couple upstairs. "For gosh sakes, Reba, I'm trying to get the door open." The old door was pulling one of its stubborn tricks, but Tally finally managed to open it.

"Oh." She strained to see the tall figure who'd stepped back as the door opened. His face was obscured by the shadows but Tally thought he was probably the Jaeckals' son, who was expected home for Easter break. "I'm sorry, I thought you were a friend coming in. It's the upstairs apartment you want. Just go around back to the stairs. The Jaeckals have their own entrance, too." She would have closed the door, but the sound of her name froze her in her tracks.

Tally closed her eyes, denying the familiarity of the voice. It was a trick; a sick, ghoulish trick of her imagination. She opened her eyes and opened the door wider to allow the light to play over the features of the man who was still whispering her name over and over.

"Tally!" As Tally worked to overcome her numbness, Reba came pounding up to the door, her eyes full of excitement and not seeing the figure who had stepped back into the shadows.

"Are you okay? Eric Jaeckal from upstairs came in Manuel's just now and said some guy was lurking around your apartment. Do you think we ought to . . ." Reba stopped cold as she realized Tally was looking very strangely at something behind Reba. She turned slowly and saw, then, the man standing in the shadows.

"Nick!" Reba's scream cut through the night and Tally was dimly conscious of lights going on upstairs, spreading illumination on the figure standing outside her door.

"Nick?" she whispered, not believing that it was really he. "Nick?"

He stepped forward and then she could see his face. "Tally," he said, his voice cracking with emotion. His control broke then, and he grabbed her and Reba both, hugging and crying and saying their names over and over while they did the same with him. "Oh, God, I never thought I'd see either one of you again."

Tally ran her hand over his face, weeping and laughing at the same time. "It's really you. Nick, you're skin and bones, but you're real—dammit. You're real! Reba, pinch me, so I'll wake up. No, don't pinch me. I want it to be true. Is it true?" Tally gripped Nick's arm hard and pulled him into the apartment so she could look at him better. "It's really you. Nick, they told us you were . . . oh, God, Reba, you see him, too. It is Nick. It really is Nick, standing right here in my living room."

"It really is," Reba said, her face glowing with happiness that matched Tally's. "I'm gonna get us all a drink. I'm sure Nick needs one and I sure as hell do."

"Make that coffee," Nick said, his eyes devouring Tally, his hands making sure she was flesh-and-blood real instead of a dream. "I can't get enough of that stuff. Or you," he whispered to Tally. To Reba, "And if you've got Luzianne, I'll feel like I've come back from hell and this is heaven."

"It is heaven," Tally whispered as she and Nick had their first kiss while Reba went to make coffee in the kitchen.

Nick had been her ghost when she and Cane made love the first time. Now, it was Cane who haunted her thoughts as Tally began to accept the miracle of Nick's return. Her first lover, the father of her child, was back, but Tally knew with a sinking heart that even a miracle could not make things the way they were before Nick had gone down in that helicopter. . . .

20

"I still can't believe it. Is it really you? Are you really here, or am I dreaming?" Tally reached out and for the hundredth time touched the arm of the man sitting beside her to make sure it really was Nick Cantrell. "You're so *thin*" was a refrain interspersed with the wonder of recognizing that her old sweetheart was actually sitting in her apartment.

She was grateful to Reba for discreetly going off to bed, after they'd had coffee, leaving Tally and Nick alone to absorb the miracle of his being back—alive. Her emotions had been restrained until the bedroom door had closed behind Reba, leaving the other two to themselves. Then Tally had burst into tears, which hadn't stopped until Nick's arms had made the reality of their reunion an occasion not for tears but for joy.

"Let me look at you," Tally said for the tenth time. She ran her hands up and down Nick's arms, then up the sides of his face. He was not quite gaunt, but there was a haggard, even haunted look about him that made her long to cuddle him in her arms as though he were a wounded child. "Oh, just let me look at you. Nick—how. . . ? I tried to listen when you told Reba about the release and all the weeks of negotiations, but all I could think about was how happy I was to see you alive and—well, not in the same shape you were when I last saw you but—alive! Oh, Nick. Was it just awful?" Tally buried her face in Nick's chest and wept again. He was so different, so changed.

There was a new patience about him, too. He waited until she was quiet again before telling her the story of how his release from the prison somewhere in Asia had finally come about after months of frustrating negotiations. "When my mother heard about the Doughty case and how they had opened the door to relatives of captured Americans, she didn't rest until I was freed. It was touch and go, but finally, with Cane's help, they broke through. . . ."

"Cane knew about this? All this time?" Tally felt the cold knife go through her, paring away much of the joy of Nick's return.

"He had contacts. And when they made the final arrangements, he met Lucy in Washington to help her cut through the red tape. They could have kept me for a much longer debriefing session, but he arranged it so that I only stayed three days. Then he let us have his plane to go home. There was a problem with clearing the Atlanta airport, though, so we came back to Cane's place." Nick's face took on a troubled expression. "My mother lied to me about you, and Cane backed her up. You were the first one I asked about, Tally, the first one I wanted to know about. They told me you had left several years ago, that they didn't know where you were now."

Tally held her breath, not surprised that Lucy would lie so blatantly—but *Cane!* He had known that Nick was alive even when they were making love—and had not seen fit to tell her. The sense of betrayal gave her a sick feeling in the pit of her stomach. "So you went to Cane's house tonight straight from the airport, you and Lucy. But how did you find out I was here?"

Nick picked up a strand of her hair and held on to it as though it were his link to life. "I saw your picture," he said softly. "In Cane's bedroom. And at first . . ." He kissed her hair, holding it against his lips so that his words came muffled. "At first I was angry at you, thinking—well, you can imagine what I thought. But then I remembered that they'd said you were gone, and if you were gone, why was your picture in Cane's bedroom? And that's when I got really mad. I wanted to know about you one way or the other. If you were with Cane and that's what they were keeping from me, I wanted to know about it. So I called Gretchen."

Tally expelled her breath slowly, almost afraid to ask him, "And she told you that I was living here, working for Cane, but nothing more." Nothing more, nothing more, her brain repeated obstinately.

Nick nodded. "She gave me your address. My mother was furious, crying and screaming at me that I couldn't throw away

my life again, right after I'd had it given back to me and—
well, some other things." He grinned a little sadly. "But I've
been screamed at a lot. The brainwashing techniques they tried
on me used screaming, too. What I wanted was to see you,
and Mother—nobody—was going to stop me."

Tally gave a little cry and pulled him into her arms. "Poor
Nick! Poor dear Nick, to be faced with a battle with your
mother over me, after all the horrible ones you've already had
to live through."

"But I'm here." Nick raised his face, which was stained
with tears. "Here with you. And I told my mother that I would
not go home until I saw you. And now that I've seen you, I'll
tell you this, Tally: I'm through being bullied. I won't go back
to Moss Island without you."

Tally closed her eyes as she pulled Nick's head back down
on her shoulder. "But I can't go back there, Nick. Never."
And she told him about her promise to leave and stay away
from the island in return for what Lucy had done for her and
Genevieve. She did not tell him about Amalie yet, for reasons
she was not certain of. Perhaps it was because of some emotional fragility she sensed in him.

"Then I'll stay here with you," Nick said with a quiet
firmness that had a granite resolve underneath the soft words.
"They've always tried to keep us apart. Now they know they
can never do that again." He lifted his head and looked down
into her eyes, which had misted up again. "Don't cry. Don't
ever cry for me again, sweet Tally. We're together forever this
time—and nothing and nobody can ever separate us. Promise
me." He kissed her feverishly. "Promise."

"I promise," Tally whispered. When Nick's lips claimed
hers with the hunger of a starving man, she responded warmly.
But in the back of her mind the image of Cane reared again,
this time clouding with her anger. Deliberately, coldly, reso-
lutely, she shut out the image.

Cane had seduced her (willing though she was, more shame
to her) knowing that Nick was on the way home. Well, he had
made her choice now quite clear. Cane didn't need her; never
had. He only desired her. Nick, on the other hand, needed her

more than anyone. He desired her, too. Hadn't he proved that
by defying Lucy on his first few days back in his homeland?
Tally, tightening her arms around Nick, felt the tiredness in
him and responded protectively. "Nick," she whispered,
"we'll talk about this in the morning. I'll call in sick and we'll
spend the day together." She put her lips to his ear and blew.
"I'm going to put you in my bed with me, but I don't think
either of us is up to anything serious tonight . . . Nick?"

She lifted the heavy head from her shoulder and laughed
softly when she realized that her returning hero was fast asleep.

Tally managed to lead him to her bed, and after he'd been
arranged as comfortably as one could arrange a deadweight
six-two frame, she stood looking down at him. He was so
exhausted and vulnerable-looking, she wanted to burst into
tears.

But she didn't. She crept gently into the other side of her
bed and very carefully turned out the light. Her last waking
thought was not a noble one: Won't Lucy's nose be out of joint
after tonight?

Cane's frustration at waiting until almost noon to catch a commercial flight home was unloaded on Lucy when she met him
at Hatfield Airport. "Dammit, Lucy, I can't believe you just
let Nick go like that. I told you it was a mistake to lie to him
about Tally. And now she probably knows I kept everything
from her." He slammed his bag down on the seat next to her
in the chauffeured limousine. Frank waited patiently until Cane
realized he was waiting for instructions. Cane looked at Lucy.
"Is there still no answer at Tally's apartment? Did you try
again on the way out here?"

Lucy looked at the car phone and back at Cane and shook
her head. The tiny lines that were showing around her mouth
were intensified from the strain of the past few days. "Yes,
I've called everywhere. Tally's office said she'd called in to
say she'd be back on Monday. Gretchen doesn't know anything, and Reba isn't to be found, either. Cane, if that girl has
got my boy in her clutches again. . . !" Lucy's hands curled
into little fists and her eyes glittered dangerously. "He's so

fragile, so vulnerable. And all he could talk about from the time I got him back to the States was how anxious he was to see Tally Malone. I wish I'd gotten rid of her for good when I had the chance!''

Cane was momentarily distracted from his determination to find Tally before she got the wrong idea that he'd been in cahoots with Lucy. ''What do you mean, 'rid of her for good'?''

Lucy backpedaled smoothly. ''I mean that I almost talked Tally into seeking an overseas position that she was quite interested in. Cane, the man is waiting for you to tell him where to take us and those people behind us are getting surly.''

''To my place, Frank. I'll make some calls from there and let Vanessa throw something together for lunch. That damn cardboard meal I had on the plane was horrible.'' Cane opened the bar and poured himself a stiff drink. He wasn't an alcoholic but was beginning to understand what turned a man into one. ''Drink?'' At Lucy's negative head shake, Cane asked her, ''What makes you think they haven't struck out straight for the island? That would be my first instinct if I were Nick.''

Lucy had no intention of revealing to Cane her reason for knowing that would not be the case. Tally's promise that she would never again set foot on Moss Island was in writing, but Lucy knew the promise was deeper than that. As much as the two women despised each other, they both knew that they were women of their word. ''Just call it woman's intuition. Darling, don't look so glum! The Army psychiatrist said that Nick would be prone to erratic behavior until he completes therapy to counteract all that horrible incarceration and brainwashing. We're not to upset him—which is why I lied to him about Tally in the first place. That woman has always had a terrible impact on his emotions, and I thought he just needed peace and quiet.''

''But you made me lie to him, too, about her. And you know good and well that I cooperated only because I've got my own reasons for believing Nick's relationship with Tally could only lead to disaster. . . . Dammit, Lucy, we've got to do something!'' Cane leaned forward and said sharply to the driver,

"Frank, do you think you could do a little better than this slow crawl? I don't want to spend the rest of my life on the expressway."

"Sorry, sir, but the road-repair crew has got traffic down to one lane. There was a lot of damage from the ice storm. There's not much I can do."

"Terrific," Cane growled, pouring himself another drink.

"How did your meeting with Litzenberg go?" Lucy asked, trying to keep her mind off the fact that her son was with Tally and may have already been told about Amalie. Her heart's worst dread was that Nick would learn the truth about Amalie and believe it, with the inevitable result of hating his mother for her part in the secret. "What did he and Colonel Mayer say to you?"

"They're afraid for the remaining prisoners if the publicity over here is too strong over Nick's release. There are mothers who've been going over there for over a year, trying to bring about their sons' release. It wouldn't look good if it came out that strings were pulled for one serviceman and not another. Mayer promised to give me his report on the brainwashing success stats, with Litzenberg's support, if I would keep the newspapers from making Nick's release a big issue. I agreed, of course. The important thing is having Nick back, but they don't want us to screw up the negotiations for the other captured Americans." To say nothing of alerting the public to our involvement in Southeast Asia, he thought to himself.

Lucy shuddered. "Those poor mothers. I met the Doughty woman. She's been through hell."

"They all have." Cane sat back, watching the skyline of Atlanta coming into view and remembering his whispered promise to Tally to take her to the opening of the city's first skyscraper restaurant, the Polaris on the top of the Hyatt-Regency. He had had so many plans, and now they were all in limbo. Tally would never forgive him for keeping the hope about Nick from her. She would never be able to understand that his stepped-up wooing of her had been an attempt on his part to make her acknowledge her feelings for him before Nick's return threw her back into an untenable relationship.

Cane's gloom lay on him like a gray cloud all the way back to his house. He feared that he may have lost his chances with Tally Malone forever.

"Here we are," he told Lucy brusquely when they pulled up into his driveway. "I'll have Vanessa fix some lunch for you. I'm not hungry."

"Vanessa?"

"My housekeeper. She's wonderful and I hope you won't try bossing her around like you do the blacks at Camellia Hall, Lucy. Believe you me, this one will put you in your place so fast it'll make your head spin."

"I have enough to think about without spending my time trying to train your staff for you," Lucy said with a sniff and a toss of her head as she marched into Cane's house ahead of him. Cane shook his head as he heard her asserting herself in the kitchen, declaring what she would have for lunch. Cane would put book on Lucy's being served whatever Vanessa had prepared with no variation on the menu.

Alone in his study, he called Tally's apartment again. No answer. Then, on a sudden inspiration, he called the Autumn Oaks Home in Monroe. The director was cautious until she found out that Cane was the man responsible for the regular weekly delivery of fresh flowers to Genevieve Malone's cottage. "Oh, Mr. Winslow, it's *you!* I can't tell you what those flowers have meant to Genevieve. Her eyes light up like stars every time the delivery boy shows up with that order."

Cane expressed his appreciation and led the director into a discussion about recent visitors. "I know her daughter is very constant about taking her for drives on weekends. Has she been there today?"

"Oh, no, but she'll be here bright and early tomorrow, sure as sunshine. That girl's faithful about coming to see her mama, I don't mind telling you. Why, there's some got folks out here that haven't been to see 'em in . . ."

Cane listened politely, but at the first lull in the diatribe against ungrateful children, he said, "The times that Tally hasn't made it for her visits she called ahead, didn't she?"

"Mr. Winslow, not a weekend has gone by since Tally

moved here that she didn't visit her mother—except that weekend of the ice storm.''

Cane remembered that weekend well. "Mrs. Cagle, I have a big favor to ask of you. I haven't been out to see Vieve in a long time, and I very much would like to see her. If I placed my order with you for a nice little lunch to be served at her cottage, would you take care of seeing that it was something she would really enjoy?''

Mrs. Cagle almost choked up over the phone. "Oh, Mr. Winslow, if only there were more people like you in the world. Genevieve would be so delighted. I can just hear her now chattering like a little girl about her gentleman caller and how her papa always liked it when she entertained in her very own home. Maybe she'll be in one of her clear spells.''

That was exactly what Cane hoped for—one of her clear spells. He would never hurt Genevieve Fontaine Malone, but for Tally's sake (and Nick's) he needed some answers about the past that had serious bearing on the present.

Lucy was not hard to convince that she should go back to the island in case Nick showed up there. Cane promised to keep her posted. He didn't tell her about his planned visit to Autumn Oaks, but he did ask her a question that had been bugging him since she'd first approached him about helping her get Nick freed. "Lucy, have you told Nick about adopting Amalie? That's not something you need to spring on him out of the blue, you know.''

"I planned to do that on our drive home, but Tally's messed that up like she's always messed up everything that had to do with me and my son.''

"But what do you plan to tell him?''

Lucy looked her stepbrother straight in the eye and said brightly, "Why, the truth, of course. I'll tell him that he now has a precious little adopted sister whom he's sure to adore as all the rest of us do.''

"And when he sees—as all the rest of us do—that little Amalie is the spitting image of his mother—what do you say then?''

"Thank you for that—I adore being told Amalie looks just

like me. As for what I'll tell Nick if he wants to pry into my little secrets, I'll decide when the time comes." Lucy still looked pleased; Cane decided she enjoyed the prospect of shocking her son with evidence of a serious love affair at her age.

"If I hadn't seen Harm making an absolute fool of himself over that little girl, I'd wonder what you told him, too. Lucy, I hate it when you get that funny little smile that means you are thinking something totally unrespectable."

Lucy patted Cane on the cheek and picked up her bag. "I heard the driver toot for me. Ta-ta, darling. Must go. Call me the minute you hear anything."

Cane hurriedly kissed her, holding her by the arm as she was about to run out the door to the car he'd ordered for her. "Not so fast. What's the private joke?"

Lucy reached up and tweaked Cane's cheek. "It should amuse you as much as it did me. The rumor around the island is that Amalie is my child by *you*, Cane Stephen Foster Winslow."

She left him standing there, his chin on the floor.

On his way to the office later, he had overcome his astonishment sufficiently to wonder who Amalie's real father could be. That she was Lucy's daughter was no longer doubtful in his heart of hearts. There had been a time when he had a terrible suspicion involving another possibility, but he had never allowed that dark seed to germinate.

Cane enjoyed the drive out to the little town of Monroe, Georgia, the next morning. Even with his mind in a turmoil, he could drink in the spring beauty of a thawed-out countryside in the serious process of leaving winter behind. He approved of Autumn Oaks, too. A peaceful place for people with gentle mind disorders, was the way Tally had described it. Privacy and seclusion were the rule at Autumn Oaks. Each of the cottages dotting the grounds had its own enclosed yard; most had little gardens and shade trees.

When he checked in with the head office to get directions to Genevieve's quarters, Helen Cagle told him that the catered meal Cane had arranged for had already been delivered to Genevieve's cottage. "She wanted to serve it herself, Mr. Winslow, on her own china, so I told the caterer and her staff that I was sure this would be agreeable with you." Mrs. Cagle smiled as she handed Cane a little map of the grounds, on which she had marked "Dogwood Cottage" with an X. "Genevieve was so thrilled at the prospect of having a special lunch with a special visitor."

"Did she seem to be aware of who her visitor is?" Cane remembered Tally telling her that Jim-Roy had never been able to explain to Genevieve who he was and why he was there. Tally herself had given up long since trying to disabuse her mother of the strange illusion that she and Tally were the same little girl of long ago.

The smile faded. "I'm sorry, Mr. Winslow, but I honestly must say I don't think she recognized your name when I mentioned it. But perhaps when she sees you in person . . ."

The door of the cottage was ajar. Cane tapped lightly and went inside, softly calling out "Vieve? Genevieve Fontaine Malone?"

She called out from the kitchen. "Oh, my goodness, you're here already and I haven't even got my apron off."

She came bustling out and put out her hand. "Welcome to my little home, Mr. Winslow." Her eyes held no recognition of him, just warm interest in an anticipated but unknown visitor. "It's not easy getting used to being away from our big old house, but Papa said closing it down for repairs was necessary. And I do declare it's sort of nice not having all those servants around bothering me about this, that, and the other. But where are my manners? You'll have a little sherry, won't you, Mr. Winslow?" Vieve's eyes clouded. "Winslow, Winslow. I declare, I know I ought to know that name. There was a family on the mainland, used to buy some of Papa's rice for their household, but I can't seem to place your face in that family."

Cane said gently, "Lucy Cantrell is my stepsister, Genevieve." He wasn't sure that wouldn't get him thrown out. He took the glass she handed him and waited.

"Cantrell, Cantrell. Lucy Cantrell." Vieve's face showed

the struggle with her memory. "I didn't know there were any girls in that branch of the family. Hugh Cantrell was Papa's best friend. They hunted together, and, land, how they did love their bourbon and branch! Oh my, once they gave Harmon a glass, and him only sixteen. . . ." Genevieve laughed, her face almost young again. "Harmon and I, we were sweethearts," she said shyly, with a coquettish look that made Cane smile. "Papa says there's never been a Cantrell yet that can hold on to his money, but they can sure charm the bark off a pine tree."

"You really loved each other, you and Harm, didn't you?" When Vieve nodded, he decided it was time for a minor shock treatment to her memory. "And then the Cantrells were in financial distress and Justin Randolph, my stepfather and Lucy's daddy, bought poor Harm off so Lucy could have the husband she wanted. . . ."

Genevieve drew herself up, her eyes shooting fire and her whole face quivering with anger. "Don't ever mention that bastard's name in this house again! You hear me? If Justin Prelutsky—Randolph, hell!—sets foot in this house one more time to try to buy our property, I'll blow his damned head off." A chill ran down Cane's spine when he realized Vieve was parroting her long-dead father's damnation of Lucy's daddy. "And now," Genevieve said with a bright sweet smile that made Cane wonder if he'd imagined her coming out with the string of vituperative words straight out of a dead man's mouth, "shall we have lunch?"

Cane was a native son of the South, but he had never witnessed what Genevieve did after they had eaten. Washing the fine china at the dining table was a ritual that Vieve's mother and her grandmother before that had always performed at the table after a meal. She brought in a white enamel pan of soapy water, shooing Cane away when he wanted to help her, and placed it at the end of the table; then, with her cloth held ready in a delicate hand, she beckoned to Cane. "Now you can help me. Just hand me those dishes one by one—careful, dear! They were my great-grandmother's old Limoges."

Since the plates had "Made in Japan" on the back and were

obviously not fine, Cane decided Vieve's fantasy extended to her surroundings. He made a resolution to have Rich's send out a set of antique Limoges for Christmas. "They're very pretty."

"Thank you." Vieve held up the last dish and cocked her head from side to side. "Maybe after my baby comes and if it's a girl—and I'm sure it will be, since Essie Mae says it's too high for a boy . . ." She was looking dreamily at the plate and not noticing how Cane's hand had frozen on the drying towel. "Maybe I'll put these up. But he says he has a set of old Wedgwood that the witch doesn't know about and he'll give them to our little girl. . . ."

Cane let out his breath. "Are you saying that Harm Cantrell is the father of the baby you're expecting?"

Genevieve looked terrified. "Shhh! Don't let Papa hear you say that word. . . . He'd blow his brains out if he knew I was . . . uh, you know . . . in a family way, and me not even . . . oh my, if this isn't the dearest little gravy boat! Just look at these little handles."

"Genevieve." Cane wished he knew if Vieve meant her father would have killed Harmon if he'd discovered he, a married man, had seduced young Genevieve; or if she meant he would have blown his own brains out. "Genevieve, what about—"

The sound of a car driving up made Vieve's face light up and Cane's heart quicken. Tally! She had come! "Here, you finish drying while I go to the door. It always aggravates Papa if we're late for our Sunday drive." Cane stood there, towel in hand, his heart pounding as Vieve ran to the door and opened it.

"Well, my goodness, I was wondering if you'd ever get here. And here, you've brought that nice young man you're sweet on. Papa will be pleased. Is there a lap robe in the car for our legs? This spring weather can turn on you. Just you two wait for a moment while I get my coat and hat."

"Mama, don't go get anything. We're not going for a drive today. I have some important news." Tally leaned over and kissed her mother, then took Nick's hand and pulled him with her to face Genevieve. "You remember Nicholas Cantrell, Mama? He and I have something to tell you."

"He's a handsome boy," Vieve whispered in a stage whisper to Tally. "What relation did you say he is to Hugh Cantrell?"

"I didn't say, Mama, but that was his granddaddy. Harm is his daddy and Lucy Cantrell is his mother."

Cane's mind screamed out silently. *Now, Vieve. Tell her now. Tell Tally why she and Nick Cantrell can never be more to each other than they are now.*

"That's nice," Vieve said, patting Nick's hand and putting it back in Tally's. *Oh God*, Cane was telling himself with a sinking heart. *It's going to be up to me to tell her*. "Now tell me about this surprise you've got for me."

"It's not a surprise, Mama, not exactly. Nick came back after a long, long time away, and we decided we never wanted to be apart again. . . ."

Cane stepped forward then, and Tally's face turned pale. "Tally, I have to talk to you. Alone."

"We have nothing to say to each other, Cane Winslow. The only reason I'm not handing you my resignation from Tri-Com right this minute is that Nick needs time to find something for himself."

Cane moved closer to the little triangle which, in some back area of his mind, struck him as being closed against him. "Tally, you're talking as though you and Nick can just pick up where you left off years ago. It won't work! He's got a long road ahead of him and you can help him, but not this way, Tally. For God's sake, Tally, not like this!" He felt Nick's bewildered eyes, like two burned holes in a blanket, staring at him. "Tally, don't make me tell you things, and Nick, too, right here, in front of Genevieve. Come outside and listen to what I have to say. Please."

Nick spoke up in a voice edged with anger. "Tally and I know what you're trying to do, Cane—you and my mother both. You want to keep me away from Tally, even to the point of lying to both of us. Well, you had your chance, and now I'm back and Tally and I are together, like we belong. And this time, nobody can keep us apart."

Genevieve spoke into the tense silence with a little-girl pique that was almost comical, "Well, if somebody doesn't hurry up and tell me my surprise, I'm going back to my room and take my nap."

Tally took Nick's hand in one hand and her mother's in her other. "Mama, the surprise is this: Nick and I got married."

Tally did not see Cane's face when she made the announcement but she heard the almost animal sound of pain that he made.

Genevieve Malone had very little reaction to what was, to Cane, the most devastating news he had ever received in his life. She was nodding like a dormouse and Tally used the distraction of putting her to bed for a nap as a way to get through her own shock at finding Cane waiting for her.

She returned to the living room and strained silence. "Cane, I know you don't approve of Nick and me getting married like this."

Cane's smile was bitter. "I would have expected something elegant from you, Tally. Going down to Folkston through that marriage mill isn't your style—or Nick's."

Tally slipped her hand into Nick's and held it tightly. She could feel him trembling and her chin went up. "Style wasn't a consideration, Cane. Nick and I made this decision together and we're very happy with it. Aren't we, darling?" Cane's heart constricted at the look Nick and Tally exchanged. They were united against him as their joint enemy and the realization cut him to the quick. "Reba was our witness, then she went on down to the island for a visit. Nick and I had our wedding night at the King and Prince."

Salt in the wound. Cane had had all he could take. "Lucy doesn't deserve to be left out of this. It's going to be a shock hearing about your getting married, but the least you can do is call and let her know that Nick is okay."

Tally nodded. "We called her from Saint Simons on our way back this morning." She smiled crookedly. "Don't ask me to repeat what she said. But don't look so worried. Nick's going down next week to make up with his mother while I'm on that new executive-training program. In the meantime, I guess I'd better ask you if I'm still a part of the company."

"You signed a contract," Cane said quietly. "I don't remember anything in it saying that getting married was a cause for termination. And I won't be around very much during the next few months. Tri-Com needs you."

"Thank you. But you said earlier that you needed to talk to me about something. You can talk in front of my husband. We're not going to keep secrets from each other."

Cane opened his mouth to utter the shattering words, but he could not. "It wasn't important."

"But you had something to discuss with me privately," Tally insisted.

He could tell her. He could lay it bare and cold and ugly right out there in front of them, six hours after they'd spent their honeymoon night in each other's arms at the King and Prince. He could watch their faces, one of them that of the woman he loved more than life itself, and the other that of a vulnerable, heart-torn, brain-weary, and scared young man. He could feel their anger, shock, the gamut of acknowledgment of being perpetuators of the South's most famous sin. And then he could walk away with the heavy guilt of having been the one to split open the secret closeness of two people who deserved hurt less than any other two people he knew. . . .

"It can wait." Cane held out his hand to Nick and choked up inside when the younger man ignored the hand and wrapped his arms around his step-uncle's neck.

"Congratulations," Cane finally managed. To Tally: "Be happy. Keep Tri-Com on the up and up. I probably won't see you for quite a while. The Guam operation promises to be a real bear to get off the ground."

"What about that international newspaper you wanted to work on?"

"It's like a lot of other things in my life. Everything I want most retreats from my grasp just when I think I've got it. That dream has to wait its turn like a lot of others. Besides, I'm the only one who can pull together this operation. Good luck, you two. And keep on knockin' 'em dead at the company, Tally."

"Thanks," Tally whispered. "And good luck. Let's try hard not to have hard feelings—you, me, and Nick, I mean." She held out her hand.

Cane looked down at it and gave a bitter little laugh as he shook her hand. "Hard feelings?" He looked at Tally's face, committing it to memory for the long, cold months of loneliness ahead. "No, there won't be any hard feelings, Tally. Good-bye, Nick, and good luck to you."

He left, the lunch that Vieve had served him chewing away in his stomach as hopelessness chewed away at his heart. And somewhere in the mess nestled love and pity for the two young lovers whose chances for marital bliss were about on par with those of Romeo and Juliet. Could Lucy be blind to the fact that Harm was Tally's father? Would she tell them? No, her plan would no doubt be to work on Nick.

21

Tally was not feeling like a triumphant bride when she returned to work the following week. Throughout the bursts of congratulations from everyone, she was aware of the underlying surprise. Blake Edenfield, perhaps, expressed it most openly when the two rode the elevator together on their way up to a First Wednesday meeting.

"You caught us all with our pants down," he said suddenly and without preamble. "If I were a betting man—and I am on occasion—I would have made book on it that you were out for the big game."

"I'm not a huntress," Tally responded coolly. "And if you're referring to Cane Winslow as the 'big game,' I hope you know I resent the implication that I'm one of those women who try to sleep their way to the top."

Blake shrugged. "Apparently you don't have to. From what I see and hear, you're almost a certain shoo-in for the vice-president-for-programming slot that Bob Frazier will be leaving empty when he moves to Seattle. Eden is thrilled about getting

he 'Newpoint' show all to herself, but she made no secret
about not wanting any of the shit-work that goes along with
the other part of Bob's job.''

"Again, I hope you're not trying to say this is a case of
favoritism where Cane and I are concerned. He's leaving the
appointment up to you and the board. You can rest easy that
he won't try to influence you about me—and he's left the board
to make its own decisions.''

Blake's famous thin smile appeared. "Oh, he could influence us all. Don't take Cane's love for company autonomy too
far. But he doesn't have to use his influence in your case. The
whole board is singing your praises to the skies, especially
since you came up with that advance-rerun plan. Imagine,
getting the best sitcoms on air now locked down for reruns five
years from now—at under three hundred an episode.'' Blake
made a mockingly flourishing bow as he allowed Tally to
precede him from the elevator. "My hat is off to you, along
with everyone else's. Who knows, you could wind up with my
job.''

"I wouldn't care for it,'' Tally said with a sweet smile. "I
can't stand the sight of blood.''

Tally had not married Nick Cantrell for his money, but she was
still shocked when she discovered how totally Lucy had cut
her son off from any financial assistance. The fact that Nick
was under regular psychiatric treatment at the VA hospital had
made it easy for his mother to continue custodial control of his
share of the Cantrell estate. She had advised Tally of that with
poorly repressed glee when the latter had approached her about
Nick's legacy rights.

"You should have investigated Nick's affairs more thoroughly before you shanghaied him into marriage, my dear.
Nick's affairs have been under my power of attorney for some
time now. But after all,'' she concluded sweetly at the end of
the unpleasant phone call, "Nick has told me you two are so
idyllically happy, you don't need his money. Are you trying
to tell me the romance has cooled?''

Tally closed her eyes and silently cursed the woman on the

end of the line. "I'm not asking about this for my sake, Lucy but for Nick's. For God's sake, he's your son. And he ha special needs—this apartment, for instance. We're so crampe for space, and he keeps having these nightmares. . . ." She didn't tell Lucy that the people upstairs had called the police twice about the screams. Bedtime had become a nightly horror "All I'm asking is that you give him his rightful portion of his estate and let him feel like a man instead of worrying himsel sick when I take care of all the bills."

"You made your bed, Tally. Now I suggest you lie in it lumps and all."

Lucy hung up then and Tally could feel the older woman's self-satisfied smirks all the way from the island.

Damn her to hell. Tally was glad that Nick was with his support group at the hospital and couldn't witness her tight-lipped march to her desk where her accounts were. He would hate to know how much his moving in with her had already depleted her checking balance. The money she'd realized with the lucrative freeway deal was tied up in Tri-Com stock, excep for the part she'd advanced to get Reba off to a good start in her boutique on Tenth Street.

Nick came home about ten to find his bride on the sofa with her feet tucked up under her, sipping her nightly Ovaltine and scratching the head of the scruffy cat she and Nick had taken in over the weekend. The feline reminded her of long-gone Mothball, except he had a black patch on his left eye. She and Nick had agreed on naming him "Out Damned Spot"—Odie-Spot, for short.

"Hey." They kissed and Nick wiped his thumb over a smudge under Tally's eye. "I hope that's for a sad movie and not for me. I had a good session tonight and I'd like to talk to you about it." He sat down and took Tally's cup from her and drained the last of it. "Umm. That helps. I had so much coffee, I'm wired. Want to hear? You really want to hear what we talked about tonight?"

Tally laid her head on his shoulder. "I think so—unless it's more of that terrible stuff about the brainwashing sessions.

Nick, I'm not a coward about that, but I can't stand to think about you going through all of it."

"Nothing about that crap. I just thought you might like to know that I'm not the only one to have the kind of problem I have." Nick cracked a couple of pecans from the bowl on the coffee table and picked the meat from them. Before popping it into his mouth, he said, not looking at Tally, "It's not uncommon with vets, you know, having a bad time with sex. They left their sweethearts, wives, whatever, and then they come back and want it to be just like it was before they left. And it's not. It's just not. Everything's different. Everything's changed. So is everybody, including the girl you left behind." Nick pulled Tally toward him and held her face while he looked down into her eyes. "God knows I've changed, but look at you. Tally, you've grown up since I've left you. You've turned from a simple little island girl into somebody who kind of scares me. Tally, I wouldn't say this if I hadn't just been with guys who came back to find that their wives, sweethearts, what-have-yous have become *strangers*."

Tally felt the sense of dread again she had first felt during her wedding night, when she knew she and Nick had something serious to confront. "Honey, I know you're tired. I am, too. Maybe this could wait till tomorrow night."

"No, it can't." Nick took Tally's cup from her hand and put it on the coffee table, then pulled her over close to him. "We need to talk about it, dammit, about how I disappointed you since our honeymoon. Tally, look at me! I couldn't do it, God help me. I couldn't make love to you, after almost five years of dreaming of nothing but that—making love to you. And all the nights since then—Tally, they've been sheer torture. Lying there, feeling you awake and hurt and wondering. . . ." He looked around the apartment. "Part of it is that this place has your name written all over it. It's yours—not ours."

"I thought you liked the apartment." Tally thought about her diminishing funds and wondered how Nick would feel if he knew she was scraping the bottom of the barrel just to keep a small apartment going.

"Oh, it's okay, but you're a Cantrell now. I want more for you. We need to move into something better. I'll call the realtor in the morning while you're at work. And then I plan to start looking for a position." He laughed. "Job, I mean. The people in my group talked about that, too, about how vets don't always get the best breaks with jobs. You'd think so, but that's not how it works."

Tally moved into his arms, hugging him so tightly she could feel the bones that still didn't have enough flesh on them. "Jobs, smobs. As for this place, it'll do for now. And, Nick, do you really feel the need to look for a job? You've spent several years of your life serving your country, after all. Take some time off from worrying, for goodness' sake."

"Goodness has nothing to do with it. Not with what I've been through. Tally, we can't ignore what's happened to me. You've been understanding, patient, loving, everything I could ever ask for in a wife, but you know damn well we've got a problem." Nick put his head in his hands. "No, change that to I've got a problem. You haven't said anything, which makes it even worse."

Tally pulled his head onto her shoulder. "I love you," she said softly. "I love you. You love me. Doesn't that count for anything?"

"Yes, dammit. But it doesn't change the fact that I'm impotent." Nick lifted his head and looked at Tally, his eyes filling with tears. "There, I've said it out loud. Impotent. Do you know how much I've wanted you all those nights? How much I want you right now?" He buried his head again. "And how ashamed I've been that I can't do anything—any goddamn thing but think and dream and want and cry and curse the world that took my loving from me?"

Tally felt that her heart might break at the torment behind his words. "Look, once you start the regular therapy sessions with Dr. Lewis, things will get better." She kissed him tenderly. "I can be patient for as long as it takes. You've got to be patient, too. Nick, you've got to learn to be gentle with yourself. Shame has no place in our marriage. For God's sake,

do you think I married you for what you could do in bed?''
She squeezed him hard and mussed the gray-blond hair. His
experience as a prisoner had robbed him of more than his
youth, she thought with a new pang.

"Why *did* you marry me?" Nick asked, his voice muffled
against Tally's bosom. "It can't be for my money, since Lucy's
seen to it that we see very little money from my trust fund.
Physical attraction is out, since I'm hardly the boy who left
you behind. So what is it—pity?"

Tally held him harder, hoping he wasn't aware of the increased thumping of her heart as she considered the tough
question. She had mercilessly probed herself for the answer to
that, not wanting to think she had married Nick to hurt Cane.
Her resolve to be a good wife to Nick strengthened. "Not
pity—fear. Fear that you might get away from me again before
I had a chance to lasso you and hog-tie you down." She
tweaked his thin cheek and grinned. "Once I fatten you up a
little on some of Essie Mae's old recipes, every Buckhead Pink
in town will be after you."

Nick's face crumpled, then he slowly put his arms around
his wife. "You're trying too hard again. We both do that. I
know it's as tough for you as it is for me to pretend that
everything's okay." He gently pushed her from him and
sighed. "You were right, it's no good talking about it. What's
on the tube tonight?"

"Nick!" Tally cried in anguish as the blaring television
drowned out the pain still lying like a wounded animal between
them. But Nick's eyes were carefully bright and blank on the
screen and she slumped in despair.

"It's your friend Eden's 'Newpoint' with the new feature
you said you were trying out this week. Say, she looks pretty
good."

" 'Viewers Bite Back,' " Tally said tiredly. "Why don't
you watch it and tell me what you think so I can pass it along
to the Tri-Com folks." She got up and went into the kitchen.

"Do you really think a shell-shocked vet is any kind of
critic?" Nick called out sarcastically. "Maybe that's what I

can start doing, so I don't feel so useless while you go off to work every day. I can start watching all the shows and writing down my opinion. . . ."

"Nick, stop it." Tally closed her eyes and leaned against the stove edge, the pot she was lining with oil for the popcorn gripped so tightly her knuckles showed white. "You don't have to worry about getting a job," she finally said when she could trust her voice to sound normal again. "We're doing fine." They were not "doing fine," but Tally hadn't told her husband about her futile talk with Lucy concerning the trust fund. Dr. Lewis had cautioned her about discussing traumatic issues of any kind. Nick was still fragile, he had warned, and had all the emotional input he could handle for a while.

She had also asked Dr. Lewis when she could safely tell Nick about their child. The psychiatrist had strongly advised against breaking that news to Nick until after he had recalled the circumstances leading up to and surrounding the receipt of Tally's letter about her pregnancy. While she planned ultimately to claim her child, with Nick as the declared father, she agreed that this was not the time to bring Amalie into their life. Nick had not once mentioned the letter she'd written him about being pregnant; she was sure it was one of the buried pieces from his pre-prison camp life that would resurface when Nick was ready to deal with it.

When she came in with a bowl of steaming, buttery popcorn and coffee, Nick was already engrossed in the evening movie. "How did Eden's show go?" Tally sat down to watch the old Bette Davis film, *Dark Victory*. "I did the editing on this one and got so interested I burned my finger on the splicer." She gave Nick a large handful of popcorn. He hardly seemed to notice. Tally said conversationally, "Bette's got the movie-star disease—no diagnosis, no name, no cure—only certain demise at the end of the movie."

Frowning, Nick turned to her and said, "Sh-sh." And when Tally wanted to snuggle against him, he shifted restlessly away from her.

"Honey, I thought we might go to bed early instead of watching some old movie," Tally said, trying again to snuggle

up to her husband. Maybe, since Nick had broached the subject
of his impotence, they could begin trying to regain their old
status as physical lovers.

But the curtain had been dropped between them again. He
pushed her away—less gently, even with a touch of anger.
"You go on and turn in. You've got that executive-training
business next week. I'm having trouble sleeping, as you know.
Besides, I want to see how this turns out." He patted her arm
and gave her a peck on the cheek. "We didn't have movies
back in the camp."

*Neither did you have a warm-blooded wife who wanted to
comfort you and help you become a man again*, Tally thought
with a good deal of hurt. "Well, don't stay up all night. And
turn off the coffeepot before you go to bed." She didn't try to
kiss him again, not wishing to experience another rebuff. "As
a matter of fact, I'll turn it off myself. Too much coffee will
add to your insomnia. I know—let me fix you a nice cup of
warm milk. That's always good for making a person sleep
well."

Nick caught her by the arm as she got up to go to the kitchen.
"Would you listen to yourself?" he said furiously. "I'm not
an invalid and I hate the way you treat me like one. Don't keep
telling me what's good and what's bad for me, Tally. I'd like
to decide some things for myself around here."

Tally waited for the coldness in his blue eyes to turn to
apologetic warmth, but it didn't. "I'm sorry, Nick," she said
meekly, though something deep inside her rebelled at being
put in the position of having to make all the decisions—and
then being resented for it. As for treating Nick like an invalid—
well, wasn't he? "Well . . . good night." Bedtime had been
awkward for a long time, but at least both had made the pretense
that it was not to be dreaded.

Up until now. Tally went to the bedroom and closed the door
very, very gently. For the first time she acknowledged the
strain that she had been under to keep up the pretense that she
didn't mind Nick's impotence, that at any moment theirs would
become a loving, normal relationship.

The frank admission acted as a soporific. For the first time since the wedding she slept well. The next morning, when she reached out to touch Nick as she always did upon waking, his place next to her on the bed was empty. There had been no screaming, sweating, nerve-screeching nightmares.

She tiptoed into the living room to find the sofa bed made up and Nick sleeping on it in front of the early-bird news report. Tally waited to hear the weather report, since she was flying in the company plane to Gatlinburg, Tennessee, with Blake and others, and the airport had been fogged in twice the past week. Then she turned off the TV so Nick wouldn't be awakened by some blaring commercial.

When she was dressed, had her weekender packed, and had written a note telling Nick the number at the Mountainview Hotel, where her group would be staying for the management seminars, she started to kiss his cheek.

But then she decided against it. Nick needed his sleep more than he needed a kiss from his wife. In fact, Tally thought with a new sadness, she wasn't sure anymore that Nick needed anything from her.

22

The year 1964 kept American press people busy trying to figure out Lyndon Johnson's chances against Goldwater in the Presidential election, to define the role of the United States in the increasingly disturbing Vietnam situation, and speculating whether the Surgeon General's report that cigarette-smoking was linked to cancer would have any effect on a widely addicted public.

Tally Cantrell had her own dilemmas to deal with. She had been the wife of Nick Cantrell almost two years and interim programming vice-president for a year now. She felt she had answered the challenges of her job better than those of her marriage.

In fact, though she had not yet been given the official title for the job she was doing at Tri-Com, she knew it was sure to happen when Blake Edenfield and the other corporate officers met with Cane. She often thought, ruefully, that it would have been a good idea for her marriage to have been on a trial basis, too.

The job was a life-saver emotionally, since she knew what to expect from it, in contrast to her relationship with her husband. She had even worked out a practical relationship with Cane Winslow. Although his newspaper branches were increasingly far-reaching, he still stayed in close contact with Atlanta. Dallas and Miami were his two latest giant acquisitions. There were big problems with the once family-owned newspapers, according to Gretchen, but Cane was managing to pull them more tightly into the growing Tri-Com network. He spent a great deal of time in Guam, too. Tally suspected that remained one of Cane's pet projects, along with the huge Tex-Ark acquisition that was still in the early talking stages. On the few occasions that they got to talk on Cane's visits to the home office, he indicated that Blake Edenfield was handling deals that Cane ideally would have handled himself.

Tally's thoughts about Cane Winslow and what he had been doing lately had to be put behind her when she entered her office this warm September morning. The station was already crackling with the usual problems. She began to tackle the day with revived energy.

"Thanks, Rachel," she told her secretary, who handed her a cup of coffee as soon as her light coat was shed. "What's on for the morning?"

"Your mail's opened on your desk; I'll be in for dictation as soon as you get a crack at it. You need to give orders for the new program insertions. There's a salesman with a made-for-TV package coming by at ten. . . ."

"Hold him off, will you, till I meet with Grady. What's this on your calendar about a college kid? Not another communications student doing a term paper, I hope."

" 'Fraid so. 'Impact of Television on the Suburban Housewife,' or something like that. Plus, you've got another film salesman at eleven." She ignored Tally's groan, consulting her notepad. "He's coming about those new first-run game shows

Mr. Lunt thought might work in the local slot until we got a firm price on the Dobie Gillis early reruns.''

"Well, just so he doesn't take forever. I've got lunch with Gretchen and I don't want to miss seeing her before she goes on vacation. Tell you what—see if you can put the college student off on Eden. She's got files and files of demographics and big boobs to boot.''

"Okay, but just don't *you* take too long over lunch with Gretchen. You've got to be back here for a three-thirty closed-circuit screening. Speck's nervous that it might have a lot of objectionable stuff and wants your opinion. . . .''

"Fine. I'll be there.'' If Gretchen tried to make it a three-martini lunch, Tally would just hop a taxi back to work. "Who's this you've got on hold for me?'' She sipped her coffee and paused at the door to her office, watching the blinking intercom light with suspicion. Nick had taken to calling her almost immediately after she got to work, ostensibly to ask her when she would be home that day, but really, she knew, to make sure she was where she'd said she'd be. He was vacillating these days between indifference and paranoia. Tally had not decided which of his attitudes was easier to deal with.

"Some viewer who wants to talk about the new weather girl.'' Rachel grinned over the sheet of paper she was inserting into her typewriter. "I think it's the same jerk that gets turned on by collarbones. He said he could see Nancine's panty line under her skirt when she was writing on the board.''

"Oh, brother,'' Tally murmured, as she went into her office to take the call. "What's he got, X-ray vision? Well, at least he's still watching us. Okay. I'll take it.''

"All right. Out with it. I've sat here and watched that brave little smile that shows up every time I ask about you and Nick for long enough.'' Gretchen leaned across the table and jabbed a long magenta-tipped finger at Tally. "You can't do this with an old friend like me. I want to know what's going on with you in that so-called marriage of yours, and I want to know *now*.'' Gretchen leaned back and waited, nursing her second martini. The "1401" was full of advertising people, all heavy lunch drinkers, and Gretchen had broken her lunchtime abstinence rule that had kept Blake off her neck so far this year.

"All right," Tally said with a sigh of defeat. It was no use trying to fool Gretchen. Anyone who knew Tally could tell that all was not well in her marriage. "I'll tell you, only you're not to let anything out at the office or in any way indicate that I'm having trouble—especially to Cane when he calls you."

"Cane hasn't called me in three months. I hear he's having dreadful problems in both Miami and Dallas. Miami wants to use the paper as a political horn for a candidate Tri-Com exposed in other papers as a crook, and Dallas has had a big ad slippage that no one can explain. But forget Cane. He's there and we're here. What the hell is going on?"

"Well," Tally started in hesitantly, "Dr. Lewis says Nick is showing some signs of adjusting. He's stopped having those horrible nightmares, for one thing." Tally didn't mention that she had no way of being certain of that, since she and Nick now occupied separate bedrooms. Nor did she mention Nick's increasing paranoia. "And he doesn't switch moods from one moment to another—well, not as much, anyway. I guess the worst thing that still happens is his reaction to any kind of yelling, or even a voice raised. He goes into his room and shuts the door—and he doesn't come out for as long as two days."

"Poor kid."

"I know. I just feel so sorry for him sometimes, I . . ."

"I mean poor kid *you*." Gretchen leaned over. "Honey, why don't you let Lucy take him in charge? She's the one that warped him so much those brainwashers didn't have much more of a job to do on him." She put her hand over Tally's. "Let him go, Tally. You said he's been going back to the island every weekend now for four months, ever since he and Mother Medusa made up. Let 'er have 'im!"

"I love Nick," Tally said quietly, tearing her napkin methodically into shreds. "He needs me, Gretchen. And he *is* making progress. He held down his last job almost two months. It wasn't until the manager yelled at him about selling a floor-model car at cost without getting the okay that he lost his temper. I have to stick it out, Gretchen. I can't throw him to Lucy and all the other wolves out there."

"In the meantime, you're killing yourself trying to make ends meet and taking care of all the cripples from your little island. Oops!" Gretchen put her hand over Tally's, forcing it to stop its compulsive destruction of the napkin. "That wasn't intended as a dig at your friend Reba. I'm glad she's doing well with her shop, glad she appreciates your help, and wish her all the best. But, Tally, you've got to call a halt to this business of playing Salvation Army to the world. There's you to look after. Who's doing that?"

Tally grinned crookedly. "Me, I guess. But it's okay. Really, it is. What about you? Is it some new man that you're flying out to meet in Puerto Rico? I haven't seen you so secretive since you went around planning my surprise birthday party. Why won't you tell me where you're staying so I can at least find you if something happens and I need a friend?"

"Because," Gretchen told her, fishing out the last olive from her glass, "I want to surprise you when I come back all tanned and gorgeous and maybe even happy."

"You're not having a face-lift?" Tally asked. "Gretchen, you know how desperate you were when that eye job left you unable to close your lids."

"Not a face-lift," Gretchen answered mysteriously. "Here, I'll get that check. You need your money to finish fixing up that adorable house. How's it coming, anyway?"

"Well . . ." Tally thought about the enthusiasm with which she had bought the run-down but still elegant house in Ansley Park. She had paid for it with money she'd got from selling some of her stock. Nick had been in one of his up moods when they'd made the offer and had been enthusiastic about doing most of the renovations himself. Tally was encouraged, hoping that their spending weekends painting, papering, repairing, and generally having something to share might reinstate their old closeness.

It hadn't worked out that way. Tally had wound up doing what work she could on weekends while Nick went down to the island. The more serious renovations were being done by local subcontractors. The drain on her financial reserve was horrendous. Hard, too, not to express the resentment she'd felt ever since Nick had left the work on the house entirely in her hands.

There were other growing resentments, none of which she could freely share with Gretchen. Nick had still never mentioned the letter Tally had written about being pregnant, or indicated he remembered any of the important phases of their previous relationship. The psychiatrist had warned her about bringing up painful memories, reminding Tally that the selective lapses Nick had were self-protective. She kept waiting for the right moment to tell her husband the truth about Amalie, but something always stopped her. Perhaps it was the promise to Lucy. She would have to have it out with Lucy and Nick both there. Amalie's birthday was coming up soon; Essie Mae had told her over the phone that there was to be a big celebration at the Cloister.

The resort hotel was on Sea Island, not on Moss, which would free Tally from the ban on visiting the island. Tally vowed to herself that she and Nick would go together to face Lucy and reclaim their child.

Gretchen was waving her hand in front of Tally's face. "Well? I'm waiting for you to come back from that private place of yours and tell me about the house you're fixing up."

Tally pushed her chair back suddenly and rose. "I've got a better idea. Let's go over there right now and you can see it for yourself. I don't have anything at the office until three-thirty, and you're off till your plane leaves tonight. Let's go."

"Tally, it's a jewel—on the outside, anyway. I love that old grillework on the door."

"You should," Tally said, noticing as she fit her key in the lock that Nick's new Olds that Lucy had bought him was parked in the one-car driveway. It had been parked on the street when she'd left that morning, so maybe that meant he had kept the appointment she'd made for him with another employment agency. "It took me an entire Sunday cleaning off the rust and repainting it. But the parking out here's hell, as you noticed. We're going to have to figure out something to do about—"

She stopped at the realization that there was conversation, dotted with laughter, in the living room off the foyer where Tally and Gretchen stood. Whoever Nick's guest was, she was apparently engrossing enough to keep him from hearing the front door being opened.

A warning sounded deep inside. Tally said brightly and a little too loudly, "Well, aren't you in luck! You get to see my handsome husband as well as the house." As she and Gretchen walked into the living room, Tally saw Nick's surprised face. Then she saw the woman sitting next to him and experienced her own surprise.

"Reba! For goodness' sake, what are you doing here?" The warning bell got louder. *Don't make something of nothing. Reba's Nick's friend, too.* "I didn't see your car out front."

Reba got up to kiss Gretchen on the cheek, then Tally. "That's because Nick picked me up to come out here for lunch." She looked back at the man on the sofa and grinned. "Your husband's getting to be a mean cook, Tally. I'm surprised you're staying so slim now that he's started taking over the kitchen."

"Nick isn't really taking over the kitchen," Tally said, accepting the peck on her cheek that Nick rose to give his wife. "Are you, darling? Gracious, Nick, if Gretchen and I had known you were serving Reba one of your scrumptious meals, we'd have joined you and saved our money."

"You don't ever come home for lunch," Nick said in the new accusing way he used when he was out of a job. "Or for dinner a lot of nights."

Tally could feel Gretchen looking from her to Nick and she spoke brightly into the uncomfortable little silence that had ensued. "Well, I will be tonight after I wrap up things at the office and take Gretchen to the airport."

"Tally, you really don't have to—"

"Nonsense. Of course I'm going to take you." Tally turned to Reba. "Can we give you a lift back to your shop? It's not out of the way."

Before Reba could answer, Nick spoke up. "I'll take her back. She's making me one of those soft loose shirts I like and needs to take some measurements." Nick put his arm around Reba. "Did Reba tell you her good news? She's got a contract with one of the exclusive Sea Island shops for her Island Princess line. They want all she can send them."

"Reba, that's wonderful!" Tally's enthusiasm was sincere. "No wonder Nick wanted to help you celebrate."

"It *is* wonderful, since it means I can pay you back what you lent me to get started—I hope within the next few months."

"Reba, you know that's not important."

"It is to me," Reba said quietly.

There was another strange little silence which was again broken by Tally. "Nick, you didn't forget about your appointment this morning, did you? Claudia Byers is a friend of mine and she made a point of fitting you in this morning when I told her that—"

"No, I didn't forget it," Nick said shortly. "We'll talk about that at dinner tonight."

"He was laughing," Tally said, as she maneuvered her car onto the Hapeville turnoff to the airport. "Nick was laughing, talking, sounding like the old Nick. Gretchen, I'm not kidding about this—Nick has not once laughed since we've been back together. Not once." She pulled up in the departing-flights lane. "I know he and Reba are old friends, but why can't he be like that with me?"

Gretchen gave her tickets to the baggage handler and got out. "Park in the short-term, won't you, and come for a drink? I've got loads of time."

In the bar they watched a plane taking off before either spoke. Then Gretchen said, "Tally, I have kept quiet until now and maybe I should keep it that way, but I think it's time you took a long, hard look at your marriage. It's not a storybook romance anymore. Sure, it started out that way. Boy and girl fall in love on beautiful island. Evil mother comes between them. Boy and girl vow to love each other forever. Boy goes off to war. . . ."

And girl finds out she's pregnant, Tally inserted silently.

". . . Girl goes off to school, makes good, gets job, makes good. Boy comes home after terrible experience, and, like in a Hollywood movie, marries girl, gets job. . . ."

"Loses job. And the pattern repeats itself. Okay, I know what you're getting at. I'm not the sweet, naive little island girl he left behind." Tally sighed. "And he's not the sweet, sexy boy I loved. We've both changed. My God, how could we have not? Look at how different my life has been. And Nick—dear Lord, the things he went through! Sometimes I feel so sorry for him I could die."

Gretchen played with the lemon peel on her napkin. "And what could be deadlier to a man like Nick than knowing that the woman he loves feels nothing but pity for him?"

Tally felt the knife of her friend's words cut through her, leaving the cold blood of truth. "Gretchen, what can I do? How can I help him?"

"You're asking me?" Gretchen shook her head. "My best advice is to leave off trying to turn him into one of the gray-flannel-suit brigade. Enjoy having a house husband who stays home and cooks dinner. Screw his ears off every night."

Tally sputtered over the last of her drink. "Gretchen!"

The older woman shrugged. "You asked. I gotta go. They just called my flight." She kissed Tally, then said, "You're not very good at hiding how miserable you are. Better start practicing in the next couple of weeks."

"Any particular reason?"

"A very good one," Gretchen said, gathering up her carry-on and fishing for her cigarettes out of the huge bag she had stuffed with everything she couldn't live without in case her bags got lost. "Cane is due to settle back in the Atlanta office soon—and you never were very good at fooling him, either."

"Gretchen, if you're thinking what I think you're thinking about Cane and me, forget it. Nick is my husband. Cane and I don't see each other very much, and when we do, it's strictly business."

"Bullshit." Gretchen looked at her, sadly shaking her head.

"Oh, you fifties girls! You really do have a knack for fooling yourself into thinking the man you marry is it, and there'll never be another man to make your twat twitch."

Tally laughed and swatted Gretchen, then hugged and kissed her. "The forties girls are better? Get out of here. And try to leave Puerto Rico the way you found it."

Gretchen waggled her eyebrows. "As long as that doesn't include those delicious beachboys. Bye, darlin'." The scared look was back under the bravado. "Remember to water my plant in my office and stick map pins in my Blake doll. Like MacArthur, I will return."

"I certainly hope so."

Tally stayed to watch Gretchen's plane take off. When a good-looking pilot on a layover invited Tally to his room, she considered the offer seriously. Uncomplicated sex might be just the ticket for what she was feeling—dread at going home and struggling through an evening with Nick, with both of them trying to pretend their marriage wasn't a fairy tale gone sour.

But she turned down the proposition with a smile. "My husband and I are having dinner tonight. He's a pilot, too."

"Lucky guy. An ace with a beautiful wife. It doesn't get any better than that."

He left her sitting at the bar contemplating the sad reality of her marriage. She and Nick had not made love successfully once since their honeymoon.

Tally ordered another drink and was just taking her first sip when a jovial voice spoke in her ear. "Well, if it isn't my little Tri-Com pal! How's the prettiest little female this side of Texas?"

Tally moved her purse so Darwin Redwine could sit down next to her. "That's a big territory to cover, Mr. Redwine. Can I buy you a drink?"

"Now, you know better'n that, after all you've done for me. And that last little bit of info you slipped to me?" The man chuckled. "Made me a pile. Who'd ever think of Winslow getting into producing those cheap little radios? Whoo-ee. Let's don't sit here, honey. I got a solid hour till my flight to Miami to meet up with the little woman. Let's go get us a booth and drink. Flying scares the pee outta me, tell you the truth."

When they were settled in a booth and Darwin Redwine had several bourbons tucked inside his good-sized belly and Tally had discreetly switched to club soda, the Tri-Com board member started talking. Tally listened carefully, knowing that what she was hearing could help her sort out the rumors she'd been hearing. She was fairly sure that Darwin's trust in her was heightened by the rumor that Cane Winslow and Tally Malone Cantrell had had a falling-out.

"You and me's friends, right? Well, I'll tell you this: That boss of yours is smart, but he ain't staying close to home as much as he ought. And that ain't smart. No sirree. He's got somebody after his ass, and that somebody has got some other folks stirred up that'll fall right behind 'im when the stockholders' meeting comes up." Darwin Redwine leaned over close enough for Tally to smell the bourbon on his breath. "It's that Tex-Ark deal that's gonna bring 'im down. There's a rotten smell to it, has been all along. Other folks are smelling it, too, talking about it, wondering why so many eggs are being put in one real shaky basket. . . ."

"Mr. Redwine, Cane Winslow isn't one to let things that big go unnoticed."

"Ain't no Indian chief big enough or with eyes and ears enough to keep watch over every one of the teepees in his reservation. I'm talking too much, girl, I know that, but I'm gonna tell you something else. There's a no-name little pissant company down in Alabama that's buying up big chunks of Tri-Com from every stockholder that'll deal. What do you think about that?"

"I think somebody is using the Alabama company as a front. Who? You?"

"Naah. I made enough on interstate land spec to put me and Miz Redwine in clover till we push up daisies. I admit I kinda like the idea of a takeover, just to keep from getting bored, but it ain't me setting it up. It's somebody big inside."

"Blake Edenfield?" Tally's fingers tightened on her empty

glass. "Is he the one behind the dummy company? He's the only one with enough power to have a hand in the Tex-Ark acquisition. And Cane trusts him—even more so now that he's gone so much."

Darwin shrugged and finished off his double shot of bourbon. "Shouldn't do that. Shouldn't trust a snake like Edenfield or be gone so much." He leaned over and looked at Tally with a shrewdness undulled by alcohol. "You gonna tell your boss all this I told you, gal?"

Tally thought about that. "I'm not sure," she answered honestly. "One thing I learned at Katharine Gibbs was that you don't undermine a superior to his boss unless you've got a pretty good case. But if I do tell Cane anything, I'll leave you out of it."

Darwin Redwine patted her on the shoulder. "That's my little buddy. Don't know what it is about you, about you and me and the way we hit it off right away, but I'm damn glad you and me's friends. You scratch my back, I scratch yours. There's some fancy foreign way of saying that, but damned if I can say it."

"Quid pro quo. Hadn't you better get to your gate? I wouldn't want your wife to wait in Miami and you not be on that plane."

"Hell, she'd just go shopping at one of them fancy import places and go home happy." But he got up and pulled out some bills from his wallet. "Here we've been talking, talking, talking, and I haven't got one tip from you about what's going on at Tri-Com. Anything happening on that coast deal everybody's been so hushy-hushy about? I got connections down there that run the newspapers and there's a good chance I could buy up some stock real cheap. . . ."

Tally teased, "Thought you had all the money you needed." She shook her head. "That's out of my bailiwick. But if I hear anything good, I'll let you know." Cane had made it clear the last time she had talked to him about her odd little liaison with Redwine that he didn't want her giving him information that wouldn't be made public the following week. The coastal merger was months off. "Hurry up, you'll miss your plane."

"Well, it was nice of you to see me off." The man looked puzzled for a minute, then sheepish. "Come to think of it, you didn't come to see me off. What are you doing at the airport anyway? Going somewhere?"

"I sure as hell hope so," Tally said.

23

Tally was lonely. The realization of how lonely struck her when she was dining alone on the little closed-in patio off her living room. Nick had left for the island the evening she'd returned from taking Gretchen to the airport. Now, two weeks later, she had talked to her husband, who had called to tell her he planned to stay through the following week as well.

"Nick, shouldn't you be here in case they call from the agency? You can't expect to get a job if you aren't available for interviews." Tally hated the chipping tone in her voice, but dammit, Nick was behaving like a child these days. "Besides, I miss you."

She had heard Lucy call out, then, "Darling, we'll be late for the Bullochs' party. Do hurry."

Tally had felt a sick feeling go from her ears to her toes. "The Bullochs' party? Nick, you never could stand those snobs. What on earth is happening to you?"

"Kathy Bulloch needed an escort, and to be perfectly honest, I've enjoyed being treated like a hero around here instead of . . ." He had paused, and Tally's anger rose to the point of making her voice shrill.

"Go ahead. Finish your sentence. What do I make you feel like around here?"

"Like a white nigger, if you want it blunt. I'm no Poke Taylor to be sanding walls and painting and Sheetrocking. You even had me putting in a stupid toilet."

Tally almost laughed, but restrained herself. "Nick, it's your house, too. And as long as Lucy keeps your trust fund tied up till you're thirty, we have to try to do as much as we can with what I make.''

"She said you'd be starting in on me about the money I'm coming into," Nick said in the stranger's voice that sometimes took over the conversations he and Tally had. "I told her you didn't care about it, but I'm beginning to wonder if I was wrong about that, too."

"Too? Nick, please come home and let's discuss these things like two civilized people. We can't talk about all this over the phone."

"We can't talk together, period, it seems like. Just like we can't do a lot of things together that most married couples do."

Tally felt agony, knowing Lucy was probably listening in over an extension. "Nick. Please. Just come home."

"I'm staying to help Mother with Amalie's birthday party next weekend." His voice softened. "Now, you talk about a little sweetheart! My baby sister is a princess, a real doll."

And she's your daughter! Tally wanted to scream. "Nick, that's another thing. I want us to be together for that party, because after it's over, there's something deadly serious we have to discuss with Lucy. Together. United."

Lucy's voice came on then. "Nick's gone to start up the car. He's been so sweet. I declare, it's like having my son back with me the way he used to be." *Before you* was the implication. "By the way, I've decided to have Amalie's party here on the island instead of at the Cloister."

Tally quietly put down the phone without saying good-bye. Lucy Cantrell was a monster.

Tally took her coffee into the living room and settled in on the sofa after she put on the new Bartók record she'd bought on another of her lonely nights. Odie-Spot settled in with her, purring in tune to the music. "I'm lonesome," she whispered to the feline, who cared not a whit for human emotions. "I'm so damned *lonesome*."

At least Gretchen was due in tonight. She'd promised to call the moment she touched stateside, but Tally was sort of glad she hadn't offered to meet her plane. She was feeling blue as deep water, and right now the home she'd worked so hard on was a refuge in a world of uncertain events.

The cat's ears perked up suddenly at the same moment that Tally heard the doorbell. "Maybe that's Gretchen now," she said, shifting the cat gently from her lap. "God, how I do need company."

It wasn't Gretchen after all. When Tally opened the door and saw Cane Winslow standing there, she wondered if she had conjured him up out of her loneliness. "What . . . what are you doing here?" she finally managed.

"Waiting to be invited in." Cane moved into the foyer, putting down the light carryall bearing his initials. "And if you don't invite me in, I'm damn coming in anyway. I've just about had it with you, Tallulah, and your way of screwing up my life."

They hadn't seen each other alone for over a year. Both drank in the moment as though that time apart had been a desert they'd finally crossed and now they had reached an oasis together.

"How have I screwed up *your* life?" Tally asked meekly, her breath leaving her at the impact of his closeness as he swept past her into the foyer, then into the living room.

"You have made every night of my life miserable since Nick returned. You have never paid one damn iota of attention to what I've told you since the first time I met you, not one, and I'm damned sick of it. You jumped into a marriage that was all wrong from the beginning, and now you're standing there looking so adorable I . . ." Cane threw his coat and bag on the sofa, narrowly missing the cat. "Dammit, I'm going to kiss you. And if you don't kiss me back just like I want you to, I'm going to carry you off into that bedroom in there and screw you without bothering to take your clothes off first."

When he swept her into his arms, Tally could no more have pulled away than she could have flown to the moon. Her hunger was a palpable, panting animal that was unleashed at the first touch of Cane's mouth on hers. The nights of lying in her bed of silent tears had piled up countless frustrations inside her;

Cane's touch was like hot ice, igniting and chilling parts of her being at once, loosing feelings long stored away.

Nick Cantrell saw the blue-blue of the flashing lights up ahead and starting fishing for his wallet. He'd heard the cops around Jackson, Georgia, were bad, but he wasn't too worried. The battered lifetime veteran's driver's license usually brought a salute of respect from the patrolman and almost never an accompanying traffic ticket. . . .

"This your wife?" The cop's flashlight pinpointed the girlish photo of Tally that Nick had carried with him throughout his incarceration.

He felt a chunk of time slide away from him and the patrolman became Pigeye, his interrogator, and the outskirts of Jackson, Georgia, the dung-pile village of Ho Chu Kien.

Pigeye had not been one of the cruelest of his tormentors, but he had been one of the stubbornest. Since Nick had been classified as one of the reconnaissance team on a level with the infamous U-2 Russian incident, he had not been physically mistreated. Pigeye, however, had taken fiendish delight in tormenting him about his personal background. . . .

"This picture, this girl, GI Joe, she very important to you. Got big boobies, yes?" Pigeye had loved running his fat little fingers over Tally's glossy breasts. "Oh, oh, they feel good to me, GI Joe; they feel real good. Big. BIG." He had taken the picture out of Nick's billfold and propped it on a stool in the interrogation room. And while he talked to Nick about what he and the Chinese could do for American soldiers who had given up their lives, families, and freedom in exchange for being forgotten in their homelands, he jerked off, finally pointing his penis at the picture. The big sticky globs had mostly missed the photo, but one had hit Tally's smiling face and Nick had spent countless hours rubbing the spot, until it was almost white. . . .

"Sorry. I was listening to something on the radio. You asked me how far I was going? Just to Atlanta." Nick took back the billfold with Tally's picture still exposed and quickly folded it up. "That's my wife. Pretty, huh?"

The patrolman winked and patted Nick through the open window. "Can't blame you for trying to get home before morning. Well, keep it in the road, son. We need our vets and we don't need nothing happening to keep 'em from their little females. Git on home."

Nick did just that, though when he pulled up in the driveway of the Ansley Park residence, he had second thoughts about this impulsive trip back home. It was just that Tally had sounded so damned hurt. He was used to that, almost, but something in her voice tonight had tugged at him to get back and see what had to be done to patch up the marriage that was fast becoming a nightmare to both of them.

No parking place was available, of course. Nick cursed and backed out into the street, leaving the driveway clear for Tally to get out the next morning. He found a place and parked, sitting there for a minute cursing and unfairly blaming Tally for taking his inability to make decisions about anything, much less real estate, as positive acquiescence to buying a house.

There weren't many lights on. Nick realized that if he sat out on the street much longer without making some kind of movement, he would be reported by a suspicious neighbor for loitering. He reached for his duffel bag in the back seat and then reconsidered. There were plenty of clothes in his closet in the house.

When he got up to the front door, he hesitated, looking down at the leather Jesus shoes that he'd bought at the shop next to Reba's Tenth Street boutique. A whiff of perspiration odor wafted up from his armpits and Nick had a sudden image of Tally, dressed in one of her "at-home" long-skirt-and-silk-blouse ensembles, opening the door. She would have that pinched-nostril look that he was beginning to dread, and prevail upon him to let her fix him something to eat, hungry or not, and then start in on him about how far he'd gotten with the new résumé.

The feeling of dread felt like a chunk of ice in Nick's stomach.

He stood there, staring at the grillework door that Tally had wound up repainting after Nick had given up on it amid terrible cursing. Then he looked down at the key in his hand. It was easy to talk himself out of going inside. "Shit. If I go in there, we'll just have ourselves another row. Then she'll be tired when she goes to that damn job of hers and I'll sleep all day to get away from thinking about it, and then where'll we be? Back in shitville, that's where."

He went back to his car and started the motor with a grinding urgency to get away from the accusations that were the worse for not being voiced by his accuser.

Tally was now Pigeye. Nick's psychiatrist had pointed this out to Nick, but he had tried to deny it. He could deny it no longer. He could no more make love to Tally than he could have put his dingdong up fat old Pigeye's butt. Nick felt the sweat pouring down his face as the terrible transmogrification of Tally into the despised Pigeye was complete in his brain. Then he took out the picture of her with shaking hands and tore it into little pieces and burned it in his ashtray. "I'm sorry," he said to the curling ashes. "It's not your fault, but it's not mine, either."

Where could he go? He hated the idea of driving all the way back to the island this late. Besides, he had to face Tally sometime, maybe the next day at lunch, on neutral ground. (He hated the Ansley Park house even more than the old apartment.) Lucy had mentioned some things that were burrs under Nick's tender saddle, things that needed to be brought out in the open with Tally.

But not now. He just couldn't face Tally right now. In fact, there was no one whose company seemed desirable right then, unless it was . . . the image of Reba Taylor came into his mind's eye. Of all the people he'd been with on his reentry to the real world after incarceration, Reba had been the easiest. Easiest to talk to, easiest to be with, easiest to laugh with. Why? Nick frowned into the night, trying to figure that out. And then the light broke through, making him laugh out loud. "Hell, that shouldn't be hard to understand. We're both cripples, goddamn cripples."

He sat for a minute, racing the motor a little as he looked at the semi-dark house that he shared with his wife. Then he

turned up the radio so that "She Loves You" by the Beatles
split the air as he headed toward Peachtree and Tenth. Reba
would put him up for the night; he was sure of it. Unbelievably,
he was getting an erection, the first in so long, Nick couldn't
believe it. He touched himself, the excitement growing deep
inside him at the thought of seeing Reba. Unlike Tally, Reba
knew what to do with scared little boys.

Unaware of anything going on outside her house, Tally could
only think of the man holding her and the tumultuous emotions
she was undergoing in his embrace. "Cane," she cried, over
and over, trying hard to fight her own desires. "We can't do
this," she finally said through the hungry kisses which answered the thirst for closeness that she had suffered for months.
She pushed Cane away, moving to the sofa and letting her
weak knees collapse beneath her as she sat and stared at him.
"We can't do this to Nick. It's wrong. You know it is and I
know it is." She started crying. "How could you just come
bursting in like this, bursting in on my life again and trying to
come between Nick and me? How could you? Sometimes I
think I hate you."
    When Cane moved over to sit beside her and put his hands
gently on her cheeks to wipe away the tears, she started beating
at him with her fists. Cane let her fight him, then, when she
was exhausted, he pulled her head onto his chest and stroked
her hair, murmuring against it, "Don't keep fighting me, Tally.
Don't fight what you feel for me. Fight Lucy. Fight the world
that put Nick into the hell-pit he's fighting his way out of right
now. Fight the demons that keep good people like us from
having an easy time getting what we deserve. But don't fight
me. And never again pretend to hate me when we both know
that's a lie." He put his lips on her hair and stroked her
shoulders, her back, aware that every touch was as much like
fire to her as it was to him. He was being selfish, he reminded
himself. All the lonely nights during his travels, trying to avoid
thinking of Tally had left him war-weary and longing for the
arms of the woman he loved. It had been even worse here in

Atlanta, seeing Tally from afar and even talking to her, but never about anything but business. They were never alone together. Even in his dreams, he saw her with Nick.

He knew full well that the marriage was not working. Lucy had gloated to him too many times about the way Nick was turning away from Tally and her "domination of my poor boy." Cane had tried not to be glad of the news that Nick and Tally's marriage was turning out to be the disaster he had known it would be, but he could not help feeling triumph at this moment. Tally needed him, wanted him and, yes, loved him. If only he could convince her of how much she needed, wanted, and loved him.

"I don't know what to do," Tally whispered between quiet sobs. "I'm scared. For the first time in my life, I'm really scared."

"If it's the first time you've been scared, you're way ahead of most people." Cane raised her head and looked down into her eyes. "It's not me, is it? It's not me you're scared of?"

"I don't think so," Tally said in a little-girl voice. "I think it's me."

Cane groaned. "You know what I want to do, don't you? Right now. I want to make love to you. I feel like a deprived man, and you're the only person in the world who can give me what I want at this moment. Tally, don't keep denying what you surely know now is the truth. You and I belong together. We always have. We always will."

The kiss was a melting together of their mouths, bodies, and souls. Tally felt more guilt at its rightness than at its wrongness. Finally, when she could speak, she said weakly, "I'm waiting for Gretchen's call. If you start something with me, I swear it won't be finished. If it's not Gretchen, it'll be some other excuse. Cane, we aren't free to do anything. Not anymore. I'm a married woman."

Cane buried his face in her breasts. "Do you have to remind me of that?" he whispered, his unproved secret a spur in his belly. "If only, if only I had not been so stupid and kept quiet about Nick like Lucy asked me to, you and I would be married now.'' His arms tightened around her. ''Think about it. You and me, together for always. Oh, God, Tally, the mistakes I have made where you're concerned!''

''You're making one now,'' Tally forced herself to say, so that the words came out stiff and insincere. ''If I let you make love to me, you'll never be sure that it's because I want you instead of that I want to move up in my job.'' The lie was sand in her mouth, but she uttered it. Anything to get away from him before he recognized her deep yearning for the closeness she had been denied in Nick's ambivalent embrace!

Cane's arms dropped away like stones. ''That's a cheap shot,'' he said quietly. ''You know I gave over the executive management of the Atlanta offices to Blake for the time being. I don't have more power over you right now than the next man up the ladder from you.''

She thought about what Darwin Redwine had said about Cane's giving up too much of his power. What if Cane had no inkling of what Blake was planning, hadn't heard the rumors about the secret stock buy-up?

''Tally? Have I lost you?''

''No. Yes. I keep having this terribly anxious feeling about Gretchen. I should have heard from her by now. It's worrying me. I know she was planning to go in tomorrow to get set up for 'Woman Alive!' ''

''Then why don't you give her a buzz? Set your mind at ease so I can have your full attention for a change.''

That was dangerous, Tally thought. If she let herself get wrapped up in the situation of Tally and Cane to the exclusion of the real world of Tri-Com and Nick, she'd never come back down to earth. ''I think I will do just that—call Gretchen, I mean. She may want a debriefing before she goes in tomorrow. I haven't had a vacation yet, but I've heard reentry can be tough.''

''You haven't had a real vacation?'' Cane looked thoughtful. ''We'll have to do something about that. Can't have you getting too indispensable around—''

The shrill ring of the telephone stopped him. Tally nearly

broke her neck getting to the instrument. Her anxieties were, she was sure, mostly based on worries about Nick, but Gretchen's situation was high on the list.

"Hello?" Tally knew there was someone on the other end, but she could not make out the words. "Gretchen? Gretchen, is that you? For God's sake, say something! Is something wrong? Gretchen, I can't understand a word you're saying. . . ." Cane had come up silently behind her and Tally cupped the receiver, her eyes wide as she looked up at the man next to her. "I can't make out anything. She's crying and trying to tell me something at the same time. Cane, she's in some kind of terrible trouble!"

"Tell her we can be there in ten minutes. We'll take my car."

Tally spoke into the phone as calmly as she could. "Can you hear me, Gretchen? Cane's here. We'll be over at your place in ten minutes. Just hang on, whatever's the matter. We'll be right there."

"No!" Gretchen's voice came through shrilly on the desperate command. "Don't let Cane come with you! I swear it, Tally. If you don't promise me that, I'll . . . I'll be gone when you get here and you'll never find me." She added almost normally, "Tell him anything you can think of: that I've got a miserable case of the 'Revenge'—or am devastated over a man I met in Puerto Rico." The desperation rose again. "Just don't let him come here with you, Tally! Not if you're my friend!"

Tally thought for a moment and turned back to Cane. "She wants me to come by myself. It's . . . it's some kind of female crisis, one she says you'd be no help at all in."

Cane looked skeptical, but he was aware of Gretchen's stubbornness—aware, too, of her penchant for forming unhappy liaisons during her vacations. "Well, tell her I'll see her at the office tomorrow." He leaned over and put his hand over the receiver so Gretchen couldn't hear. "As for you, I'm putting you on fair warning. This conversation we had just now is not finished. I'll call you later tonight."

He kissed Tally hard on the mouth, looked at her for a long

moment. "Give Gretchen my love . . . and sympathy, if all this is really about a love affair," he said. "I'll let myself out, my darling—but not for all time. Remember that."

He was gone. Tally quickly wound up her strange conversation with Gretchen and broke a few speed records getting over to the Howell House penthouse. . . .

A few miles away, Nick sat in Reba's tiny apartment on Fifteenth Street and looked around. The girl was in the cupboard-sized kitchen making coffee; Nick found the sound of Joan Baez coming from the kitchen radio annoying and said so. "Shut that damned thing off, will you? I can't stand that woman or anything she stands for." Actually he was anxious to go to bed with Reba before he lost precious ground.

"Well, she has a pretty voice," Reba said as she came back in and put down two steaming mugs on the old coffee table. She was dressed in one of her own designs—a flowing caftan that had the bright colors of a tropical garden. She'd let her hair grow out long and straight; it reached almost to her waist. "And you can't hate somebody for speaking up against war." She sat down next to Nick and pulled her leg up under her, looking at him from under a falling curtain of hair. "What are you thinking about that has you looking so grim?"

Nick was embarrassed to tell her so he looked around the room, at the scarred furniture, at the spattered rug, at Reba. "I'm wondering how you can stand living here. It's god-awful, Reba. You're making money now. Why don't you move into something nicer?"

Reba looked down into her cup. "Because," she said quietly, "I'm trying to pay Tally back every cent I owe her. And if the line down in Sea Island does well, I'll be free and clear by the end of the year. Then I can think about moving into more elegant quarters." She laughed softly. "It's not so bad." She gestured gaily toward the door. "There wasn't even a door when I moved in here. The Tech student who rented this place before we took it with him when he moved. It seems my landlady charged him for damage that was already here when he moved in, so he decided to take what he'd bought. And the roaches. Yech! I kept my dishes in the icebox—refrigerator, I mean—before, so I wouldn't be eating after those little devils. Nick, aren't you even going to give me a smile?'' Reba reached over and playfully pinched Nick's cheek.

He pushed her hand away roughly. ''Don't do that. I feel raw and sore from people patting me and telling me how happy I ought to be just because I'm back home.''

Reba's smile faded. ''Well, excuse me. I thought you were here tonight because you needed a friend. Why are you here, Nick? Another fight with Tally? If that's it, don't feel like you're flattering me by running here.''

Nick's jaw tightened and twitched. ''I can leave right now if that's what you want.''

Reba looked at him and saw the hurt behind the anger, anger that she knew was not directed at her. Her heart melted away the guilt that had gnawed at her ever since Nick had begun turning to her instead of to Tally for the comfort he so desperately craved. ''You know that's not what I want.'' She held out her arms and welcomed Nick, who came into them with an agonized moan. ''You know this is what I want,'' she whispered when Nick buried his head in her breast and wrapped his arms so tightly about her that she thought her ribs would break. *Forgive me, Tally. But he needs me more than he needs you. And I need him.*

''Are you sure?'' Nick pulled his face away and held Reba's head between shaking hands, looking into her eyes searchingly. ''I'm not much of a man right now, Reba. I can't satisfy my wife, myself, anybody. And I'm not just talking about screwing. Those gooks took everything from me; I've got nothing left to offer a woman like you.''

''Nick, are you trying to tell me that you've been impotent with Tally?''

Nick put his head on her shoulder and Reba could feel the flowing dampness of his tears seeping into her caftan. ''Yes,'' he whispered. ''But not with you. Not now. Feel of me, Reba.'' He unzipped his jeans and guided her hands to his cock, almost boyishly proud at the little gasp of pleasure from Reba when she closed her warm hand around him. ''You were the first,

Reba. I dreamed about that night on the beach with you. I dreamed about that more than I dreamed about being with Tally." That wasn't exactly true, but Nick *had* thought about her being the first one. It was symbolic that he was here now, back at his sexual beginnings.

Reba felt her heart swell with the joy of being desired. There was no room for guilt about Tally and friendship as she silently led Nick to her bed. There was only room for elation at once more being needed by the man who had always resided at the core of her secret passion.

"Oh my Lord. Sweet heavenly days, what did you let them do to you?"

Tally stood looking at Gretchen's ruined face in the lamplight. The older woman had finally let her turn on a light, and it revealed the relentless truth of what she had been up to in Puerto Rico. "If you think this looks awful now, you should have seen me before they peeled off the scab." Gretchen was shaking all over, but she was no longer hysterical. She even managed a semblance of a grin. "When I was leaving the hospital, a little boy looked up at me and screamed while we were in the elevator together. His mother tried to hush him, but I saw the horror on her face, too." Gretchen walked away into the shadows, her back to Tally. "They wouldn't let me have a mirror while I was in my room. When I got back to my hotel, I looked in the bathroom mirror and screamed even louder than the little boy had."

Tally sank to the sofa and hid her face in her hands. "What in the name of God did you have done, Gretchen? I've seen face-lift patients before—the bruises, the swelling—but nothing like this." She lifted her head. "We have to get you to a doctor. A real doctor. Let me call and . . ."

"It's no use," Gretchen said quietly, with a jerky sob. "I knew the risks, and I took them anyway. There's no infection. I got the antibiotics I need; the healing—such as it is—is already underway." Gretchen's hands hovered over her raw skin, not lighting, but expressing her need to cover the discolored ugliness of cosmetic disaster. "You asked what I had

done. I had a face peel. They use acid, burn away the top five
layers, taking wrinkles, splotches, blemishes—or, hopefully,
that's what it burns away. Only I have the wrong skin type.
Wrong color. The oil in my face mixed with the acid and
sizzled like a bed of hot lava. I could hear it when they were
pouring it on my face! Even through the deadening, I could
hear it!''

"Oh, Gretchen," Tally cried softly. "Your beautiful face!
What will happen? And why would they do this if you were
the wrong skin type, the wrong color?''

"Money. Of course. No one legitimate would do it, but I
had to be stupid and stubborn. I thought if I could smooth out
all my wrinkles and get rid of those horrid pits . . ." Gretchen's
bravery and voice broke and she crumpled on the sofa, against
Tally's shoulder. "Oh, Tally, what am I going to do about my
show? Can't you just see how Blake will react when he sees
me? I'm down the tube. I'm definitely down the tube. They
can't have the bride of Frankenstein hosting a glamorous
woman's show. I'm dead. I'm dead, Tally.''

"Gretchen, get hold of yourself. You're not dead. You can
go to a doctor here, a good one. I'm sure they can correct the
damage." Even as she said it, Tally was heartsick with the
realization that Gretchen's face was irreparably disfigured.

"No," Gretchen whispered, starting to cry again. "Of all
the ironic things, I sat next to a stateside doctor coming back.
I had on a scarf and glasses but he still noticed the shape I was
in. He . . . he didn't want to, but I made him tell me what I
could expect. He said I would have ridges as the flesh grew
back unevenly and . . . and some pretty serious discoloration,
but . . ." Gretchen broke down again. "Oh, Tally, why didn't
I listen to Dr. Tillman here when he told me I wasn't . . .
wasn't a candidate for cosmetic surgery? Why did I have to
run off to another country and do something so stupid?''

Tally held Gretchen's shaking shoulders and pulled the ravaged face down to her own shoulder. "Because," she said
quietly, "the business expects its women to be young and
beautiful forever, while it's perfectly all right for someone like
Walter Cronkite to get silver-haired and 'distinguished' instead

of older. It's a crock, this double-standard business, and don'
be so hard on yourself for trying to stay up with what's expected
of us out there." Tally considered briefly getting one of her
Dixie Mafia contacts to go hunt up the Puerto Rican "doctor"
and nail his knees to his office floor. But the more important
consideration was Gretchen and what could be done to get
her through this nightmare. "Can you imagine Marlin Perkins
getting *his* face done?"

Gretchen gave a weak giggle. "Tally, it really does hurt
when I laugh. God, what am I going to tell Cane? And Blake?"

"Nothing." Tally led Gretchen back to the sofa and sa
down with her, still holding the cold hands, which were no
shaking quite so much now. "I'm going to do the talking for
you. But you have to be brave, braver than you've ever had to
be about anything in your life. Now, listen carefully, Gretchen
Your show's set for next Thursday—right?"

"Yes." A fat tear slid down Gretchen's cheek and wet her
clenched hands. "But how could I possibly go on now? Like
this?"

"Eden Thorpe filled in for you while you were gone, as you
know—and did fine. The guests are all set for this week's
show. We'll get her to take your spot again while we work on
the show for the following week, when you take over again."

"Tally, I can't go on in two weeks! Two years, maybe, but
I'm looking at never, ever, ever showing my face on television
again!"

"I have an idea. If we work at it, we can pull everything
together by next week's show. Now, listen to this. . . ."

Gretchen listened as Tally talked, and gradually, as Tally's
ideas for the upcoming "Woman Alive!" edition were un-
folded, began adding her own ideas to what Tally was sug-
gesting. . . .

Tally picked up the phone on the first ring, not wanting an
interruption to what was likely Gretchen's first peaceful sleep
since her ordeal. "Hello?"

She had known it would be Cane and she was glad—not jus

because she was emotionally exhausted and needed to hear his voice, but because he was the only one who could help her with Gretchen. "I thought I would find you still there. Is she all right? Do I need to come over?"

"No, but I need to talk to you first thing tomorrow about Gretchen's show."

"Tally, I've told you I don't tread on Blake's boundaries. If Gretchen's got a problem that affects his bailiwick, I've got to stay out of it. You've never tried to pull strings with me, even though you knew you could. Don't do it now."

Tally's hand tightened on the receiver. "I'm only asking you to let Gretchen have a few days at home to pull herself together. She can put 'Woman Alive!' together from here, with a little help from her friends. Blake is leaving for Texas tomorrow and won't be back until Thursday week. I have to go over his head on this, and I'm asking you to do it."

"Is this week's show all set?"

"All we have to do is get Eden the script and make any changes she wants. Cane, Gretchen has all kinds of unused vacation leave she's never used. Let her have this time at home."

Cane paused, thinking. Then he said, "I'll have Marsha write a memo for Blake to have on his desk when he returns." Cane waited for Tally's murmurs of thanks to subside before asking shortly, "What's this about Blake going to Texas? How do you know these things before I do?"

"You've just got back into town. I bet you haven't even been by the office yet."

Cane softened. "There was another place I had to go first."

Tally caught her breath, remembering that first moment in Cane's arms. She knew he was thinking about it, too. "Marsha was glad to hear you're back. I called her ten minutes ago to get her to put me down first thing on your morning calendar."

Cane said huskily, "You're always the first thing on my morning calendar. And I hope someday that you'll be the last on my evening calendar. Tally, this business with Gretchen broke up some pretty important business between you and me.

But as I warned you, I'm not letting it drop. We're going to have it out, you and I. And I'm not leaving this town until you admit that you screwed up everybody's life by marrying Nick.''

Especially mine, Tally thought. "All right," she said wearily. "We'll have that talk—though I'm warning *you* that it won't do any good. I'm not admitting anything that would hurt a man who's already been hurt enough. But tomorrow morning over breakfast we'll be talking shop. Now, Cane, if you don't mind, I'll say good night. I'm really tired and still have to hunt up one of Gretchen's nightgowns.''

"If you were with me, you wouldn't be hunting one up," Cane said emotionally. "And we sure as hell wouldn't be getting up to go to work.''

Feeling the rush of heat to her body, Tally quickly said good night and laid down the receiver.

What would Cane say if he knew how often in the past year she had lain awake wanting his arms around her again?

"Nick, please come home soon," she half-prayed as the warm images of Cane filled her mind. "Please be the man I loved once and don't let me hurt you.''

But Nick was on the island with Lucy, Tally reminded herself. It was wearing enough to fight Nick on her own turf without trying to tackle their problems with Lucy looming in the background like a deadly spider.

"Good night, Nick," she whispered. Then she glanced over at the woman sleeping on the adjoining twin bed. "Good night, Gretchen.''

Poor Nick. Poor Gretchen. "Poor Tally," she added sardonically as she switched off the bedside lamp. What was it Gretchen had said once about her being a one-woman Salvation Army? Well, maybe it was time she shut down the soup line. She was getting low on emotional nutrients.

24

The atmosphere on the set of "Woman Alive!" was tense, even electrifying, and Tally held her breath, as did the cameramen, prompters, and everyone else as the lead-in music came on.

"There's Blake," she whispered to Eden, as she saw a small group of lookers-on break away to let the executioner come through. "Oh, God, I was hoping he wouldn't get back until it was all over." She crossed her fingers and gripped Eden's hand tightly. "There's Gretchen. Dear Lord, she's so pale, and look at what the lights are doing to her face." Tally covered her own face, praying as hard as she'd ever prayed before. "Tell me when it's over," she whispered.

"She's going to be fine," Eden whispered back. "Blake just did his double take and is over there having a hissy with Grady Lunt, but you know how laid-back Grady can be. . . . The lead-in's over, now Gretchen's on . . . oh, God, Tally, she's just great. She's taking all the light, just look at her, and she's coming on with the old smile . . . attaway, Gretchen!"

As though she had heard the sotto-voce murmurs of encouragement, Gretchen lifted her scarred face into the unforgiving lights of the strobes and led into her show with a voice whose underlying tremor was noticeable only to those who knew the hostess of "Woman Alive!" far better than the audience ever would.

Tally's long-held breath eased out as she watched her friend get into her professional stride, bringing in the special guests she had lined up for the show. The two other "victims" of cosmetic surgery disasters, along with Gretchen herself, were balanced by two women who had had successful, legitimate operations and a well-known plastic surgeon. Soon, the small live audience was deeply involved in a discussion of the risks versus the benefits of cosmetic surgery and the controversial area of human vanity. There wasn't a dry eye backstage and

not many out front. As soon as she was sure that Gretchen had
herself and her show completely under control, Tally slipped
away from the studio back to her office. It was a good time to
dictate the report she'd promised to have in Cane's box by the
end of the day.

At her desk, Tally switched on the dictating machine and sat
thinking, composing the words in her head as she always did
before dictating.

It was during that contemplative moment that Blake Edenfield burst into her office. His cold gray eyes had taken on the
hue of molten steel. "What the shit has been going on here
while I've been in Texas? You're the one behind that freak
show, Cantrell. I know you and how you sneak around behind
my back every chance you get. . . ."

Tally let him rant on. Then, when he paused for breath, she
asked calmly, "Blake, what were we supposed to do—cancel
the show? You yourself once said that while national disasters
are the lifeblood of live TV, personal disasters are its adrenaline. Well, we pumped a little of that adrenaline into Gretchen's
show—or she did, rather. Check with Chrissie at the front
desk. I understand the switchboard's been jammed with calls
since 'Woman Alive!' went on the air."

"People are fascinated by freaks, but they don't want them
in their living rooms every week."

"Maybe that's why you should have stayed to see our
'freak's' bye-bye today," Tally pointed out sweetly.
"Gretchen is even now, as we speak, bidding her very loyal
audience and friends farewell."

Blake's jaw dropped. "She's *quitting?*"

"Not Tri-Com itself, just the television part of it. Hell's
bells, Blake, I shouldn't be the one telling you all of this! Wait
and let Gretchen be the one to share her good news." In fact,
Gretchen had beseeched Tally to be the one to break the story
to Blake about her new enterprise. Tally did so now with great
satisfaction. "But since I've already blown the secret that this
is Gretchen's swan song with 'Woman Alive!' I'll give you the
rest of it. She's going to be given her vice-presidency at last,
and she'll write a syndicated column now, called 'Woman

Alive!' It could be a lot bigger and more lucrative. Already several other chains are trying to buy syndication rights.''

The executioner was, for the first time in Tally's recollection, totally speechless. For the first time, too, he had been robbed of his favorite occupation—personally delivering the message to someone, especially an on-air ''personality,'' that he or she was fired. When he had recovered his equilibrium, he looked at Tally long and hard. Then he said, slow and mean, ''Don't think I don't know who was behind this little . . . shall we say, coup. Don't think, either, that I'll soon forget it. You know, I liked you. I really liked you. You've always been a gutsy little split-tail, full of spit and vinegar and not afraid of the devil himself. I even thought once of fucking you, just to see if you were as good at whipping ass in bed as you were out of it.''

''I'm glad you thought better of that,'' Tally said, her own temper rising at the insulting words that were the more insulting because Blake thought they were backhanded compliments. ''I'm really glad you didn't indulge your sexual fantasies involving me. Because, let me tell you something—''

Blake stepped up close to her, so close that when he spoke to her through clinched teeth, little specks of saliva flew onto her suit jacket. ''No, you let me tell you something. We're not having our shoot-out here where there's nobody to see the blood. I like it out in the open, mean and clean. I'm going to bring you down, Cantrell. I took you up slow, but I'm going to bring you down fast and hard. You know what?'' He relaxed a little, now that he had his target fixed. Gretchen had squirmed away, but now he had a new one, an even more worthwhile one, since Tally had Cane Winslow in her pocket. ''I don't like women in this business. I don't like women in any business. They're stupid and bitchy and petty and they smell bad when they sweat. Like you're doing now. You're sweating, Cantrell, and you stink.''

Amazingly, Tally kept her tongue civil. ''I could tell Cane about this personal abuse, you know. I've never tried to influence him about one of his people before, but that doesn't mean I can't tell him about this. It's abuse, Blake, pure and simple. Even discrimination. Not that I'm surprised to hear your opinions on women. It's just the sort of narrow-minded attitude I'd expect of you. The board is voting on contracts next week after the big stockholders' meeting. I suppose you'll make sure mine gets lost in the mail.''

Blake smiled. "I told you it would happen in the open. I'll have such a good reason to get you busted at a First Wednesday that you won't even stay long enough to clean out your desk. Subtlety isn't my style, honey.''

That was when Tally realized she had the bastard by the short hairs. Her dictation tape was still running, and if she could get Blake to keep on spilling his guts, she'd have enough tangible evidence on him to get him fired. She had to play it carefully, though. Blake was no fool. But he was mad right now and not as completely in control as he usually was. He wouldn't think about this conversation being recorded. But Tally did, and couched her digging little comments accordingly.

"Oh, no? You were subtle enough to keep it quiet about that dummy corporation in Alabama that's been buying up Tri-Com stock like crazy. Subtle enough to keep it quiet about your secret dealings on the Tex-Ark deal. There's something queer about that deal, Blake, and I'm surprised Cane hasn't looked into it before now. As a matter of fact, I'm surprised a man as smart as Cane has trusted you with anything involving Tri-Com.''

Blake grinned widely, showing the big yellow teeth that he never bared until he was out for blood. "Your fucking hero is not as smart as you think. He doesn't cover all his bases. He doesn't know I came into his business knowing everything about him—his weaknesses, everything. He doesn't know it, but he's coming down, too, when I get ready to pull the chain.''

Tally encouraged the boasting. "You and Cane aren't that close. He's made the mistake of trusting you, but I know him well enough to know any weaknesses you've perceived are just that—your own warped perception.''

Blake's smile was sly. "I have my sources.''

"I have mine, too. And I fully intend to tell Cane about this little talk we've had. . . .''

"Tell away. And while you're at it, tell him about the way your daddy *really* died. And tell him about the little bastard baby you had for your half-brother."

Tally reeled from the shock of what she had heard. *Daddy? Half-brother?* "I . . . I beg your pardon?" The polite tone was born of complete incredulousness. "What did you say?"

"You heard me." Blake wandered over to the window and looked down into the parking lot. "I make it a point to dig up the dirt on people I may need to bury later under that dirt. There are those who said old Harm would never have had the balls to play around on your pal Lucy Cantrell, but your mother indicated otherwise." He turned around, enjoying his revelation of power too much to notice that Tally was still paralyzed from shock. "Pretty woman, your mother, even now. Don't know why she was so terrified of me. I guess she thought I was somebody her papa had sent to make her tell who got her pregnant." The yellow smile reappeared. "Or maybe she thought I was her papa himself."

Tally made a little sound that was half-pleading. "Please, don't say any more."

Blake was enjoying himself thoroughly. "Bet you didn't know, did you, that your grandfather—that fine, upstanding southern gentleman, who was famous for treating his slaves like white folks—beat it out of your mother who the daddy was. Beat her till she came out crippled. She lied and told him Daniel Malone. That's why the old man made her marry your so-called daddy."

"How do you know she lied?" Tally whispered, wondering if this was all really happening. Who was Blake? She felt as though she were being circled by him, that his dripping yellow fangs and gleaming eyes were all around her, that he was just about to pounce on her to finish tearing her apart. "Daniel was my father."

"Oh, no, he wasn't. Your mother sipped that fine Crown Royal I took her till her tongue was tripping all over itself telling me all about the 'good ole days.' Honey, you may spread your legs for anybody coming around, including kinfolks, but your mama was real class. She said she didn't want Lucy mad at her, so they were just real, real discreet, her and her 'lovely, red-haired gentleman.' She told me that she lied to her papa about the real daddy so he would stop beating her."

Tally thought about Harm's faded red hair and closed her eyes in anguish. *Harm her father! It couldn't be! It mustn't be!* Because that would mean that Nick and she were . . . she couldn't say it, couldn't think it. It was the ugliest of all the ugly things in the world. Incest. Tally's mind shut out the hideous word but could not prevent the shattering opening of equally sickening windows of revelation. Amalie! Amalie!

She couldn't bear to be in the room with Blake another moment. The sickness engulfing her was threatening her equilibrium. Her head spun with the need to be away from there, away from Blake, away from the horrible things he was saying. . . . "I don't want to talk to you about this anymore, Blake. Do your worst at the stockholders' meeting, do anything you want. But just get out of my way." She pushed past him, her mind glazed by the need for fresh air, fresh, gulping gasps of fresh air.

She didn't hear anything else he said. When the elevator door closed behind her, she pushed the parking-lot-level number and collapsed against the cool, smooth wall, hardly able to breathe. All she could think about was getting out of the building, getting into her car, and driving far, far away from the ugly words that had been buried into the quick of her like long, rusty nails.

She had left her bag in her office, but there were extra keys under her floor mat. She started up the Mustang with shaking hands and screamed out of the parking lot onto Peachtree, not even noticing when a delivery truck almost hit her and its shaken driver sat on his horn until she turned off onto the freeway.

Instinctively, she turned off on Riverside Drive, her thoughts dead set on getting somewhere quiet, anyplace where she could be alone with the dread of what she had to face. There was an isolated bluff on the winding road overlooking the Chattahoochee. She and Nick had once gone there for a picnic, had talked about their future, about plans for a home overlooking the

river. It had been one of their nicer times together. . . . Tally
lurched the car onto the side of the road and almost fell getting
out. By the time she'd climbed to the vantage point, she was
breathing like an asthmatic, her stockings were torn and her
skirt had twigs clinging to the expensive fabric.

"Nick," she whispered, closing her eyes and breathing in
gasps of cleansing air. "My half-brother. The father of my
child. Dear God, how can I tell him?" For there was no longer
a doubt in her mind. Blake had been cruel, but Tally believed
he had not lied. Too many things from the past, too many hints
from her mother, from other people suddenly fell into place.
Even Cane had suspected the truth; she was sure of it now.
Only she and Nick had been ignorant. Tally, her back against
a hardwood tree, slid limply down, unable to stand any longer.
"I have to tell Nick," she said numbly. "We have to do
something about the marriage. Neither of us can live with
this."

It changed everything. The fantasy of one day claiming
Amalie, with Nick, and living out the storybook marriage had
turned into a horror story. "He doesn't have to know," she
whispered. "He doesn't have to know about Amalie. Lucy
would never tell him about that. At least she's my ally in this."

But she had to tell Nick what she knew about their unholy
liaison. Or did she? How else could she communicate the
urgency of ending the farcical marriage that was now worse
than unsuccessful? Tally raised herself with new strength. The
first step was getting to Nick and somehow figuring out what
they had to do to salvage their lives.

The phone rang several times before Essie Mae finally answered. Her voice spread smiles through the line to Atlanta
when she recognized Tally. "Honey chile! I so glad to hear
your sweet voice." Her own voice dropped conspiratorially.
"Guess who I got eating cookies in my kitchen jest like another
little girl I once knew. She's full of herself right now, our little
Amalie, just plumb full of herself. Made the best grades on her
report card of anybody in the class."

Tally closed her eyes, giving thanks. Essie Mae had no

way of knowing how grateful she was to have this immediate assurance that her child at least did not have the mental taint of incest. "Give her a special kiss for me. But, Essie Mae, I need to talk to Nick. I hope he's around somewhere there. Can you get him to the phone?"

"Law, Tally. Mistuh Nick, he done gone to Atlanta, shoot, it's been over a a week. Ain't you seen him?"

"Oh." Tally managed a little laugh. "Oh, of course I have. My mind's going, with all I have to think about at the station. I just came home to the house being empty and forgot Nick called on his way up about a little side trip he was making. And then I've been so busy with Gretchen's show." Nick had been in town over a week and she hadn't even seen him. Tally felt numb. The emotional Armageddon had already begun and she just hoped she had the strength to survive it.

Essie Mae wasn't stupid. "You all right? You sound kinda funny to me." She added suspiciously, "You ain't startin' in to drink them martoonis like Miss Gretchen is always swigging at all hours of the day?"

Tally fought the hysterical urge to laugh. "No, I'm not drinking, Essie Mae." Maybe that's what she needed, Tally thought laconically: a gross of Gretchen's "martoonis." "I'm just working so hard I'm like one of those frizzled chickens of yours."

"Well, you better slow down," Essie Mae cautioned darkly. "Ain't no good nebber come of a person burning the candle both ways. You want I should fetch Miz Lucy for you? She been outside gittin' on the convicts about her 'zaleas, but I 'speck she'd come right to the phone if I ast her."

"No, don't call Miz Lucy to the phone," Tally begged weakly. "And don't tell her I called asking about Mr. Nicholas."

"I sho' won't, that what you want. How 'bout if I get little Amalie on the phone? She's the cutest thang about her birthday comin' up you ever seen."

"No," Tally said in a choked voice. "Don't get Amalie on the phone, either."

She managed to say good-bye before she burst into tears.

* * *

Tally had reached the eye of her emotional storm by the time
she pulled into the cluttered parking area off Fifteenth Street
where Reba's little battered Volkswagen sat. The busy phone
signal she'd gotten from Reba's apartment had not deterred
her; Reba would have heard from Nick if anyone had.

Several minutes passed before Reba opened the door to
Tally's insistent knock. "Tally!" Reba smoothed her mussed
dark hair and held the neck of her gaily-colored kimono close.
"Good gracious alive, I expected almost anybody but you to
be showing up here. I was sure you'd be out celebrating with
everybody else at the station. Wasn't Gretchen just great? But
why did she have her face worked on like that? Everybody who
came in the shop today was talking about it."

Reba's nervous chatter was unusual, but Tally had her own
thoughts on her mind. "I'm looking for Nick. Do you have
any idea where—"

Tally's question froze on her lips when she saw her husband
emerge from the tiny bedroom, his chest bare and his hair
tousled, as though he had just recently awakened.

"I'm right here, Tally," he said. "I was afraid you might
do something like this—I told Reba you might—so I can't
really say I'm surprised."

Tally's first reaction to her realization of the true situation
was that of righteous anger. And then she wanted to laugh,
because she realized that the role of the betrayed wife and friend
was ready-made and waiting. "I must say I am—surprised, that
is," she said with a careful undercurrent of wifely hurt. "My
best friend, my husband, caught in flagrante."

"I don't know what that means," Reba said, shooting worried looks in Nick's direction.

"It's a fancy way of saying I've been caught with my pants
down," Nick said, his smile reminiscent of the old days when
he and Tally had made gentle fun of Reba's disdain for literary
sophistication. "I'm sorry, Tally," he said softly, his eyes
almost the old Nick's. "But maybe it's better this way. You
and I were all wrong for each other, and we were both killing
each other coming to that realization."

Reba gave a little cry. "Tally! I never meant this to happen."
She started crying. "I swear, I didn't mean for this to happen.
You must think I'm just horrible. After all you've done for me,
here I am sneaking around behind your back with Nick."

Tally still felt that numb urge to laugh at the easy way out
she had been provided. "Don't cry, Reba. It's always the wife
who's the last to know. I can't blame Nick for turning to you.
God, look at the kind of wife I've been! Gone half the time,
not there even when I'm there, preoccupied with my job even
when I'm not on it." She looked at Nick, her sympathy genu-
ine. "Nick needed so much more, so much that I was unable
to give him. I'm surprised he stuck it out as long as he did."
She was amazed at her calmness and, encouraged by it, laid
the final bricks of logic. "Nick left the island a boy and came
back a man. Only the girl he'd left behind had become a bossy,
ambitious, sharp-tongued businesswoman who had let go of
the simple values he craved more than anything I could give
him."

"Tally . . ." Nick's blue eyes were sad. Tally was afraid
that perhaps she had made a case for too much sympathy toward
herself. She couldn't have that.

"Nick, don't say anything else. I've been trying for months
to figure out a way to tell you I wanted out. There's another
man, you know. Your having Reba makes it so much easier."

She felt as much as saw their relieved exchange of glances
and felt her own relief at lightening the darkness that had
engulfed her with Blake's terrible revelation. How long had
she known that she did not love Nick in the way that a wife
should love her husband?

"I was going to tell you how I felt, Tally. I wouldn't have
been a coward about it forever. Reba and I talked about it
tonight, about how hard it was going to be, but how we had to
tell you what we'd decided."

"And what have you decided?" Tally moved over to the
sofa and sat down. It had been a very long day and her legs
were wobbly beneath her. "Have you thought about Lucy, for
instance?" She smiled tiredly. "I'm not your mother's idea of

the perfect daughter-in-law, Nick, as anybody with half-sense knows, but what will she say about you and Reba?''

Nick and Reba exchanged glances again. Then Nick said a little apologetically, ''We hope to be long gone before she has a chance to put in her two cents' worth.''

''Long gone? Reba's got her ties here and to the island, and so do you. Are you talking about cutting those?''

''Yes. I don't feel the same way you do about living there, and neither does Reba. Hell, Tally, that's your home, not mine. It's not Reba's, either. People there have treated her like shit.'' Nick put his arm around Reba and faced Tally defiantly. ''Tally, I'm sorry this is happening like this. I . . . I had very different plans for telling you that I want a divorce. But then it came up that Reba has a chance to work with a top designer in Italy and I realized I didn't want to be separated from her and . . .''

Reba looked as if she was on the verge of tears. ''Nick, you make it sound as if you and I have been lovers and we haven't, not really, not till . . .'' She looked at Tally and burst into sobs, then ran from the room.

''She's telling the truth. We weren't lovers until I came here last week. I started to come home, Tally, but I couldn't force myself to go in and face you.'' Nick choked. ''I'm sorry, Tally. I know how much I've disappointed you, how much I'm hurting you now, but I can't take this storefront marriage any longer. Reba's given me my manhood back.'' Nick looked at Tally's unmoving face and got angry. ''For God's sake, can't you scream or yell or call me names or something? Tell me you hate me, call me an SOB, or shoot me between the eyes, but don't just stand there with those big eyes looking like a dying doe.''

''I don't hate you, Nick,'' Tally whispered, tears rolling down her cheeks. ''On the contrary, I love you more than ever—only in a different way. And I'm not saying much because I'm scared to death for you and Reba, scared about what Lucy will do to you.''

Nick's face turned a little harder. ''You're thinking about

the 'taint' that Reba's rumored to have, aren't you? Well, you needn't worry. Reba and I will be together in a place that doesn't have the kind of prejudices that Reba's had to live with. My mother can rant and rave all she likes. It won't change my plans to spend the rest of my life with Reba, who's better than any mainland deb I ever met.''

"I agree with that," Tally said in a choked voice. "Nick, I know you've always had special feelings for Reba. I'm just sorry I got in the way."

"You didn't get in the way," Nick said tenderly. "I was the one who messed things up from the word 'go.' I guess I had more of my mother in me than I realized. Reba wasn't somebody she could accept, and I just went right along with that. But I'm glad I did. Tally, you and I had something special together that I'll never forget."

I wish I could, Tally thought despondently. "Yes, we did, Nick. But you and Reba will have something even better, I know you will!" She wiped a tear off her cheek. "I want to be the godmother to your children."

"I don't even know if I can have any," Nick said sadly. "God knows nothing else about me has been normal since I came back."

"Oh, Nick." Tally thought about Amalie and felt her heart burdened even heavier with the secrets she could never reveal now. "Where will you live?"

"Italy—Milan, it looks like. Reba has an offer with a designer over there. She really wants to make the big time and I want it for her. I'll find something, maybe in a consulate. Cane can probably help me with that."

"I'm sure he will," Tally said. "I will, too, any way I can."

"You're taking this better than I ever dreamed. Reba and I agonized over how you'd feel about us. Tally, I guess you know I feel like hell about what we're doing to you. But I'll make it up to you. You can keep everything. I won't give you a minute's trouble over the house or anything else. God knows they should be yours by rights, anyway. And I've already talked to my counselor about the divorce. He says with my shrink's records about our . . . problem, he's sure we can probably get an annulment.'' Nick moved closer to Tally and leaned down to kiss her wet cheek. ''Maybe when I come back you'll be happily married with a houseful of kids. God knows, you deserve to be happy.''

''Maybe so,'' Tally said between gulping sobs.

''I'll drive you home.''

''Home.'' Tally dabbed at her eyes and looked up at Nick with the closest thing to a grin she could manage. ''Sometimes I wonder where that is—or if I really have one.'' At Nick's attempt to embrace her, she stepped away quickly. ''I'm all right. Just let me know what we have to do about a divorce or annulment. And let's think up a better story to tell Lucy than the one about you and Reba running off together to find fame and fortune in Europe. Maybe if you told her you walked out on me for good because you couldn't stand hearing another word about mean ole Lucy . . .''

''You're serious?''

Tally wondered if the feeling inside her was the beginning of the healing process. ''I'm serious. Somebody's got to come up with the money for your airline ticket—and damned if it's going to be me.''

For the first time since Nick and Tally had been married, they laughed together.

25

Nobody knew where Tally was when Cane went into her outer office to check. Rachel had been answering phone calls and taking messages when Tally dashed out. ''Her bag's still here,'' Rachel called out to Cane when she opened Tally's closet. ''She must be somewhere in the building—probably in Eden's office, gloating over Gretchen's send-off.'' Then she went back to the phone and Cane was left alone in Tally's private office.

He picked up the picture of Nick that she had on her desk. ''This is the way she wanted you,'' he told the smiling likeness of the young Nick. "Untried, heroic, uncomplicated. A handsome, perfect Ajax."

The sound of whirring caught his attention. Cane tracked the noise to Tally's open desk drawer and realized the dictation tape was at an end. He pushed the "stop" button, then, realizing Tally must have been in the midst of dictating when she left the office, pushed the "rewind" button. Then the "play" button. Maybe he could get a hint as to where she'd run off to.

A few seconds later, when he heard Blake's voice, he realized that what he was hearing was more than the report about Gretchen's future with Tri-Com. Cane walked over and quietly closed Tally's office door. Rachel did not need to hear this, but he did, he realized when he got to the part about what Blake was up to. . . .

Cane sat at Tally's desk for a long time after he'd finished listening to the tape. Then he took it out and put it in his coat pocket. Rachel was off the phone for once. Cane pushed the intercom button and when the secretary came on said quietly, "Rachel, place a call to Texas for me, will you?" He gave her the name. "Marsha's got the number upstairs. Call her and buzz me when you've got the party on the line. And, Rachel . . ." Cane thought about Blake Edenfield and what he had said to Tally and a wave of white-hot rage rippled through him. "Don't say anything to *anybody* about this call. Not to anybody."

"You got it, boss." Rachel started to hang up and then added, "Oh . . . did I hear you listening to Tally's dictation for me? Just leave it where it is and I'll type it up for her soon as I get you and Texas taken care of."

Cane gave a little embarrassed laugh straight out of drama school. "Would you believe I messed up and erased the damn thing? I was trying to hear if she had said anything about where she was going and somehow or other I pushed the wrong button. She's gonna kill me."

Rachel agreed. "Well, I'm just glad it's you and not me."

Cane was glad, too.

* * *

Tally's house was dark, but Cane knew she was there. Not only was her little Mustang convertible parked out front (slightly askew), but he could feel her pain all the way out to the sidewalk. He found the door unlocked and walked into the house.

"Tally? Tally, where are you?"

"I'm in here, in the living room." She was sitting in the dark, watching "The Flintstones" on television. Her cat, Odie-Spot, was in her lap and Tally's hands were methodically rubbing the thick fur. Cane could hear the feline's loud purring from across the room. He stood there, waiting for Tally to acknowledge his presence.

Finally she said, "Why didn't you tell me that Nick and I were half-brother and -sister?" Her words were so soft he could hardly make them out. "You knew all along. Why didn't you stop us?"

He marched over to the TV and switched it off. "I tried," Cane said hopelessly. "I did everything I could to keep you two apart except tell you what I thought to be the naked truth. Why should I have been the one to open up such an ugly can of worms? But I was going to anyway, when Nick came back. And then you got married and the worst was done and couldn't be undone. . . ." He rushed over to sit beside her, taking the cat from her lap and putting it on the floor. He took her hands in his. They were cold as ice, even after stroking the warm cat. "Tally, look at me. It's not the worst thing in the world. You can get a quiet divorce now, put it all behind you, and go on with your life. At least there were no children to complicate things. . . ." He stopped, remembering Blake's other shocking revelation on the tape.

"But there was Amalie," Tally whispered, a fat tear sliding down her cheek. "Amalie is my child—and Nick's."

Cane closed his eyes for a long moment, recalling his pain at hearing that shocking truth on the tape. But his mind was trained to sort out quickly the salvageable parts of any hopeless situation. Little Amalie was bright as a new silver dollar, had none of the taints from the brush of too-close kin. "Does Nick know this?"

Tally shook her head. "No, and I've decided not to tell him. Not about Amalie, not about his father Harm being my father, too, not about anything that could tear down the fragile healing he's undergone the past year."

"I think you have to tell him. There has to be a divorce, Tally. For God's sake, you can't go on living with him as his wife now that you know the truth."

Finally, Tally told him what had occurred at Reba's. When she finished, Cane was quiet for a long time. Then he said, "That must have hurt you a lot. Even knowing your marriage had to be ended, it must have hurt to hear that Nick and Reba . . ." Cane stopped in mid-sentence, his eyes suddenly wide and puzzled. "Wait a minute. You said *annulled*. How the hell can you get an annulment when you've been married as long as you and Nick have?"

Tally looked at him and said quietly, "Because we were barely man and wife in the biblical sense. Nick was impotent right after our honeymoon and throughout our marriage." She added with mild bitterness, "I think he's healed now, with Reba."

Cane looked at her with disbelief, then, as the implications sank in, he let out a deep groan. "You poor kids. You poor, tormented, star-crossed kids." And yet, Cane thought as he pulled Tally into his arms, the torturously imposed celibacy had its positive side. There was only Amalie, no more children.

They stayed glued together, unable to let go even when the cat jumped on the back of the sofa and meowed to remind them that the phone was ringing off the hook. "Don't answer it," Cane whispered. "I can't think of a single solitary soul you need to talk to today—except me, of course."

"I can't, either." Tally put her face up for Cane's kisses, feeling the warmth of his caring. Already, after only a few moments in his arms, she felt better. "Cane, you heard everything on the tape, didn't you? About Blake and his plans to cause trouble for you?"

Cane leaned back just far enough to push her hair away from

her forehead so he could kiss it. "I've known about that for a long time. I was giving him enough rope to hang himself before I did anything. As for what he said about you and 'bringing you down,' don't give that another thought. You have a job with Tri-Com as long as you want it, but I was kind of hoping you might want to take a short sabbatical and take on another career for a while."

"For instance?" Tally's mouth curled against Cane's cheek, knowing perfectly well what "career" he was talking about.

"I'm not getting any younger, you know. We'll work out something with Lucy about little Amalie, but in the meantime, what would you think about getting married and starting our own little conglomerate?"

Tally considered, her hand going up to stroke the slight stubble on Cane's cheek. She loved the strong planes of his face. She hoped they would have sons who looked just like him. "Wel-l-l . . . I did have some exciting ideas for next year's programming schedule, if I get the permanent appointment, that is."

"You will get anything you want, my darling," Cane murmured, kissing her lingeringly and trying unobtrusively to shove the cat off his neck. "As long as it includes me."

"Ummm," Tally murmured. "Just so you realize that I plan to keep on working, even after we have babies." She had no desire to lose control of her existence as the women of her mother's generation had done.

"Babies. I like the sound of that. Personally, I think we ought to start practicing so we can get it right on our wedding night." Cane's exploratory kisses were getting warmer, and Tally was not made of stone. She heard him breathing heavily as he started running his hand down her side.

One thing led to another and they were soon in each other's arms, with no thoughts of the day's horrors, no thoughts of anything or anyone but each other. Tally watched Cane undress after he'd undressed her, a process that had taken a long, long time, since he had to caress lovingly every part of her as he bared it to his gaze. She, too, wanted to linger in the delicious twilight preceding passion. "You're such a beautiful man," she whispered, admiring the long, flat muscles of his thighs and arms and wondering how he had maintained that gorgeous tan as busy as he stayed at his job. "When Reba and I used to talk about the man of our dreams, I always described you, right down to that funny little crook in your nose."

Cane pretended to be hurt. "Take that back about my crooked nose." He was on the bed with her there, then, and had her pinned down.

"Not only that," Tally said, giggling, as Cane started exacting sweet penalties for her "insult." "Not only that—it's even bigger than mine."

"Haven't you learned anything out in the business world? You can't trust people with little, squishy, no-account noses. . . ."

The subject of noses took a definite backseat to the delights of Tally's body, which Cane was rediscovering with the zest of a man who had been too long denied. When he had brought her to the point she could not bear to postpone ultimate closeness, Cane looked deeply into her eyes and asked gravely, "Are you sure you feel okay about this—now, I mean? I don't want anything to happen that you don't want as much as I do."

Tally put her hands on either side of his face. "I know it's not the proper time for us to make love, Cane—not in the light of all that's happened. But I have never wanted or needed you more than I do at this moment."

Cane set about proving how much he wanted Tally. Now that he knew she would soon be his forever, he could not forget or forgive the years of deprivation. "You'll never be far from me again, Tally," he murmured hoarsely between passionate kisses. "We have so much time to make up, and we're starting right now. You belong to me, you always have. I'll never let you go again."

Tally had no inclination to go anywhere. Cane's passion was matched by her own. She welcomed the fire of his kisses and moved her flesh against his wantonly till neither could think of anything else. "I want to be deep inside you," Cane whispered as he released her mouth. "But first I want to memorize every inch of you. And when I'm inside you, I'll think about how

beautiful, how sweet you are, and then I'll want to start all
over again at the very beginning, starting with your toes, those
delectable little . . .''

He was incredible, Tally thought, shivering as Cane slid
down the length of her and took each of her toes, one by one,
in his mouth and slowly and sensuously sucked. She would
have giggled, but it felt too wonderful. And then she had no
desire at all to be frivolous as his tongue reached her inner
thighs. She felt his strong hands on her knees, pulling them
apart wider and then wider, until her most secret core was open
and vulnerable to his desire. She moaned as he brought her
again and again to moist, pulsating longing. When he slipped
a pillow beneath her buttocks, making her ready for his final
conquest, she whispered, "I love you, Cane Winslow."

"And I love you, Tally Malone Cantrell soon-to-be Winslow."

He was inside her, then, and Tally's breath left her as Cane
filled her body and soul, leaving no room for the pain of the
outside world. The intensity of their need and desire for each
other made the union so satisfying that, at the point of surren-
der, Tally wished she could stretch out the moment of ecstasy
for a lifetime. . . .

In the delicious aftermath, the sweet sweat of passion glistening on their bodies, they lay entwined, talking about the miracle
of their love. "If I didn't have you, Cane . . ." Tally whispered. "Oh, God, if I didn't have you with me like this . . . I
can't even bear to think about it."

"You have me, my darling, for the rest of your life. I won't
choke you or smother you, but I'll always be there for you,
good or bad. Forever, Tally. Forever."

"Forever." Tally whispered the word aloud and smiled and
closed her eyes in total exhaustion. Then she slept, Cane's
arms around her protective and comforting.

"Cane. Cane, wake up!" Tally shook the shoulder of the man
sleeping next to her. "It just came to me, what Blake said."
When Cane sleepily reached for her and Tally realized he
hadn't comprehended, she said more clearly, "I know Blake

went to see my mother, to see what he could get out of her
but she couldn't have told him everything about that nigh
Perrie died. Even Mrs. Cagle, the director, says it's all rea
fuzzy in Mama's mind about that night. There's only one
person who knows what happened—clearly, I mean—tha
night. Lucy. Cane, is it possible that Lucy and Blake have beer
seeing each other? Maybe even that they're lovers?''

Cane sat straight up, fully awake now. ''Lucy and Blake'.
Tally, that's not poss—'' He rubbed his eyes and stared at her,
realization of what she was hinting at dawning on his face
''Or is it? Lucy came up for that big corporation reception I
held for my new board about ten years ago. And it wasn't long
after that that she started making regular trips to Atlanta. I
heard she had a guy on the side, but . . .'' Cane stopped and
cursed softly. ''Of course. That's what he's up to. He's beer
courting Lucy all these years so he could have his private tap
into my family life. Now he's probably working on her to ge
her stock. He's already bought up stock through that dummy
Alabama corporation that he thought I didn't know about. Well,
he's in for a surprise—Tri-Com's Japanese transistor affiliate
is on the verge of making a takeover of Alabama Electronics.''
He snapped his fingers. ''That's it! He's bamboozling Lucy
into selling her chunk of stock to Alabama Electronics, which
means she probably doesn't know she's really selling to
Blake.''

''Cane, you always give Lucy too much credit for loyalty.
Why do you think she wouldn't knowingly sell to Blake, since
she obviously has a thing for him and has had for a long time?''

''Because I know Lucy.'' Cane reached over Tally for his
shirt and kissed her on the way back. ''Umm. Boy, do you
feel good to wake up to. By the way, we'll be honeymooning
on a deserted island that I bought in the Fijis, and you can
brace yourself for nonstop sex for at least a month.'' Cane
kissed her again, then said regretfully, ''But right now we have
places to go and people to see. Maybe we can stop Lucy from
closing the deal with Blake and losing her shirt, plus a big chunk
of Nick's inheritance.'' Cane started pulling on his pants.

''Cane, where are you going?''

"*We* are going to Moss Island, my darling. The regular stockholders' meeting is Tuesday. If I'm right, that's when the shit's supposed to hit the fan. That means Blake's got to get his deal with her closed sometime today—Friday—or Monday. I know for a fact all Lucy's shares were still in hers and Nick's names as of yesterday, when I had all my major stockholders' Tri-Com assets checked out." Cane tossed Tally her stockings, which she looked at with a grimace and promptly threw in the trash can. "Had your assets checked out, too, my darling. They don't hold a candle to the assets I checked out last night."

Tally cuffed him for that, then got serious again. "I don't understand. I know you don't want all Lucy's stock being turned over to Blake Edenfield, but he would be paying her top dollar. So how do you figure she'll lose her—and Nick's—fortune?"

Cane tossed Tally her underwear, putting it to his lips first and pretending to swoon. "The deal will be on paper. Blake doesn't have the liquid assets to pay Lucy for her stock. And when his dummy corporation carpet is yanked out from under him, Blake will be lucky to have the money to take a cab to bankruptcy court—much less pay the people he owes."

Tally zipped up her skirt and reached for a fresh blouse. Lucy and Blake lovers! It boggled the mind. "Pardon me if I don't seem overly enthusiastic about saving Lucy's skin. Why do you?"

Cane looked at her for a long moment, mulling that over. "Because she's family," he said with a quiet finality. "But more than that, Lucy stood up for me once in a way that made all the difference in my life. When my mother died, old Justin was ready to pack me off to her relatives in Mississippi, boot me out of any kind of inheritance. I wasn't his boy, he said. But Lucy made him take responsibility for my welfare. She made him set up a trust fund, made him turn over the money my mother had left me. If it weren't for Lucy, there wouldn't be a Tri-Com. There might not even be a Cane Winslow."

Tally hugged him silently. She still had no love for the woman, but she could finally understand Cane's devotion to the detestable Lucy Cantrell.

26

When Cane's Mercedes pulled up to the ferry dock, Tally froze. "I can't go over there. Lucy swore if I ever broke our agreement, that she'd have me arrested. Cane, I can't do it!" Tally's eyes were wide and frightened. "I know you have feelings for your stepsister that I can't share. She hates me, Cane, hates me with a passion. She'll live up to her promise of causing the biggest, ugliest scandal in the world. All the horrible business about Daniel will be brought up. She'll probably have that dreadful Sheriff Waymon dig up Daniel's body to show that he was shot before the fire. My mother, my poor mother will be dragged into it, and you know what that could do to her. . . . Cane, why are you looking at me like that?"

"Shot? Daniel Malone was *shot*?" At Tally's nod, he eyed her with a speculating look that he used often in pinning down the truth about something. "Genevieve Malone shot and killed her husband, didn't she? And Lucy found out about it, maybe even saw it happen. That's Lucy's hold over you. She knows that Vieve shot Daniel."

At Cane's quiet finality, Tally burst into tears. "Yes," she sobbed against Cane's shoulder. "She didn't mean to, Cane! She was trying to kill the snake. But Lucy could have made it look like . . . could've had people thinking . . . Cane, even Mama doesn't remember. That was what kept me from ever bucking Lucy and letting her do her worst. But Lucy will bring it all out in the open now. Lucy hates me enough to dredge it all up and drag poor Mama into it. Poor Mama doesn't even remember that night or what she did! Think what it could do to her!"

"You've forgotten one thing. I'm with you now—all the way." Cane patted her on the shoulder and handed her his handkerchief. "There's the ferry, with poor old Poke looking more grizzled than ever. Chin up, my darling. We'll face Lucy together, you and I. I just wish you had come to me all those years ago when Lucy was squeezing you under her thumb. She needs a strong hand, my stepsister does—and always has. Since Justin died, I've been the only one who could control her.''

They drove onto the ferry at Poke's signal, and Cane got out to talk to Poke while Tally sat in the car pulling herself together. Despite her dread of what lay ahead, she savored the early-morning view of the island. It was even more beautiful than she remembered. Tally felt the lump in her throat at the breathtaking sight of a brace of gulls taking off into the dawning sun. On the waiting dock she saw two little girls, one fair and one dark. A long-ago memory rushed back of her and Reba standing there, giggling as they threw bread crumbs to the dive-bombing birds.

You feeding the gulls, Tally?

Naw—I'm feeding the boys.

Ghostly laughter was all around her. Tally blinked her eyes as the ferry pulled closer and the two little girls did not vanish as she'd expected.

The fair one was Amalie. Tally got out of the car and stood at the railing, hands clenched, her hair streaming in the wind, and drank in the first sight of her daughter. She hardly felt Cane's hand when it covered hers on the railing. Finally she let out her breath. ''How can I love her so much already?''

''Easy, darling.'' Cane squeezed her hand again. ''We'll work things out, I promise, but right now you must be careful.''

''I wouldn't hurt that little girl for anything in the world,'' Tally said in a trembling voice. ''Cane.'' She turned to the man next to her, her eyes holding a new brightness that had come with her first glimpse of Amalie. ''I know now that it's not right to keep the truth from Nick. He has to know, too.''

Cane threw his arms around her and squeezed her joyfully. ''Oh, God, I hoped you'd see that. But right now we've got other things to attend to.'' He looked down at Tally and reminded her, ''We've got to save our company so our children will have the inheritance we want them to have.''

Our company. Our children. Tally liked that. She turned back to watch Amalie run onto the ferry as soon as Poke had secured it. Suddenly shy, Tally waited for the little girl to approach. She knew that Amalie was eyeing her curiously even as she was being swung around by Cane, who was apparently, judging from the happy squeals, a big favorite.

When Amalie had been deposited groundside, she went immediately up to Tally and started tugging on her skirt. "Hi. You're pretty. What's your name?"

"Tallulah. But most people call me Tally. And you must be Amalie."

"That's my friend Jolamine over there hiding behind the tree. She's scared of white ladies. And this is my doll, Felicia." Amalie held up her very pretty, very blond and blue-eyed doll. "Did you play with dolls when you were a little girl?"

"Oh, yes," Tally said, biting her lip to keep her voice from shaking. "Not very fancy ones. They were made out of corncobs and rags, but I loved them very much."

"Corncobs and rags! I bet they weren't this pretty. My big brother Nicky built me a house for my dolls. Want to come see it?"

Tally looked at Cane for help. He stooped down to talk to Amalie and brushed back the flyaway blond hair. "Could Tally and I do that after we've seen your mother? And is it possible that the delicious odor I smell right now is some of Essie Mae's famous Luzianne?"

Amalie made a face. "Yuk. Coffee."

"Can we meet your little friend? You can tell her I won't bite."

Cane and Tally smiled at each other when Amalie marched over and firmly pulled the little black girl out from behind a live oak. "How do you do?" they both said solemnly, shaking the pigtailed child's hand in very serious fashion.

"Jolamine can play with me out here but she can't come in the house." Cane saw Tally's distressed look over Amalie's head and suddenly swooped a giggling Jolamine up on his back and went galloping off with her to the kitchen stoop. Amalie watched a little jealously. "Mama says little white girls need to be real careful around the nigras."

"Well, I don't know about that," Tally said, taking Amalie's hand and swinging it as they walked up to join Cane. "I grew up right here and Jolamine's mother F'Mollie and I made cookies in that very kitchen every Saturday morning. Oh my gracious, who is that I'm looking at?"

Essie Mae had come out with her apron full of pea-hulls. When she looked out and saw Tally, she flung the whole mess to the wind and made a run for her "chile."

Harm did the official greeting, after Tally had had her reunion with Essie Mae and she and Cane had fortified themselves with the black woman's strong coffee. "Lucy knows you're here, but I have to talk with you before you go in to see her," he told them, his freckled hand running nervously through the vestiges of faded red hair. "Let's go into my den and talk."

Essie Mae brought in a tray of cheese straws which were left untouched while Tally and Cane joined Harm in snifters of brandy. Tally was secretly thrilled that Amalie seemed reluctant to leave her lap, where she had curled up like a kitten, but gave the child over to Essie Mae when she declared it lunchtime.

With Amalie's kiss still warm on her cheek, Tally found it hard to concentrate on what Harm was telling them. "Lucy hasn't been herself lately. She ran me out of my study, took it over for herself, and locks herself up in there for hours every day, talking to someone about her Tri-Com stock. Cane, I'm worried. I sneaked in there when she was out the other day. She had the whole portfolio out, with transfer papers already drawn up just waiting for her signature."

"That's why I'm here, Harm. I have to talk Lucy out of selling. It would be disastrous for her, for Nick, and for Tri-Com. Where is she?"

"In her room. She says she's not feeling well. She might be lying down. Cane, do you know someone named Edenfield?" At Cane's nod, Harm said, "Well, I heard that name on one of her phone conversations." Harm cleared his throat. "Look, I'm a pretty good-sized stockholder in your company, too, Cane, and I want to know if there's any truth to some rumors I've heard. Word's around that this big Tex-Ark acquisition is putting the whole conglomerate at risk financially, that the land title to it is as murky as the Altamaha River. Can you comment on that?"

"I can and will." Cane reached out and took Tally's hand in his, intertwining her fingers with his. She could feel the restored confidence flowing from him to her. Things were under control again, they had each other (or would soon), and the fight that lay ahead wouldn't be the fixed kayo that Blake Edenfield had in mind. "This is just between you and me—I guess you can understand the need for that—Blake's managed to pull in a few board members on his side, so the quieter we keep things, the better."

And then he told Harm what he had learned about Blake's plans to pull the rug out from under Cane's empire, setting himself up as the logical replacement for the discredited and unseated president of Tri-Com. "I wasn't sure about the dummy company that was buying up stock all over, not until I heard Blake admit it on Tally's dictating machine. . . ." At Harm's quizzical look, Cane said with a sardonic grin, "Don't ask. That's another story, one happily erased for all time. No, I didn't trust Blake completely, not ever, but I wasn't sure what he had in mind until Tally mentioned that he's been tight with Lucy." At Harm's uncertain look, he added quietly, "I'm sorry, Harm. I don't want you getting hurt in this."

"It's okay. I always knew there was somebody else. There should've been. I was never enough man for Lucy."

Tally would have protested, but Cane interrupted. "Tally, Harm doesn't like being treated like a blind fool, so let's not cover up for Lucy. At the moment, the big issue here is my credibility as Tri-Com's head. I want you both to know that I've got things under control and that Blake will eat shit at that stockholders' meeting next Tuesday. He did his best to stir up things so I would be tied up and unable to get back in time for the meeting, but I took care of that." To Harm he added, "You're worried about the murky title to the Tex-Ark property. I'm perfectly aware that the lawyer who initially laid the groundwork for the deal was Blake's shill. He slicked the deal ast my desk while I was traveling, but I'm not one to sign apers without doing my own checking on what's what.''

"So you knew we were getting stuck with an unclear title,'' Iarm said, his blue eyes shining with the pleasure of business ılk, which he dearly loved. "You knew it all along.''

"Not all along. Just in time to get some of my sharpest eople busy buying out the heirs that had the land title fucked p. I've got quit-claim deeds from every mother-loving one of em—and Blake doesn't know a damn thing about it. And on't, until I show up at that meeting with 'em.'' He pulled ally to him and kissed the top of her head. "And Tally, here, s going to feed Blake's chief crony, Darwin Redwine, a little nisinformation about my alleged 'panic' as soon as we get ack to Atlanta.''

"I'm not so sure Darwin is in Blake's pocket, Cane. I think e's playing both sides, seeing which one will come up on top. Vhy else would he have let the cat out of the bag to me that ime at the airport?''

Cane kissed her. "Because you're irresistible. The Sphinx vould tell you its secrets if you turned those big, beautiful eyes n it. I'm not worried about Darwin Redwine. It's Blake's hide 'm after. And after that stockholders' meeting, it'll be nailed o the barn door.''

Harm looked at Cane with admiration and shook his head lowly from side to side and then chuckled softly. "That'll ;ive me some personal satisfaction, I don't mind telling you. 'd just like to see that bastard's face when you sock it to 'im hat Tri-Com's got clear title to the biggest news media property n Texas. What about this Alabama outfit that he's got buying ıp stock? What happens there?''

"Well, I've already had my legal boys check out Alabama Quad-Tech to see if it's phony through and through or a viable :ompany. Turns out it's solid granite, except for Blake's shady iaison. My Japanese friends have already made an acceptable •id that carries the stipulation that Blake's front man in the :ompany will be ousted the minute the contract's signed Mon-lay morning. There'll be no more underhanded stock buying, and Tri-Com's Japanese subsidiary will own a vigorous new little company to handle our electronic import-export outlet.''

Harm laughed. ''You're a wily SOB. How'd you pull that off without Edenfield getting wind of it?''

''There are a few secrets I'd like to keep to myself. Harm, why don't you come see the show? You're a stockholder and entitled to a ringside seat. Blake honestly thinks he's going to have me ousted as a weak president who doesn't hold tight reins on the expansion funds, but he's got a shock coming. Two of the board members he thinks he's got in his pocket have already come to me secretly with their balls in their hands. He has maybe three votes—including his own—left for bringing me down—and that is not enough.''

While Cane and Harm were talking, Tally became aware of a sound drifting in from the open window, a sound of excitement—mostly children's voices. Curious, she walked over to the window and, her own voice filled with hushed excitement, called back to the two men, ''Cane—Harm—come look. You've never seen anything like this. Hurry! Come look!''

The men rushed over, not having any idea what to expect.

''Well, I'll be goddamned,'' Cane swore softly. ''It's Aunt Monday, come up from the swamp.''

Harm shook his head in amazement. ''She's never come up here, not since I was a boy. I can't believe it.''

The swamp obeah was drifting toward the big house, her bright-colored caftan streaming out behind her, the small children from the quarters were dancing around her and touching her skirts like little elves circling their fairy queen. Some of the adults had come out to see the phenomenon and had lined up in solemn curiosity so that Aunt Monday swept down the human corridor like royalty ascending to her throne.

All at once, Aunt Monday came to a stop and looked up at her white audience staring down from the open window. She seemed unaware of the small black children who milled about her, touching her clothes and staring up at her as though she were all the island legends come to life in one form. ''Tallulah," she called up in her rich voice. "Tallulah Fontaine. You have come home to your island."

Tally's voice rang out clear and strong. "Yes, Aunt Monday. I've come home."

Aunt Monday bent down to pick up a tiny black child who had tumbled over at her feet and started crying. The child stopped crying immediately and played happily with the glittering shell ornaments in the obeah's long braided hair. "I would speak with you and Miss Lucy," the woman called out distinctly, adding firmly, "Alone. Just the two of you and myself."

Tally looked at Harm and he nodded slightly. "Would you like us to come down?" she asked Aunt Monday, then whispered to Harm, "Do you think Lucy would do that?"

As if the whisper had carried down to Aunt Monday, the old woman called, "No, please. I would very much like to come up there. Let me see to these children and then I will come up to you."

She dispersed her fascinated audience with a kiss here, a whispered word there, until she was finally alone. Looking up, she saw that Tally still watched from the window. Her face broke out in the wonderful warm smile that Tally had only seen twice in all the years of their acquaintance. "Don't look so worried, child. I am not here to bring darkness. I have come to bring the light of truth. Wait there. I will come to you."

Harm and Cane left, the latter planting a soft kiss on Tally's head before he did so. Then the obeah walked into the room. "Aunt Monday." They embraced and Tally said worriedly, "Lucy is not well. She may not receive us."

"She will receive us," Aunt Monday said, and swept through the door and up the stairs. Tally followed obediently. On the way up, Aunt Monday tossed back casually, "I am grateful to you for sending me word about my grandchild. It pleases me that Reba has found her place in the white man's world."

In front of Lucy's door, the black woman waited for Tally to join her. "Do not be pained at what I have to tell you," she said, putting her hand against Tally's cheek. "I was bound to this many years ago."

They walked in without knocking and Tally, expecting Lucy to be pale and wan, lying on her bed, was surprised to see the blond woman sitting at her little desk, perfectly dressed and coiffured, leafing through a magazine. Lucy, for her part, was visibly surprised to see her uninvited guests. She half-rose than sat back down. "I would invite you in," she said sarcastically, "but I see there's no need for that."

"Lucy Randolph Cantrell, I have come to speak with you and Tallulah. You will listen and you will say nothing until I have finished."

Lucy's mouth crooked. "If it's about your property taxes, I'll tell you what I tell everyone else who lives on this island. If you own your land, you pay your own taxes."

"It is not about taxes." Aunt Monday wandered over to Lucy's dresser and picked up the small framed picture of Justin Randolph, Lucy's father. "It is about your father, whom you loved perhaps best of all men, and about you and about Tallulah, whom you love least of all women."

"Aunt Monday, if you've come to cast one of your island spells, please spare me. You know I don't believe in that hocus-pocus. I suppose you've heard I haven't been feeling well and have brought me one of your magic potions." Lucy's lip curled. "Well, I'm sorry to disappoint you, but I'm perfectly fine now. It was a simple case of indigestion from one of Essie Mae's spicier dishes at last night's dinner."

"I am not here as a doctor, even if I were so qualified. I am here to bring the truth, which was entrusted to me by your father. That is why I am here. Mr. Justin wished you to be spared until the last moment, but he was adamant that you too, would know the truth."

Lucy set back to thumbing through her magazine. Tally saw that her hands were trembling and knew that the casualness was part of the woman's bravado. "The truth is that the woman standing beside you has no right to be here. No right to be in this house."

"She has every right," Aunt Monday said, moving to stand between Lucy and Tally, as though to provide a human shield for the vitriol that emanated from the woman at the desk. She continued more softly, "Long ago, when you and Mr. Harm came here and Mr. Justin was trying to buy everything that pleased you, he saw something that pleased him, and he moved to make it his."

"No," Lucy whispered, putting down her magazine. "Leave my room. I don't want to listen to you."

"He and Miss Genevieve, poor thing, fell in love. Her father hated him for all the things he stood for, and your father, he hated Mr. Fontaine right back. But he did love Miss Genevieve and wanted to do right by her. When she got pregnant, he knew the babe was his and he wanted it. He wanted to marry her, but all he could think about was how unhappy you would be to think of him finding somebody to love more than you. He talked to me, night after night, about how it had to be kept secret, how you hated to think of him marrying some silly woman, and how his sweetheart's daddy couldn't stand giving anything to a Yankee bastard like him—least of all, his only child. After all, Mr. Justin had forced Mr. Fontaine into selling his property to him—before he fell in love with Miss Genevieve, of course. 'They will make my Vieve's life a living hell,' he said to me. 'And mine, too, but I can bear it and my darling cannot.' "

"I don't want to hear any more," Lucy said, her hands over her ears. "I don't want Tally hearing this."

"No, but it's time it was all heard. Secrets can't be kept for all time. A secret's something that has to be let out someday." Aunt Monday looked at Tallulah. "Are you all right, child? I see your pale face dreading what's coming out before you."

Tally said honestly, "I feel a little sick, but I want to hear what you have to say about my mother and Justin." She closed her eyes and whispered, "I thought it was Harm my mother loved."

"It was! It was!" Lucy shouted, her face as scarlet as the hibiscus in Aunt Monday's hair. "Harm was always silly over your mother, and vice versa. It was my stupid husband who got Genevieve pregnant, if anybody did, and this crazy witch woman won't convince me otherwise."

So many things were coming clear to Tally that she didn't know where to start sorting them out. "If . . . if Aunt Monday's right, and Justin Randolph was my real father, that means . . ." Tally buried her face in her hands. "At least I'm not Nick's sister."

"You're his aunt," Aunt Monday said sympathetically. "Legally, too. I'm sorry, Miss Lucy, but the time for truth is here. Your daddy loved you and wanted you to be happy, but he didn't want his unborn child to be left out."

Lucy and Tally both lifted their heads at the same time and stared at each other as the realization dawned on them. They were *half-sisters!* Sisters! "There's no proof of it," Lucy said finally, her voice almost back to its normal arrogance.

"Oh, but Miss Lucy, there is proof. You see, Mr. Justin really loved Miss Genevieve and wanted things to be right, even though you hated the idea of his loving anybody else and Mr. Fontaine was crazed with anger. Your daddy came to me, he and little Genevieve, and asked me to help them make it legal."

"I'm calling my lawyer right now. Stop where you are. I won't listen to another word."

"Then don't listen. Look." Aunt Monday reached into her voluminous caftan pocket and pulled out a yellowed paper. "This is the marriage certificate, Miss Lucy. Your daddy and Miss Genevieve were married by a boat captain, just days before your daddy went back east and died of a heart attack. I'm not ashamed that I was the one who arranged the wedding, secretly, aboard the vessel that had come in for my shrimp catch." Aunt Monday looked at Tally with a smile. "Your parents were married by a nice man, Tallulah. They all knew you were coming, that crew did, and celebrated till dawn, me with them."

Tally was in shock, unable to react. All she could think about was that she and Nick were not brother and sister, after all. Their innocent incest had still taken place, her numbed brain reminded her, but somehow being Nick's aunt seemed better than the closer relationship of siblings. . . .

Lucy's voice took on a new shrillness. "She can't be my sister! I won't have it. And she won't get a penny, not a dime from this place. You hear me?" She came over and stood trembling in rage in front of Tally. "You hear me? Not a dime. Not an inch of this place."

Aunt Monday said gently, "Mr. Justin wanted his child—whom he never got to see—to have her share. I'm sorry, Miss Lucy, but you have to accept the fact that Tally is legally entitled to half this place. I kept quiet all these years because Miss Genevieve made me promise. When her daddy forced her to marry Daniel Malone, she was already widowed. She didn't dare tell him or anyone else that her child was by another man—a man who was the cause of her daddy's ruin and whom he hated like the devil himself."

Lucy's nostrils were pinched and her face so red Tally was sure she might explode at any moment. But her voice was hard and strong. "That paper's not proof. It could be forged. Besides, Tally could easily be Daniel Malone's child. We all know that Vieve was a little southern tramp."

"Not so," Aunt Monday said, shaking her head sadly. "She was a victim of her time, like a lot of other women who followed their hearts and not their heads. And I don't think anybody ought to shortchange Daniel Malone in that whole business. He stayed quiet when Vieve named him as the father of the child she was carrying and went through a shotgun marriage without a single solitary complaint. Daniel Malone was a good man, Tally. He loved your mother and didn't ask questions most men would've asked. And she loved you and was trying to bring you into the world the best way she could." Aunt Monday looked at Tally with sympathy. "Your mother was so unhappy, child. And then when her father shot himself and she thought it was her fault . . ."

"Her fault!" Tally cried. "Aunt Monday, what are you saying?"

"Oh, darlin', how I hate it that you should hear all these things from me, but it's time, long past time. Miss Genevieve

found her daddy in his study the night before he would be
turning over this place to Lucy and her husband. He had lost
everything else in a foolish rice deal that he'd entered into in
hopes of getting everything back. He sat in that big black chair
and held his gun to his head. Poor Vieve tried to take that gun
away from him and it went off. She saw it all. She never got
over blaming herself for what happened. In her mind, it was
all her fault.''

"Oh my God," Tally breathed, closing her eyes against the
memory of her mother's face after she had pulled the Luger's
trigger and shot Daniel. No wonder Genevieve had withdrawn
from the horror of a second traumatic death; no wonder she
had never faced reality from the moment of Daniel's accident.
"My poor mother," she whispered, tears streaming down her
cheeks.

Aunt Monday smiled wryly. "I'd say it's you who deserved
pity more than your mother. You came into the world shorn of
your inheritance and doomed to suffer for your mother's sin."

Lucy Cantrell made a sound of derision. "Maybe I'm the
one who deserves pity for having to listen to this . . . this
ridiculous drivel. I have to ask—why on earth have you decided
to come forth with this fictional trash at this particular time?"

"Because I saw my death in the tea leaves, perhaps early
fall, and I wish to see justice done before I leave this plane."
She ignored Lucy's snort of derision. "I have strong feelings
about the soul in the afterlife. I felt I had the obligation to tell
you the truths I've just told you, Miss Lucy, so you, too, can
have the opportunity to do what's right to redeem your soul."

Lucy laughed harshly. "You people and your stupid backwa-
ter religions! I don't believe in hell, old hag. You don't scare
me. I'm sure Tally helped you cook up this little witch-doctor
scenario to do just that. I suppose you can predict my exact
season of death, too," she said sarcastically.

Aunt Monday bowed her head and Tally knew that the black
woman's death was not the only one she had seen in the tea
leaves. Lucy knew it, too. Her face grew pale as flour. "Damn
you!" Lucy screamed. "My son is heir to this place, and that
bitch will never get it! Never—do you hear me?" Tally saw

the blue vein at Lucy's temple jerking like a worm under the skin.

"There's still time for you to make your peace, Miss Lucy," Aunt Monday whispered softly. "The spirit that leaves this plane full of hate and evil lives with that torment forever."

"Damn you!" Lucy yelled. "Get out of here! Both of you— get out!" She picked up a pillow from her bed and flung it at the obeah, who stood implacably as the object passed by her head. "Get out. And you!" This to Tally, who felt as if she were paralyzed. "You know what I can do to you. Your mother shot your father. I can have her put away tomorrow with one call to the sheriff."

Aunt Monday's eyes met Tally's and the latter knew that the black woman knew everything about that, too. "I'm calling your hand, Lucy Cantrell." She reached deep into her pocket and brought out the blue-black Luger that Tally recognized with a pang as the one she had flung out the window that terrible night of Perrie's death. "If you plan to call the law down on Genevieve, you'll need this as evidence."

She placed the gun on the desk in front of Lucy. The latter stared at the gun as though it were a snake that might strike. "How did you. . . ? I searched everywhere. . . ."

"One of my people brought it to me a few years back. It still has the bullets, all but the one. I leave it with you gladly. I have never liked having man's instrument of death in my possession. God's ways are better." Aunt Monday smiled as Lucy kept on staring at the gun. "There won't be any finger-prints, of course, after all this time. But perhaps you can use it to bring about what you might call justice."

Tally looked at Aunt Monday in distress, but the black woman signaled to her across Lucy's head. *It's all right, child.*

Tally wasn't satisfied with that. "Why didn't you come to me, Aunt Monday? For God's sake, why?"

Aunt Monday's lips twitched. "You needed a nudge to get you off your pretty little duff, child. I declare, I was beginning to get worried that you would wind up living here forever and not ever get out in that world that has your name carved on it somewhere. I didn't want you to be another Genevieve, vegetating like a gardenia that never spreads its wonderful fragrance beyond a tiny spot in a southern garden."

"Your scheme cost her Amalie," Lucy spoke up sharply. "She may finagle Nick into giving her this place someday, but she can never have Amalie—never. I saw to it that the records at that home were lost. It cost me a pretty penny, but I—"

"Wrong, Lucy."

The sad voice from the door was that of Harm, who was flanked by an angry-looking Cane.

Lucy's face showed momentary bewilderment, then crumpled in its well-practiced little-girl fashion. "Cane! Cane, if you could hear the lies they're trying to scare me with!" Lucy ran to her stepbrother, who stood like a stone as she embraced him. "You've always loved me like a sister. Tell them to stop telling their horrible lies and go away."

"Lucy . . . the director at the home has a greedy streak," Harm said, looking at Lucy. "When I found out about Tally having her baby there, I made my own contribution."

"You?" The utter contempt in Lucy's voice and face made Harm cringe. But then he straightened to his full dumpy height and looked her squarely in the eye.

"I followed you to Savannah when you went to sign the final papers at that home. You brought little Amalie here, expecting me to accept anything you did as being just fine with poor, mild old Harm. But I couldn't accept not knowing the child's background. That business about your cousin was phony as the devil. For God's sake, Lucy, I'm a Southerner! Blood's important to me!"

"Blood!" Lucy spat out. "You and your stupid 'blood.' I'm sick to death of hearing about it. So you found out about Tally having little Amalie in Savannah and you paid that bitch to go against her promise and keep the records of the real mother . . . you interfering bastard. If you had any balls, I'd pinch them off. But none of that matters. Tally signed Amalie over to me and she's legally mine."

"Lucy, Amalie is Nick's daughter, too. And I guarantee if he finds out that you kept him in the dark about this, he'll never want to see you again.

"Poke said you stole Tally's letter to my boy about her being pregnant. That letter might've brought Nick back safe and sound instead of him winding up in some prison camp." Harm looked at Tally. "I'm sorry, girl. I should've stood up to her about that a long time ago. But that's why I wanted to know the truth about little Amalie. I had a feeling she could be your and my boy's little girl."

"All of you get out and leave me alone!" Lucy blazed. "My little girl is staying with me in this house as long as I live!" She looked at Aunt Monday and said coldly, "And that'll be longer than the devil himself, old hag. Take that back and put it in your witch's brew."

"Lucy, you're just making things hard on yourself. Tally's not planning to kick you out of Amalie's life—or this house now that she knows it's half hers. As for my part in this, all I'm asking is that you hold on to your Tri-Com stock that you're planning to sell to Blake Edenfield's fake corporation."

"And *you!*" Lucy's venom was turned on her stepbrother. "You're no smarter than Harm when it comes to women. You're just like all the other men I've known—stupid and weak and lily-livered when you're faced with a strong woman!" She smiled—a terrible smile—at Cane and said almost sweetly, "I'm so sorry, brother dear, that I can't refuse Blake anything he wants—including your precious Tri-Com stock. He's a real man. Maybe if you'd taken me to bed like I always wanted you to . . ."

The sound of the stinging slap across Lucy's face was like a gunshot in the suddenly quiet room. Harm looked down at his hand and then at the other people in the room. "I apologize. My daddy always said a gentleman should never hit a lady, but I think my wife has just disqualified herself from that injunction."

While Lucy stood there staring at Harm as though he were a lamb who had sprouted horns, everyone filed out of the room slowly, leaving her alone. When her bedroom was emptied of visitors, Lucy went over to the mirror and stared at her face in the vanity mirror. The imprint of Harm's hand stood out in sharp pink. "It's that little bitch, Tally, who made all this

happen. I will get you for this, Tally. I *will!*'' She walked over
to the desk and picked up the gun Aunt Monday had left. She
held it to her stinging cheek as though it were a lover's hand.

"You swore that you'd never set foot on this island again,
Tally Malone, and you broke that promise. What happens now
is all on your head, you . . . little . . . bitch."

Even with all the tension of the day, the delicious picnic supper
Essie Mae brought over to the lighthouse for Tally and Cane
gave the occasion an air of festivity. "Mistuh Harm, he done
took Miss Amalie over to stay with her little school friend on
de mainland, and Mistuh Harm say he gone stay over, too."
Essie Mae rolled her eyes back. "Law, I prayed down in the
kitchen lak I ain't never prayed before, but Miz Lucy, she be
acting plumb normal. She tole me that she had come to see the
light and wanted to make ever'thing right agin. I took her some
soup and that cottage cheese she likes and she was just sittin'
in that big ole black chair in your granddaddy's study, smilin'
and chattin' at me lak none o' that screamin' and yellin' and
fightin' I heard y'all doin' upstairs never happened."

"If she gets a call from Atlanta, Essie Mae, you make sure
you come get me," Cane said, taking out a chicken sandwich
and handing half to Tally, who was sipping her wine and trying
hard to forget Lucy's parting look of sheer venom.

"Ain't been no calls, in or out, Mistuh Cane. But I got a
message for Tally from Miz Lucy, and I'm hopin' it means
that there won't be no more of that turrible yellin'. She say she
want you to come see her in that ole study and see can you and
her work out something together so's that precious little girl
you both love won't git caught in the middle."

Tally put down her sandwich before she'd even taken a bite
and stood up. "Oh, thank God! Cane, I knew when I saw the
look on her face when we all walked out on her that she'd
finally realized she can't win against all of us."

Cane put his hand on Tally's arm, restraining her. His face
was worried. "Honey, she hates you. I didn't know how much
until today. To tell you the truth, after what I saw in there
today, I think Lucy's got a cog loose. I'll go with you."

"No. If you do that, we'll get all involved with other things, and all I'm interested in is trying to get Lucy to agree to let me see my little girl from now on." Tally said to Essie Mae, "You stay here with Cane and keep him company. I really think it's time Lucy and I faced these things that have hit us both pretty hard. After all, we are half-sisters." As Essie Mae and Cane both looked at her dubiously, Tally laughed a little nervously. "Oh, come on. What can she do? Chop me up into little pieces and throw me to the sharks?"

Cane and Essie Mae looked at each other and then back at Tally, and, in unanimity, nodded.

"Lucy? It's Tally. Why have you got it so dark in here?" Tally peered into the study that had once been her grandfather's, and then Harm's, and now had been commandeered by Lucy. She could make out the death chair and avoided it, feeling her way to another one closer to the flickering kerosene lamp that barely illumined the room.

"I'm here at the desk," Lucy said. "I didn't want you looking at the mark my husband made on my face. It's bad enough giving in to you about everything without having you pitying me." Tally was accustoming herself to the dim light and could see Lucy rise from the desk. "Come over here. I'm giving you back the gun. Take it."

Tally walked over and gingerly picked up the Luger. When Lucy said quietly, "It's loaded, you know," Tally put it quickly back on the desk and stepped back.

"Don't be so jumpy." Lucy carefully slid the gun by its barrel to a safer spot. "I thought and thought about you and me being sisters and decided it's time we put all our differences behind us. I always wanted a sister," she said a little plaintively. "It makes it better, you know, in working out things about Amalie. We can both be her mothers!" Lucy's little tinkling laugh was not quite right. It set Tally's teeth on edge, but she waited to hear what else Lucy had to say. "I'll have my lawyer on the mainland draw up a joint-custody agreement tomorrow. And I'll have him do something about recognizing your share in the property, too."

"That sounds fine to me, Lucy," Tally said, rising. She really didn't like sitting with Lucy in this eerie darkness. It was spooky as hell. "You let me know when they're ready and I'll sign whatever I have to. But I have to go back to Atlanta Sunday, so . . ."

"Oh, everything will be finished by then. Everything." Lucy went around the desk and sat down in the big black chair. "We all need to work on being friends again. Poor Cane is probably devastated by his big sister's silly little fit up there today. Please assure him I won't be selling to Blake Edenfield. I was just teasing."

"You could have fooled me. But I'll tell him," Tally added quickly. "Lucy, I'll be going now. Is there anything I can get Essie Mae to bring you? I know it's been a tough day for you, too."

"Not a thing," Lucy said airily. "I have all I need right here."

Lucy smiled at the door after Tally left, then counted slowly, "One . . . two . . . three . . . four . . . five . . ." before she picked up a heavy paperweight, Tally's grandfather's, and threw it through the window. The lead missile crashed through the glass, splintering it into a thousand shards that echoed in the dark silence of the room. Lucy picked up the Luger, her handkerchief delicately covering the handle. She waited until she heard Tally's pounding steps come close, then placed the Luger against the fleshy part of her shoulder. Grimacing in anticipated pain, she pulled the trigger just as Tally burst through the door.

"Lucy, for God's sake, what do you think you're doing?" Lucy screamed at her. "It didn't shoot! The fucking thing wouldn't shoot!" She looked at the gun and then pointed it straight at Tally, pulling the trigger again and again. "It won't fucking shoot!" she screamed. And then her eyes stared at Tally as if they were popping from her head and she put her free hand to her throat. "Ah . . . ah . . . ah . . ." she mouthed, her neck arching against the high-backed chair.

"I'll get somebody," Tally cried, grabbing the phone and praying that the running steps she heard were those of Cane and Essie Mae. "Hang on, Lucy. They're coming. Just hang on!"

But by the time Cane and Essie Mae got there, Lucy was dead, the Luger dangling ludicrously from her hand.

"Stroke," Essie Mae said sadly. "I kept telling her she ought to go to de doctor for them turrible headaches, but you know Miz Lucy. She didn't like nobody tellin' her what to do."

"What was she doing with the gun, Tally?" Cane would never have figured Lucy to be a suicidal type. He turned the gun over in his hand. His and Tally's eyes met at the moment of comprehension. "Someone had removed the firing pin. That explains why she couldn't shoot herself and then blame you with it. Somebody did you a big favor, Tally, and I think we can both pretty well guess who that was."

Tally went over to Cane and pulled his arms tight around her as they heard the sound of the ambulance siren coming up the front drive. "Maybe you'll agree with me now that Lucy didn't make much of a sister."

"Time to go to bed, honey," Aunt Monday said, sticking her head in the room where little Jolamine was playing with her cornshuck doll. The old obeah had been afraid to leave the sensitive little black girl around the Hall where so many unpleasant things were happening. "What in the world happened to that poor thing?" she asked, seeing the crushed stuffed head of the blond-haired doll. "And what's it doing on the floor anyway?"

"It just fell outta my hands, Aunt Monday, and I stepped on its head."

Jolamine stood there looking up at her and Aunt Monday finally shook her head, a little smile playing along her lips. She knelt down and picked up the doll, smoothing out its mussed corn-silk locks very gently. Her eyes met the little girl's as she said softly, "Do you know what juju is, Jolamine?" The child nodded slowly. "And have you ever seen a goofball do its work, or a horseshoe that was turned upside down so the luck wouldn't run out, or . . ."

She talked on, softly and unceasingly. There was so much
to talk about with little Jolamine before the coming fall took
the leaves from the trees and the current island obeah with
them.

27

Spring! The universally welcomed season brought with it not
only the poetic promise of fresh new beginnings, but also
some pragmatic changes. Tally, with Tri-Com's president's
full approval, took a six-month leave of absence. "I want our
wedding to be the biggest, happiest celebration that Moss Island
has ever seen," Cane told his bride-to-be when they were
leaving Atlanta to start the preparations. "And I want every
damn person on the place to be there in full regalia—including
that crazy swamp witch."

Tally had laughed at that. "Aunt Monday has already promised not to make a die of it until after the wedding—and she's
a woman of her word. I just wish Nick and Reba could come
home for it."

"He still feels a little funny about things, I think." Cane
kissed Tally again (for at least the twentieth time since they'd
gone out to her car prepared to drive down to the island). "I'm
glad you broke it to him—the whole truth, I mean. It's a
good thing, too, that he agreed Amalie doesn't need to know
everything. Dealing with Lucy's death and finding out she has
another mom was enough for even a very smart little girl."

"Nick has been great. It's nice he's got Reba and that they're
getting married. I hope her designs take off like Nick seems to
think they will." The price Tally had paid Nick for his share
of the island property had enabled them to invest in the salon
where Reba had become a designer. Lucy's fortune had not
been as extensive as everyone had believed. Even Harm was
perplexed over the cold realization that his wife had apparently
squandered much of her funds. Maybe, Cane had pointed out

charitably, that was why she had felt pressed to consider selling out her Tri-Com stock.

"I'm sure it will be—with Reba's talent and Nick's determination to be a hardworking business manager. Hey, I guess you noticed that Blake Edenfield was noticeably absent from your farewell luncheon today." Cane's mouth twitched. "I sent him a wire to his ratty little office in Boston, telling him I'd send up the company plane if he had a notion to come down."

Tally chuckled. "I'll never, as long as I live, forget that day at the stockholders' meeting when you blew him out of the water. He really didn't think we'd get there, with Lucy's funeral coming like it did. Cane, I wish we had a picture of his face when he heard that copy of the tape you played for him afterward."

"He'll never make any more nasty threats about you. I took care of that."

"Well, he's made history around here as the classic SOB who got too big for his britches."

"Word is from up Boston-way that his new employers aren't too happy with him, either. But that's old business." Cane kissed Tally lingeringly one more time. "On with the new. What is it we have left to pack? The kitchen sink?"

"Just Socrates. Oh, and the groom." Tally wondered if this much happiness was unlucky before the main event. She couldn't wait for the wedding. "Mama and Amalie have been planning their dresses for the wedding for two months. I don't think the bride is going to get much attention from anybody with those two around."

"She will from me," Cane said huskily, his eyes dancing at the happiness in Tally's voice. He knew how much it meant to her that her mother was back home—really home—at Camellia Hall and responding beautifully to the love of an unexpected granddaughter. The psychiatrist Cane had arranged for on a weekly basis in the comfort of Vieve's very pleasant surroundings had privately told Cane that Genevieve's progress with dealing with painful old traumas had been expedited incredibly by her liaison with Amalie. The child had helped Vieve regain her perception of herself and those around her.

The ferry was waiting for them when they reached the mainland landing. Tally looked over at the half-completed bridge that would one day soon make the old ferry crossing obsolete and felt a pang of sadness. But now that many of the Ducktown residents were selling their property to developers who hoped to turn Moss Island into another Hilton Head resort, it was inevitable that the island would be made more accessible to the outside world. Even some of the blacks in the quarters were negotiating with would-be buyers; only a few of them (including Essie Mae) had remained stubborn about not giving up their homesites for quick money.

"Poke?" After Cane had driven the car onto the ferry she got out, expecting to see Reba's long, lean father, his yellowed teeth gaping wide in a grin of welcome. But the stocky figure that came to greet her was not Poke Taylor.

When she recognized who the ferry captain was, Tally broke into delighted laughter and held out her arms. "Jim-Roy! As I live and breathe—I can't believe it's really you!" She turned to Cane, who had solemnly exchanged handshakes with Jim-Roy. "Do you mind, darling, going on up to the veranda and waiting for me? I'd like to talk to Jim-Roy just a minute or two, but I don't want you going into the house before I get there."

Cane kissed her. "Anything you want, sweetheart. This is your goose—I'm just holding the tail."

After he'd gone off, Tally found out that Jim-Roy had something he wanted to discuss.

". . . I just finally couldn't take no more of that big-city stuff, Tally. I reckon I'm born to be right here on this island. And when I heard you and Cane was thinking of coming back down here to live after you was married and all, I just ast myself—why not put it to Tally plain and simple that you want back down here, too?"

"Jim-Roy, I can't think of anybody I'd rather have running the place than you! Shoot, I can't believe you'd want to go back to farming, after all those times you told Reba and me you'd dig ditches before you'd work in tobacco again.''

"Well, we all say things we don't really mean. Tell the truth, I'd like my young'uns to grow up like you and me did. Right here on God's island.''

"Two children—right? A boy and a girl?''

Jim-Roy grinned proudly. "And one more bun in the oven. Betty Lou says she'd like three more, but I'm thinking about putting a stop to the young'un business after this'un.''

"Well, I'm glad you'll have a big family to help with the suckering,'' Tally said, laughing. And then she sobered, thinking about the bridge, about the lots already sold and the ones being put up for sale. "But Jim-Roy, are you sure you want to give up that big mill job to come back down here to work for me? I can't promise anything real definite, and you already know how much work there is in it.''

"I ain't ever been scared of work. And I like being back here. A person needs to feel attached to a place. That place where I was, how could I do that? Drinking beer on Friday nights with fellers that didn't know what they wanted from one week to the next? Paying rent to some jerk-leg that didn't even know my first name, much less what family I come out of? Having folks treat me like I was redneck trash one minute and trying to sell me fancy insurance the next?'' Jim-Roy shook his head as he pulled the ferry up into the slip at the island landing. "Uh-uh. I'm part of this island just like you are. I plan to lay my bones down every night in my own bed on my own land, and when them bones rot out on me, I'm gonna let 'em be laid to rest right there in that old cemetery.''

"It's not going to be the same as it was when you and I were coming along,'' Tally said, handing Jim-Roy the bags she and Cane had packed. "Jim-Roy, if you don't mind driving our car off the ferry and leaving it right next to the commissary, I'll go catch up with Cane. Just put our bags on Poke's porch and we'll send somebody over for 'em later.''

"Sure thing.'' Jim-Roy stopped Tally just as she was about to strike off toward Camellia Hall. "Tally, you're right about it not being nothing like it was when you and I was growing up, but you know what? I think it's gonna be just as good, even with all them tourists coming in and all. I mean, you and me, we're here, ain't we?"

"We sure are," Tally said fervently, taking a deep breath of the fragrant spring air. "We sure as hell are. And if Cane and I have our way about it, we'll provide some more little ones."

She stopped at the end of the walkway up to the veranda of the mansion, drinking in the beauty of it as though she were seeing it for the first time. The lights were on everywhere and from a downstairs window she heard the sound of the piano and her mother's high, soft voice. She smiled when she heard Amalie join in "Too-ra-loo-ra-loo-ra" . . . This would be her safe place, hers and Cane's. It would not be her only world, but it would be the one she could always come back to. She and Cane had other worlds to conquer, but this one was already hers—really hers.

A tall dark figure stood waiting for her on the veranda, a four-legged one by his side. The dog broke away from Cane and bounded down to greet her. As Tally patted the Great Dane, happiness engulfed her.

"This is the place I told you about, Socrates. Think you can be happy running rabbits all over this island? Potlikker sure had a lot of good times." The dog cocked his big head, and Tally decided that the expression on his face was as close to a smile as a dog could manage. "Odie-Spot will be here, too, soon as Gretchen brings him down. We'll all have wonderful times, fella, your master and me most of all." She laughed as Socrates streaked off after a squirrel who was much too swift for a city dog.

Then she walked toward the house, toward Cane, toward the warmth and love and music awaiting her. "Guess who's home," she called out as she stepped through the polished front door into Camellia Hall.

The historical romances of
JEANNE WILLIAMS
from St. Martin's Paperbacks